Summer Winds

By A.J. Questenberg

Acknowledgments:

To God who made a way where there was no way, and for making a path in the wilderness then leading me through it; and for perfecting all that concerns me. I am forever grateful.

Dedicated to: Hailey Jo, Landon, Thomas, David, Kaitlyn, Levi, Hailey Mae, Brody, Xavier, Ashley, Mike, and Kya.

Thank you to: Tim O'Malley, assistant superintendent for the Minnesota Bureau of Apprehension, for technical assistance.

Chapter One

This is where Holly's folks decided to move? Not much like Holly's letters, Renee Good thought as she got out of her parent's car and stepped onto the hot sidewalk in front of the Sand's Cafe. The twelve-year-old, on that hot, muggy July 3 afternoon in 1963 had imagined Rutledge, Minnesota to be a big metropolis, bustling with activity because of Holly's letters. The only traffic in sight—a listless, big black fly buzzing her sweaty, dark brown locks she held off her shoulders in a ponytail. She stood next to the car on Main Street in front of a restaurant that from the outside looked as dead and as the motionless as the streets surrounding her.

"Now you behave yourself, do you hear?" Her mother said.

Jeez! I'm twelve years old! Doesn't she think I have any sense? Renee thought, angrily.

During the interminable drive from their farm in Makinen to Rutledge, ninety-five miles southwest, her parents had done nothing but fight. Her father had actually used the "f" word yelling at her mother, and though she didn't know exactly what the "f" word meant Renee knew it had to be bad. Everybody in the car had gone unnaturally quiet when he said it including her mother, and brother, Mike, and her mother didn't shut up for much.

Neither the sight of the tiny hamlet, nor her mother's contentiousness on the hot, muggy, ninety-degree day could dampen Renee's happiness, however. It had been two months since she and Holly had talked face to face, two months since she had laid eyes on Holly's brother, Sam, the major love of her life, which began for her when she was ten and first laid eyes on him. To her, the then thirteen-year-old Sam was so handsome, smart, and worldly she darned near swooned when he came around her.

Even if Sam were not in the picture, Renee missed Holly tremendously. Since the Spurs moved from the little farming community of Makinen, situated 100 miles south of the Canadian border, Renee had been having the loneliest summer of her life. Sure things were changing. A new family had moved into the neighborhood. They had already befriended her folks and had kids her age, which was nice, but she and Holly had been so close that the new friendships couldn't compare. Now, for two weeks at least, the two girls could pick up where they left off.

As Renee stood on Main Street, which, in 1963, was the main thoroughfare traveling south to the Twin Cities, another ninety miles further down the road, she was glad Rutledge appeared so tiny. For the little country girl who had never spent any length of time in any town, this was to be her first big adventure away from home. Smaller seemed safer, not much different from home, and, she thought, it would be easy to get to know everybody.

And even though the village was tiny, it seemed worldly to her. Maybe that's why it seemed so big in Holly's letters, she thought, taking in as much as she could while she waited. As she stood on the sidewalk in front of the café, Renee looked across the street up at the apartment building she knew the Spurs lived in. Three floors of apartments stared back at her with glass eyes, some curtained, some not, as if winking in shared secrecy at her. Somewhere on the third floor was the Spur's apartment. Renee stared up at the windows, which stared coldly back at her, then she turned to look in through the big glass eyes of the Sands Café stretching across the front of the entire block. Sheltering her eyes against the sun's glare, she saw that inside the restaurant bustled with customers, belying her first impression that the town was devoid of people, and the fact that the streets were so still. She wasn't surprised the restaurant was popular. The Spurs were a captivating family.

As Renee took in her new environment, her mother insisted on standing on the sidewalk next to her, embarrassing her because she would not leave until one of the Spur family members saw her daughter across the street and into their apartment with her luggage. There her mother stood, tall, regal, her strawberry blond hair done up in a bee-hive hairdo, her Pokka-dot dress impeccably neat even after riding in the hot, humid car all day, her winged black eye glasses adding to what she hoped was a glamorous façade, her one vanity. She never wished to be known as a "hick" so she cultivated all the popular looks from glamour magazines making dresses from patterns she designed just by looking at them in the magazines.

God, she is such a pill, Renee thought trying, and failing, to remain patient with her mother. Good girls don't sass their parents. Her mother had told her that often enough. She wanted to sass—and sass some more.

Mike, with his Elvis like hair-do slicked to the sides and hanging out over his forehead into his eyes, stuck his tongue out at her from the back seat. She rolled her eyes. How Holly could ever have a crush on him was beyond her. Renee had to admit he was cute. He was funny, too, but he was her brother and she was sick of him. She knew that Mike, too, hoped to see Sam before the folks took off, but Sam was still nowhere in sight.

Just then Holly threw open an upstairs apartment window and yelled down, "Hey you! I'll be right down!" giggling, setting Renee off in titters, too. And even though her mother heard Holly call out that she was coming down, the elder Good remained waiting with Renee until Holly came alongside the car before she would get back into it.

Holly was glad Mrs. Good had stubbornly waited on the sidewalk with Renee; it allowed her to drink in as much of Mike's face as she could in the few seconds he remained within her sight. His dark brown hair and eyebrows set off his bright, hazel eyes alongside his perfectly Grecian nose above his perfectly molded lips. Holly tried as discreetly as possible to savor every pore of his face, to indelibly imprint them in her head, so when he was away all she had to do was call it up and wallow in the beauty of it when the desire hit her. She saw, too, that he seemed to be drinking her in as well.

Renee, too, saw that Mike was happy to see Holly.

Renee's father by that time stood outside the car with his driver's-side car door open, leaning his rock hard, six-foot-four inch frame against the car's frame, tapping his toe on the hot tar, an unfiltered cigarette dangling from his lips, and an impatient expression creasing his sun-bronzed brow while he stared at his wife. It was easy to see where Mike got his looks.

The elder Good dressed in antithesis to his wife. He wore jeans, T-shirt and engineer boots, just to get on her nerves. He wanted to wear his bibbed-overalls, but she put her foot-down to that and told him he would dress civilized or she would make his life miserable. Didn't she do that anyway, he wondered as he smoked his cigarette, staring at her? He wanted to hit the road.

Renee practically read his mind, but couldn't fathom for the life of her why he'd want to hit the road with her mother. All her mother ever did was to tell her father to slow down and nag at him while he drove. Each time she barked a driving order, he drove faster and it was getting scary riding in the back seat. He had started taking unnecessary chances in passing way too closely other cars along the two-lane highway just to annoy his wife. And she still wouldn't shut up. Meanwhile, in the backseat, Mike and Renee clung to anything they could find in fright.

Of the five children still living at home, Renee was the second oldest, Mike was three years her senior. Tad was three years her junior, Sam, four years, and Rachel, the youngest, was just a year old baby. She sat in the front seat on their mother's lap. Mike and Renee sat in the middle, while the two younger Goods sat in the back of the station wagon.

Mike and Renee both thought that one-day their parents would get them all killed on a road trip, and begged not to go most of the time.

On this trip, the elder Goods headed south to visit their two eldest daughters and one son, all married and living with spouses in the Twin Cities. Neither Mike nor Renee had ever been there, the reason Mike had refused Sam's invitation to visit along with Renee for two weeks in Rutledge. Mike wanted to experience Minneapolis, St. Paul and all the other things his elder siblings had promised to show him.

Renee smiled as her mother finally climbed back into the car and it drove off out of sight into the horizon. Amen, she thought. She was thankful they were gone and that they wouldn't be back for two whole weeks, and that she no longer had to ride in the strife-riddled car in the middle of a heat wave with no air conditioning.

As her parent's car drove out of sight, Renee turned and looked long and hard at Holly, who was looking back long and hard at her. Holly's hair shown golden in the summer sun. Her pale skin belied the fact that she spent a great deal of time outdoors. The two laughed simultaneously at nothing, grabbed Renee's two suitcases, and started for the apartment building across the street. The tarred highway, so hot their feet sunk lightly into its scalding surface, urged them to hurry.

Inside the Sand's Café, Mrs. Roberta Spur saw as the Good family car pulled up. She was disappointed the elder Goods had not come in to say hello. In fact, she was angry they hadn't. She had so many customers, she could not get outside to speak with them, so she busied herself taking care to hide the disappointment she felt. Maybe they'll stop in on the way back, she hoped; she missed Mrs. Good, her husband, how the two families had gotten along so well. Mr. Good was the one man her husband didn't suspect was trying to chase her, she thought.

Mrs. Spur was angry most of the time anymore, anyway. Sometimes she couldn't seem to help it. The man she married spent most of his time being jealous of her, afraid other men would steal her away from him. He chased off couples wanting to be friends. She was so lonely she could scream. She never could understand his abject jealousy. She had never even considered another man in terms of adultery, but he constantly accused her of it. It was so bad, he didn't believe any of his sons were his, justifying his nasty treatment of them to himself, she suspected.

As Roberta Spur poured him another cup of coffee, Pine County Sheriff Ernie Hansen watched her, trying to keep his crush on her to himself, although he had a hard time not beaming every time she came around. He had never dated a married woman and would not consider the possibility, but he couldn't help himself when it came to finding excuses to come into the restaurant so Mrs. Spur would wait on him, and he could be near her. He saw something there, someone as lonely as he was. He wondered if she sensed that in him.

Besides, the Sands Café had the best coffee for miles. The cooks were pretty darn good, too. Since his wife left him, Hansen didn't get home-cooked meals like those that he was used to. The Sands was the only place around that could compare to her cooking. Besides, if he kept his mouth shut and his ears open, he could always learn a thing or two from the gossip flowing through the crowd that always seemed to be there.

His deputy, Andy Freboni, sat with him amid the hustle and bustle of the cafe. He wasn't paying attention to anything inside the restaurant. Instead, he was watching the scene unfolding in front of them on Main Street. A new kid in town, not a big deal, still, for reasons unbeknownst to him, he noted it. And when Freboni noted something, it was as if it had been chiseled into the hunk of granite that was his brain. He had the memory of an elephant, Hansen often thought, and had come to appreciate since taking office.

Criminally, not much happened in Pine County. Kids were the worst of Hansen's problems and mostly the sheriff's office just wanted to keep them alive until they could grow up and get out of town; drinking and driving where his biggest headache. There was not much else for the kids to do with the exception of the Fourth of July weekend, that weekend. Kids saw that weekend as an excuse to drink and drive. He and his deputies dreaded it for that reason, but at the same time looked forward to it as it brought a much-needed break in their routine. He really didn't like the fact that he'd have to reign in the local kids more so than usual.

Something told him though, that this July 4 would be different, anything but routine, and he'd been on edge because of it. People scoffed at things like psychics, but he didn't. Cops were often psychic, the good ones, anyway, picked up on things, little things, real easy, like when someone was lying to them, or a story that didn't ring true, things like that.

Now he was getting a feeling that he and his men needed to be on top of things over this holiday weekend. Something big was going to happen, something he might want to prevent.

He did not mention this to anyone else though. He just kept his eyes open as he drove the highways between Rutledge and Willow River.

Hansen lived in Willow River, just four miles down the road from Rutledge, which was where his office was located. Willow River was twice the size of Rutledge, boasting 600 souls to Rutledge's 350. It was also a place most kids couldn't wait to grow up and leave.

On the other side of Main Street, Holly and Renee reached a dirt side street that led to the back of the apartment building. The dirt side street continued up to Willow River just east of town. A metal bridge covered the river's expanse not one hundred yards away from Holly's back door as willow and hardwood trees stood languidly along shore, while a beautiful bay horse ate contentedly in a field next to the river.

When Holly turned right to start for the stairs, Renee looked at the rickety structure with trepidation. The back stairwell looked like it was constructed in the dark ages of wood, very old wood. As they climbed each floor, the rickety staircase creaked, and groaned swaying gently under their footfalls, and at each floor they came to an enclosed porch like awning that covered the turn in the steps leading upwards. The enclosures were equipped with wood-boxes where once inhabitants of the three floors of apartments stored their winter heating supply. In 1963, tenants no longer stored wood, but the awnings with their wood-boxes underneath remained and looked as though they would be good places for someone to hide. As she looked around at the gloomy, rickety staircase with not a little fear, Renee asked, "Isn't there another way inside?"

"Nope. This is creepy isn't it? Sam used to scare me all the time jumping out at me from behind those," Holly pointed to the wood boxes, "so if I were you, I'd be prepared for him to try it with you. You might want to watch out for his friends, too. They still try and scare me."

"Oh, great! Now, every time I walk through here I'm going to think the boggy man is going to jump out to greet me!"

"Don't worry about it. Pop got pretty mad at Sam for scaring me all the time, so I don't think he's going to bother you too much. Wasn't much Pops could do about Sam's friends except forbid them to come around here, and you know how that went," she said raising her eyebrows and turning back to look at Renee. They both knew Sam didn't pay much attention to anything his father said.

Renee was glad when they climbed the final flight of stairs passing through the kitchen, then down a long hallway leading into the living room of the apartment. It was nice and well worth the trip up Rickety Hill to get to it. Holly led Renee to her bedroom and helped her unpack so they could get back outside right away and over to the diner. Her parents had prepared a meal for them, and after that, Holly was taking her to meet some of her new friends, the Thompson sisters. When the girls finished they ran out the back door of the apartment not watching where they were going. So engrossed in talk were they that they ran smack dab into Sam and his friends. Renee was first out the door and ran right into Sam's arms.

"Hey, you," he teased, "you need to watch where you're going!" He smiled as he looked down at her, still holding her lightly in his embrace although he could have let her loose.

"Did I miss Mike?" he said in all seriousness releasing her.

She melted with regret as he took his arms from about her growing frame, and said, "Yes, he's gone with the folks. He was looking for you, though. They'll be back in two weeks."

"Hey, you guys, this here is Renee Good. She's a friend of Holly's. Her brother Mike is a good friend of mine." Sam turned back to Renee, "I'm sorry I missed him."

Renee couldn't find anything to say as Sam looked down at her with his beautiful blue eyes shinning and his blond curly hair falling about his face. He wore the uniform of the rebel, a white T-shirt with cigarettes rolled up in the sleeves, tight blue jeans and engineer boots made of black leather with a heavy sole and a studded belt strap across the ankle. He looked tough, but the girls knew he wasn't. Holly was crazy about him and her other two older brothers, Ernie and Rob, both gone from home and living somewhere on the East Coast. They hardly ever wrote and Holly told Renee many times how much she missed them. Renee did to; so did her oldest brother, Frank who was a good friend of Ernie's.

Now though, Renee's heart fell when Sam took his friends inside; she and Holly were alone once again to make their way downstairs. She forgot him soon enough, however, because when they got to the second floor landing, out from behind a wood box jumped a young man screaming, "Boo!" at them.

"Dennis Hanson, you idiot! How many times have you been told not to do that to me?" Holly's hands were on her hips as she yelled at this stranger to Renee. Since Dennis wasn't paying any attention to her, and staring at Renee, Holly introduced them. He just smiled at the two without saying a word and went upstairs and inside the apartment with Sam and the rest of Sam's friends.

"He's been waiting for you to get here," Holly said over her shoulder to Renee as they made it to the bottom floor landing and jumped off the porch to walk back to the dirt road that would take them to Main Street. "You might need to watch out for him; I don't know. There aren't too many new girls around here and he might just get ideas."

Ideas—what kind of ideas, Renee wondered as they again crossed the hot tar over into the cool air-conditioned restaurant?

Mrs. Spur, who saw the two crossing the street, waited for them from behind the front counter. It was noon and the restaurant was packed, so she didn't have time to talk, but when they came in she sent them to the back room where Holly's father, Old Man Spur (as he was known to his sons), had two cheeseburgers with French fries ready and waiting. Mr. Spur insisted that they drink milk with their meal, too.

The back room, a bar, was magic for Renee. It smelled of grease and food and liquor as the two sat at the bar eating. Renee had never seen a bar. Her parents never drank, except that one time on their twenty-fifth wedding anniversary when they had champagne (her mother got tipsy).

Sitting alongside them at the bar were others who were quite accustomed to their surroundings. Renee tried to absorb everything so she could remember and write about it later. She studied the bottles that lined the bar and wondered what was in each. She could see the kitchen through the open door, and the fry cooks working, watching as they pulled up more French fries out of the deep fryer. She saw as they filled plates full of shrimp and fried chicken and placed them on a counter where Mrs. Spur could get them and serve them to people sitting in the front, customers Renee could not see. She noticed a couple of old men sitting at the bar sipping something out of small glasses that smelled sickly sweet. Four men sat in a booth next to a pool table near the back door. They had on dirty clothes and were eating burgers and fries and had beers bottles in front of them that where covered with ice. Renee wondered what the whitish colored dust was that covered their clothes.

A woman, older than either her or Holly's mothers, and wearing more make-up than Renee had ever seen on one woman, sat by herself in a booth next to the Wurlitzer jukebox, which separated the front of the diner from the back bar. Renee could smell her perfume all the way over at the bar. The woman was talking to someone although no one shared the booth with her.

"Don't mind her," Old Man Spur said when he noticed Renee watching the lone woman. "She's sort of lost her mind. Husband died in a car accident, son died in a separate car accident not two weeks later. She hasn't been the same since. That was two years ago, they tell me. We just leave her alone and get her what she wants. Most of the guys," he nodded at the four in the back by the pool table, "keep her in liquor while they're here. They were friends with her son."

Renee couldn't imagine what it would be like to loose a son and a husband like that. She looked at the woman again, trying to keep her gaze discreet. She seemed nice enough, she thought as she took another bite from her burger. Man, this was too much. She had never heard of such tragedy, couldn't imagine it, yet here she was sitting in the same room with someone who had lived it!

Renee turned her gaze to Old Man Spur as he stood at the corner of the bar smoking a cigarette, his hawk eyes dancing about the room as ash from his cigarette fell onto the bar away from the ashtray. He kept close watch on the barroom customers and made sure they had all they wanted and that the cooks in the kitchen were doing things his way.

Renee often wondered about her friend's father. She had the misfortune of witnessing some of the things he put Holly's mother through, although she never said a word about any of it to her own mother.

She was there the night Holly's mother came home from work, sleeping in a bed across the hall, in a house where all the bedroom doors where left open, when loud noises woke her up. She heard Old Man Spur banging on the metal pipes of his wife's bed and screaming insults at her. He kept it up most of the night, not letting her sleep calling her filthy names. Renee didn't really know what the names meant, she had no one she could ask, but she could tell they were filthy by the way he said them. She often wondered, too, why they slept in separate beds; her parents didn't, but she had no one she dared ask such a question sensing it was full of information she wasn't ready to hear.

She also saw how Old Man Spur treated his sons, which wasn't much different from the way he treated his wife, but he was his nastiest when dealing with Sam. He accused Mrs. Spur of having an affair and said Sam wasn't his son in spite of the fact that Sam looked just like him.

Sam hoped that was the case and that he really wasn't his old man's son. He hated his father. The odd thing about all of it was that Old Man Spur never ever said a mean thing to Holly, and he was always nice to Renee.

As they finished their meal they told Old Man Spur they were going over to the Thompson's house, but as they spoke, the Thompson sisters came through the back door into the dimly lit bar. Squinting in an attempt to adjust to the dark lighting, it was a short time before the three Thompson sisters could see either Holly or Renee.

Holly was up from her stool in a flash with Renee right behind her to greet the girls. But before introductions were made, a mild disturbance at the front of the diner drew everyone's attention. At the sound of a plate crashing to the floor, Renee and Holly turned to look, as did Old Man Spur and the others at the bar.

Mrs. Spur yelled, "You get out of here! I've taken all I'm going to from you." The next thing the girls heard was the sound of the front door slamming.

"What is going on?" Old Man Spur demanded as he tottered to the front of the diner. Twenty years older than his wife, he was now getting on in health as he had spent most of his life drinking booze and smoking cigarettes. At sixty years of age the extra weight he carried on his short body was most pronounced on his stomach making him look as if he were nine months pregnant and slowing him down considerably. When he reached the threshold between the back and front of the restaurant, he gazed down at a hamburger steak and its accruements littering the diner floor.

"It was just Mr. Hanson again. He said we didn't cook his steak right. It's fine. It was fine when it came out of the kitchen. He's just had too much to drink again. Can't admit to himself that his stomach is rebelling against food because of the booze." Mrs. Spur seemed sad as she spoke of the unseen Mr. Hanson. The girls watched everything from behind Mr. Spur's rotund backside.

"Well, just pick up the mess and stop making such a spectacle of yourself!" Old Man Spur growled as he went back into the kitchen. He did not appreciate his wife's sympathy for the town drunk.

Chapter Two

The Thompson sisters, Shannon, eleven, Kathy, twelve, and Judy, fifteen, stood behind Renee and Holly watching the mild disturbance, and as the girls turned around, Holly remembered she wanted to introduce Renee to them.

"Looks like your folks are having another . . . spat," Judy said smirking at Holly. Renee took an immediate dislike to her.

"Oh, like Mom and Dad never fight," Kathy snapped at Judy, who, in turn, gave her a dirty look.

"Renee, this is Shannon, Judy and Kathy," Holly said pointing to each girl in turn. "This is Renee Good, my old friend from up north that I told you about," Holly said pointedly to Kathy and Shannon deliberately leaving Judy out.

After a brief moment of awkwardness, Judy suggested they go over to their house because their parents were out shopping and would be gone all day. The girls trooped outside into the hot July sun and walked the three blocks to the Thompson house.

"Where's Sam today?" Judy asked as sweetly as possible as they walked across the old ball field, ducked through broken fencing and crossed onto the walk in front of the Thompson house.

"Don't know. He doesn't need to report his whereabouts to me," Holly snapped.

Renee went on red alert. Her hearing seemed sharper as did every other sensory preceptor she possessed, while she wondered what that simple exchange between Judy and Holly meant for her and her Sam fantasy as they walked into the air-conditioned Thompson home, the nicest home in Rutledge.

Mr. Ralph Thompson, a lawyer in nearby Willow River, and husband to Mrs. Viola Thompson, was one of Rutledge's most outstanding citizens in 1963. His wife, Viola, served on any and every local committee she could, including the Rutledge school board. Renee wondered about the pair as she got the fifty-cent tour of the Thompson home from Judy.

A three-story Victorian, Renee thought the house a mansion as she compared it to the simple farmhouse she lived in. Judy, very much her mother's daughter, noted with satisfaction the look of appreciation on Renee's face as she brought her through the house. Holly was not impressed, Judy could tell, but of course, she'd been in the house many times since moving to Rutledge.

Tastefully decorated, the Thompson house was loaded with fine furnishings and paintings and had every modern appliance known to man abounding in it. Mrs. Thompson was the first in Rutledge to own a dishwasher and a modern washer and dryer, something she liked to point out to the other women who served on as many committees as she did. The others served in an effort to keep up with her, and she knew it.

When the sisters took Renee upstairs to their bedrooms, Renee had to pinch herself to keep from gasping, the rooms were so lovely and feminine. Judy invited them into her room first hoping to get a reaction from Renee there as well. Holly remained mute. Renee noticed the uncharacteristic hostility coming from her friend toward Judy and worked to follow her lead. She had to work very hard, as Judy's room was even nicer than all the rest; one like she dreamt would someday be hers. The canopy bed was covered in pink taffeta. Judy's French provincial, white dressers were cluttered with pretty jewelry boxes, music boxes, perfumes, and other various sundries boggling Renee's mind with their numbers. She had never seen so many pretty things in one space before.

Upon the bed were three chiffon evening dresses. Judy had been trying to decide which to wear that evening to a function at the country club her parents belonged to in Willow River. Kathy had declined her parent's invitation to attend; Shannon was happy to do whatever Kathy planned on doing, so she wouldn't be going, either. They planned to stay home for the evening, and since Kathy was twelve and very reliable, the elder Thompsons didn't worry about leaving Shannon with her.

Judy grabbed up the dresses hurling two of them onto a sitting chair. Kathy and Shannon sprawled out on the bed with Holly as Judy took one dress and held it up in front of herself admiring both it and her figure in a mirror, asking Renee what she thought of the dress. Renee was too tongue tied to offer an opinion, the dress, she thought, was stunning.

"Come on you two; let her pick out her own dress. You know she doesn't listen to anything we have to say anyway," Kathy said jumping off the bed and grabbing Holly's hand steering her out of Judy's room. Kathy garnered another dirty look from Judy for her efforts; she wanted to continue to wallow in Renee's admiration.

Shannon, as usual, tagged along behind Kathy and the others. Kathy's bedroom was also beautifully decorated, and much neater than Judy's was. There Renee found something much more to her liking—books, and lots of them. They lined the walls. She scanned titles as Kathy sat on her bed with the others.

"Judy can be such a pill sometimes. Just ignore her," Kathy said as she watched Renee looking through her books. "Hey! I got some new records; do you want to hear them?"

"Sure, what have you got?" Holly asked.

"Roses are Red," by Bobby Vinton and "Sugar Shack." Kathy put one of the 45 RPMS on a small record player and turned it on.

"My folks just put those on the juke-box," Holly offered.

"How do they know what records kids like? I mean, they're kinda' old," Kathy said.

"Me and Sam tell them what we like . . . My mother's not that old."

"I didn't mean anything by that. It just seems like your dad is old."

"Let's drop it, okay? My dad might be old, but your sister's a jerk."

"You're right, she is, and I'm sorry, Holly. I didn't mean anything against your dad."

Holly smiled at Kathy and the two started dancing around the room to Sugar Shack trying to imitate the steps they saw American Bandstand kids doing on the weekly television show. Shannon and Renee soon joined in, but none of the girls had mastered any of the dance steps to the Swim, or the Jerk and looked so silly to themselves, they all started laughing.

"What say we sneak out of here, leave Judy to herself and her mirror, and head to the lake at Willow River to go swimming. It's a perfect day for it!" Kathy's eyes were big and hopeful as the other girls nodded in agreement. She and Shannon grabbed their swimsuits and headed downstairs on their tiptoes in hopes of eluding Judy. They needn't have bothered, Judy was so busy looking at herself in the mirror trying to decide which gown to wear, and she never heard them leave.

The four girls jumped on two bikes and rode over to Holly's with Holly and Renee riding shotgun behind Kathy and Shannon. When they got there, the group ran upstairs forgetting completely the fact that Sam and his friends were there.

They ran into the apartment laughing and letting the screen door slam as they burst into the hall and down to the living room where the boys sat. Sam was up and staring down the hall at Holly and Renee smiling. "You two think you could get a little louder? I don't think Old Lady Conway heard you."

"Oh shut up." Holly said running for her bedroom on the other end of the rectangle living room.

"And what about you," Sam said smiling at Renee. "Do you always run through someone else's house like an elephant?"

"About as much as you do." He sounded so much like Mike she couldn't help but sting him back.

"Oh, getting smart are ya?"

"How could you tell?"

Sam hooted with delight at Renee's deadpan comeback. He had never noticed before that she was smart and wondered why.

The other boys let out a hoot, too. No one had ever smarted off to Sam and lived to tell about it, so to speak. They admired the gangly kid that so nonchalantly forced him to take some of his own medicine. No one bothered to introduce any of the boys to the girls, or the girls to the boys.

"Holly, what are you up to?"

"We're going swimming at Willow River Lake; do you mind?"

"No, I don't mind," Sam said as he watched the girls run into Holly's room and shut the door. When it closed, he motioned to his friends to follow him and they thundered down the narrow hallway, and out the door and down the rickety stairs to Henry Samson's 1955 Chevy convertible parked by the dirt side road. Henry had already given Sam the keys to the car although his parents had expressly forbid it.

Henry, Hank Hall, George King and Smiley Rains were all from Willow River and the bunch of them jumped into the car along with Sam and Dennis Hanson.

Sam started the engine screeching the tires as he peeled out from the side street tearing up the dirt road as he turned onto Main Street heading north to Willow River. He hoped everyone in town heard him peeling out enjoying the thought that he might be pissing off the adults. As he flew down the four miles to Willow River traveling at speeds just shy of 100 miles per hour, he wondered if the girls would be surprised to find him and his friends at Willow River Lake when they got there.

Inside Holly's bedroom the girls changed into their bathing suits putting their street clothes on over top because there were no dressing rooms at the lake. While they were changing, they heard the boys thunder out of the house and Sampson's car roar out of town.

The four-mile bike ride to Willow River Lake on the dust covered, sandy road next to the railroad tracks got so hot the girls removed their shirts and tied them around their waists as they peddled their bikes leisurely down the road.

"You couldn't have picked a better day to get here, Renee," Holly said as the girls peddled their Schwinn bikes over gravel and rock. "Tomorrow is the Fourth of July and the town's having a big celebration. There's even a rodeo this weekend. It's just outside of town. We can ride bikes to that, too. I don't think it costs anything to get in, either." Holly was excited about the rodeo. She loved horses as much as Renee did.

"You know what else? Our landlady, Old Lady Conway? She lives on the first floor? She's got a horse! She just lets it run around in a fenced in field next to the river. I'll show it to you when we get back. He's real pretty, but she won't let anyone ride him. She's like 100 years old or something . . . what the heck does she want with a horse?"

"Yeah?" Kathy chimed in picking up on Holly's excitement. "She has to be 100 years old at least! Some people in town say she's a witch, too!" She let that information drop on the stranger to see what kind of reaction she would get. Rutledge might be small, but the residents were not uninteresting, she hoped to convey to Renee. Holly nodded her head in agreement.

"Why do you think she's a witch?" Renee asked, intrigued.

"She knows stuff. She says it's the Lord talking to her. Makes you wonder cause she's right so much it creeps people out. She never goes to church. Says the pastor is a hypocrite and more of a sinner than his congregation is! She makes a lot of folks mad, too, especially my mother, because it was my mother that talked the church into hiring the guy! Anyways, she's old and she's strange."

Holly and Shannon were both nodding their heads in agreement. This was all very exciting to Kathy and Shannon. Not only had a new friend arrived in their midst just a short time ago, (Holly) but now she was bringing in another stranger, one they already liked and they wanted her to be impressed with them.

Shannon, being the youngest of the four, felt she had to agree with the group on this, even though secretly she liked Mrs. Conway very much, and agreed with her 100 percent about the pastor. Her mother always got mad at her for saying she didn't like him, but she felt uneasy around him. Shannon didn't change her mind under the pressure her mother applied to get her to do so, either. She knew a creep when she met one. For now though, she just wanted to make friends with the new girl.

By the time the girls finished talking, they had arrived at Willow River Lake and couldn't wait to jump in the water. They were so hot from the bike ride, they dropped their bikes in the sandy mounds of the beach, and tossed their clothes in the dirt as they ran laughing to jump into the water from the dock. They were in such a hurry to get into the water, they never noticed Henry Sampson's car sitting in the parking lot, or the older boys standing outside the beach area watching the swimmers enjoy the summer sun.

The girls were a sight. Unconscious of their looks, they had no way of knowing what an impact they were having on onlookers. Each girl in separate ways was a vision of beauty about to bud out. Holly, Renee and Kathy were all approaching young womanhood; none of the three was there yet, though. Their bodies only hinted at what they would become. Their breasts were small and their legs long. Silky blond, (Holly), raven (Kathy), and dark auburn (Renee), hair bounced as they ran, and glimmered in the sun like flax, copper, and ebony. Shannon, raven haired like her sister, approached young womanhood with potential, too, yet retained the ungainliness of youth tripping over her own feet as she bounded for the lake. None of the girls cared.

The boys did. Sam watched Holly and Renee with new eyes. When it struck him just how pretty they really were, he turned to see if his companions had noticed. He didn't like the look he saw in Dennis Hanson's eyes. He turned again to look at the girls. His heart leapt as he watched Renee jump around on the dock frolicking with his sister. He watched as they dove into the water, climbed back out on the dock squealing with laughter and jumping once again into the coolness of the lake. They were such a sight Sam did not give a thought to Judy. When he could finally take his eyes away, he impulsively herded his followers into the Chevy and they took off into Willow River proper to see if they could pick up girls. He didn't want his friends watching his sister or Renee anymore.

Holly, Renee, Kathy and Shannon never knew the boys were there. They swam the afternoon away, and at five p.m. hopped back onto their bikes and rode back to Rutledge. By the time they got home, they were as hot as they had been before going swimming.

Once inside the city limits, the girls went their separate ways. Holly and Renee went back upstairs to Holly's apartment to change clothes. They lounged around in Holly's bedroom for quite sometime until they heard someone coming down the hall. Mrs. Spur brought them dinner at 6:30 p.m. and told them that she and Mr. Spur wouldn't be home until late. She left money on the table and told them if Sam came home, maybe he would take them to the drive-in movies at Willow River. Holly doubted that would happen, but she took the money just in case. Aside from the drive-in theatre, there wasn't much for teenagers to do in either village.

None of that mattered to Renee. She had not talked to Holly for so long she just wanted to catch up with her friend's life and was happy to have some time alone with her. They could play music, watch TV or something if they wanted entertainment. She was hoping Sam would come home to take them to the movies though, but if he didn't it wouldn't matter too much.

As they ate, curiosity plagued Renee and she asked, "What about this Conway woman? Is she really a witch?"

"I don't know, but she is spooky. She'll tell you things about yourself. She calls herself a prophet. She knows things. It's creepy."

"Do you believe in God?" Renee did and didn't know why. Her parents never took her to church. She used to ride the Salvation Army bus to Sunday school every Sunday, but that was the only religion she had ever heard.

"I don't know." Holly said staring out the window so intently, she seemed transfixed. She had attended those same Sunday school classes but neither girl had spoken of the subject of God outside of church.

Something was troubling Renee about the subject and she had been dying to talk to Holly about it, but she didn't know how to broach it.

Holly came out of her revere and began to check out the latest Movie Star magazine hoping to find something written about the Beach Boys. Renee decided it was a good time to jump into what she had on her mind.

"I heard a voice the other night—at home. It called my name—three times," she whispered.

Holly looked up from the magazine at Renee to see she was on the verge of tears.

"I don't know what it means. My mother told me to shut-up about it and never to mention it to anyone. She's always telling me to shut up every time I try to tell her anything that I've seen. Like that time I was in church and the pastor was talking. I saw the earth on fire, orange, and red and yellow flames lapping up everything in sight. It scared me. When I tried to talk to my mom about it, she told me to shut up about that too, and said my imagination was playing tricks on me."

Holly looked puzzled, then her eyes lit up, "Hey! I know! Talk to Old Lady Conway! Downstairs? She says she knows about this stuff. And you know, Renee, if your mother is telling you to shut up there's probably something to it. She doesn't usually get things right about that kind of stuff you know."

"I thought you said the woman downstairs was crazy?" Renee was not eager to meet someone the other kids called a "witch."

"Everybody says she's crazy 'cause she isn't like them. Sam figures she's probably right on the money if she isn't like most folks."

"Well, I'm game, but I'm not ready to talk to her now."

"Let's wait until after the Fourth and we can both go and see her."

Renee nodded her head in agreement. By now, it was eight p.m. and Sam Spur still wasn't home. The girls doubted if they'd see him that evening. Instead of going out, they set their hair, poured over the latest fashion magazines, called Kathy Thompson, then went to bed about eleven p.m. The Spur elders had not yet come home by the time the girls were fast asleep.

Outside the apartment, standing behind the wood box on the third floor landing was Estelle Conway. She smiled to herself and watched for a while as the girls slept. She saw the stranger arrive earlier that day and knew she was the one. She would wait, though. The girls were coming to her in one day's time. That was best. Slowly Mrs. Estelle Conway, now 111 years old, stepped down the three flights of stairs to get to her apartment on the first floor. She was as spry and as healthy as a seventy-year-old, and enjoyed walking up and down the stairs when no one was watching. She went inside her apartment and warmed a glass of milk before going into her bedroom. Inside her room, she retrieved her tattered and worn Bible from the closet, moved over to sit in her tattered and worn rocker, seated herself, and began to rock turning to Revelation and reading, smiling as she did and thinking, yes, she's the one, all right.

Chapter Three

When Holly and Renee awoke at six a.m. the next morning, they were greeted by sweltering heat inside Holly's tiny bedroom, which had only one window that faced onto the landing. It was not open. Holly's mother didn't allow the window to be opened at night since access to Holly's bedroom would be too easy for an intruder. Holly kept it open during the day and now hurried to open it and get a little relief from the heat.

As she did, Renee wiped the sleep from her eyes and stretched out her long limbs while still lying in bed. "What time is it?" she asked.

"Time to get up," was all Holly said dashing off into the bathroom before Renee could. When she was out of sight, Renee's mind wandered back to Sam, and she wondered if he was home. His room was right next to Holly's, so she would find out soon enough.

She jumped out of bed and searched her wardrobe for the perfect outfit. She wanted to look nice, in case she saw him at breakfast. She studied her hair in the mirror and brushed it to bring out its sheen. When Holly returned, she rushed into the bathroom and dressed as quickly as she could. When she finished, she found Holly in the kitchen getting out cereal and milk for the two of them.

"The folks never came home last night," Holly said to Renee. "Neither did Sam. None of their beds are slept in."

Renee tried to hide the shock she felt. Never had her parents ever stayed away from the house all night leaving the kids alone. "Where do you think they all are?"

"The folks are probably sleeping off a drunk at the bar. Sam probably spent the night with Judy Thompson. They've been seen together numerous times."

Renee's heart ached at what Holly said about Sam. She wasn't experienced enough to keep the hurt from showing in her face and Holly said, "You should have known he'd be like that. He's messed up Renee, but that doesn't mean he doesn't like you; he does. He's older than we are is all. He can do things with Judy he can't do with you."

"Like what!" Renee demanded. "I would kiss him if he wanted me to. What else is there?"

Holly said, "There's other things we don't know much about yet, but

Questenberg—16—Summer Winds

I'll tell you this; before this summer is over, I'm going to find out. Somebody is always saying something about good girls or bad girls, and I want to know what they mean, and what makes good girls different from bad girls, don't you?"

"I've heard that! I've been wondering about it myself. I've tried to ask my parents, but they just get red in the face and leave the room. What is that about?"

"I don't try to find out from mine. I've been listening to Judy Thompson. She's been saying plenty. That's the only reason I put up with her. She's and encyclopedia of information on that subject let me tell you! But she still hasn't told me everything. Even Kathy and Shannon are waiting to hear that!" Holly raised her eyebrows as she talked igniting Renee's curiosity to a fever pitch.

"Like what?" She breathed eager for any enlightenment on the subject of sex.

"No, I'm not saying anything cause I'm not sure what she meant, but just wait and see if she doesn't start telling us stuff when we're alone with her. I can't stand her otherwise, but the information she gives out is very interesting," Holly's eyebrows rose once again to indicate to Renee that this mystery was juicy.

Renee couldn't wait to find out more. Still, she wished Sam were home. She got her wish soon enough. Sam came stumbling into the kitchen as the girls where cleaning up the dishes from their breakfast.

"You two are looking pretty dashing this morning," he winked at Renee who instantly got angry.

"How would you know? I doubt if you can see your own nose!" She was angry with him, jealous of any time he might spend with an older, more sophisticated girl.

Holly giggled.

Sam looked at her. "Okay, what's so funny?"

"You are! Look at you. You can hardly stand up! What have you been doing?"

"Oh, me and the guys were drinking beer by the lake. Must've had too many," he belched. They girls both giggled. "Saw you guys there, yesterday. Looking pretty cute in your swimsuits. Some of the guys thought so, too. Renee, you've got an admirer."

Her heart lurched to her throat. She thought Sam was going to tell her he liked her. Instead, he said, "Yep, old Dennis Hanson's really got a thing for you."

Sam was perplexed by the deflated look that fell across Renee's face. "What? He not good enough for you?"

"Oh why don't you just shut-up, you idiot!" Renee said storming out of the kitchen to the back porch balcony.

"What?" Was all Sam could say to Holly who stood in front of him shaking her head?

"Why don't you go sleep it off? By the time you get up, the parade will be going on, so will the rodeo." Holly turned and left heading for the back porch.

Sam found himself alone in the kitchen still looking bewildered. He shook his head in wonderment then decided to take Holly's advice and go lie down. He passed out as soon as he sprawled across his full size bed.

"Well at least you know he wasn't with Judy last night," Holly said to Renee as the two stood atop the landing watching the big bay gelding run alongside Willow River to the end of the fence and back. The animal held his tail high, tossed his head and snorted as he flew across the paddock rearing up, then bucking as he appeared to revel in the morning sunshine. The sun glistened off his well-brushed hide. Renee couldn't take her eyes off him. She loved Sam, but right now Sam couldn't possibly compete with the vision racing before her.

"And he did say I looked cute in my swimsuit," Renee giggled as she turned to look at her friend. This was not a time for sorrow. She only had two weeks to be with Holly, and she'd make the very best of them if it were the last thing she ever did. So what if Dennis Hanson had a crush on her? He wasn't the first boy to like her. Maybe Sam will get jealous! She realized in a revelation that buoyed her spirits higher than they had been yet that day. Yes, things were indeed looking up!

The two ran down the stairs and jumped off the bottom step to run across the street to the café. There they found Holly's parents busy cooking and waiting on customers. The Fourth of July would be a big day for them.

"Hey you two," Mrs. Spur greeted as they walked through the door, "did you have your breakfast?"

"Yeah, Mom, we had cereal."

"Good. You both can get aprons on and give us a hand today. We've been busy all morning. We spent the night here getting ready for today and we could use a little extra help right now."

"How come you left us in the apartment by ourselves?" Holly didn't like the fact that she and Renee were alone all night, although she didn't let on to Renee.

"You weren't alone. We had someone watching you."

"Who, nobody was inside the house but us!"

"The same woman who looks out for you every time we leave the house—Mrs. Conway."

"What! I never saw her! Mom, you know everybody in town calls her a witch!" Holly bent at the waist looking at her mother with eyes blazing fury.

"Who do you think you're talking to young lady? Do you really think we would go away and leave you two with no protection? Now you take your attitude and get to work washing dishes, and I better never here you call Mrs. Conway anything other than her given name, do you hear me?" Holly was no match for her mother's fury, rarely in evidence.

"Yes Mom. I'm sorry. It's just a shock. I didn't know you knew her even."

"We rent from her silly, of course I know her, now you go and get to work." Mrs. Spur turned her attentions on Renee.

"Renee, have you ever waited on anyone in a restaurant before?"

"No." Renee looked around in a panic. Holly's mother couldn't mean she should serve food to total strangers! She could hardly talk to them for crying out loud! Mrs. Spur knew that!

"Don't go getting upset now; nobody in here bites and I'm going to be right with you teaching you what to do. You might be surprised. People coming in here tip pretty well."

"Tips? What are tips?"

"You wait on people, they pay their bill, and they usually give the waitress a little something extra for themselves. You'll make more than enough money to go to the rodeo with Holly. I hear there might be a carnival coming, too. You can go on the rides." Mrs. Spur stood in front of Renee hoping to spark something in her daughter's shy friend. She knew well that there was no job better than waitressing to alleviate a child's shyness.

She stood behind the counter in the front of Renee assuming Renee would yield to her will, and began her first lesson. Renee stood there looking bewildered as Mrs. Spur started teaching her what she had to do. Renee worked hard at take in everything Mrs. Spur said.

If what Mrs. Spur said about tips was true, that meant Renee wouldn't have to spend the little bit of money her folks had given her to pay for playful expenses. They didn't have a whole lot to spare, she knew, her father being a farmer, but they managed to give her some cash anyway. The family never wanted for anything, but money for extras, that was a sacrifice for her parents and Renee knew it. If Mrs. Spur was right, maybe she could save what her parents gave her and give it back to them. She liked that idea, but when she looked around at all the customers, her heart raced. It would be difficult to greet a bunch of strangers.

In her forty plus years Mrs. Spur had seen a thing or two and knew a shy child when she met one, which is how Renee was three years ago when she and Holly became friends. When the Spurs first visited the Goods, Renee had been so shy she wouldn't come out of her bedroom until Mike forced her out over an hour after the Spurs had arrived. Of course, Renee and Holly had been glad that he had.

Now Mrs. Spur saw a chance to bring Renee further out of her shell. "I tell you what. Do you see that old guy in the back booth next to the juke-box?"

Renee nodded her head yes.

"I want you to go over there, take this glass of water to him and this small notepad, and write down what he wants to eat. Can you do that?"

Renee's heart leapt, but the man looked nice enough, so she took the glass of water from Mrs. Spur and brought it to him. Renee placed the water in front of the elderly gentleman, and cleared her throat, "Can I help you?" she asked, terrified.

Sam Brown hadn't looked up from the menu until Renee spoke, and when he did, he saw a little girl shaking pretty badly, so he smiled his biggest smile at her. His brown eyes lit up and he good naturally, said, "Why, yes, Ma'am, you surely can help me. I'd like these here pancakes, a short stack, with two eggs over easy, some black coffee and maple syrup for my cakes. Can you get that for me?"

Renee's response to Sam Brown was immediate. His brown eyes held her hazel ones and they knew they could be friends. "Yes, sir," she said smiling. She ran back to Mrs. Spur and asked, "What's a short stack?"

"That's two pancakes, dear. Here's how you write it," she took the green notepad from Renee and wrote on a new piece of paper, short stack with two over easy. "See, that's all you have to do with this one. Now take the notepaper and place it on this rotating rack here for the cooks, then come over here. Here's the coffeepot. Most times in the morning, most everybody wants coffee. If you aren't waiting on anyone, you should take the pot around and fill cups for anybody that wants more. Keep them full. They like that. "

"Now, for Mr. Brown, you get a cup out of here," she pointed to the coffee cups stored on a shelf beneath the coffeepot, "and you bring it empty to him. When you get there, that's when you fill it. Now you didn't ask if he wanted cream or sugar; he only wants sugar, by the way, but next time do that, too. See, we keep the creamers and the sugar down here," she pointed to another shelf, this one under the counter. "Now take a tray, they're right here," again, pointing under the counter, "and put the creamer, sugar and coffee cup on them. Carry that in one hand and the coffee pot in the other." She showed Renee how to balance everything and watched with anticipation as Renee successfully completed her mission in serving Mr. Brown his coffee. When she came back to the counter, Mrs. Spur showed her where the silverware was and schooled her on how to lay that out in front of Mr. Brown. She pulled it off and even tallied up the tab when he was finished. Renee found math easy and surprised Mrs. Spur with her quickness in accurately tallying the cost of the meal.

Mrs. Spur schooled her on how to use the tax table, and when all was done, Mr. Brown congratulated Renee and tipped her one dollar, which in 1963 was substantial.

By the time the morning was over, Renee had decided she had found her vocation. The people were fun, for the most part, and she learned the process of waiting tables easily, of course the noon hour hadn't arrived, so she had no experience with a rushed crowd. Being as it was a holiday, the Spurs knew better than to rely on a green recruit to handle the noon rush hour crowd. As Holly worked happily in the kitchen alongside the fry cooks who treated her like a queen, Renee worked out front and earned ten dollars in tips and the skill to earn more in the future. As eleven a.m. rolled around, the two girls were relieved of their duties and brought into the bar to be served lunch. There would be no more work for them that day. It was time for the pros to take over. They didn't care. If it were like this every day, they would be happy. There was never much to do in the mornings anyway.

That afternoon would be another matter. There was to be a parade and a rodeo, even a carnival, Mrs. Spur had told them. They ate excitedly in anticipation, but the parade wouldn't start until two p.m. and the rodeo not until five p.m. No one knew when the carnival would start up, but it was supposed to be at the fair grounds all weekend, which were right next to the rodeo grounds.

Renee had been too absorbed in her waitress lessons to give much thought to Sam, but now as she and Holly finished their meals, she wondered what he was doing. Maybe they could bring him some lunch and just as she thought it, Mrs. Spur came into the bar with a Styrofoam container and told Holly to bring it home to Sam. That happened to Renee so much, thinking something only to have it come to pass moments later, that she didn't perceive it as extraordinary.

The girls hustled across busy Main Street at noon to run Sam his food. People were already vying for choice spots along the roadway. Rutledge was small, but they put on one of the best parades the local communities had ever seen. Floats and bands from all around the county lined up for the Rutledge Fourth of July Day parade.

This angered many travelers heading south to the Twin Cities. Initially, they didn't want to stop; they just wanted to reach their destination. They had to stop, however, and most would take in the parade, one of the reasons it had grown in such popularity. The strangers told their friends then they all came the next year and multiplied the previous year's crowd exponentially, simply by word of mouth.

The 1963 Fourth of July air was festive. Excitement rang out as the girls made their way though the crowd and crossed over to the other side of the street. They ran up the backstairs to the apartment yelling out to Sam that his food was on the table, then they ran back outside again, not caring if he heard them or not.

He heard all right. He was in the bathroom shaving when they cried out startling him so that he almost cut himself. He was let down when he came out of the bathroom and found the apartment empty again. He saw the Styrofoam box on the table, but without his sister and her friend, it held no appeal even though he was hungry. He went to the windows overlooking Main Street to take in the sights below. No wonder they wanted to get back outside, he thought. Still, they could have waited until they saw him before they ran out.

As he gazed out on the street looking through the faces for someone he might recognize, he saw Holly and Renee talking to Judy, Kathy and Shannon Thompson across the street next to the restaurant. He smiled. He had a date with Judy that night. When he could take his eyes off her, he looked further south and saw Dennis Hanson walking up the street taking in the crowd. Behind Dennis came Gloria Wilson, Judy's friend.

Sam forced himself away from the window after looking at Renee talking to Judy and her sisters. He compared her to Judy and thought she would outshine Judy in the very near future. He turned his attention back to the elder Thompson sister, but she didn't draw him in as she used to. His eyes kept refocusing to Renee. Finally, he looked down at his wristwatch, saw the time, and rushed back into the bathroom to finish dressing. He wanted to get downstairs and mingle with the crowd just like everybody else.

Chapter Four

Joseph Wilson crept out of his fifteen-year-old daughter Gloria's bedroom at three a.m. that Fourth of July morning and went back to bed with his wife, Prudence, Gloria's mother. He wanted to get some sleep before finishing his preparations for Sunday's sermon.

It was getting on his nerves that Gloria didn't go to church. "I don't feel well," she would say to Prudence who would let her stay home because she "looked pale."

Inevitably, Prudence would call to Joseph to come check on Gloria, who would lie in her bed stiff as a board when he sat down on the edge of it.

"You'll feel better soon," he'd whisper in her ear dancing his fingers lightly over her breasts. Prudence always stood directly behind him effectively blocking from her sight what he was doing—deliberately—he sometimes suspected.

He felt no shame at touching his daughter. It was his right to do as he pleased in his own house. After all, he was a man of God and the head of his own family. Still, he wished his wife would back him up and make Gloria go to church. What kind of mother was she anyway, to deny her daughter the word of God? How did Gloria's rebellion look to the congregation who depended on him for spiritual guidance? That is what he'd like to know! After all, he had some important parishioners who depended on him; besides, Gloria would change her tune about him if she saw him in action. He excited women, he knew, once he got on that pulpit. He wanted his daughter to see how magnificent he was up there. Then she would be like the rest, he was sure of it.

There was another whelp getting on his nerves a lot lately, too. Shannon Thompson did not like to be around him, he could tell. She would cringe if he touched her shoulder, or bent down to whisper something in her ear. She was lovely though. There was no reason he shouldn't be the one to "break" her in.

Her mother was easy enough—not that she'd bed him—he didn't want to bed her, she was too old. He courted her for a different purpose. She was the most important congregation member he had. She thought so highly of him, she helped him get elected parish pastor. She was a stellar leader in the community. With her backing, he could do anything he liked, but little

Miss Shannon was another matter, and just the right age.

She made excuses to get away from him, and wouldn't come to any of the children's programs if he led them. He would handle her easily enough, he decided. He'd just have to wait for the right moment and the right moment always prevailed eventually. If after that moment arrived she were to say something about him to her folks, they wouldn't be too hard to dissuade. After all, he was the pastor, she, just a hysterical little girl entering into puberty. It was always that easy.

Later on that day, and downtown, Gloria walked across the street behind Dennis Hanson to catch up with Judy Thompson, but the crowds were so thick, she visually searched them out but couldn't see Judy.

Judy stood next to the Sands Café tucked behind those close to the street watching as Gloria walked past her. She called out, "Hey, you, I'm over here!" She yelled at the top of her lungs because of the size of the crowd. Everyone turned to stare at her. She didn't mind; she lived for attention.

"What's up with you?" She said when Gloria got close enough so that they could talk quietly. "You look down in the dumps?"

Gloria smiled. She wasn't about to tell Judy what was wrong with her, what was going on at home; she knew Judy wasn't anybody's friend. Judy hung around with Gloria because she thought she could outshine her with her fancy clothes and pretty looks. Gloria didn't care. She needed to hang around with someone and Judy was obligated to make friends with her. Judy's mother had brought their family to Rutledge. Gloria was glad Judy adopted her as companion for the summer. She was easy to be quiet around, and so self-centered she didn't look too hard at Gloria, which gave Gloria the anonymity she craved. She didn't want any attention.

It was also through Judy that Gloria met Sam; now there was someone she felt she might be able to confide in, someone she suspected was abused, and knew was an out-cast, shunned by a lot of townspeople. She doubted he'd look down on her if he knew, but still she doubted that she could open her mouth to speak of what her father was doing to her; it was too horrible to tell.

"You don't look so good," Sam said, hitting Gloria's arm playfully. He liked her, better even than Judy, but Judy put out and he found he liked that best of all.

"What's it to you?" Gloria said playfully. She really wasn't in the mood for horsing around, but she liked Sam enough to spar a bit. Deep down, she was really wondering how everything could look so normal, so nice, when at home her own father was raping her. Why aren't their ragging fires, devastating earthquakes, and title waves crushing cities into the sea? How can the sun shine so beautifully? How can so many people have a look of joy on their faces in the midst of her devastation? She wondered how her father could treat her like a whore and not care. While those thoughts flitted through her mind, she stood erect and looked out into the crowd without saying a word.

Sam didn't hold her attention long, and it grieved him as he watched her slip away into herself gazing about at the crowd. He wondered at the sudden change in posture, why her chin jutted out a bit in defiance. Whom was she defying? She reminded him of him, and he wondered what her story was? Was her old man as bad as his was? Maybe it was her mother. He doubted it though. Gloria's posture was just like his; did she have a chip on her shoulder, too?

When she turned her attention back to the group, she looked angrily at all the boys there, including Sam, and wondered if he would do the same things to her as her father given half a chance.

"You look different," Sam said staring into Gloria's angry eyes.

Gloria glared back silently.

Judy didn't like Sam fixing his attention on Gloria, so she slipped her arm though Sam's batting her eyelashes up at him. She looked at Gloria feigning concern at Sam's comment, although she didn't say anything.

Gloria recognized Judy's phony behavior and knew her so-called friend couldn't care less what was going on with her, so she blatantly ignored her.

Without a word, Gloria walked across the street to sit in front of Conway's Grocery. The store's stoop was the best place in town from which to watch the parade.

Everyone else followed without comment. As they crossed the street, Sam watched his friends from Willow River pull up to their usual parking space next to the apartment building. Henry saw Sam, Judy, Dennis and Gloria and joined them with the other Willow River boys in tow.

Renee and Holly stayed next to the restaurant to watch the parade. They saw Sam join up with Judy and Gloria and the others. Renee's heart lurched in her chest at the sight of Sam and Judy arm in arm. She shook her head wondering what Sam could possibly see in Judy.

Kathy noticed. "Judy is just playing with him. He doesn't mean a thing to her. She just likes the fact that he's wild. She thinks he's a big shot 'cause he drives his friend's convertible, but just you wait and see. If they get through two more weeks together, I'd be surprised."

"You sound like you don't like your sister much," Renee observed. She knew why she didn't like her, but Judy wasn't her sister.

"Judy has only one person she cares about, herself. It doesn't matter to her what I feel. And you're right, I don't like her much. She's still my sister, though."

"I hope you're right about her and Sam." Renee turned to Holly who was looking down the road.

At the south end of town, Highway 61 stretched Rutledge's Main Street on toward the Fair Grounds where Holly could see horse trailers arriving. After them came big semi-trucks and the girls guessed that the carnival was arriving, too. How long would it take them to set up, they wondered as they giggled with excitement. This was going to be a BIG weekend!

From the north end of town, music could be heard slowly gaining in volume as the first entry to the parade, the marching band from Willow River, stepped off a side street and made their way down Main with baton twirlers twirling and drum majorettes marching. Behind them came the floats with prom queens and homecoming royalty waving prettily at the crowd. Behind the floats came local politicians riding in open convertibles hoping to get more votes in the next election.

The Shriners and Elk Clubs had entries all decked out in their club jackets strutting down the street, as well. Volunteers and clowns walked the parade route throwing candy to the kiddies as venders lined the side streets selling hot dogs, potato chips and pop.

At the curb, children stood enthralled with parade entries, but Holly and Renee waited for the Appaloosas, Arabians, Quarter horses, Paints, and Belgians pulling big wagons loaded with people that peppered the parade.

Each girl stood there dreaming of the day when each would ride a fiery black stallion down the middle of the street. They'd be so beautiful that a hushed silence would still the throngs and all would watch, mouths agape, at the sight of the girls and their horses. Master animal handlers, each would wave nonchalantly as they sat regally upon their horses that would wear sliver-embossed saddles. The girls would dress in black cowboy shirts with fringe at the cuffs and necklines, and pearl snaps down the front and on the cuffs that would glisten in the sun. Their silver-toed cowboy boots would rest in the stirrups matching perfectly the saddles, and white cowboy hats would don their heads. Their fiery black stallions would prance and snort their majesty before everyone.

As they watched the parade, that is what each girl saw. Everyone else saw that behind the horses and riders came the fire engines, police cars and ambulances from five neighboring towns all blazing sirens as they crept down Main Street.

This Fourth of July hundreds of strangers had flocked the tiny hamlet of Rutledge in anticipation of the festivities that weekend. Besides the parade, there would be a town picnic known for its good food. Add that to the rodeo and carnival, and everyone from many miles around turned up to participate in at least one of the activities. Every business in town vied for the business of the strangers. It was always the most lucrative long weekend in the year for the tiny hamlet, ensuring that more than one business would stay open another year.

The Sands Café was no different. They had specials on food during the day; after nine p.m. they would run a happy hour where customers could consume their favorite cocktails two for the price of one. The place was over crowded with strangers. Old Man Spur appreciated the boom in his business because the money of strangers swelled his pockets. This was the Spur's first year at the Café and their first Fourth of July celebration in Rutledge. Neither husband nor wife had anticipated such crowds even though fellow business owners had assured them it would be an excellent weekend.

Strangers were happy and in a generous mood for they lavished tips on the humble townspeople who served them up their food. Mrs. Spur was in her glory as she floated across the Café floor being the perfect hostess and making sure all her customers' needs were met beyond their expectations.

Among the happy strangers, there to enjoy the day only, came the predators, the type of people most folks in small towns are blissfully unaware of, the type of people that like to take advantage of any situation that presents itself. Purse-snatchers, pickpockets, child molesters, rapists and those that preyed on the elderly, were all present and in abundance.

Sheriff Ernie Hansen and Deputy Andy Freboni walked amid the crowds too, watching, as did scores of other police officers from various departments across the county. They knew what to expect from the predators, and determined that very little would happen to any innocent bystander this weekend. Hansen and Freboni were like hawks flying above a hayfield waiting to swoop down on unsuspecting field mice, their keen eyesight missing no unsavory activity.

Rutledge's Fourth of July holiday was to predators a field day with all types of fruit for the picking. As teenagers milled the streets, and played the jukebox in the Sands' Café blissfully unaware of any clear and present danger, there were those watching their every move waiting to take advantage.

It was then, on that hot, humid, ninety-two degree above zero day, amid friend and foe, that Renee's body decided it was time to grow up. She had no clue what was happening. As she and Holly and Kathy and Shannon walked around enjoying cotton candy from the vendors and watching as prom kings and queens floated by on floats, Renee started cramping just after she ate a hot dog. The girls crossed over the street to sit in front of the grocery store when a cramp grabbed Renee so severely, she moaned in pain and slumped over. She couldn't move.

By this time, Sam and his friends had disappeared into the crowd.

Holly was alarmed at Renee's countenance, which was pale, and she was obviously in a lot of pain. "Are you all right? What's the matter?" She asked fearfully.

Mrs. Conway, who watched the parade from inside her store, saw the girls stop on her front steps, and Renee double over apparently in a lot of pain. She guessed the source of the problem simply by watching her. She had had her eyes on the girls all afternoon, although they didn't know it. Mrs. Conway was well aware of being in the midst of evil, but she was confident of her place in Christ. Though she sensed the evil all around her, she made it her business to see to it the chosen one and her friends were not hurt in any way. She did all she knew to do to protect them.

"I don't feel so hot," Renee said looking up at Holly, her face pale, in spite of her deeply tanned skin.

"Come on, I'll take you upstairs. Maybe you should lie down? You don't look so good." They started for the rear staircase where Renee doubled over twice more, and had to stop before finally making it upstairs and inside the Spur's apartment. Her stomach ached badly.

"I'll lie down for awhile," she said to Holly as Holly dabbed a cold washcloth over her sweating brow. "Maybe it was that hot dog I ate. Go on. Go have some fun with Kathy. I'll take a nap and come down and find you when I wake up."

"Are you sure? I can stay here with you?" Holly was torn. She didn't want to leave Renee, but she really wanted to get back to the parade.

"Yeah, I'm sure. I'll look for you after while. But don't go to the rodeo without me—please! I got to get better to see that!" Renee laughed then doubled over again on the bed. She fell asleep shortly thereafter and Holly went back outside. Before she resumed her fun, however, Holly went into the diner and told Mrs. Spur what happened.

Mrs. Spur said, "You go on and have some fun with Kathy, like Renee wanted you to. I'm going home in a little while and I'll check on her myself. If she's really ill, I and your father will take her to the doctor."

Mrs. Spur smiled as Holly left the diner. She wondered when it would be her daughter's turn to lay ill in her bed thinking she ate a bad hot dog. She went in the back, and talked to her husband then grabbed her purse and headed for the grocery store across the street then upstairs to the apartment. Renee was asleep. She left her purchases on the bed beside her along with a note instructing the child how to use what was in the bag. There were painkillers there, too, if Renee needed one. Mrs. Spur pushed Renee's long dark auburn hair away from her face, bent and kissed the girl, and went back to the diner to work.

Renee woke up two hours later. She felt better but something was wrong. She felt wetness between her legs gasping when she found bloodstains on her inner thighs. She ran to the bathroom to wash and stood shocked to find the blood still leaked from between her legs. She screamed, but no one heard. She took toilet paper, bundled some to stick between her thighs, and ran back into the bedroom for clean clothes. There, she striped the bed so she could wash the stained linen. She prayed no one would come home until she could cover this shame. Then she saw the package Mrs. Spur had left on the bed. She opened it. Inside were a package of pads and a bottle of pills. Entangled in the coverlet was Mrs. Spur's note. When Renee saw that the coverlet had blood on it, she retrieved it and all the other bedding and took it all into the bathroom with her along with the package. The note fell onto the floor on the far side of the bed as she removed the covers. She never saw it. In the bathroom, she opened the package and saw some things that looked like long Band-Aids.

Hey, these will work to hold the blood back! She thought as she secured one to her clean panties with small safety pins. She put the panties on and was quite pleased with herself for being so resourceful. She looked at the bottle of pills and read that they helped with monthly cramping. She didn't know what monthly cramping meant, but since she was cramping, they might help her, too. The bottle said the pills were safe for twelve-year-olds. After she took the amount recommended, she grabbed the soiled clothing and washed it out in the sink.

Since she was the only daughter left at home, she was accustomed to helping her mother with the laundry and knew how to get bloodstains out of underwear. She often did that for her mother, although she had never asked her mother why there were bloodstains on her panties. Maybe her mother was dying, and if that was a fact, she, too, was now sentenced to death. That thought didn't occur to her until she finished cleaning up the soiled bed linen.

She took her panties and shorts and hung them on the back of a chair in Holly's room. She prayed they would dry before anyone got home. The coverlet, she hung outside on the balcony where there was a clothesline. It didn't matter if anyone saw that. Everything was clean now, anyway, but how could Holly explain her wet under things and shorts? She'd hide them until she knew what to do. She was thankful she had the apartment to herself.

When she finished with the chores, she sat on the bed and made sure there were no traces of the blood there. There weren't. She went to the bathroom and checked her Band-Aid to see if there was any more blood coming out of her. There was. She filled with dread believing she too was now going to die, just like her mother.

She trembled as she sat there by herself on the toilet inside the bathroom. What was she going to do? She realized that the thing she had pinned to her panties was doing a good job of keeping the blood from seeping onto her outer clothes. She thought about this for a moment. When it got soaked with blood, how could she dispose of it inside the apartment? If she put it in the trash, someone was bound to notice it. She would find a way. In the meantime, she would take some extras with her and the bottle of pills, get out with the rest of the girls and see if they knew anything about this. Was she dying? She needed to know.

Renee went to the living room, and looked out the window facing Main Street after deciding what to do, and saw that the crowd was now in the park enjoying the picnic lunch and free bandstand music. The parade was over. She couldn't see Holly from the window, but knew she had to be somewhere close by. She turned to leave and there standing directly behind her was Dennis Hanson.

He smiled.

All the hair on Renee's neck stood on end. Dennis lunged at her, grabbed her and put his lips to hers forcing her mouth open then stuck his tongue inside her mouth trying to French kiss her.

Renee pushed back hard enough to unlock the embrace, and with all the strength she could muster, she slapped him across the face, which shocked him so much, he let go of her. She took the opportunity to run for all she was worth, down the hall and out the door and down the back stairs hurling down them two at a time. She didn't stop running until she was on Main Street and into the park in amongst the crowd of strangers crying in fear that she was both dying (the blood) and pregnant (the French kiss).

Chapter Five

After Renee went upstairs to the apartment, Holly, Kathy and Shannon watched the rest of the parade with its many floats, gazing at the prom royalty and wondering if one day one of them would be able to ride a float as queen. Holly mingled with horses and riders in the aftermath of the parade festivities when they milled about the streets on their steeds.

Oh how Holly wanted to have one of the wonderful animals nuzzle her cheek, and be her best friend. She loved to smell the animal's scent as owners graciously let her stroke their horses. Some even invited her to go for a ride as they led their animal around in front of the cafe with Holly sitting in rapture atop it. She was in heaven and could have mingled with the other horse lovers the rest of the day, except for her other friends who were nowhere near as enamored as she was.

"Hey, come on! It's time for the picnic!" Kathy tried to draw Holly's attention away from the horses. She did her best to wait out Holly's infatuation with patience. It wasn't difficult because she took the time to do one of the things she loved to do, watch people. As she did, she saw many familiar faces and many faces she did not know.

As her eyes scanned the crowd, she saw him, a young man sort of hidden inside the doorframe of the gas station across the street from the café. When her eyes met his, her heart leapt in fear; he was staring back at her! There was something not right in his eyes. It sent a chill down her spine. It wasn't as if Kathy could see him real well from her position in front of the café, but she saw enough to make her skin crawl. She turned aside quickly asking herself if she knew him. Try as she might, she couldn't recall ever seeing him before. She took another sidelong peek to her left to see if he was still there. He was, and now he was talking to another creepy looking guy who was watching her then, too. She saw them point in their direction and sensed they were checking out Holly and Shannon as well. She didn't like it.

Just then Sam and Judy walked up, "You know, Kathy, Mom said to be home by 2:30. You're supposed to help with the party tonight."

"Why don't you quite lying! That's you that's supposed to be home helping Mom, so just trot on over there yourself!"

This fight was not a new one between the sisters. Judy repeatedly tried to make Kathy do her chores, trying to make Kathy the families' scapegoat every time something went wrong. Kathy learned how to stand up to Judy long ago, and knew Judy couldn't do anything to her. Oh, Judy tried. Like that time she took their father's leather belt, pulled the covers off Kathy's bed when she was asleep, and began beating her with it to try to make Kathy get up and go do the supper dishes she didn't want to do, even though it was her turn. Kathy wouldn't budge though, and she managed to take the belt from Judy and slap her with it a good one right across the back. God, she had loved doing that.

As the girls argued, the two men who had been eyeing the younger girls slipped off to the picnic grounds to enjoy the free food that women of the Junior and Senior Chamber of Commerce of Willow River and Rutledge had prepared.

By the time Kathy finished her argument with Judy, she had forgotten the men. When she did remember them, she looked in the direction of the garage. They weren't there. She was relieved. They had made her so uncomfortable that when she saw them again filling plates at the picnic, she talked Holly and Shannon into going to the restaurant instead. Just as they were heading inside, Renee, breathless, found them and joined the group.

"Hey you! How are you feeling?" Holly was happy to see Renee up and about. They had so little time together she didn't want to miss any of it. Renee looked funny, though, as if she had been crying. "You don't look so hot," Holly observed.

"I feel better," Renee prayed Kathy and Shannon would soon leave, so she could tell her best friend in the entire world all that was happening to her. How could they be away from one-another for just two hours and in that time have their lives change so completely? What was Holly going to think when she found out Renee was pregnant! He French kissed me! God, how could he do that? I don't even know him! Renee was distraught thinking that was how girls got pregnant. That's what her friends at school had told her. How could this happen to me? I haven't done anything wrong, and what about the bleeding? Am I dying? Whom can I talk too?

Inside the restaurant, the girls seated themselves in the booth where just yesterday the crazy old lady had sat. The thought of so much change in so few hours had Renee in a tailspin.

Mrs. Spur supplied the girls with quarters for the jukebox and music filled the restaurant. The back room burst at the seams with kids dancing, milling about and eating.

Old Man Spur wouldn't be serving liquor until that evening at nine p.m.; a city ordinance forbade it, so kids from Willow River and Rutledge filled the place ordering burgers and cokes, dancing, playing pool and arcade games. Renee had never seen so many teen-agers in one place at one time. As the youngest bunch of kids in the room, the girls sat quietly watching the older teenagers socialize. For them, it was a sight to see.

They watched Sam, Judy and Gloria in one booth talking to some of Sam's friends from Willow River, kids the girls didn't know, not his usual crowd. He had his hand across the back of the booth over Judy's shoulder. Renee ignored it. She had too many of her own problems to worry about

Sam Spur. How he could be anywhere near Judy was beyond her anyway, but if he wanted her, he could have her. She felt deserted in her most dire hour of need.

Renee turned her attentions to Gloria, and after watching her for a little while sensed something was different about her. She didn't appear to be one of the crowd, and some of the looks she gave Judy didn't look so nice, either. Renee liked her immensely wondering what her story was. The more Renee watched the more Gloria intrigued her. She didn't banter with the boys, who obviously thought she was something. She was pretty, Renee noted, yet she held back and didn't use her beauty as Judy did. Judy seemed to thrive on male attention using her good figure and pretty face like weapons.

As conversations raged, Gloria was bored. The young men vying for her attentions were out of their league. She felt spoilt, like a piece of filth. When she showered that morning, after her parents left, she scrubbed her skin until it bled trying to wash away that filthy feeling, but to no avail.

Before she would ever allow herself to get naked in her own house, however, she would fearfully wait until she heard her father start the car and back up out of the driveway. She often sat in the bathtub crying and debating about whether or not to tell her mother what her father was doing to her, but she always decided against it. Her mother never stood up to her father. She always gave in to anything he said or did, saying that he provided for them and it was her duty as his wife to be submissive to his wishes. Gloria snickered, thinking about her refusal to be submissive. Well I'm not the bastard's wife, she thought.

Finally, she got tired of thinking about her situation at home and tapped one of the boys on the shoulder asking him to dance. He looked flabbergasted at the invite, but was on the dance floor in seconds.

In the kitchen, back by the bar, Mrs. Spur watched the booth that her daughter and Renee occupied and wondered what the girls had been up to that afternoon. She wondered if Renee had found the note. She called her into the kitchen and asked her.

"What note," was all Renee said.

Mrs. Spur guessed what might be going through Renee's mind. "Come on Dear, let's go outside for awhile." Mrs. Spur took Renee to a picnic table at the back of the restaurant. Surrounded by a high wooden privacy fence, they were sheltered from view by anyone outside. Restaurant employees took their breaks on the little veranda oasis not even a block off Main Street. Mrs. Spur took out a pack of cigarettes she had in the pocket of her apron, shook one loose from the pack, and lit it. She took a can opener out of the other pocket, the kind they used to call a "church key," and opened two sodas she brought with her to share with Renee. After just a few moments, as she took a long, hard draw off her Pall Mall, Mrs. Spur said, "Did you find my package?"

"Oh, you left that?" Renee said barely above a whisper. She was very uneasy. How could her friend's mother know she was in so much trouble just by looking at her?

"Do you know what those pads are for?" Mrs. Spur watched the child's face closely.

Renee broke down crying, "I'm bleeding!" She pleaded. "I am using them like a Band-Aid to stop the blood! What's wrong with me?"

Mrs. Spur smiled as she pulled Renee close and put her arms around her saying, "Nothing, Dear. You just started your period, is all. That means you're growing up. Every woman bleeds once a month. Bleeding lasts about five, maybe six days, it varies with everybody. I just guessed that was happening to you when I saw you on the steps of the grocery store across the street. I bought you those pads and left them upstairs while you were asleep. That medicine I gave you will put a damper on those cramps you are probably having, too. Did you take any?"

"Yes, I did, and they did work. But you mean I am not dying?"

"No, Dear, you're not dying." And to her amazement, Renee started blubbering again and saying, "I might as well be. I'm pregnant!"

"Pregnant! How can you be pregnant?" Mrs. Spur was so shocked at the statement, she momentarily forgot that having a period automatically nullified pregnancy. "Why in God's name do you think you're pregnant?"

"Dennis Hanson grabbed me and French kissed me, upstairs, shortly before I ran down here. He was behind me in the apartment in the living room when I turned around from looking out the window onto Main Street. I didn't want it to happen!"

"I have no doubts about that, dear," Mrs. Spur said quietly, while fuming internally. She stood up and took Renee's hand to bring her to her feet; then drew her close and hugged her again kissing the top of her head. All the while, her fuming at Dennis Hanson escalated, much like a pressure cooker, and she pushed Renee back down onto the bench beside the picnic table as she paced the patio. "He should not have been in our apartment in the first place, and in the second place, you don't get pregnant by French kissing!" It was then that Mrs. Spur stopped, looked down at Renee's stricken face, sat back down on the bench across from her and took it upon herself to tell the child the facts of life. She had yet to tell Holly.

"You mean that's what those animals on the farm are doing? If a bull does that to the cow, the cow will have a baby?"

"Yes, dear, that's exactly what's going on."

"Oh my God, I am so embarrassed!"

"Don't feel too bad Dear. Most of us, when we're your age don't know what's going on, either." Mrs. Spur took another long draw from her cigarette as Renee gazed up at her with thankful, loving eyes. In one fell swoop, Mrs. Spur had taken her from a dying, pregnant wretch, and turned her into a girl that walked among the living as a whole human being once more without shame. She would be forever in her debt.

"Please don't tell Holly I didn't know," Renee crossed her fingers beneath the picnic table praying Mrs. Spur would let this be a secret between them.

Mrs. Spur looked across at the young girl and nodded her head. "It's between us," she said. What she didn't say was that the Dennis Hanson business was now between her and Sam as well. She would not have any more of that, and was sure Mr. Spur would feel the same way. He wasn't the one to handle it, however, Sam was, and she would ensure that's how it would play out. Dennis wasn't a bad kid, she knew, but he needed reigning in, of that, there was no doubt.

When Renee went back inside to join her friends, she found the back room of the restaurant the same as it was before she went outside, only now she could enjoy it being that the pall of death and pregnancy had lifted off her shoulders!

Kathy and Holly were enjoying chocolate malts Old Man Spur had made for them when Renee sat back down beside them. As she did, he crossed the floor with a malted for her in his hands. "Thanks Mr. Spur," she said smiling at Holly's father. He smiled back and started back for the bar.

"Where did Shannon go?" Renee asked turning back to her friends. Shannon was nowhere in sight.

"She wanted to go home, so I told her to go ahead and go. Sometimes she needs me to tell her things," Kathy said smugly.

"She also said she was afraid, Kathy, and you wouldn't even walk her home, remember?" Holly gave her friend a stern look. She would give anything to have a sister, older or younger, she didn't care, and if the wished for sister was younger she'd have walked her home.

"Why don't we go check up on her," Renee suggested. For some reason a strong feeling of foreboding came over her. She looked across the room and saw Sam and Judy still sitting together, which meant if Shannon did go home, she was there by herself. "Come on Holly, ask Sam and Judy to come with us." Renee felt a sudden urgency, pushed her malted aside, and was up out of the booth and walking toward Sam and Judy before the others could respond.

"Okay." Holly said to Renee's back as she walked away. That suited her fine because she didn't like the look of fear that had passed over Renee's face when she learned Shannon walked home by herself.

"Hey Sam," Renee said as they approached his table. "Seems Shannon went home by herself earlier and we've decided to go check and make sure she's okay. Will you come with us?"

Normally Sam would have become angry at the interruption, but he had a soft spot in his heart for the girls, so he said, "Sure, come on."

"Sam, baby, we don't need to go check on the little baby Shannon. She is just fine, I'm quite sure. Mommy and Daddy are probably home by now. Come on, baby, stay with me, here." Judy padded the seat hoping Sam would sit back down.

"If you want to stay here, go ahead. Me, I'm going to walk my kid sister over to your house with her friends and make sure your kid sister is okay. You guys coming?" As if on cue, Henry, Hank, George and Smiley got up from their seats and followed Sam out the back door.

They were a sight, the boys, as they walked behind the girls. Henry, Hank, and George looked like they could play offensive linebackers for the Green Bay Packers, and they all dressed in the uniform of rebels, just like Sam. In fact, they always followed his lead. Even though Hank and Smiley were one year Sam's senior, they looked up to him. As they crossed the picnic grounds and walked through the swarms of Fourth of July picnickers, adults moved out of their way. The boys displayed no outward signs of malice, but they looked as though they were on a mission.

Many Rutledge residents didn't like the newcomers, the entire Spur family, looking down on Sam in particular. They were scared of them, being strangers and all, and instead of inviting the family into their homes; they bolted their doors against them creating a hostile environment especially for the teenage boy who was already up against more than he knew how to handle with his father.

As he saw the looks on the long time Rutledge resident's faces, the hatred in their eyes, Sam threw his shoulders back and walked as if he were invincible.

When the group of youngsters trooped into the Thompson house, the boys made themselves comfortable in the living room while Kathy ran throughout the house calling Shannon's name without garnering a response.

Judy, being angry because everyone had left her alone inside the Sands, came through the back door as Kathy walked down the back steps into the kitchen.

"She's not here," Kathy said to no one in particular, but as she spoke, she looked at Judy. Judy's presence there was not registering and Kathy looked right through her.

Holly was in the kitchen and said, "What? She went home over a half hour ago."

Renee stood by the kitchen sink trying hard not to let the fear in her heart show, but she was getting an even stronger feeling of foreboding standing inside the house. A dark cloud sat over the kitchen like a shroud. She could see it. "Does everything look okay in the house?" She asked praying that her fear didn't make her voice crack.

"Everything looks fine," Kathy said.

But Renee "knew" it wasn't.

"Look, if the house is fine, it doesn't mean much if Shannon isn't here," Judy said. "She probably went over to visit some of her own friends. She has them, you know." There was so much disdain in her voice for Kathy, that Kathy gave her a dirty look. She had to admit that Judy was probably right. She was not about to say that though.

Renee latched onto that possibility as if it were a lifeline. Of course! She thought. Shannon is just visiting her other friends! It is just like Mom said. I needn't tell anyone what I see. I have to keep my mouth shut. Who wants to think the worst has happened to someone they love anyway! Reasoning away what she knew in her heart to be true, Renee felt much better. Still, she would glad to get out of the house.

Sam walked into the kitchen asking if Shannon were there.

"No," Kathy told him, "but Judy says she has probably just gone to visit some of her other friends. There doesn't seem to be anything out of place in the house, so maybe Judy is right." Kathy, too, wanted to believe Shannon was just out visiting, so she clung to Judy's reasoning as if it were a lifeline rescuing her from a raging torrent. She effectively blocked out what she saw when she went through Shannon's room. The clothes Shannon had been wearing were lying on the floor, her dresser drawers laid open, the speckle of blood in the bathroom sink, upstairs. The single shoe lying near the backdoor, one of the pair she had been wearing earlier, while the other shoe was nowhere in sight. She said nothing.

"Well, come on then since that mystery is solved. Let's all go to the rodeo. Since you girls have been so good today," Sam said to Holly and Renee, "you two can ride with us. We'll even bring you home, deal?" He pointedly left Judy out of the invitation.

"You get to sit in the front seat with me," he said turning and winking at Renee as he walked back into the living room to get his friends. None of them minded if the young girls tagged along TO the rodeo, just as long as they knew they were not to tag along AT the rodeo. That was off limits. Renee didn't care. Just to be able to sit next to Sam in Henry Sampson's car was cause for celebration.

Judy didn't appreciate Sam's offer to the young girls, but it didn't matter too much to her in the final analysis. Kathy was right. She was supposed to be at home when her parents got there to help with the party they planned to give that evening. Besides, the party was much more interesting to her than any old smelly rodeo.

Renee rode in the 1955 Chevy convertible as if it were her chariot and Sam her prince. Holly and Kathy just laughed, but not aloud. Holly hoped that one day she could sit alongside Renee's brother Mike in the same way. Kathy had yet to find that certain someone who would inspire such romantic love; she only hoped it would happen soon.

For Renee, the rest of the day was a blur. Yes, she loved the horses, loved the rodeo, but she was so high on love, she didn't really see any of it. Kathy, too, was distracted. She couldn't get her mind off Shannon, prayed all the while she was at the rodeo that her kid sister was okay. Holly alone was blissfully happy watching as horses and riders performed a myriad of wonders before her eyes.

At the Thompson house, Judy neglected to tell her parents when they got home that Shannon was not with Kathy, and that no one knew where she was—for sure.

Chapter Six

After the rodeo Friday night, Sam dropped Holly and Renee off at home; he went over to the Sands Cafe to tell his mother where the girls where and that he and some of his friends were headed to Willow River Lake. Mrs. Spur took that opportunity to tell Sam what Dennis Hanson had done to Renee earlier.

Sam was livid. How dare Dennis try to steal a kiss from Renee! Renee was a kid, like Holly! Her brother Mike was like a brother to him! Sam stomped out of the restaurant bent on thrashing Dennis within an inch of his life. One look at his face, and Sam's friends went silent, riding in terror as he drove like a manic to Willow River and tore into the dirt parking lot next to the lake. Sam was looking for Dennis. Many of the kids from Rutledge and Willow River congregated at the lake so he expected to see Dennis there as well, but he was nowhere to be found and those Sam asked all said they hadn't seen him at all that night.

Henry Sampson was relieved that Dennis wasn't around. As angry as Sam was, he thought Sam might go too far if he started a fight with Dennis. He was relieved for both of them.

His anger finally spent for lack of target, it wasn't long before Sam got bored with hanging out at the lake, and with driving, so he had Henry drive him home where they cruised around Rutledge a short time halfheartedly looking for Dennis. Dennis was still nowhere around, but they did see that the Thompsons were giving a party, and from all the cars parked in front of their house, and in the old baseball field across from it, they guessed it was a real big party. Sam knew then where Judy was and knew, too, why she hadn't invited him or even let him know her parents were giving a party.

He didn't really care though, because he dated Judy for the same reasons she dated him—to piss off the neighbors.

When Henry dropped Sam off at the apartment building, Sam climbed the rickety apartment steps as quietly as he could. It was midnight and the night was beautiful with a huge moon casting its glow over everything. When he got to the top floor, Sam stopped, pulled out his cigarettes, turned toward the river, leaned on the porch railing, and stood their smoking as he gazed out on the water, which shown like glass under the moonlit sky. He could see Mrs. Conway's horse in the field. It stood there like a statue staring out at something almost as if it too were enjoying the beautiful evening and the moonlight on the river.

Sam took drag after drag off his cigarette as slowly the embers burnt down to his fingertips, and just as he was about to stub it out against the creosote covered wood railing, he heard a shuffling noise to his right. With a start, he turned to face the noise, and from out of the shadows, in a corner near the girl's bedroom window, crept a tiny, stooped over figure. Sam fought to keep calm even though his heart leapt in his chest.

"You just settle down there, Sonny. It's just me. I've been waiting for you to get home."

Sam couldn't believe his eyes as he watched old Mrs. Conway totter toward him. When he was finally able to get his voice, he asked, "What are you doing here?"

"That's original," she said as she snickered and stepped in closer to him. "What I'm doing here is what I've been doing here since the day you folks moved in. I'm keeping an eye on them girls."

"You've been babysitting?" Sam couldn't see his parents leaving Holly with Mrs. Conway. Man, she's old! He thought, as she tottered underneath the solitary light bulb that dimly lit the back porch. He could clearly see the wrinkles embedded deeply into the folds of her face.

"What's the matter Sonny? You thinking maybe I'm not up to it? I'm in a lot better shape than most folks figure. I am 111-years old you know. I'm still climbing these here stairs—every day—for that matter—still out there taking care of that horse. You see anything wrong with that horse? You smell a manure soaked barn, do ya'? Who do you think mucks his stall? Yours truly, that's who!"

"I'm sorry; you just startled me is all. I didn't know anyone was watching the girls," he paused, "I don't think they know it either."

"That's the point, Einstein. Your mother didn't want them to know someone was watching out for them."

"So where were you this afternoon when Dennis Hanson snuck up here and into the apartment? Renee was here by herself and he stole a kiss!" Sam was still livid about what his mother had told him.

Inside Holly's bedroom facing the outer wall, Renee lay wide-awake listening to everything. How did Sam know about Dennis Hanson? She was humiliated.

Too, she had no idea that Mrs. Conway, the one everyone called a witch, had been keeping an eye on her and Holly. They had never seen her in the apartment or anywhere near them. She wasn't worried about that though, barely giving it a second's notice.

She was reeling with the knowledge that Sam was angry with Dennis for kissing her! After he said that, she heard nothing else but his voice as he talked to the old woman. She could make out none of the words, she was so elated. Sometimes, she wished she could be anyone but herself, so she could talk to him as freely and openly as all the other females, old and young seemed to, even Old Lady Conway. But right now, none of that mattered. He was angry with Dennis for kissing her! She heard that from his own mouth! She drifted into blissful sleep to thoughts of kissing Sam.

Even if Renee had stayed awake, she couldn't have heard as Mrs. Conway made her way downstairs, the woman was so light on her feet. Sam wanted to help her down to her apartment, but she would have none of it. No charity for her, thank you very much, but before she would let Sam from her sight completely, she turned back on the stair and looked up to him and said, "You are up against a great deal. If you turn to the Lord, He will save you. Let no one keep you from Him—not even yourself."

The wisp of a woman turned back to the stair and was out of sight before Sam could say anything. What did she say? She couldn't have said what I thought she said, could she? He pondered while taking another cigarette from the crumpled pack nestled in his T-shirt sleeve. He lit it pulling hard and exhaling slowly as he looked back out onto Willow River watching it move slowly downstream lazily lapping at its shores while the moon danced its light off the river's crystalline surface. By the time he had finished smoking, he doubted that Mrs. Conway had ever been on the third floor landing with him.

It was an unusual morning for everyone inside the Spur household the next day. Holly and Renee didn't get up until ten a.m., a rarity for the early birds. When they did get up, they found the elder Spurs in the kitchen, where Mrs. Spur was cooking up an enormous breakfast for everyone.

Rubbing the sleep from her eyes, Holly sat down at the table next to her father smiling up at him as she moved. He had his nose inside the Willow River Gazette catching up on the local gossip. He peeked out from the side of the paper and winked. Holly, still dressed in pajamas, waited for Renee to get out of the bathroom, so she could get dressed.

Renee came to the kitchen table in shorts and a sleeveless top. She walked on air still thinking about Sam. Shortly after she sat down to the table, Sam, too, came into the kitchen being, he said, awakened by the smell of breakfast.

"It's about time you got your lazy ass out of bed, boy," Old Man Spur said from between clenched teeth as he looked at his son at the other end of the table. "Everyone else works their fingers to the bone around here while you just run around with your friends acting like a big shot."

"Don't start on him this morning, Wally! You promised!" Mrs. Spur stood by the stove with a spatula in her hand flipping pancakes.

Old Man Spur ignored her. "We have to hire help to take over for us at the restaurant so we can have a day off—and why? Because my lazy assed son can't get out of bed until 10:30, that's why!" He snarled at Sam. He had yet to shave or dress, so as he sat at the table, his morning shadow grew deeper while his wife beater T-shirt reeked of body odor, and food stains left behind from the soft-boiled eggs consumed at breakfast, which dotted down its front along with syrup, grease and coffee. They all took up space on his once snow white T-shirt that barely covered his rotund stomach. His appetite for food had been sated. His appetite for war with his son just whetted.

Sam stared at his father, glaring, daring him to say more.

Old Man Spur didn't like that, acting predictably. "It's a good thing you get summer vacation, boy, 'cause you're so damn dumb I'm surprised them teachers let you stay in school." He stopped then to measure the reaction he was getting. When he didn't appear to get any response, he started in again. "When you gonna' grow up, boy? I'm getting tired of feeding your useless face. When's the last time you contributed to this family, huh? Where's your paycheck? I ain't never seen one. Doubt if you'll ever earn much more than a dime. Dig ditches, that's what your lazy ass will have to do, too damn dumb to do much else."

Sam didn't say a word.

"You shut your filthy mouth, Wally! I'm sick and tired of you picking on Sam the same way you did Frank and Ernie! Sick of it, you hear!"

"Oh, stop shouting you stupid bitch! Get back to the stove and finish cooking, you ain't good for nothing 'cept whoring around and bringing home these bastard boys for me to feed, anyway! Get too it! And shut up before I shut you up!"

Holly, who had gone into the bathroom to get dressed, came running when she heard the fighting start up again. Before Renee had arrived to spend two weeks with her and her family, she had prayed fervently that they wouldn't fight in front of her! Why couldn't they just leave each other alone? As Holly knew he would, the minute she walked into the room, Old Man Spur shut up. He grasped the forgotten newspaper and put it in front of his face blocking everyone from his sight.

Renee was aghast. She had heard their fights before, but never this early in the morning, and on such a beautiful day! It was as if the old man couldn't resist ruining what had started out to be glorious. She looked at Sam who still sat calmly at the other end of the pine table staring at the paper now in front of his father's face. Sam's eyes fixed on Old Man Spur; he scared her. His youthful muscles rippled beneath his T-shirt, so taught they looked ready to fly into action at any given moment. The corners of his mouth twitched, as if he fought to keep his tongue in check.

Mrs. Spur dropped the spatula, turned off the stove, and moved over behind her son massaging his shoulders as he sat fuming. She wanted to calm him and knew it would take a great deal of soothing. She also wanted Old Man Spur to see her comfort their son. She was tired of his accusations about her. Sam was the spitting image of him when he was young, so each time her husband denied Samantha, he drove a stake into her heart. Everyday she cared less and less if he lived or died.

Finally, Old Man Spur got up from the table, smirked at his wife and son at the other end, and went outside and down the steps. The tension abated. Nobody knew where he was going, but everyone was delighted he was gone.

Renee, Holly, Sam and Mrs. Spur ate the now cold breakfast in silence. What could anyone say to clean the filth that had polluted the air?

Sam wondered if this was what Mrs. Conway meant the night before when she told him, "Don't let anyone keep him from the Lord, not even yourself." Right now, his thoughts were anything but godly. He was fantasizing about the old man being dead. He would use the old bastard's ashes for traction every time he was stuck in the snow. He'd take over the restaurant and run it right! Hell, the old man was the one who wouldn't let him work there—wouldn't let him earn a few dollars! Whom was he kidding? Sam could stand it no more. He got up from the table and in silence walked out onto the back porch and down the steps slamming the kitchen door behind him.

He went out looking for Dennis Hanson and found him in Old Man

Hanson's garage working on a car. Old Man Hanson was off on another drunk and Dennis took charge of the family business as usual. It was always like that for him. He couldn't do much of anything the other kids did because of his father, his mother, and his sister. If he didn't work the garage, how would they eat, or pay the note on the house, pay the light bill, keep the phone connected, or have any clothes for school. The old man sure didn't give a damn if any of them had anything; he was too busy drinking!

As he pulled the carburetor out of Mrs. Jenkins' Ford Fairlane, Dennis Hanson wanted to scream. He wanted to be with his friends. He wanted to meet a girl, someone who didn't know about his father and look down on him because of the old man. Hell, he didn't have anything to do with the old man's drinking! Why was he such an outcast because of it?

As he slammed a large wrench down on the counter, Sam walked through the open garage doors. The sun blinded Dennis to the menacing look on Sam's face.

"What were you doing sneaking up on Renee yesterday in my house and kissing her?" Sam's quiet demeanor belied the volcano about to erupt just below the surface.

Dennis didn't realize that at first, saying, "Hey, man, I was just having a little fun. That Renee is one sweet number, know what I mean?"

Sam did know. That's why he laid back his fist letting it fly into Dennis' jaw faster than Dennis could move out of the way. One blow and Dennis lay sprawled out on the garage floor. "Don't you ever come in my house again unless I invite you, and if I see you anywhere near Renee, or Holly, for that matter, I'll bust you faster than you can blink, got that?"

Dennis nodded. He was smart enough not to attempt to get up. He was having a very bad day, but from the looks of it, Sam's day was going much worse, and it wasn't even eleven a.m.

Sam left the garage and Dennis got back up and went back to work. No wonder I don't have any friends, he thought as he picked up the wrench and went back to work on the Ford Fairlane.

Chapter Seven

Saturday wasn't going well for the girls. If it started out this bad how much worse was it going to get, they wondered. Hoping they'd seen the worst of it, they happily anticipated the carnival, refusing to let the morning's unfortunate events throw a depressing hamper on their plans. They busied themselves in cleaning the kitchen, making plans as they washed dishes.

Mrs. Spur had gone off to the restaurant to work. That's what she did every time she got upset—she worked. Holly wondered aloud if her mother gave much thought to how the arguments she and her father had affected her or her brothers; she didn't seem to, she told Renee. What she didn't say was that she often questioned her mother's love for her because of it. Her father, as ugly as he could get, always gave her plenty of loving attention, but not her mother. She wasn't mean; she just didn't seem to care much. Left alone, often for hours in the day, was one of the reasons she was so happy to have Renee with her for two whole weeks.

Renee pointed out that Mrs. Spur seemed to treat Holly absentmindedly while she showered attention on her sons. It was just the opposite of what her father did. They both thought on this awhile. Holly concluded Renee was right. "It kind of seems that way for your mother, too. Do all women do that? Pay more attention to their sons than their daughters?"

"Hey! You're right! She does! But I'm glad of it! She can be a pill." Renee said thinking about her mother's nagging and her father's dangerous driving habits.

The girls let the matter drop, refusing to get into a bad mood over any of it. Holly had often had to fight off feelings of resentment toward her mother and today she'd do it again.

The rodeo the night before reawakened Holly's excitement about horses, something that always lifted her spirits, so she ran outside to the paddock, and Mrs. Conway's horse, Sugarplum. Like every other time she was feeling low, the horse brought her out of it. She straddled the wooden fence to feed the animal carrots. He loved to have the back of his ears scratched and she contented herself with this.

When Renee joined her, Holly shared her carrots with her and the two of them patiently waited for the horse to get his fill. In the bright glistening sunshine, the animal's coat shown like freshly brushed silk.

As the girls stroked his face and fed him, they didn't notice Mrs. Conway come up behind them. This was their day to talk to her anyway. In the excitement of yesterday, Renee almost forgot that sometimes she saw things that her mother had warned her never to talk about, the things Holly urged her to talk to Mrs. Conway about.

"Ahhhmmmm," Mrs. Conway cleared her throat and continued, "little girl, it is so nice to meet a sister spirit."

Renee turned to find herself face to face with Mrs. Conway who was no taller than she was. Mrs. Conway's gaze held hers and Renee knew instantly that this was no witch. In a blink of an eye, Renee fell in love with the elderly saint standing in front of her. When she realized she was staring, she said, "Oh, I'm sorry. You're Mrs. Conway, right? My name is Renee Good. I'm a friend of Holly's." Renee turned to include Holly.

By this time, Holly had turned toward Mrs. Conway, too. She looked into the old woman's eyes and wondered how the kids could call her a witch, her eyes overflowed with warmth and love. She felt shame wash over herself recalling that just yesterday she had told Renee that the old woman was a witch!

"Stop beating yourself up, dear," Mrs. Conway said to Holly. "All kids do that, you know. God doesn't hold grudges."

Holly's mouth fell open; she couldn't think of a thing to say. The woman knew her thoughts! Maybe she was a witch. Unconsciously she took a step backward.

"Scared ya', didn't I? It ain't me that knows these things, Dearie; it's the Lord. He just lets me in on them sometimes, is all."

"I see you like old Sugarplum there. He's a nice one, he is, must be nineteen years old now. That's old for a horse," she said and the girls turned back to the paddock. They did like old Sugarplum. He liked them, too.

"Will you let us ride him someday?" Holly asked shyly. Everyone said she never would, but Holly doubted that anyone had ever asked her if they could.

"You ever ride horses before, Sugar?" Mrs. Conway asked Holly.

"Just a little. I know I could do it!"

"Well, I'll tell you what. If you don't have much experience riding, Sugarplum there is the best place to start. But you can't ride him until I get a note from your parents saying that you can. They also have to agree that you ride at your own risk."

Holly almost took off across the street to the restaurant before Mrs. Conway could finish speaking.

"Now hold on there, Dearie; we got all day. I was just going to tell you that you're lucky I'm the one that owns him—see? I used to ride horses all the time. I'll teach you everything you need to know, more than you may want to know, but for letting you ride him and all I'll expect payment."

Holly's face fell. She doubted her father would pay for riding lessons.

"You have to come down here twice a day and muck out the stable. You have to take care of Sugarplum every time you ride him. That means you have to cool him down, brush his coat, and make sure he has plenty of feed and water when you're done riding. You agree to those terms?"

Holly was so ecstatic that Mrs. Conway wasn't asking for money, she jumped up and down and exploded with "Yes! Yes!"

"Will you teach me, too?" Renee hoped beyond hope that she, too, could ride the horse.

"If you help your friend here take care of him, I'll do the same for you while you're here. On one condition."

Here comes the catch, Renee thought.

"You sit with me outside this paddock while your friend here has her lessons. You have other lessons to learn that are going to be far more important for you in the end. The horse there can be ridden a couple of hours a day; it ain't going to hurt him, and I promise you that you'll get a turn. Agreed?"

"Oh yes! Thank you!" Renee was so happy she didn't give much thought to what the old lady meant about the other lessons that would be more important to her latter.

"Your brother," Mrs. Conway said to Holly. "See if you can get him to come see me. Otherwise, I'll have to find another way."

"Well, don't just stand there; go get that note from your parents if you want to ride that horse today. Your first lesson will be how to saddle and bridle him. Hurry up!"

The two girls ran across the street finding Mrs. Spur sitting at the café counter smoking and drinking a cup of coffee. She readily agreed to let Holly take the lessons and vouched for Renee as well as long as her parents weren't there to do it for her.

When they got back to the barn, Mrs. Conway set them to work immediately to find out if the two had character. Neither girl minded mucking up the horse manure and cleaning the stall. When they finished, it was as clean as if Mrs. Conway had done it herself. Neither girl complained once about the hard work Mrs. Conway noted with approval. She would be glad to help two such as these.

Mrs. Conway took the girls into the large box stall with Sugarplum after she fetched him from the paddock. The horse looked twice as large inside the stall as he did outside. All at once, the girls felt intimidated by him. But tiny Mrs. Conway, who, the girls noted, was really, really, old, didn't seem a bit unnerved by the horses' size, so if she could handle him as old as she was, they surely could do it, too.

As she talked, Mrs. Conway showed the girls where all Sugarplum's grooming supplies were and how to use the equipment. Next, she taught them how to put the bridle on. Each girl had to use a stepladder to reach the top of his head, but Sugarplum patiently waited for both as they put the bridle on and took it off, getting comfortable with the process.

Next, Mrs. Conway showed the girls where she kept the western and English riding saddles she had used in the days when she actively rode horses. She decided that she would show them how to use the western riding gear first. Each girl practiced putting the western saddle on and taking it off.

Sugarplum patiently waited for the girls to learn their lessons twitching his ears back and forth, listening as Mrs. Conway instructed them. His left back leg and rump rested lazily, as he closed his eyes in sleep while the girls practiced putting the saddle blanket and saddle across his back and cinching it up then taking it off only to do it all over again.

When each girl had completed the task twice, Mrs. Conway told Holly to leave the saddle on and to lead the horse out into the pasture, which she did. There, she was shown how to mount, which she had to do repeatedly until Mrs. Conway was satisfied that she could do it confidently. Next, Mrs. Conway showed Holly how to use the reins to guide the animal and how to stop him once she got started.

"Now dear, today, all I want you to do is walk Sugarplum here around the parameter of this here fence. I want you to get comfortable handling him."

Holly was delighted.

Sugarplum, a thoroughbred jumper mix, was quite tall, and even if she had ridden before, she had never ridden a horse as tall as he was at seventeen hands. Even with the step stool, Holly had to leap to get onto his back. His height was intimidating at first.

Meanwhile, Renee and Mrs. Conway stepped outside the paddock standing alongside the fence rails to watch Holly as she worked the horse. Sugarplum was the perfect teacher as he patiently endured all mistakes Holly made. He even stopped still once when she accidentally pulled too hard on the reins while trying to get him to speed up.

Mrs. Conway throughout encouraged the girl. "You're doing fine Honey," she yelled, "just take a little pressure of the reins is all. You accidentally told him to stop. That's it; give him a little nudge in the ribs. See, he's going forward again."

After circling the enclosure once, Holly rode up to the fence and Mrs. Conway said, "You just keep going Honey, by the time you've made the rounds a couple of times you should be feeling pretty comfortable with them their reins. How you doing so far?"

"It's great! He smells so good and he's so big! I love him!"

"That's good, Honey, now you keep riding!" Mrs. Conway turned to Renee. "Don't fret too much Dearie, your turn is coming. Meanwhile, help this old lady to that lawn-chair right over there and come sit beside me. We got some other things to discuss."

Renee wasn't happy at the sounds of that, but she readily helped Mrs. Conway to her seat. She could hardly take her eyes off the sight of her best friend inside the paddock with the wonderful Sugarplum, though.

"They're a sight, ain't they?" The old woman mused as she nestled herself into the lawn chair.

Renee had to agree. She was finding it difficult to wait her turn. "You ever hear your name called out in the middle of the night when no one is around to be calling it?" Mrs. Conway asked unexpectedly.

Renee, whose mind was on the horse, and whose eyes riveted to the paddock, answered without thinking, whispering, "Yes. My mother said never to mention it to anyone. They'd think I was crazy. She was worried about what the neighbors would think."

"She ain't too far off in her assessment of the neighbors. They probably would think you're crazy. They think I'm crazy. But I'm not, you know. They are. 'Many are called, but few are chosen.' Do you know who said that?"

"No Ma'am."

"God, that's who said it, Him and his Son, Jesus. Do you know them? I learned of them 'cause I went to Sunday school at the Salvation Army. I actually got to know them later. That's the thing. You can know them personally. Something else—you're going to make mistakes along the way, but they'll forgive you."

"When you heard that voice calling you? That's who it was; the Father knows who you are. That's what I want to tell you. He knows your friend, Sam, too. It's a shame God's chosen ones have to go through so much on this earth, but if he calls you, he knows you're strong enough to get through it."

"And you and your friend?" She pointed to Holly who was now blissfully trotting around the paddock. "You two have something coming up that's going to require God's strength. I'm here to help you as long as you're in Rutledge. I want you started off on the right foot. There are things going on you won't understand. You—both of you—you come talk to me about them. With God's help, I'll help you through them."

Renee wasn't sure she liked the sound of this, but said, "Why does everyone dislike you so much? I think you're nice."

"Thank you, Honey. They don't like me 'cause I tell them the truth. It's been a burden. I say things most folks don't want to hear. Folks have always been afraid of the truth."

"You got yourself a Bible, Honey?"

"No."

"Good. That means I can pick one out for you. I'll give one to your friend there, too." With that, Mrs. Conway said no more about God for the day.

Holly came around for the third time and Mrs. Conway called for her to stop the horse, which she did without incident.

It was Renee's turn. Renee, too, had to mount and dismount the horse until Mrs. Conway decided she was confident enough to ride around the paddock. Then, as Holly had, Renee took three turns around the enclosure. When they finished riding, both girls walked the big horse until he cooled down then fed and watered him as Mrs. Conway instructed. They were so happy in their work they took no notice of the time, so by the time they finished it was 2:30 in the afternoon and they were famished.

Mrs. Conway had long since gone inside for her afternoon nap so the girls went over to the restaurant to eat. Mrs. Spur was still sitting at the counter smoking and drinking coffee. She told the cooks to fix the girls a big salad each, and then asked them how their day of riding had gone. She didn't seem to be listening as they bubbled over in their enthusiasm for both Sugarplum and Mrs. Conway.

Periodically all Mrs. Spur said was, "That's nice dear," or "Good, I'm glad."

The girls, in their turn, were too excited to be disheartened by her reaction. And as if the riding lessons weren't enough, they were going to the carnival that afternoon. Sam said he would drive them.

By the time they finished eating it was 3:30 p.m. They sat in a booth in the front of the café and over Cokes, they decided to call Kathy and see if she could go, too. They were also wondering about Shannon.

Holly called the Thompson house talking to Kathy on the restaurant phone behind the counter. Renee could tell by the look on her friend's face that something was wrong. She couldn't remember ever seeing Holly's complexion go so pale.

Mrs. Spur, too, watched her daughter talking and wondered the same thing. "What is it dear?" She asked as Holly turned her back to her to hang up the wall phone. Renee moved over and sat down next to Mrs. Spur. She was afraid all of a sudden. Holly looked horrible.

Holly turned to them both as tears streamed from her eyes. "It's Shannon, Mom! They found her . . . dead!" She barely spoke above a whisper, as she choked out the horror of what Kathy had just told her. "The police are over at Thompson's house now. They just told Kathy's folks that they found Shannon dead. Kathy doesn't know much else." By this time, Holly was sobbing, as was Renee.

Mrs. Spur's face went ashen. No one knew where Mr. Spur was, so she comforted the girls alone.

As she did, Sam walked through the front door.

"Hey, what's going on? Why is everyone crying?" He was alarmed at the sight of his sister and Renee so obviously distraught. "Did someone hurt you guys?" He was at the counter in a flash placing an arm around each of the girl's shoulders, bending between them to look them in the eyes.

"No, dear, but we've got something to tell you," Mrs. Spur said to her youngest son.

Sam looked about him noticing there were no customers in the restaurant. Joey, the day fry cook was in the back obviously trying to hear what had happened as he kept coming to the order window to look out at the counter. He was there when Mrs. Spur said to Sam, "It's Shannon, Dear. Kathy told the girls that she has been found dead. We don't know much else."

"No! You can't mean that! That cute little kid? She was just out front hanging around with all of us yesterday! How can she be dead?" Sam found the news very hard to believe. He sat down at the counter on the far side of Renee facing her and Holly, who sat between Renee and their mother. After his initial outburst, and by looking at the three of them, he could tell there was no joke in what they were saying. "I've got to go see Judy," he said jumping up from his stool.

"No! You sit back down!" Mrs. Spur ordered. She had no use for the eldest Thompson girl, and would not entrust her son to her. She heard the exchange in the restaurant the day before when Renee asked Sam to take her, Kathy and Holly over to the Thompson house to look for Shannon. She heard Judy trying to entice Sam to stay right where he was. No, Judy Thompson was just the person Sam needed to stay away from right now. Mrs. Spur knew Judy was the type who would try to pin the blame for her lack of concern over Shannon onto someone else, and she would do everything she could to ensure that the person blamed was neither her son, nor her daughter, nor Renee, for that matter. Mrs. Spur fumed at the thought of her beloved children, or their friend, being implicated in anything so ghastly.

She was also well aware of how the town looked down on her family, the fact that they were strangers having lived in Rutledge only a few months. She was not about to have her children subjected to any kind of anger because of something as horrible as this. She could not entrust their well-being to the Thompsons. They liked to think of themselves as pillars in the community, above any type of concerns the lesser peons might enjoy.

No, it was best that her family stayed there by her side where she could protect them to some degree. If police wanted to question the kids, they could come there and do it. Most likely, they would, if, as Kathy told Holly, Shannon was dead by suspicious means. Was she murdered? Who could harm that precious little girl? Mrs. Spur shuddered at the idea and drew Holly and Renee even closer in a hug. If it were her daughter, she'd want somebody's hide.

As for Sam, he never knew of a kid being dead, let alone someone he knew. How had she died? What the hell was going on? He was about to get answers to that question when the Sheriff and one of his deputies walked through the front of the restaurant and approached Mrs. Spur at the counter.

"Ma'am," they said in unison. The older officer looked at the younger one with impatience and then continued, "Ma'am, are you Mrs. Wally Spur?" he asked.

Since he came into the restaurant all the time, he knew who she was, which alarmed Mrs. Spur. Why all the formality? She nodded yes, and he continued, "We understand that your daughter," he looked at his notebook for the name, 'Holly,' was a friend to Shannon Thompson and the other Thompson girls. Is that correct?"

"Yes sir, it is. This is Holly," Still hugging the two girls, she nodded at Holly with her head. "This is Renee Good, Holly's friend from the Iron Range. She just came to visit us yesterday, and the young man at the end of the counter is my son, Sam."

The police looked at Sam with a wary eye. Neither officer liked the way he dressed. They would get to him later. He wasn't a suspect anyway.

"Can we talk to your daughter and her friend, Ma'am?"

"Yes, but you can do it right here in front of me."

"That's fine, Ma'am, but I think it would be wiser to talk to them in that booth over there," and he pointed to the booth furthest from the kitchen. He noticed Joey the cook straining to hear every word. When she noticed Joey stealing looks at the counter and hanging around so he could catch what was going on, Mrs. Spur knew he was spying again. How he loved his gossip.

"Yes, I think your right. You girls go sit with the police over there in the booth. Sam, you help me bring the officers some coffee and get yourself and the girls each a Coke. You can join us, too."

She gave her son a stern look, so he did as he was told without complaint.

The police noticed his behavior towards his mother and modified their initial reactions to the teenager—a bit. Sheriff Ernie Hansen and Deputy Andy Freboni had to put on their professional faces even if they were regular customers of the Sands Café. They had work to do, serious work. They were glad to be able to sit down with a cup of coffee, the first one they'd had in hours.

It had been a busy night, what with a missing child and two car accidents on Highway 61. In twenty-four hours, they had witnessed the death of five people, and it hadn't been easy. Four of those were mangled beyond recognition in a car accident with body parts scattered everywhere. It wasn't easy informing their loved ones, either.

But when they stumbled onto the body of that lovely little girl laying in the ditch, the girl who obviously didn't belong to either car involved in the accident, they knew that their night was going to be a long one.

Sheriff Ernie Hansen found her. She wasn't but a few yards away from the accident, on the other side of the road, lying in a culvert in a manner that he found suspicious the moment he saw her. She was placed on display with her legs spread apart and her vagina exposed. Her blouse was up over her head and though initially he couldn't see her face, Hansen could tell by the small body and the tiny breasts that this was a very young girl.

The coroner would determine if she was even old enough to be having her period yet, but he doubted it. As he looked around the crime scene, which he immediately determined was one, Hansen could tell that she hadn't been killed there. He couldn't determine how she died because of the way she was displayed, but that, too, the coroner would tell him.

After discovering the body of the little girl, he went back up to his cruiser and called headquarters. They would need more deputies. Some would handle the accident investigation, while he and Freboni would handle the murder, knowing in his gut that it was a murder.

Willow River and Rutledge were quiet, respectable places for parents to raise their children, places that rarely saw violence of any kind let alone murder, although they did have one every thirty years or so in and around Pine County, but never had there been one involving a child. It had made him sick to his stomach when he saw the little girl lying there, posed as she was.

Whoever did that to her had to be some kind of monster, something he had never seen before and never wanted to see again. When he looked at the little girl lying in the ditch, all he could see was his own eleven-year old daughter, Jessie. "There but for the grace of God," he said. Like a bulldog, he set his mind on catching the killer, and wouldn't quit until he did.

Freboni, too, had been shocked at the sight. He heard the sheriff say, "There but for the grace of God," knowing he had a little girl. Freboni understood what he meant and made the same vow to himself to bring in the perpetrator if it were the last thing he ever did as a cop.

As Hansen and Freboni sat in the restaurant with Renee and Holly, two little girls obviously terrified of them, all Hansen could do was smile inwardly. He was grateful for the doughnut and coffee Sam brought him and Freboni deciding to finish both before tackling the questioning.

"Holly?" He asked looking at Renee. Renee pointed to Holly as a way of saying he had the wrong kid. She got the impression he wasn't too smart. Mrs. Spur had told him not ten minutes ago who was who.

"Holly," Hansen started again, "I was told that you, Renee here and Kathy Thompson were with Shannon Thompson yesterday afternoon. Is that correct?"

"Yeah. We all watched the parade together. Or we did once Renee came back downstairs. She got sick and went upstairs to take a nap. When she came back down, we all watched the parade together."

"You weren't with the group the whole afternoon?" Hansen turned to Renee and asked.

"No, sir. I got sick about noon, and went up to Holly's room and took a nap. I got up about two and came back down to watch the parade with them then."

"You got sick? What was wrong with you?" Freboni interrupted.

Renee shot Mrs. Spur a stricken look. She didn't want to have to say.

"She had female problems," Mrs. Spur answered giving Freboni a stern look.

"Oh!" he said, his face turning crimson.

"Her first time, you understand. It can be difficult."

Freboni was still blushing. Renee was glad that Mrs. Spur shut him up without saying much, but she knew that now everyone in the booth with her understood she was having her period. She didn't like it and when she looked up to see Sam staring at her, she stuck her tongue out at him. Whom is he staring at? She thought. He better not say anything smart! Mrs. Spur looked at them both telling them not to start anything without opening her mouth.

"Okay," Hansen continued, "When you came back down, you said it was two p.m. Is that correct?"

"Yeah, that's right." Both she and Holly were nodding their heads.

"We stood out front of the café here and watched the parade."

"Did anyone say or do anything funny while you were there?" Hansen probed studying the girl's faces, hard. He knew what Kathy had told him about the men hanging in the garage door watching them after the parade. He hoped these two saw them, too.

"When I was coming inside the café to use the bathroom, two guys were trying to get me to come over to the garage," Holly pointed next door, "but I ignored them. They looked funny to me."

"Funny? How did they look funny?" Hansen asked quietly without expression. Inside his heart raced as he hoped for a real lead.

"Funny, you know. Something about them didn't seem right."

"Oh! I know who you're talking about! They tried to talk to me too as I was walking past them and coming up the street to get to you, Kathy and Shannon. They were greasy looking, sorta'," Renee offered. Hansen's heart thumped in his chest. Although he and Freboni hadn't partnered too long, Freboni could tell that his commanding officer was onto something and he picked up on the lead.

"Okay, girls," he said calmly. "You are being a big help. Now try to remember what the men looked like, where they old? How did they dress?

That kind of thing."

"Oh, they were old!" Both girls said in unison, "They had to be at least twenty-five," Holly offered while Renee nodded her head in complete agreement.

Freboni let Hansen pick it up; he was aghast to know that kids thought he was already over the hill.

"That's good. Can you tell me what they were wearing?" Hansen asked in a fatherly way trying not to laugh at the girl's idea of old. It's no wonder Freboni can't say anything, he thought, and had to bite his lip to keep from laughing.

Renee warmed to Hansen but wondered why he was biting his lip. She tried to remember the two men in her mind. "One wore jeans and a jean jacket. I thought it was odd because it was so hot yesterday. I wondered what he was covering up. His breath smelled bad, too. I couldn't tell from what, didn't want to know. He was just too close, I ran off. He stunk, you know, like sweat. My skin crawled when he got close to me. He didn't shave; he just looked—you know—dirty. Understand? The other guy didn't. He looked clean, nice, actually. He was kinda' handsome, too. He smiled at me. I smiled back."

Hansen's skin crawled with that comment. Had Shannon smiled back?

"How do you know Shannon is dead, anyway," Renee wanted to know. "She was our age, almost. How could she be dead?"

"I'm wondering that myself, officers," Mrs. Spur said.

Hansen didn't like bringing this kind of news to anyone, but these kids where that little girl's friends. If he didn't tell them, they, if they weren't cautious, might end up just like her. "Okay, I'll tell you," he said after a few moments of silence. He looked at the girls. "Shannon Thompson, eleven years of age, was murdered." He never took his eyes off Shannon's friends as he spoke to make sure his words had the effect he wanted them to have, which, it appeared, they did. No one said a word.

Thinking they had gotten all they could from the girls, Hansen and Freboni got up to leave. When they reached the front door, Hansen bent down to Mrs. Spur and said, "You do know you were damned lucky yesterday. From what your daughter and her friend just got through saying, they probably came mighty close to being victims, too. If I were you, I'd keep a close watch on them until we get whoever did this."

His words sent chills down Mrs. Spur's spine. She believed the moment the girls started talking that they had been inches away from Shannon's fate.

That is what everyone inside the Sands Café thought that day after Shannon Thompson, eleven-year old friend of Holly Spur and Renee Good, was found murdered.

Chapter Eight

"Sounds too pat to me," Hansen mumbled to Freboni as they got into their cruiser and headed back to their office in Willow River. "How convenient two strangers were in town."

"Do you think the kids were lying?" Freboni didn't.

"No, they weren't lying, and they need to watch out for those two yahoos trying to talk to them. No, that's not it. I just don't think those guys were up to murder. My guess is they were up to sex, maybe, or something to do with pornography, but this kid, the dead kid?" he turned to look at Freboni as he drove north, "No, this kid knew her killer. She got into his car with him, something like that. She didn't expect that kind of trouble." He turned back to watch the road.

Freboni didn't say a word; he let what the sheriff said sink into his steel trap of a mind. They drove the rest of the way in silence. By the time they arrived at the office, Freboni sensed Hansen was right on the money. The kid had to have known her killer.

Back in Rutledge, Mrs. Conway paced the floor. She heard from a close friend that Shannon Thompson had been found dead, and though no one had yet mentioned murder, she "knew" that is what happened.

She got the news from the one woman in town that she had befriended. They had become friends because everyone in town thought that woman was crazy, too. No one took her seriously. Well, she does talk to her husband and son a lot even though they're both dead, but hell, Mrs. Conway thought, that's sorrow talking.

When her friend told her that she saw the little girl the day before, Mrs. Conway urged her to talk to the police. It would take some doing, she knew, because her friend knew what people said behind her back. She was afraid to talk directly to anyone other than children or Mrs. Conway.

When Mrs. Conway hung up the phone after talking to her friend, a vivid scene flashed through her mind concerning Shannon's death, disturbing her greatly.

It happened that way sometimes. She had open visions, knowing that's what they were from studying her Bible, but she didn't want to have them, couldn't stop them, they'd just pop into her head. She didn't always understand them immediately, either. She'd pray about them because sometimes they were parables, not to be taken literally; and she needed discernment. Sometimes the visions were literal though, like the one she was having at that very moment. She saw a mass of red, knew it was blood, a little girl's face, Shannon, and the back of a man. He had on dark clothing and though she couldn't see his face, she heard him laughing, saw him lifting his arm and bringing it down with great force. He held something in his hands, which she couldn't see, but she sensed that he was doing great harm. Then a thought repugnant to her flashed in her mind; she saw the man naked with an erection forcing the same young girl onto a bed to rape her. The girl was screaming.

All this happened in a matter of seconds; when it was over Mrs. Conway went into the bathroom and vomited.

Over at the restaurant Holly Spur and Renee Good remained in the same booth they had shared with the police long after they left. Sam sat with them for a time. None knew what to do. The girls grieved for Shannon silently, each lost in their own thoughts, remembering how the day before they had all ridden their bikes to the lake laughing, and having a good time.

It wasn't long before the other kids from town started drifting into the restaurant, one at a time. Sam drifted off to talk to some of the guys that stopped in. None of them knew how to deal with the loss of Shannon either, one of their own. Awkwardly, many tried to comfort each other. The boys turned to Sam for support, the older girls, each other. Many, having lived in Rutledge all their lives, were uncomfortable around Holly and Renee, relative strangers, even though they knew the two were friends of Shannon. That left the two with only each other for support. Sam found himself pulling away from Rutledge natives who talked to him, boy or girl, to stay close to Holly and Renee as he watched all the other kids avoid them.

It was later in the afternoon when Gloria showed up. She sat down in a booth with girls that went to the church her father pastored.

Sixteen-year old Francine Hanson, Dennis' sister, said, "You sure are lucky to have Pastor Wilson as your father." She looked dreamily at Gloria. "He's so nice . . . Isn't it awful about Shannon? How could anyone do such a thing? I heard she was raped." She whispered the last sentence. The pimples on her rotund face disappeared into the wrinkles she made frowning. She covered her ample bosoms with crossed arms as she shivered at the thought of Shannon, little Shannon, being raped, and although she would tell no one, she fanaticized about being raped by Gloria's father. She liked that idea.

Gloria just looked at her. She thought Francine was the biggest hypocrite she had ever met, second only to dear old Dad. Francine wanted to get in bed with the pastor that was why she went to church every Sunday and Gloria knew it. She was in no way spiritual. Francine was every bit as carnal as her father was.

Pastor, what a joke, Gloria thought. Hell, if he comes from any supernatural place, it is hell! She smiled at the irony of that thought.

Gloria looked across the booth at Sharon Fry, who sat next to her best friend Francine, and wondered what the mousy brunette really thought of Francine. Since Sharon was tall and skinny, she looked funny next to Francine, too; who was big, although she wasn't fat, with large breasts, large hips, legs, backside, and an even bigger mouth, but Gloria had seen

Francine in gym shorts and there wasn't a fat dimple on her. She was just big.

Sharon was the exact opposite. As Francine never shut up, Sharon barely ever opened her mouth. She wasn't dumb, Gloria knew, because every now and again, when she did decide to say something, it was usually profound. Where Francine used the church as a place to socialize, Sharon actually read and understood her Bible. That's why Gloria couldn't understand how Sharon could tolerate the likes of Francine. Maybe she's just really, really, lonely, Gloria thought.

"Hey, Sharon. What's your take on the Shannon Thompson thing? Got any suspects?" Gloria asked.

"No, she doesn't Gloria, and why do you talk like this is no big deal?" Francine was giving her one of her superior looks.

"I don't recall asking you your opinion. I was talking to someone who actually uses her brain, so shut the fuck up."

Francine blustered, but did not open her mouth again. Sharon smiled. So did Gloria when she got Sharon's reaction.

"Actually, everyone is talking about some strange men, but my guess is Shannon knew her assailant. I'm betting she went with him willingly." Sharon said.

"You keep saying 'him.' Are you certain it wasn't a woman?" Francine asked.

"Well, if it's true she was raped, well, that can only mean a man, right? All we have is second hand information, though, but going by that, I'd say, yeah, it's a man and it is someone she knew. We probably all know him," Sharon commented.

Gloria was amazed at the insight Sharon showed. "You're pretty smart, you know that?"

Sharon blushed and never said another word. Francine scowled, sitting back in the booth as far away from Gloria as she could manage as she continued to give her dirty looks. She resented the compliment just showered on her friend.

"Hey, sweetie," Sam said to Gloria stopping to rub her shoulders as he spoke in her ear. "Why don't you come join us?"

Gloria turned, and saw Sam point to the booth he and his friends shared. Even Dennis Hanson was there.

"Okay, she said, but don't get any funny ideas. I don't put out like your girl-friend does."

Sam's eyebrows shot up as if offended. Actually, he knew that, and that is why he wanted her to join them. Something about Gloria always drew him to her as if they shared something no one else in the room did.

As Gloria got up to join Sam's friends, Sam walked to the front of the café to find Holly and Renee and to check and see if they were okay once again. Old Man Spur had not yet returned from wherever it was that he went, and Mrs. Spur was at the counter drinking coffee and smoking cigarettes. Holly and Renee sat at the corner booth silently staring out the café windows. The streets of Rutledge were exceptionally quiet for a Saturday. It was as if the world knew the small hamlet was in mourning.

"You two okay?" Sam asked.

"We're okay, I guess," Holly said.

His heart lurched in pity for the two they looked so crestfallen. He sat down next to Renee and hugged her shoulder. She tried not to cry.

He gently wiped her tears belying his tough persona, hugged both she and Holly once again, got up and went back into the back room where his friends waited. There wasn't much he could do for the girls other than that.

Dennis Hanson felt pretty down, too. First his sister, Francine was in the restaurant, a place she rarely went, and secondly, Renee was up front and all upset about her friend dying; and then there was that, the little girl being dead, murdered ta' boot! Jeez! How could that happen in Rutledge, of all places? He wished it hadn't. He wished a lot of things. He wished his family didn't embarrass him, but they did. He wished he didn't have to work so much, but as long as his father was always on a bender, he did. He wished he hadn't snuck up on Renee and kissed her, but he had done that, too. As he thought about everything he wished hadn't of happened, he managed to work up the courage and go to the front of the café and apologize to Renee. The restaurant was so busy Sam didn't notice him as he passed by on his way up front to see the girls.

Renee accepted his apology, gracefully. Her mother had taught her that if someone apologized for something, it was only right she (anyone, actually) accept. It showed good manners to apologize. It also took courage. She made sure Renee knew that, too.

Renee looked so sad, though, Dennis was at a loss for words other than the apology. He went back to the booth in the backroom where his friends were and sat down feeling more dejected than before.

Sam saw Dennis cross the room to return to the booth. His eyes bore steel knifes at him, so Dennis told him what he had done. Sam visibly relaxed, and Dennis sighed with relief. The last thing he wanted was to be punched out by Sam again. Sam had a killer left hook. Beside, Dennis genuinely liked Sam; he didn't wish to jeopardize their friendship. Sam was the only one in town who didn't put him down because of his family.

At the Thompson house, Mrs. Thompson had been sedated and was upstairs asleep. Mr. Thompson kept staring out the dinning room windows at the back yard. Judy and Kathy were distraught while neither one knew what to do about it.

When the police had been there Judy tried to blame Shannon's disappearance on Kathy because Kathy let her go home by herself, but Kathy wouldn't let her older sister scapegoat her, not this time. She told her parents, and the police, how Judy didn't want to come to the house with the rest of the kids the night before and look for Shannon. How Judy was the one to insist that Shannon was just off with her other friends and that no one had anything to worry about.

Kathy also told everyone how it was Sam who insisted on walking her, Renee and Holly over to their house the night before, so they wouldn't be alone. He had been worried about Shannon too.

Whether or not any of these things registered in their parent's minds, the girls couldn't tell. Neither parent said a word to their daughters after the police left. Judy ran upstairs to her room and slammed the door as their parents sat mutely. She was already feeling shame at her neglect of

Shannon the night before. How could she have let her go off by herself? She could have stopped her when she saw her leaving the restaurant. Why hadn't she? She never told the police she saw her leaving, either. She couldn't. She had been so nasty to her.

Judy was also so jealous that everyone's attention centered on Shannon, and not herself, that she wanted to scream her frustration as she paced her bedroom floor. Shannon was gone, forever, what could she do about it? The kid never did make much of an impression, and once she calmed down enough to consider her circumstances, she thought that perhaps, she could use Shannon's death to garner attention for herself.

After hours of sitting around the silent, mourning household, Kathy could take no more. She, too, needed comfort, but wasn't getting any at home. She ran the three blocks to the restaurant hoping to find Holly and Renee. She went running in through the back door to be greeted by a myriad of eyes staring back her. She froze there, like a deer caught in an oncoming car's headlights, shocked to see so many people looking back at her. She never considered that all the other kids in town would be at the restaurant.

None of the kids doing the staring could believe what they were seeing. Here was the sister to the kid who was murdered! They hadn't expected to see any Thompsons. What were they supposed to say to her?

Sam jumped up out of his booth and grabbed Kathy by the shoulders. "The girls are up front," he said as he took her arm and helped her to the front of the cafe. Once there, Mrs. Spur caught Kathy's attention. The girl could not take her eyes off the woman at the counter. When Mrs. Spur motioned for her to sit beside her, she did. When Mrs. Spur took her in her arms and held her, Kathy broke down and sobbed. No one in the back room came out to the front, although they all heard the sobbing. Holly and Renee joined Kathy and Mrs. Spur at the counter where they all grieved over Shannon.

Judy saw Kathy sneak out of the house and decided to follow her. She, however, guessed that the restaurant was packed, so decided against going inside. Instead, she walked behind the restaurant to Main Street then crossed it and slipped down the dirt road to Willow River.

She sat on the river's edge watching the water roll downstream. She quietly cried when the full realization of what had happened to Shannon came down on her. No more did she feel the surreal numbness of unbelief that she felt earlier. She was ashamed of her earlier jealous thoughts concerning Shannon. She felt horrible about the night before when she thought her youngest sister had gone off with other friends and how she had tried to stop the others from looking for her. If she had not done that, maybe Shannon would be alive right now. She bowed her head and sobbed into her hands wiping her nose with the underside of her pleated skirt after discreetly looking about to see if anyone else could see what she did.

She was so focused on Shannon and her own grief, she didn't hear the footsteps approaching her from behind.

Tears spilled down her cheeks sliding into Willow River as she sat there on the bank. She could see herself and the trees of the riverbank reflected lazily on its surface. The summer sunshine beat down upon the river and upon her back warming her. She wondered how the day could be so lovely when everything else was so ugly. Who could have hurt Shannon, someone who had never harmed a living thing in her short life? She had been so full of laughter and energy. Who could hurt her? A shadow fell across the water grabbing her attention with its flickering dance across the water's surface.

"Ahhhhmmm." A voice behind her cleared its throat.

Judy jumped, startled, hurtled to her feet, and would have fallen into the river if Pastor Joseph Wilson had not been there to catch her. He grabbed her arm just as she started to loose her balance on the uneven downward slope of the riverbank and drew her sharply to him. As he did, his hand brushed across her breasts.

Stunned by his sudden appearance and her near mishap with the river, she choose to believe the touch was accidental. He is the pastor, after all. It was an accident, right? Maybe I just imagined it, she thought.

A tall man, Wilson towered over Judy smiling down at her from his lean six-foot-two frame.

When she looked into his eyes, though, Judy shivered for cold.

"You have to be careful, young lady. You almost fell into the river," he said taking her arm gently and pulling her close to him. "There, there," he cooed, "no need to be frightened." He rubbed her arms gently as he embraced her drawing her even closer.

She grew more uncomfortable. "Thank you for helping me," she said as she tried to pull away from him politely.

He released her just enough so that his fingers could brush lightly over the curve of her breasts, once again as he let her step back from him. "How are you dealing with all this . . . unpleasantness?"

Judy kept her eyes glued to the grass beneath her feet. She didn't like to look at him. Why was he calling Shannon's death, "unpleasantness?" It was damn sight more than unpleasantness. "I'm fine," was all she could bring herself to say. Taught to be polite and to respect people in authority, Judy grew more uncomfortable by the second. She didn't like the pastor, but she couldn't be rude, could she?

"Here, let me help you; I'll walk you home," he said when he saw her trembling.

Judy moved away from him and thought, once, okay, maybe an accident, but twice? No, he isn't walking me anywhere. She kept her head down as she straightened her clothes. She didn't like the look in his eyes. He scared her. "Thank you for the offer Pastor, but I'm going to stay here for awhile. I want to be alone. I have a lot to think about."

"Nonsense. I'm walking you home. You shouldn't be here by yourself."

"No, really, I'm fine."

"I said, young lady, that you are going home."

"Who are you to tell me what to do? I'm staying right here! My parents don't need me at home."

"I said they do," with that Wilson grabbed her arm and attempted to force her away from the river by pulling her, but she steadfastly held her ground by planting her feet into the soil. If Judy knew how to do anything, it was how to resist unwanted attentions.

What neither one of them knew was that Mrs. Conway was making her way slowly to the river, cane in hand. She saw Wilson attempt to pull Judy away from the river and was right behind him as he did so. She raised her oak cane over her head and brought it down to hit him as hard as she could across the flat of his back.

Wilson turned, startled, fury in his eyes, drawn fists brought back ready to strike whoever had hit him.

"You go right ahead, Mr. and I'll get right back up and clean your clock." Mrs. Conway croaked. She had a look in her eye that froze the pastor to the spot. "Yeah, you may attempt to hurt me, but I've got an advocate with the Lord, and He'll make you pay for it. Bet on it."

Judy's mouth hung open as she watched the shriveled old lady, who everyone said was a witch, and who was probably 100 years old, make this man, at least three times her size and in his prime, back down. The old lady reeked of disdain for the pastor. Judy loved it.

Wilson quickly regained his composure. "I am so sorry Mrs. Conway, isn't it? I mean I'd never strike a woman. It's just that you hit me with the cane from behind. I thought I was being attacked! Surely, you understand."

Oh, he's smooth, Mrs. Conway thought. She said, "This here girl says she doesn't want to go home, she don't have to. I'm here to see to it. If she wants to sit at the river's edge all day, she damn well better be left alone so she can sit at the river's edge all day."

"The Lord be with you, Mrs. Conway, and with the Thompson family in this their hour of need. You're absolutely right about this young lady. I'll yield to your wisdom, and pray, Ma'am, that someday you'll see fit to come into the church, into the house of the Lord, and let me shepherd you."

"Don't hold your breath waiting, buster. The Lord already shepherds me and He's more than enough for anybody."

Pastor Joseph Wilson smiled a condescending smile at her gentle rebuke, looked back at Judy who stood to the side near the bridge iron watching their interaction with great interest. "You need to be careful out here young lady, what, with what happened to your sister and all. You never know what is lurking around the next corner, do you?" He smiled again, and again Judy's insides revolted. Is he threatening me? It sounds like it, but he's the pastor? Why would he threaten me . . . because I didn't go with him? And why is he so insistent I go with him?

Judy and Mrs. Conway watched in silence as Wilson walked off back toward town. He took the old dirt road up to Main Street, turned left then walked back toward his house on the south side of town next to the church. Both women could see him as he passed between buildings and continued on his way.

"He's creepy," Judy said softly once the pastor was completely out of sight.

Mrs. Conway heard her. "You're damn right he is, Dear. And might I suggest that you heed what he says about being alone after what happened to Shannon. He has a point. But, that applies to him, too," she whispered. "If I were you, I'd stay out of situations that forced me to be alone with him. He ain't right."

Judy stared at the old woman. "My mother and father brought him to this town. He's done wonderful things for the church. How can you talk about him like that? You don't even know him?"

"Neither does your mother and father. Look here, little girl, just trust your instincts about the man and remember what happened here today. Don't let reasoning talk you out of your instincts, especially in view of what happened yesterday. Nobody knows whom to trust right now, not really. Maybe it were a stranger that took Shannon, maybe it weren't. You should be real careful till the police catch whoever it was, understand?"

Judy nodded her head in agreement.

Satisfied, Mrs. Conway placed her cane before her and started the slow process of walking back home. She turned around, looked back at Judy, and said, "I'll be in that apartment right up yonder. I know you know which one it is. I'll be keeping an eye on you from there. I suggest you get out of here before dark and get back home to your folks."

Judy nodded her head again. She heard Mrs. Conway, but her mind raced with thoughts of what the old woman had just done. Who knew what she had just been saved from? And there she was an old woman who didn't even go to church, saying that the pastor was weird. Who was she to talk? Didn't everyone in town think she was a witch? Yeah, they did, but it was the old woman, who, by the way, can barely walk, who stopped the pastor from hurting you and taking you home, a small voice inside Judy's head reminded her.

"Wait up, Mrs. Conway, I'll walk you home," Judy said running to catch up with her. Judy knew Mrs. Conway was right about her being alone and thought now was a good a time as any to go home. Slowly the two walked up the dirt road behind the apartment building, and Judy saw Mrs. Conway inside. Mrs. Conway could see that the girl was coming to her senses about being alone. That's all Mrs. Conway wanted. Until that killer was caught, she would protect every girl in town any way she could if need be.

Chapter Nine

When Mrs. Spur took Holly, Renee and Kathy home to the Spur apartment, Sam went too. The girls needed to get away from prying eyes and ears at the restaurant. Everyone there listened in to Mrs. Spur as she talked to Kathy hoping to hear juicy gossip. They were like wolves on the scent of prey.

Mrs. Spur was amazed at how the young people imitated their parents to the degree that she could tell whose child was whose by how they treated Kathy. She observed closely, though discretely, those lusting after information on Shannon's death, the same way their parents lusted after other gossip right there in her restaurant morning after morning over coffee. They even did it in church on Sunday. Many envied the Thompsons so much that they were glad something awful had happened to them; she could tell by the looks in their eyes, blazed, hungry for details about Shannon's demise.

Holly, Renee and Kathy were grieving for Shannon; they needed— deserved—to get away from prying eyes and ears. Since they were so young Mrs. Spur refused to leave them alone, especially under the circumstances. No one Mrs. Spur knew had ever had to deal with a situation like this. It was a first for her, too.

When they got home, and as the girls went off to Holly's room, Mrs. Spur decided to get busy and cook a few dishes to take over to the Thompson's when she brought Kathy home later. It didn't matter if the Thompsons didn't like her family, she would do the right thing, regardless. She busied herself in the kitchen preparing two casseroles and a cake.

In Holly's bedroom, the girls cried themselves into emotional exhaustion, lying silently crosswise on Holly's bed.

"Who could do something like that?" Renee wondered out loud after a long period of silence. "I mean, she was a little girl! Who wants to have sex with a little girl?"

Holly was wondering the same thing. She had never heard of such a thing.

Kathy couldn't believe it, either. "Makes you wonder, doesn't it? I mean, how dirty can someone be to molest a little kid?" She said.

As they talked, Judy was at the river being accosted by the pastor. No one had seen Mrs. Conway walk to the river, or walk back from the river with Judy in tow. They didn't see the pastor pass below their third story apartment, either.

Mrs. Conway, though, knew everyone was upstairs. She had an uncanny sense that told her when her tenants were home and when they weren't. "Judy, dear, you need to help me upstairs."

Judy didn't protest. She took Mrs. Conway's arm and slowly proceeded up each of the three flights of stairs, even though Mrs. Conway seemed barely able to get up each step. Judy wondered just how old she was, and feared for the old woman's life at each new step.

Mrs. Conway smiled as they climbed. She "knew" everything Judy was thinking as she pretended to be feeble in body, more so than she actually was.

Finally, they made it to the Spur's back door. Judy had never been to the Spur's apartment before even though she lived in Rutledge all her life, and she dated Sam Spur. Her mother had always looked down on most of the townspeople, so Judy did too. She didn't understand why Sam Spur held such a fascination for her, but he did. She wasn't too unhappy to find that he was home, either. God, I hope he doesn't hold yesterday against me! I was such an ass in front of everyone, she thought as they crossed the threshold into the apartment.

Mrs. Spur was in the kitchen when the knock came at the backdoor. She saw Mrs. Conway, and welcomed her inside before she noticed Judy standing behind the old woman. She was more than a little surprised, and was none too pleased at the sight of her, but she invited her in, too. She didn't have much choice, all things considered, she thought.

"Well, Mrs. Conway! It's always good to see you, Dear, but should you still be climbing those stairs?" Mrs. Spur was genuinely concerned with the old lady's well being.

"Oh, don't you worry none about me! When the good Lord is ready to take me home, He'll do it no matter where I'm at, so if I want to climb those stairs out there I will. I suspect He'll come for me when I'm just lying in my bed doing nothing. As for now, He's got other things He wants me to do. Will you get those girls for me? I got something to talk to them about and I'm too damn old to be coming to them all the time."

Mrs. Spur motioned to Judy the direction of Holly's bedroom with her head and silently told her to go get them. Mrs. Conway plopped herself unceremoniously on a kitchen chair refusing to go any further. Mrs. Spur is right about one thing, she thought. I am too damn old to be climbing those steps all the time. She belched and waited for the youngsters to come into the kitchen. She had a story to tell.

The girls were surprised to find Judy at Holly's bedroom door and Mrs. Conway in the kitchen. Because of Shannon's death, however, everyone was subdued and Kathy and Judy made no rude remarks to one another as they walked back into the kitchen. Sam, who was in his room, heard all the noise so he followed the sounds into the kitchen as well. Once there, they all sat around the big kitchen table while Mrs. Spur got something for everyone to drink. Mrs. Conway joined the kids in a bottle of orange Crush, which she loved. She needed a sugar fix for the energy. She had a lot to say. "I was born right here in Rutledge, did you know that?" She started. Everyone shook their heads no. "Yep, was born here in 1852. You guessed it; I'm 111 years old. Lived a long time, all of it spent right here. Seen a lot of things, too, although can't say I ever seen anything quite as ugly as what's going on right now." She patted Judy and Kathy's hands; they sat on either side of her. Mrs. Conway exuded a sense of security, which they gravitated to.

"Nope, never seen the likes of it here. Lest not before yesterday. Didn't see it coming, neither. If I had of, I would have tried and stopped it. Yes sir. Don't know why the Lord didn't show it to me, but he didn't. I suspect we got the nasty one living right here amongst us, yes sir, I truly do. Think I know who he is, too." She looked around the table to see if her words were having any effect. "But I'm getting ahead of myself."

"When I was a girl, about thirteen or so, I fell into the river, Willow River, right out yonder. Got caught in a drop off, which drug me right down to the bottom of that old river. I was dying, couldn't seem to come up out of it. It wasn't as bad as most folks think, dying, I mean. It was real peaceful. Course, first of all I fought it, the suffocation I mean, but when I stopped fighting it, I saw a light, a real bright light, like looking at the sun directly, you know, only it didn't burn my eyes. Felt real calm, too, stopped panicking. Anybody here ever suffocate for a short time, or loose their wind and not been able to get it back for a time?"

Sam was the only one nodding his head in the affirmative.

"Well, it was kinda' like that, but it lasted longer." She paused and took a long draw from her soda bottle.

"Saw God then, as I sank into that river bottom. Won't ever forget it, no sir. It ain't like you really see Him, not in form anyway, but you hear Him, feel Him. It's like He speaks to you through every pore of your body. You definitely know you're in His presence. He talks to you that way, not through words, necessarily, but through thoughts and feelings. It's amazing. He showed me many amazing things. Next thing I know, I'm back on the riverbank and there was no one else around me. I was sopping wet, so I knew that I did actually go under, was towed under by the river current. I wasn't dreaming it. Yet, somehow, something saved my life."

"Started reading the Bible that day and haven't stopped since; everyday I read it cause no one on this earth jumped into that river to save me, no one, you understand?" She got hesitant nods, but knew no one really understood. She pushed on anyway. "It was God that delivered me from death, no doubt about it. And, no, I didn't just fall asleep on the riverbank and wake up after having a beautiful dream, like the nincompoop who pastored our little church then, said. No, when I woke up, I was soaked to the skin, my clothes drenched with water and I was exhausted. Good thing it was a hot summer day, or I'd have caught my death of cold!" She laughed then, kicking up one of her legs, slapping it, and slamming it back down onto the linoleum-covered floor, so heartily she shocked her rapt audience.

"Well, you understand, don't you? Do you think God would have lifted me up out of that river to safety then let me catch a cold and die? I don't think so." She took another draw off her soda bottle.

"Anyways, back to my story. I was thirteen when He called me, and He did not call me in any traditional sense of the word. Although, if you read the Bible, you're going to find out that women are not as lowly as mankind would like them to think they are, not in God's eyes and not in Jesus' either.

"And, as I was saying, I was called that day. Ever since that day, I've been able to see things, know things, even though I don't want to know them. I knew when my parents were going to die in the fire of 1870 that burned this here building to the ground. I was eighteen at the time. I've owned it ever since, by the way. The Lord helped me get through that."

"Since I got the call, and could "see" things, and was never too shy about saying what I saw, I scared a lot of people off. I knew when this one was having an affair, or that one was stealing from his boss, or when the boss was stealing from his employees, you see. And Lord knows I never kept my mouth shut when it came to those things, so folks just started calling me a witch. They meant bitch, I'm quite sure, but they said witch." She looked around the table to see if her language offended anyone. The kids were young, she didn't want to hurt them in anyway, but if any time was right for the truth, it was now.

The kids were all smiling, so was Mrs. Spur. This had to be a good sign. The girls thought it funny to hear a cuss word come out of one so little and so old that her eyes were almost hidden behind her wrinkles.

Mrs. Conway simply cackled at their expressions. It was nice getting old. You could get away with so damn much! "I can't get into my entire life here, I am 111 years old! But the jest of it is this. I didn't see what happened to Shannon, I mean like I could see all those other things. We're up against something right here in town and it's bigger than we are. If it had the power to block my vision, the vision God gave me, it's powerful. And though I can't be positive, if I were you Mrs. Spur, I'd keep these girls," she pointed to Holly and Renee, "away from the pastor."

She turned and looked sternly at Kathy and Judy. "You two have a worse problem. Your parents think he's okay. He's not. I don't know what it is, but he's not okay."

"I also know none of you really know how to ask God for help, but you better start. He's the one warning me, telling me to tell you. You pray. He'll answer. Whoever it was that hurt Shannon will not be able to keep his secret. God isn't going to let him. I know that for sure. He is always talking to me, and besides, you'll find that in scripture. No secrets will remain hidden. As for the Lord, He'll talk to anyone who'll listen; most folks just don't know that. He forgives any kind of sin we committed in the past, but He expects us to stop committing them. He'll even help with that if we'll call on Him. He sent Jesus as a sacrifice for us. Oh, my, am I preaching again? Sometimes I can't help it. But I mean what I'm saying."

"In the meantime, I'll be praying for everyone's protection. You can do that too. If you find yourself needing any help, if you don't know how to pray, you come to me and I'll help you any way I can. You may not know it to look at me, but the Lord has made me mighty, even now when I can barely walk. He listens to my prayers. If you can't get to me, you call out to me, I'll hear you because the Lord hears you and He'll tell me. And He may do you like he did me that time in the river, lift you out of the mess or danger or whatever it is you're in. I don't want to scare you, but whatever we're up against is strong, but the Lord is stronger. You have to call on Him."

Mrs. Conway turned to Mrs. Spur. "He's talking to those cops he sent to you. They work for Him, too, although they don't know it. They're doing His work. They will be instrumental in finding out what happened to Shannon," she turned to the Thompson sisters, "don't you doubt it. In the meantime, use any means possible to stay away from the pastor. Don't let yourself be caught alone with him, you hear me?"

The girls nodded their heads somberly. Judy didn't need convincing. The guy had already given her a major case of the willies.

Mrs. Conway turned to Sam. "You, young man, have the nasty one already pitted against you. I'm talking about Satan dear. Sometimes I think it's the kids that are treated the worst that are the ones God is really trying to reach. If He weren't, why would Satan be working so hard to keep them away from finding the truth? Anyways, your father's got problems and he's taking them out on you. You are not to blame him. The only way you will be able to save yourself is if you forgive the old man."

Forgive him! She must be crazy, Sam thought.

"No, Dear, I ain't crazy," she replied. "The words most kids hate to hear, but I'll say them anyway—it's for your own good."

How does she know! Sam worked hard not to think of anything else. He didn't want her reading his mind again.

"You'll have questions when it's at its worst. You come to me with them. I'll help you as best I can. Remember, that if your own parents reject you, you have a strong advocate in the Father. Here I go preaching again. Maybe I missed my calling after all." She laughed again and took another swig of her orange Crush. There wasn't much left.

"You kids got yourselves a Bible?" Sam shook his head no as did Holly and Renee. Kathy and Judy had the family Bible at home.

"You come downstairs with me, you three. I've got plenty. You take what you need." She turned to the Thompson sisters, "You two go home and ask God for guidance and wisdom, then you open your Bibles and see if there isn't a word in due season there for you. Remember to pray for protection. Jesus is there with you if you want Him, even if you are a novice, probably most assuredly, if you are. Got that?" They nodded their heads yes.

Judy would never have opened the family Bible on her own. What did she need to pray for? She had good looks, plenty of money, and her parents were well to do; her future was guaranteed.

But if her future was guaranteed, why wasn't Shannon's? She recalled how it had been when she sat by the river, how bad she felt, and how creepy Wilson was. No, Mrs. Conway was right. She did need help.

Mrs. Spur, having finished cooking, had each of the Thompson girls take one of the dishes, and they all went downstairs where they got into her car and she took them straight home even though they lived only four blocks away. The girls never thought to invite Mrs. Spur in when they got there. Instead, they took the meals she prepared and went into the house through the kitchen door with Kathy calling back another thank you to Mrs. Spur who waited for the door to close, then backed out of the driveway and left. Once inside their house, the girls did as Mrs. Conway instructed heading for the den where they knew the family Bible was stored.

Sam, Holly and Renee followed Mrs. Conway downstairs after the Thompson sisters left. When they got to Mrs. Conway's apartment, they took it all in with amazement. The place crawled with equestrian trophies and pictures on the walls.

"That there, next to those pictures," Mrs. Conway spoke to Holly. "That was one of the first trophies I ever won showing horses."

"You mean that's you?" Holly was more than a little surprised.

"Yes, dear. I wasn't born old."

"I'm sorry. I didn't mean to hurt your feelings."

"You didn't, and I'm not too surprised you never thought of me as anything but old. Hell, people I've known for a lot longer than I've known you tend to forget I was a girl once. Most are too young to remember about my life then. Just remember that the next time you see an old person. They weren't always that way, and their lives might be a damn sight more interesting that you can imagine." She raised an eyebrow as she spoke hoping to make an impact.

"Those Bibles I was talking about are over here." She moved into the dinning room and opened up a locked roll top desk retrieving from it three Bibles, each claiming to be the Living Word of God.

"Now, when I give you these, I'm expecting that you will use them. Do like I instructed the Thompson girls. Pray then ask for guidance. After you do that, read whatever page you open up to. The Lord will guide you through this, and any other thing you might have to deal with in your life. Right now, I'd concentrate on Shannon. Pray for her. Pray that whoever hurt her is brought to justice. Pray for them, too, this town. Pray for your friends, yourselves, your families. God listens. He listens whether or not you've ever been in church a day in your life. I know He's calling you, so you listen. He sent you to me, so, I'm assured of it. You get confused about anything? You just let me know. I'll see if I can help you. You all go on home now and do like I said, you hear?"

They did, even Sam. He went upstairs to his room thinking about his father. How was he supposed to forgive that old man after all he put him through? Surely, that was too much! Sam decided that the Thompson family situation was more important, so he began to pray for them. The girls did the same.

Chapter Ten

When Judy and Kathy got home late that hot July 5 afternoon, they slipped quietly into the house. They didn't wish to disturb their parents. As they came through the kitchen door, however, they heard voices coming from the sunroom at the front of the house. They could easily slip upstairs without being noticed, but they listened at the swinging kitchen door instead to see if they could discern who was visiting. Besides, the Bible was in the den right across the hall from the sunroom.

They could hear their mother's quiet sobbing. Their father's muffled voice, too, on occasion, but what took Judy aback were the other voices. One was that of Pastor Joseph Wilson. She'd recognize it anywhere, but there was another voice, too, one she wasn't familiar with.

Kathy whispered, "That's Holly's dad!"

"Are you sure?"

"Sure I'm sure. I'm over there all the time. He talks to me every time he sees me."

Judy could not say the same thing. She most often saw Sam away from any parental supervision. She liked it that way. Besides, Sam's father was sort of a puke wasn't he? He drank and had that horrible belly. She could think of nothing endearing to contribute to her boyfriend's father as she stood there listening to him talk to her parents. How could they even let him in the house? She wondered.

"Well, I'm going in to say 'hi,'" Kathy announced. "He's been good to me. It would be rude if I didn't speak to him when he was in my own house."

"Yes, but it's the pastor that's in there with them all. Mrs. Conway told us to watch out for him."

"You come with me. We'll both pay our respects then excuse ourselves. Mom will be pleased when she sees us taking the Bible upstairs to read," Kathy said

Judy had to admit Kathy had a point. There was no way they could hide from company now that Shannon was dead. People would be coming over continually to pay their respects. She would not allow herself, or her sister, to be left alone with the pastor. Her parents would have to take care of themselves; they probably would never listen to her if she said something negative about Wilson, anyway.

And as long as Sam's father was in the sunroom with everyone else, they wouldn't be alone with Wilson, she reasoned, so she could do Old Man Spur a favor and speak to him civilly in her own house since he was nice to her sisters. It would also be much easier to get the Bible from the den that way, too. The adults would gladly excuse them for that, especially the pastor. How could he discourage two young people from reading the Bible? He couldn't.

"Hey girls," Old Man Spur said as he raised himself from the settee and addressed the young women as they entered the sunroom. Pastor Wilson didn't bother to get up.

"Hello Mr. Spur," Kathy and Judy said in unison. "It's nice to see you."

They quickly turned their attentions to their mother who sat in a wicker chair with a box of Kleenex in her lap. She looked horrible. For a woman who normally was meticulous about her appearance, her hair was unkempt, and she hadn't donned any makeup, or, if she had, she had been crying so long, none of it remained. Even her dress was wrinkled, something she would not be caught dead in on a normal day. The girls were shocked.

Mr. Thompson looked like he always did. He was dressed in a conservative pin stripped suit with a simple white shirt and a gray tie. His tie clasp and cuffs of emerald green, matched. His hair, graying at the temples was perfectly combed, and his trim, athletic body moved about the room with the grace of a gazelle. He smiled at his daughters and took their hands as they entered the sunroom. He sat them down on the couch next to himself and the pastor.

Mr. Spur sat back down on the settee.

"I saw Judy here earlier today, didn't I dear?" Wilson, who sat to her left, tried to take her hand, but she managed to avoid him.

"Oh? Judy, did you leave the house?" Her father looked down at her.

"Yes Dad. I was down by the river trying to think things through, you know, trying to come to grips."

"I don't want you out there by yourself right now, is that clear? Whoever hurt Shannon is still out there!"

"I tried to take her home, you know, Mr. Thompson," Wilson fawned, "but she didn't want anything to do with me, I'm sorry to say."

"Judy? Why didn't you let the pastor bring you home?"

"Well, Dad, I just wasn't ready to come home. Mrs. Conway came down and insisted on talking to me for awhile. I stayed with her."

"Now what have I told you about that old woman! You know she's crazy! I'm grounding you young lady! Do you understand me?" Her father's reaction came as a shock to Judy. He never raised his voice to her, not like this.

"Yes sir," she whispered looking out the corner of her eyes at Wilson who was leering at her, smiling with satisfaction at her chastisement.

She couldn't help but defend herself, "But Dad, you know, I, we," she pointed to Kathy, "we talked to Mrs. Conway this afternoon, and she's a very nice lady. She's very upset about what happened to Shannon. She wouldn't hurt a flea. And Dad, there is nothing wrong with her head."

"Are you arguing with me?"

"No sir, I'm just saying, Mrs. Conway is okay."

"That's enough. Go upstairs to your room."

"All right, Dad, but do you mind if I take the Bible up there with me, to read, I mean."

"The Bible? No . . . go ahead. Why are you reading the Bible?" Mr. Thompson asked as he was very surprised and fought to maintain it while inquiring of the girls what they were doing.

"Mrs. Conway said it would be the thing to do, under the circumstances. May I be excused, too, Dad. I'd like to read it with her." Kathy said, hoping her father would understand that it was Mrs. Conway's influence that put his daughters to reading scripture.

Mr. Thompson was now more than surprised, but refused to show it. Although he didn't say it, he thought that if Mrs. Conway could talk his daughters into reading the Bible in one afternoon, something the pastor had never been able to do, she couldn't be all bad.

Mrs. Thompson said nothing. She remained in her chair, quietly weeping. The girls each hugged her before going into the den to retrieve the Bible.

Judy looked back into the sunroom before crossing the threshold into the den. Pastor Wilson was no longer smiling; he was menacing her with a dirty look. She smiled, turned and closed the door behind her. She'd take the book upstairs the back way, through the kitchen. She had seen enough of the pastor for one day. Kathy was right behind her.

The girls couldn't be more different in their personalities, their father thought as they walked away from him into the den. Where Judy favored her mother, Kathy took after him. Though he never thought much about it, he knew he was a simple, quiet man and often misjudged because of it. Kathy, he saw, was often misjudged, too, most everyone assuming she'd take after her mother.

What his colleagues knew about Ralph Thompson was that he was one of the most successful trial lawyers in Minnesota, this in spite of living in one of the tiniest hamlets in the state, Rutledge, then setting up his office in the next tiniest hamlet, Willow River, to practice law. He had a mighty reputation for being tough, too, even though his manner was always polite, gentle and non-threatening. Many misinterpreted his gentleness thinking it a sign of weakness.

That was usually their mistake, both in court and out of it. This most attorneys in the state were well aware of, especially when they came up against him in court. Those not working within the legal system tended to be blinded by Ralph Thompson's exterior demeanor, which was always kind and gentle, regardless of circumstances. If placed in the intolerable position of having to use his fists, Ralph Thompson was quite capable of handling himself there as well, although the idea of violence repulsed him.

Ralph Thompson was a man worthy of respect in every way. He didn't cheat, steal, or demean those less fortunate than himself, though they often demeaned him. He didn't feel himself superior to anyone. He knew, however, from the time he was a young boy that he had an overwhelming interest in the law and he thanked the Lord daily that he had been born into a family that could put him through college so he could develop that interest. He was quite good at practicing it, too.

He didn't believe that most people were blessed with self-knowledge at a young age so he had a lot of respect for anyone who went after their dreams, regardless of age, color, financial background, or circumstances. This was America. Anyone could overcome anything they needed to overcome in this country. He did not discriminate against anyone during a period in the nation's history when discrimination was popular among men. Therefore, some of his less tolerant townsfolk had no compunction about starting a fistfight with him, thinking he would be an easy target. He was not—not then, not now.

As a small town lawyer, Ralph Thompson was ahead of his time in his attitudes toward minorities and women. He believed Galatians 3:26-29, which says; For you are all sons of God through faith in Christ Jesus. For as many of you as were baptized into Christ have put on Christ. There is neither Jew nor Greek, there is neither slave nor free, there is neither male nor female, for you are all one in Christ Jesus. And if you are Christ's then you are Abraham's seed, and heirs according to the promise. (NKJV)

As Ralph Thompson sat in his sunroom entertaining two guests that in his heart of hearts, he wished would leave, and as he watched in amazement as his two daughters took the family Bible upstairs to read, he grieved for his lost daughter. He pitied his wife, who sat weeping in her chair across for him. His heart ached for her, and for Shannon as he tried to deal with their loss in the midst of strangers working hard to maintain his composure in front of them. He would give a king's ransom to be able to grieve alone, but doubted that he would be able to for quite sometime. It was best to take over, and let his wife succumb to her bereavement for the time being.

Besides, his wife was his soul mate, his life long partner and there was nothing he could do for her right now, no words he could think of that would console her. He could think of nothing to console himself.

He was not blind to his wife's shortcomings, however. One of those was looking back at him from the other end of the couch on which he found himself. Wilson was his wife's biggest vanity, and he thought, her biggest mistake.

Mrs. Thompson was not like her husband when it came to feelings of superiority. She wallowed in them, as she wallowed in pride. Anyone who paid her compliments was a friend to her, whether they really were or not. That was how Joseph Wilson came to Rutledge in the first place. Ralph Thompson could see that Wilson was cunning just by watching him. He had zeroed in on Mrs. Thompson's weaknesses like a heat-seeking missile no sooner than he met her. And since he was a pastor, he should have counseled her against her prideful attitude; instead, he encouraged it.

As Ralph Thompson listened quietly to the solicitous voice of the pastor, he knew that Pastor Joseph Wilson fell into the ranks of those who misjudged him. That was fine, because Ralph Thompson always managed to use people's misjudgment to his advantage. He didn't like the pastor; it was a blasphemy against God just to call him pastor as far as he was concerned.

He wasn't found of Wally Spur, either, although he had a whole lot more respect for him. He tolerated Spur because he knew that his wife treated the Spur family with contempt. She treated all newcomers that way unless they fawned over her.

Ralph Thompson had been more than a little surprised when he found Wally Spur at his doorstep along with the pastor, however, there was no way he could turn the men away; it wasn't in him. So he made coffee and served it to his guests while his wife wallowed in her grief.

As Ralph Thompson served coffee and cookies to his guests and Mrs. Thompson did nothing but sit in the wicker chair weeping, Pastor Joseph Wilson watched with contempt thinking that Ralph Thompson was the henpecked husband of his vain wife, a woman he couldn't stand the sight of. It did his heart good to see her weeping in the corner. She deserved everything she was getting. He only wished he could watch her husband suffer, too. Why wasn't he crying? As he watched, he tried in vain to keep his contempt for the pair off his face.

Ralph Thompson, schooled in the nature of human beings, noted the look of contempt flitting across the pastor's face as he watched his wife. Was that a slight smile of satisfaction he saw flit across the man's mouth at his wife crying in the corner? God, why was his wife so gullible when it came to people who fawned over her and at the same time such a snob? Was she so insecure that no one could say the least little thing in disagreement with her, that she felt unloved because of it? What a weakness, pride! Was she ever going to realize that? He wondered seething at the pastor's contempt for his beloved.

All Ralph Thompson could see in Mr. Wally Spur's face was compassion. He had met the Spur's daughter, Holly, and liked her. He knew Judy dated Sam Spur, but never brought him home, which angered him as well. She knew better than that, but he could see she was too much like her mother to care.

None of that mattered much this day, however. His mind kept flying back to Shannon. How could anyone have hurt her? He couldn't bear to think on it, but he would not share that with the so-called man of God sitting next to him. The good pastor may have buffaloed his wife, but he wasn't fooling Ralph Thompson. He was no more a man of God than Jack the Ripper! Funny I should compare him to a murderer, he thought fleetingly.

He was not so ensconced in his grief that he had not noticed his daughters' reaction to the good pastor, either. They didn't seem to like him, sticking up for the old woman in front of him. That showed they had courage. Any sign of courage coming from Judy surprised him, he was ashamed to admit to himself. He was not surprised to see courage out of Kathy. Now, as it was, he would have to wait for his guests to leave to question them about their Bible reading. Something was going on.

"You come over to the restaurant, you and your family one night next week, and let me and the Missus fix you up with supper. We've got some good food over there and it'll do you good to get out," Wally Spur said breaking into Ralph's reverie.

"Yes that would be nice, Mr. Spur. I'd like to meet the rest of your family. I know my daughter Judy has been dating your son; I'd like to meet him."

"Well, don't go judging us because of that boy. I've been trying to beat some manners into him since the day he was born. He don't seem to learn though."

Ralph Thompson wished Wally Spur hadn't said that. He was loosing any initial regard he might have had for the man.

"I can't seem to keep that kid out of trouble, no matter how hard or how often I give him what for. He smokes, I know he drinks, and frankly, Mr. Thompson, I wouldn't let no daughter of mine anywhere near him."

"Funny, I've seen your daughter with him. She dotes on him. He can't be that bad."

Mr. Spur wasn't happy about that comment, but chalked it up to Thompson's grieving over the loss of his daughter. He didn't hold a grudge, especially against someone in Mr. Thompson's position. It just goes to show ya', it don't matter how high up ya' think ya' are, bad news can come to you, too. And this is the worst kind of bad news, Spur thought knowing how he would feel if someone had harmed Holly.

"Well, Mr. Spur," the pastor said turning away from Ralph Thompson and looking at Wally Spur, "Maybe we should go. Ralph, you don't mind my calling you that, do you?" The pastor asked but never bothered to wait for a reply. "I and my family are going to take Mr. Spur and his family to the carnival tonight. Maybe you would let his daughter's friend, Kathy, come along?"

"No. This is not the time for her to be going to carnivals. She'll stay home with her mother and me." Ralph Thompson immediately rejected vehemently any consideration that his daughter should ever be alone with the pastor, wondering even as he did, why he was so repulsed by the idea. Right then he didn't really care. He just wanted the two men out of his house. He expected many more neighbors would be dropping by throughout the course of the day. He knew many of his colleagues would.

"I'll see you to the door." Ralph Thompson hoped his eagerness to get rid of them wasn't too apparent. Perhaps they would excuse him if he were, considering the circumstances.

Mr. Spur certainly did.

The pastor, however, was annoyed. Ralph Thompson hadn't paid him the respect he deserved, not like Mrs. Thompson always did under normal circumstances. He could forgive her this one foray into bad behavior, considering.

At home, it wasn't much better. It was the second time that day that a member of his own family wouldn't do as he told them. No matter, that would change. As long as he was in Rutledge and had an ally in the lawyer's wife, it would all change.

Besides, tonight he and his wife would be in the company of strangers, a family dying to fit into local society. What better person to share an evening with than a man of God and his family. Who better indeed? He smiled as he walked out the Thompson's front door and back over to the parish. Mr. Spur walked with him up to Main Street then turned left on his way back to the restaurant while the pastor turned right, heading home to his family.

Of course Prudence, who never liked to go out of the house, would have to be convinced that they should go have a good time in view of the town's present circumstances. To hell with the town, Wilson thought as he walked through the summer heat. He needed to be close to young people tonight, to feel alive. If Prudence decided to stay home, all the better, he could ride in the backseat of the car with the girls. Mr. Spur's daughter Holly had a friend visiting didn't she? He thought he saw a strange girl around town the last couple of days. He could ride in the backseat with those two sweet little girls. How nice, he thought, as he walked up the street smiling.

Back at the Thompson house, Ralph Thompson watched the two men walk away from his home and go their separate ways. He wanted to make sure the pastor didn't turn back before he went upstairs to talk to Judy and Kathy.

As he climbed the stairs he could hear his two daughters talking, and as he got closer to their door, he could hear them recite Psalm 23: . . . "Yeah though I walk through the valley of death, I shall fear no evil for Thou are with me." He stepped into the room to find the two of them sitting on Judy's bed, holding hands, their eyes closed and praying, something he had never witnessed either of them do before. That was not because the family never went to church. They went every week. Religion had been rammed down the girl's throats from the day they were born. The girls had always rebelled against it. He suspected that their rebellion was more toward their mother than God. Now, as he stood there watching before clearing his throat, he was moved by their prayers and didn't want to interrupt. He did though and as they opened their eyes and saw him standing there, they looked at each other as if they'd been caught doing something wrong.

"Hey, I'm glad to see you praying. I'm just surprised is all," he said when he perceived what they were thinking. "What has gotten you to do this?"

"Mrs. Conway," Judy spoke up immediately. "She told me today that I need to do this. She said something evil was in town, and that everyone should be doing this, didn't she Kathy."

Kathy nodded her head in affirmation. "It's weird Dad," she said, "but Mrs. Conway's pretty sweet. She's no witch, like we kept telling everybody. She does see things, though. That's what she said. She didn't see what happened to Shannon, though. Someone was strong enough to block her vision. That's why she thinks we need to pray. She said it has to be strong, real strong, to block her like that." Kathy rambled on as she talked as if trying to get it out of her mouth and mind all at once. She wanted desperately to protect her father and mother, everyone she knew. She only wished she could have protected Shannon. Maybe if I had of walked her home? She thought, fighting to keep her tears in check.

Chapter Eleven

"Honey, I'm home," Wally Spur mocked as he walked through the kitchen door of the Spur apartment trying to sound like Desi Arnaz from the I Love Lucy show she liked so much. He had gone to the restaurant first expecting to find his wife there then became angry when she was not.

Mrs. Spur immerged from the bedroom where she had been napping. The day's news had taken a toll on her. She couldn't understand how someone could murder a child. She wanted to comfort Kathy, who had spent a great deal of time with them that afternoon. The girl needed comfort, something her parents probably couldn't give enough of when they needed it so much themselves.

She also wanted Holly and Renee to know that things would be okay. But how could she convince them of that when she wondered how they were ever going to be okay again herself!

After she took Kathy and Judy home, she came back home and laid down hoping to ease her tired mind, which pounded inside her head. Now, to top everything off, her husband had a bad attitude, nothing new in that, she half expected it, but today of all days!

"Why have you got your lazy ass in bed in the middle of the afternoon? Why aren't you at the restaurant? Someone from this house should be there when I'm not. You know damn well the help over there is ripping us off!"

He was secretly glad she was home. He was glad to have something to rag on her about. She was too free and easy with the customers, if you asked him, smiling at them all the time, especially the men. Nothing but a tramp whore, and god knows he'd told her that enough times.

But he loved her, so what was he to do? He'd bear up under it, that's all. He'd even be good to her on occasion, after all he was her husband. At that thought, he smiled, and said, "Get dressed; get the kids dressed. We're going to the carnival tonight, and you'll never guess with whom. Well, go on, guess!"

She just starred at him. Did he say they were going to the carnival—tonight of all nights?

"Pastor Joseph Wilson has consented to be our companion for the evening, so I think you should be grateful one of the town's finest leading men has deemed us worthy enough to be seen with him. Lord knows it wouldn't hurt you any to be around a godly man for a change," he looked at his wife with scorn. He was angry with her again. Why did she have to be so pretty?

"If the pastor wants to hang out with you, there must be something wrong with him." She regretted it no sooner than it spilled from her mouth, but she couldn't help remembering what Mrs. Conway had said earlier about this pastor her husband was now forcing his family to socialize with.

Wally Spur did what Wally Spur always did any time his wife had the gall to talk back to him. He reached over and slapped her as hard as he could across the face. The sound carried throughout the apartment. His attack left a large red welt on Mrs. Spur's left cheek.

She said nothing. She turned, walked out of the kitchen, and into the bathroom where she ran cold water soaking a washcloth in it and pressing it to her face. She was good at this. She knew how to prevent a welt from forming. She had had to hide many of them over the course of their twenty-five year marriage.

Sam was lying on his bed when his father came home, heard as the old man walked through the door yelling at his mother for not being in the restaurant. He also heard the slap. At the sound, he jumped to his feet. He was all too familiar with the progression of his parent's arguments. He waited until the bathroom door closed, which he knew it would, then stormed out of his room and into the kitchen to face down his father. "You are the ugliest damn human being I have ever met," he said calmly staring into his father's eyes.

Old Man Spur raised a fist and was about to attack, much as he had many, many times before. However, as he was about to strike the look in Sam's eyes caused his balled up fist to fall limply to his side.

"Look at you standing there acting like you're somebody. You ain't nothing but the punk you've always been. You ain't shit, little mamma's boy, running to help her when you think her little feelings might be hurt. What goes on between a husband and wife ain't none of your business boy, so go cry to your mamma that her husband said mean things to you," he taunted until he could see Sam's face contort with rage. When Sam didn't erupt, he taunted all the more.

"I don't know who your daddy is, boy, but you better learn to stay out of other people's business if you know what's good for ya'."

No more would his father's taunts hurt him. Sam saw now that his old man was afraid of him. The realization knocked him for a loop inside, but he fought to maintain his composure in front of him. Sam could actually smell his father's fear. It felt good. "You know what, Pop. One of these days, I'll probably be thanking God you are the prick you are. Can't say as I can do that right now, but it'll happen. You're right, you aren't my real father. My real father is God Almighty. Thank you, thank you for sending me to Him." With that Sam walked out of the apartment and down the rickety back steps, and off into the late afternoon twilight.

Old Man Spur stood stunned and motionless. Sam couldn't have hit him hard enough to stun him as much as his words had. What the hell did the kid mean, he wasn't his father? Did he know something Wally Spur didn't? Had his mother confided in him? And what did he mean he had sent him to God the Father? What, was the kid going to kill himself or something? He breezily brushed the thoughts aside. They neither bothered nor bewildered him. He was just glad Sam was out of the house. He didn't want to take his rebellious son anywhere.

It took a few moments to gather his composure, but gather it he did. When he did, he crossed the living room intent on seeing Holly to give her the good news that the family would be socializing with the pastor tonight. The girls needed to get ready; the Wilsons would be there soon.

Holly heard it all. Even though she knew Renee had heard plenty in her house from her parents, she was still embarrassed by it. She felt pride in Sam, something Renee felt too, judging by the look on her face, but what were they going to do about the pastor? She didn't want to go anywhere near him let alone to the carnival with him. She didn't want to go to any old carnival anyway, not now that someone had murdered her friend.

"Dad," she smiled when he walked into her room without knocking. Holly was skilled at appeasing her father's tirades. She had been doing it for years. "I heard what you told Mom about the carnival, and that's a nice idea, Dad. But I don't want to go. Neither does Renee. I mean, Shannon just died, Dad. We don't feel like going out and having fun." She looked in her father's eyes pleading with him silently not to make her do this. She got her way most times by using this ploy, and prayed that it would work again, today of all days.

But it didn't.

"You know what you need?" Old Man Spur said, eager to please his daughter. In his heart, however, he was more eager to spend more time with the pastor, a man who thought so highly of him, the first one who had paid him a compliment, a well-deserved compliment at that, in a long time. Hell, he needed some praise once in awhile, he certainly didn't get any thanks for all his hard work from his family. "You need to come out and have some fun; that will take your mind off your loss for at least a little while. Do this for me tonight and be on your best behavior. Your daddy doesn't ask much of you, Holly, so this one time you could do as I ask without complaint. Have I ever steered you wrong?"

"No, Dad," Holly was pleading now, "but not tonight, please!" she whined.

"You two get dressed. That's the last I'll hear of it! You're going with the rest of us to the carnival if I have to drag you. My family can stick by me this one time, so I can socialize with a few of the bigwigs in this town. People, whom by the way, think a great deal more of me than you do, so you be ready in fifteen minutes, or I'm coming in here with a belt." Since Old Man Spur had never touched Holly, nor had he ever threatened her with violence, she was shocked. She got dressed. Renee followed suit. They didn't have much choice.

At the Wilson residence, Pastor Joseph Wilson wasn't working too hard to convince his wife Prudence that she should go with him. Prudence, a mousy little woman without much backbone who didn't like to socialize much. Crowds made her nervous, as did most things. She liked reading her Bible, her crochet, and having a few good friends over on occasion, but a carnival? No, that would not be something she'd be interested in. "Why don't you be a dear and take Gloria, Hon? She's upstairs. You need to take her. She's young; carnivals were made for the young."

Not a bad idea, the pastor thought, he kissed his wife's cheek and thanked heaven she didn't like to go out. He climbed the steps to Gloria's room with anticipation.

Gloria had spent the day at the restaurant with many of the other young people in town. She had been as shocked at the news of Shannon's death by murder as everyone else had. Also at the news, something horrible had begun to dawn on the inside of her. A shadow flitted through her mind, the shadow of the real murderer. It wasn't the strangers in town the day before! She remembered them clearly, saw the men that the girls had told the cops were trying to accost them. She had seen them leave town, watched them get into a shinny gray car after they'd eaten their picnic lunch; they drove south. She saw Shannon walking through the picnic grounds on her way home long after the men had left. She had even said hello to her.

She wondered why the police weren't asking her questions. She guessed they didn't know to ask her anything, and she thought about calling them and offering the information. Shannon was a sweet kid. If she could help in some way, she'd be glad to. She paced back and forth across her bedroom floor, while the shadow in her mind of the real killer grew clearer with each step. Just as she was about to see whom it really was, her father walked into her room without knocking. She had heard him come home, knew he was downstairs talking to her mother, but hadn't heard the creak on the steps and thought, no, God, not again, not today. Keep him from me, please! It surprised Gloria that she would bother to call on God considering her upbringing, but she would not allow her father's evil to jade her against that which she knew was good. Still, she prayed, keep him from me! She wondered why that prayer was never answered. Maybe someday she'd find out.

Wilson didn't feel he had to knock on any door in his house. He walked in, just like he had done a million times before. This time, though, she was fully clothed. Even though the weather was blistering hot, Gloria wore two shirts to hide her ample bosoms, an aspect of her anatomy that he took great interest in. She wore jeans as well and underneath them a pair of shorts to cover her panties. She wanted no one to look at her with lust.

"Gloria, dear," Wilson said brushing his daughter's shoulder with his fingers and planting a kiss on her cheek. "You smell so good. You are a temptress aren't you? You sinner you; why are you always tantalizing me with your body? Are you a harlot, Gloria? Is that it? Do I forever have to rid you of that viper demon, lust? Is that it? Is God using me to deliver you from wanton sensuality?" As he spoke, he moved in closer to her, exerting pressure on her shoulders and forcing her down on the bed with his hand over her mouth.

She didn't know what to do. She was afraid of him. If she didn't let him have his way, he'd hit her, hard. He'd lock her in the basement like he did when she was a little girl after he accused her of trying to tempt him, then.

Again, he took her, and again he told her it was her fault for tantalizing him the way she always did.

When he finished, he got up, went out the door and didn't look back. He never asked her if she wanted to go to the carnival. He didn't give her another thought.

Gloria laid on the bed hating him for what he did to her. She was beginning to believe he was right. She was no good.

When he finished with Gloria, Pastor Joseph Wilson got into his brand new 1963 Cadillac, a car Mrs. Vivian Thompson had purchased for him against her husband's wishes, and drove to the Spurs'. He would let Mr. and Mrs. Spur sit in the front seat on the way to the carnival while he rode in the backseat with the two girls. They were lovely, now weren't they? And wouldn't Mr. Spur, such a lowly man, appreciate his good will by letting him drive his new Cadillac? Of course he would. Everyone would be happy. It was a grand idea.

Although they didn't want to go, the girls were ready by six p.m. just as Old Man Spur had ordered. When they went into the kitchen, they found Mrs. Spur sitting at the kitchen table smoking cigarettes and drinking coffee. Her makeup looked funny to Renee. There was too much of it under her left eye, otherwise, she looked beautiful, as always.

Mr. Spur was getting ready. He left the bathroom door open, and the girls could see him standing over the sink in his undershirt, his suspenders hanging down around his buttocks as he shaved. He hummed, smiling at himself in the mirror.

The girls wondered what he was so happy about. For God's sake, Holly thought, doesn't he have one thought for Shannon, the little girl who came to the restaurant with me almost every day since we moved to town? She was disgusted with her father.

He didn't seem to notice the look of reproach on her face even though he could see her reflection plainly in the mirror through the open door.

Holly turned her back to him and sat at the table with her mother.

Mr. Spur put on a clean long sleeved white shirt, buttoned it, tucked it into his pants, replaced his suspenders, rolled his cuffs up due to the oppressive heat and walked into the kitchen. As he did, they all heard a car honking below.

He motioned for the women to follow, and he stepped onto the back porch. As he opened the screen door to take a step outside, Mrs. Conway hobbled up to him from the shadows, startling him. "Don't you take those girls in that car! You hear me? The one you think is your friend, ain't. He'll harm them if he gets a chance." She pointed to the girls who stood behind Mrs. Spur who had followed her husband out the door.

"Shut up you old bat! You keep hanging around my family and land-lady or no, I'll sick the cops on you. Don't be filling these here kid's heads with your bullshit, neither. You hear me?" Old Man Spur was raving mad now. Nobody was going to keep him from going out with the pastor. He had been waiting for a moment like this far too long to be stopped now.

Mrs. Conway didn't bat an eye at his tirade, neither did she back down. She stood in front of Wally Spur blocking his access to the rickety back stairs. "You girls listen to me since this man is too stubborn to. I want you to know you can come to me if anything—and I do mean anything—happens to you tonight. Do you understand?"

Both girls nodded their heads in fright. What could happen?

"I told you to leave my girls alone, now, didn't I?" Old Man Spur was about to push Mrs. Conway aside when everyone heard a voice coming from behind her on the stair.

"I see you're at it again, Mrs. Conway. My, my, my, but you like to butt into other people's affairs. What must it take to keep you from meddling where you don't belong?" The voice behind the old woman was sickly sweet, and at the same time icy cold. The children shivered in fear of it. Suddenly they were afraid for their new friend, this tiny old woman who couldn't hurt a flea, afraid she would be hurt. When she moved aside, they saw that none other than the good pastor had uttered the veiled threat, the man Old Man Spur was intent on befriending.

Mrs. Conway didn't blink an eye, nor did she back off in fear. "No weapon formed against me shall prosper," she said staring the pastor in the eye. "You should know that one now shouldn't you, Pastor?" She spoke as sweetly to him as he had her.

"Why don't you quit your meddling, you old witch, and go back to hell where you belong," the good pastor leveled her with an icy stare.

"That's your home, now ain't it? I know who your spiritual father is, now don't I? So you just keep it up Pastor. You know who is on my side. The same one that knows the rumors and lies you spread about me around town. He hears them and He knows, and you know it. So you watch your step. He'll only let you get so far. You know that, too!" She smiled as she spoke walking past him on the decrepit stairwell descending to her first floor apartment.

The pastor made no move to touch Mrs. Conway, which was what the girls feared he would do. Instead, he backed up against the stair railing as far as he could so she would not brush him as she passed. He tried to make it look as though she repelled him, but Renee knew instinctively that he was afraid of her. She smiled.

But there was no mistaking that hatred in his eyes for Mrs. Conway. If he could have murdered her with a look, he would have. The hatred frightened both girls down to their souls. Never had they seen such malevolence. They were also very impressed with Mrs. Conway. As tiny as she was, she stood boldly up to the pastor, and didn't look remotely frightened of him.

Maybe that's what made him so mad, Renee thought. She also thought that no matter what Old Man Spur said, she would visit the old lady ever chance she got as long as she was in Rutledge. She liked Holly's father less and less with each passing moment.

It wasn't until Mrs. Conway had reached the bottom porch and had gone inside her apartment that Joseph Wilson turned his eyes away from her. One of these days, he thought, then remembered to smile as he looked at his guests still standing above him on the stairwell. "Well, let's get going, times 'a wastin'," he said cheerfully. He smiled at the girls who were still standing behind Mrs. Spur.

"Here, Wally, you drive." He tossed Old Man Spur the keys to the Cadillac. "Mrs. Spur, you ride in the front seat with your husband. Enjoy the car."

By this time, they had descended all the steps and the girls were walking onto the first floor porch and had to pass by the pastor. As they did, he smiled and said, "I'll ride in the backseat with the girls." He was smiling at them like a Cheshire cat. They shivered realizing that he would be sitting right next to them, away from the elder Spurs. When they reached the car, Wilson held the door for the girls, bowing slightly at the waist as he waited for them to get in. "Now, dear, you sit by that door," he said to Renee pointing to the far side of the car. "Holly can sit next to me."

"No, I don't want to," Holly stamped her foot and pouted hoping her father would make the pastor sit up front so their mother could ride in back with them.

"You do as the pastor says, girl, and you do it now. Don't you know how to respect your elders? He's treating you to the carnival! You sit next to him and you keep your mouth shut!"

Holly was crushed.

As Renee got in and slid over to the other side by the door, she turned to see Holly getting into the car. A single tear fell silently down her friend's cheek. Wilson climbed in behind her and shut the door then turned to smile at the girls knowing he had just won a major victory. Renee wanted to hit him in the head. He looked her in the eye, still smiling, as if daring her to try it.

Chapter Twelve

It had been a long day, and proved to be an even longer night. Damn that carnival, Sheriff Ernie Hansen thought as he got ready to go out on patrol. He didn't want to go out on patrol. He had a murder to solve, but he was short handed because of the carnival, it always brought so much trouble with it. Police had to make an appearance there though, otherwise the riff-raff that the carnival attracted would take advantage of local citizens at every turn. It was the same every year.

The one thing he had hoped by patrolling the carnival was that he would get a handle on the two strangers that had been hanging around town the day before during the parade. He was betting they came to town with the carnival.

Even though his instincts told him this case was not one of stranger danger, he still had to check them out. Besides, even if these two turned out to be innocent of little Shannon Thompson's murder, they sure as hell weren't innocent, and it behooved him to check up on them.

He noted the oppressive heat as he walked across the department's two-lane parking lot to get into his cruiser. As he opened the door, heat shot out at him like a bullet from the interior, splaying him like double ought buckshot. He laughed as he started the engine and rolled down the windows. The only air-conditioning he enjoyed in his 1963 Oldsmobile cruiser was two-eighty, meaning he opened two windows and drove 80 mph. He better not let any of his deputies' catch him driving that fast; they'd ticket him. He laughed again.

As soon as he got on the highway and started cruising toward Rutledge, thoughts of Shannon cruised through his mind as fast as he was driving. He could still see her splayed open and on display. When he thought of how she looked then, he had to fight to control his anger. Whoever did that to her was a demon, they weren't human. No human could do that to a child.

His mind drifted to her father, Ralph Thompson, and his heart went out to him. Ralph Thompson was a familiar face at the police station. Even if he never showed his face at the jail, which he sometimes did to see someone incarcerated there, most of his officers had met Ralph Thompson in court. He was a formidable foe to anyone who didn't obey the law. He was also a nice guy. Even if he weren't, the sheriff thought, his little girl didn't deserve to be killed. Nope. Pine County Sheriff Ernie Hansen made a vow that come hell or high water, he'd make sure that who ever did hurt little Shannon Thompson would pay for it.

As he passed the Willow River Lake road, he noticed Henry Sampson's '55 Chevy tearing it up. He didn't have time to deal with teenage kids right then unless they were at the carnival. The kids in Sampson's Chevy got lucky, he thought, and they didn't even know it.

He also noted it was Sam Spur driving Samson's car. He knew, too, that Henry wasn't supposed to let anyone else drive his car. Hell, the Spur kid couldn't be much more that fifteen, Hansen thought. When he interviewed him, he had to admit that he had expected trouble from him based solely on how he had been dressed, jeans with a tight T-shirt, with smokes rolled up in its sleeves, shouldn't be smoking let alone driving. But the kid was polite, seemed nice, sure as hell was upset when he found out someone had killed one of his sister's friends, all of which Hansen found interesting.

Ernie Hansen didn't know much about the Spur family, but he had learned a few things since he began investigating Shannon's death. He doubted the Spur kid had anything to do with it. Regardless, he might prove to be a lot of trouble later on, he thought.

As for the restaurant, he hadn't had as much as one complaint about it staying open too late or serving minors liquor, even though he knew a lot of kids hung out there. They didn't have any place else in Rutledge to hang out. He heard the older kids were kicked out by nine p.m. and the younger ones, eight p.m. That was in keeping with state law. That's what mattered to Hansen. He hadn't been called to the restaurant to break up any fights, or anything like that, either, hadn't heard of any trouble coming from the place, so he could see nothing adverse about it. The parents had to be doing something right, he conceded. All the kids seemed to like them, even the Willow River kids, which was a stretch, considering the two villages had a long-standing rivalry going.

Hansen didn't know much about the little girl they had staying with them, either. She seemed like a nice enough kid when he talked to her. The girls seemed as innocent as his own daughter was, and he liked them right off, felt badly for them in fact because of how their friend was taken away from them. Had to be hard on a kid considering how hard it was on adults. They probably didn't understand everything, and that was for the best. Why should they? "Hell, I can't understand that sickness!" He said to the empty car.

He slowed the cruiser to 25 mph coming into the outskirts of Rutledge then slowed even further as he cruised onto Main Street carefully observing all that was before him. It wasn't much. The restaurant had its shades pulled and its lights off, the gas station was shut up tight with the doors closed, and the single grocery store with its "Open" sign still hanging in the window looked empty. Mrs. Conway must be working, he thought as he slowly drove past the front door.

There were hardly any cars driving up or down Main Street, which was odd because it was also a busy highway. As he edged closer to the south end of town, Hansen could see a myriad of vehicles coming and going from the fairgrounds, much as he had expected. Being that Willow River and Rutledge were so small, as were most all the other towns in the vicinity, there wasn't much for anyone to do for excitement. It wasn't just a problem for the kids. Adults seemed to need a little excitement, too. That's why, whenever a carnival came to any of the towns, it drew a lot of attention from all the neighboring towns.

Hansen made his way up to the entrance gate being motioned in without paying an admission charge. Everyone working the carnival gate knew not to charge the police. The county owned the fairgrounds, and they expected all local law enforcement to show up as a matter of public service.

The carnival needed them, too, although they would never admit it. It wasn't just carnies who started trouble. Sometimes it was the locals thinking they could do as they pleased to the carnies.

Most times, the carnival was simply more trouble than any of the police officers cared to deal with what with the fights, pick pockets, runaways and thieves; a carnival coming to town meant overtime whether officers wanted it or not.

Hansen pulled up and parked alongside the horse barns. He thought he'd check that out before he started strolling through the midway where all the rides were, and where the carnies hung out hocking wares and trying to get people to throw their money away on rigged games.

His daughter was interested in horses. What was it about little girls and horses? He didn't think he would ever know, but he did know that he didn't know much about horses. Since he was planning on buying her one for her birthday in August, he decided he had better research them a bit so he knew what he was doing. Besides, he didn't want to buy an animal he didn't know how to take care of.

He would have to teach his daughter to do the same, and make sure she understood the importance of pet ownership and all the responsibilities that went along with it. Besides, he didn't know what to expect when it came to cost.

He had learned enough through his research, so that now as he strolled through the horse barns, he could identify the different breeds. When he saw an owner grooming or feeding their animal, he'd stop to talk to them and ask questions about the horse's care. By the time he finished strolling through the barn, he had learned a great deal more.

Horses didn't just eat hay; they had to have grain, too, the amount dependant on what the horse would be used for. They needed plenty of fresh water every day and a field to run in. Fences also were a concern. Barbed wire worked, but wood would be better in case a spooked horse went through a fence. They did that sometimes. And how close to a main road would the horse be stabled? Insurance needed to be considered, and he learned, he could add coverage against horse accidents to his homeowner's insurance policy. Saddles—what type of riding would his daughter be doing—English or western? Bridles—what kind would the horse require—what type of bit might be best—again much of the information was use dependent.

As Hansen strolled out of the barn, he felt a tad overwhelmed. He'd have to guess at a few things, like the saddle and bridle. He decided he'd get the type most commonly used, western, and go from there. If she changed over the course of time, he'd get her English riding gear. The type of horse to buy was another matter. He had been watching the papers to see if anything caught his eye and not much had. Of course, he would want the gentlest breed there was for her, but what did she want? What was she ready for?

One local horse owner showing his horse at the fair suggested to Hansen that a good grade horse might be ideal for his daughter. He liked that idea. The man even offered to go with him on his buying trip until they found a good animal. The sheriff took him up on the offer and got the man's name and phone number. It wouldn't hurt to take someone along who knew something about horseflesh when he went to finally purchase an animal.

Once out of the barn Hansen began walking toward the midway when it hit him. Here he was planning this surprise for his eleven-year old daughter, a surprise he knew would delight her, and another eleven-year old had been robbed of any such joy by some fiend. He was angry all over again. His respite from thoughts of the young Shannon lying tossed aside like a piece of unwanted meat was short lived.

As the sheriff slowly walked past booth after booth he grew angrier and angrier, frightening more than one carnie with the look on his face. Carnies could smell a cop from a mile away, and when they saw one with anger in his eyes, those wanted by the law for some infraction, mostly minor, would slink out of sight and stay that way until the unwanted intruder disappeared.

News of a cop on the midway spread throughout the compound faster than any cop could. Those wanted by the law hid behind closed doors. Those who didn't hide chose not to offer any information to any cop that there were others amongst them that police might take an interest in.

Hansen knew this. It happened every time a carnival came to town. They had a better intercom system than his office and there were no wires connecting it. It always amazed him though, how fast news of his presence preceded him. He stopped walking for awhile; he was tired and thirsty. He chose a food stand and ordered a hot dog with all the fixings and a soda, sitting down under its awning, eating, and looking across the midway. Sitting there, staring out at the midway, eating his lunch, the Tilt-A-Whirl caught his attention, and there he found what he had been looking for. The two men running it matched exactly the descriptions given by Shannon's friends.

They fit the bill perfectly. As he ate, Hansen thought it odd that they hadn't disappeared like the rest of their cronies. They would have if they were guilty of something. Maybe these two are just bozos, he thought as he bite into his delicious dog and continued to watch. He was in no hurry, as the two appeared completely oblivious to him.

They still wore the same clothes the girls saw them in the day before. Hansen smiled. They hadn't even bothered to change. Sometimes, things were just too easy, he thought, which immediately made him uncomfortable. Things were rarely too easy. He finished his dog, drank his soda, and slowly hefted his big body up off the wooden bench. He hated to get out from under the shade the awning offered. It was a hot day.

The big sheriff, heavy laden with police paraphernalia hanging off his utility belt, ambled over to the ride observing that on the platform were many eager carnival goers waiting for their turn on the Tilt-A-Wheel. Standing to the right, in front of the ride about twenty feet from the ticket takers, he could hear real well, it was just the spot he had been looking for. He wanted to watch the two men in action before approaching them. They seemed completely unconcerned with his presence, if they even realized a cop was in the vicinity.

Each time one of the cars rolled in front of him screaming faces of people enjoying the ride with its speed and quick turns, flashed speedily before his eyes. The surreal landscape of faces made it hard to pinpoint any one person; they came and went too quickly. Some of the ride's chairs twirled faster than others, and it looked to Hansen as if the people in those seats were having the most fun. Their screams were louder, their smiles bigger.

Cheap thrills, he thought, but, hey, who was he to judge. Not everybody led exciting lives, and if they needed a carnival ride like that to give them a little thrill, what the hell, they weren't hurting anyone.

"You girls want to ride for free?" one of the carnies asked a group of four teenage girls. "Come on! We run this ride; it's okay. You'll be mine and Freddie's guests. My name is Bobby." He enticed them onto the platform where he urged everyone back so they could move to the front. The paying fair goers didn't appreciate it, Hansen thought looking at their faces.

The girls didn't look much older than thirteen, but they were wearing makeup and trying to look nineteen. Hansen wondered if Freddie and Bobby had noticed that, or him standing so close.

They probably hadn't or they'd have been more discreet. Maybe they were just dumb, he thought. That observation brought on the uneasiness he had felt while eating. Something wasn't right here.

Bobby, the one running the controls, said to the girls, "You know, you four are pretty special. Anybody ever tell you that?" He ran his fingers down one of the girl's cheeks as she blushed and the others giggled.

They like him! God, what idiots, Hansen thought.

Bobby had yet to do anything wrong, though, and Freddie, who spent a lot of time under the ride, hadn't uttered a word, let alone put his hands where they didn't belong.

When he finally came out from under the ride to sit at the controls, Freddie sat on the rail to move the lever back and forth, smiling at everyone as he worked. He would get his turn; that's how Bobby and him operated. They switched jobs each time one ride ended and another began.

Hansen observed that as the ride stopped and those on it rushed off the back stair, a new group pilled into the empty cars. That's when he saw Bobby take over the controls and Freddie turn his attentions to some new girls waiting in line for the next go around of the Tilt-A-Whirl. This time Freddie singled out which girls to talk to while absentmindedly taking paying customer's tickets.

The first four girls rode in a car twirling this way and that, smiling and laughing at each go around as they came upon Bobby, while he smiled and waved back at them. They were riding free.

Two of the girls in the first group of four, seemed to feel neglected as neither Bobby nor Freddie had been shown them any special attention. They looked dejected as the car twirled in front of the sheriff. The other two girls had smug looks on their faces as they enjoyed the ride. All that changed, however, as the car with the first set of four girls came around for about the fifth time in front of Bobby. The first two favored girls found that Bobby now had eyes for four different girls waiting on the platform for their turn at the ride. Oh well, one of them said as their car twirled in front of the sheriff, at least we got to ride for free. With that, all four girls started laughing.

Good, thought Hansen, maybe they weren't senseless after all. And they probably haven't a clue as to how lucky they'd been.

When a new group of eager carnival goers piled onto the platform, and the second group of girls were twirling around the ride free, Hansen crossed over the gravel tarmac and heavy cables, climbing the stairs, edging his way toward Freddie and Bobby, smiling as he went.

"Are you going to offer me a free ride?" He asked Freddie sweetly.

When Freddie turned looking to see who spoke to him, taking his attentions away from the girls he was flirting with, his demeanor changed instantly. Suddenly wary, Freddie scowled and slumped at the rail.

Hansen noted the change in demeanor. Freddie drew into himself gazing up at the sheriff from underneath his eyelids. He looked to Hansen as if he were hunching in an effort to hide himself. It was too late for that, though. Whatever was wrong here, he'd find out and respond accordingly, and he had no doubts that something was wrong.

"Nothing wrong with giving a couple of kids a free ride, now is there Sheriff?"

"No, there isn't. And that's all you're gonna' give them."

"Wasn't thinking about doing nothing else, nothing."

Hansen knew that was a lie. "I'll bet those girls ain't much older than twelve, thirteen. What 'ya think?"

"Yeah, sheriff, that's what me and Bobby figured."

Bobby gave Freddie a dirty look for using his real name.

"Why don't you come and join us, too, Bobby?" Hansen asked politely, but there was no mistaking the tone. It was an order.

"Now, why I'm here; I been kind of wondering what you two were doing yesterday, say about noon. You wouldn't have happened to be in Rutledge then, would you?"

"Rutledge? Where the hell is that?" Bobby chose to act dumb. It was a mistake.

"Are you going to get stupid on me, Bobby? Cause if you are I'll find a way to smarten you up. How's that?" Hansen paused looking Bobby in the eyes, daring him to say something even dumber. Bobby wised up and said nothing. "Now, I was asking about yesterday. Were you in Rutledge at around noon, during the parade?"

"Yeah, we was there," Freddie answered. Again Bobby gave him a dirty look. "Why? Any law against watching a parade?"

"No, no law against that. Tell me boys, were you two goobers trying to talk to some young girls down in front of the café?" The two men looked at each other. Bobby looked scared to Hansen, but Freddie didn't.

"We're always talking to girls, Sheriff. It's part of the job. We flirt a little, they buy more tickets, take more rides. That's more money for us. We go to town before we open, entice the locals in. You know how it works. Local small town girls are always looking for excitement. It's easy."

Hansen had no doubt Freddie was telling the truth on that score. He didn't like it though.

Andy Freboni joined Hansen on the platform, just then. Hansen had called him earlier on his walkie-talkie as he finished his soda and got off the bench to get a good look at the two running the Tilt-A-Whirl. At the sight of two cops, Bobby was visibly sweating, putting Hansen on the alert. Freddie didn't seem too concerned, though, and was cooperative.

"Well, boys, we have us a problem here. See, yesterday, sometime, don't know exactly when yet, a little girl from town got hurt. Seems you two had been nosing around her before the accident. What we need to do, in view of that, is to take you two back to the office and have us a nice long chat."

With this news, Bobby was ready to bolt. Hansen could tell, so as Bobby took his first step away from him, Hansen grabbed him, threw him up against the ticket booth, and handcuffed him. Freboni was too fast for Freddie, and on him, handcuffing him, making sure he couldn't make a break for it, before Freddie could react.

"Now Freddie, you look like you have a few more brains than your buddy, here. I would suggest you radio for someone to take over the ride for you—we'll wait—and you come along peacefully. If you haven't done anything wrong, you have nothing to worry about, right?"

Freddie just nodded his head and reached inside the ticket office to pull out a radio, while handcuffs dangled between his wrists. Within two minutes, two other carnies were ready to take over the ride. Meanwhile, everyone who had been riding the Tilt-A-Whirl got a free go-around long enough to equal two rides. No one complained.

"Now, Bobby, what are you so scared of? Trying to run from a nice old guy like me? Tsk, tsk, tsk. That just makes me wonder about you, you know? Guess I'll have to dig a little deeper than I had planned into your background. Do one of those big city background checks, you understand. Sometimes that's fun for us small time cops. I mean we get to play with the big boys once in awhile," Hansen smiled at Freboni as the two lead the carnies off the midway and he spoke to Bobby. They were sharing a private joke which every small town cop understood; no one ever gave them credit for having, or using, the brain in their heads, especially carnies.

Every time a carnival came to a small town, carnival workers thought the police were small-time rubes. Hansen had never been a stupid man, and he had always been even tempered, but he had never seen anything like what he had seen when he saw Shannon Thompson dead. Nope. Nobody was going to get away with that, not on his watch.

Freboni had parked his cruiser right behind the Fun House across the midway and both Bobby and Freddie were placed unceremoniously in the back seat of the car. Hansen climbed into the front seat alongside Freboni who gave him a ride to his cruiser. Hansen was not just blustering about doing a real thorough background check on the two in the back seat; he'd fingerprint them first, then have mug shots taken.

Chapter Thirteen

Sam watched Hansen go by, and wondered how long it would be before he called Henry's folks to tell them he was driving Henry's car. He didn't really care. He knew the Sampsons would rag on Henry about it, though. He hated to see that happen; Henry was decent to him.

Lots of things were happening, though, most a damn sight more serious than Henry's folks ragging on him about the car. He didn't know what to make of any of it, especially the fact that Shannon had been murdered. He still had a hard time trying to comprehend that.

Holly and Renee, too, what about them, he wondered? The more he thought about them, the more his mind came back to Renee. He hoped she was okay. He knew he'd be around for Holly anytime she wanted him, but Renee? Her brother Mike wasn't really there for her. He just didn't appreciate what a good kid she was.

Kid? She isn't much of a kid anymore, he thought. She sure looks good swimming, and she's so tall! Man, she was just a pip-squeak not three months ago—what the hell happened! He wondered.

As they passed the lake for the hundredth time Sam wondered about the fact that the girls were all together at the lake only the day before yesterday? Shannon, too! They were all having such a good time! They looked so pretty running for the water, all four of them. It was funny when Shannon fell; she looked so gangly and awkward. We all laughed at that—her legs got so tangled up in each other. How could someone hurt her?

Sam understood about sometimes wanting to hurt someone, though. There were times when all he wanted to do was pummel his old man into unconsciousness, the way the old man was always pummeling his mother and him, but never in a million years could he fathom actually doing it, that, or hurting a little girl. He wanted someone his own size, age, and strength, or, even better, someone bigger to fight, so he could use them like a boxing bag hanging in a gym.

But Shannon, never in a million years could he consider hurting someone like her. Someone had, and it wasn't right. He probably wasn't right in wanting to hurt his old man, either, he supposed—but murdering a kid went way beyond anything he contemplated, he felt.

Sam drove Henry's car like the thoughts racing through his mind, hard and fast.

Talk was that Shannon had been raped, too. Smiley Rains, sitting in the back seat of Henry Sampson's car as Sam roared down the gravel roads, had eavesdropped on his folks when they were talking about the murder that morning. Neighbors had stopped over for coffee thinking the Rains might know something extra since Smiley was a friend of Sam Spur's and all, and the Spur kid being the brother to the little murdered girl's friends.

His folk's Willow River neighbors hoped to be the first to hear some juicy gossip, Smiley guessed, but instead, he learned things from them. Seems the neighbors were friends with one of the sheriff deputies and he told them about the rape. The local newspaper, the Willow River Gazette, had not mentioned it, they told his folks that morning as he listened from the upstairs stairwell.

Smiley, thinking he possessed knowledge that would be of great interest to his friends, cleared his throat getting ready to tell all, "Ya' know, my folks had some friends over this morning for coffee," Smiley started, hoping to garner some attention for himself. "They was talking about Shannon."

Sam turned the radio off so he could hear what Smiley had to say.

"They thought maybe I'd know something, cause you and me's such good friends," he said tapping Sam on the shoulder. Sam said nothing, waiting for Smiley to continue. Smiley, knowing he had everyone's rapt attention, started talking even slower than normal. "They said she was raped." He let that statement hang in mid-air before resuming.

"Raped?" Sam said. He couldn't believe it. "How do you know she was raped?" He was furious that Smiley would say such a vile thing and Smiley sensed it.

"Hey man, don't take it out on me. I'm just telling ya' what the neighbors said. They said one of the sheriff's deputies, a friend of theirs, told them that." Smiley wished right then that he was anything but the center of attention, and he sure as hell didn't want Sam pissed at him. He never saw Sam strike anything, but figured if he ever let go someone would get hurt . . . bad.

Dennis Wilson, riding in the front seat, absentmindedly rubbed his nose. He hadn't told the others that he and Sam got into it over Renee, but they had all wondered how his nose got busted up. Smiley guessed right then who had done it and clamed up.

Sam was astounded. How could anyone want to have sex with a little kid? You were supposed to have sex with bad girls, not little kids! "Man, are ya' telling us one of your whoppers again? This one sucks! You're talking about a little kid, a sweet little kid and a friend of my kid sister. Ya' damn well better watch what you're saying," Sam looked at Smiley through the rear view mirror and though he never raised his voice, what he said was more menacing because of it.

"Hey, man, that's the gospel truth. I mean that's what the neighbors told my folks. I don't know any more than that." Smiley was very uneasy.

Sam watched him closely in the mirror and knew he wasn't lying, which made him all the angrier. Shannon came from the best family in town, how could anyone do that to her?

A voice popped up in Sam's head saying, "It shouldn't happen to any of My children." Sam half laughed at the irony of that. I guess no child should be abused! He thought, then looked around at his companions knowing that their parents had abused everyone of them, in one way or another. Henry was neglected; his folks kept trying to buy him off just to get rid of him. Smiley's folks treated him like dirt. Everyone knew Dennis' old man was a drunk. Hell, Dennis was the man of that house and he wasn't but sixteen-years old. Only two of the group, George King and Hank Hall were treated good by their folks, but they were made fun of by the other kids in town because they didn't have a lot of money and sometimes they smelled like the cow barns they had to clean.

When he thought about it, Sam realized that the same thing held true for the girls he hung around with, all except Judy Thompson. Maybe that's why she intrigued him. But he liked Gloria Wilson the best, as a person. Some of the other guys in school, the ones he didn't hang out with, said she put out, but Sam doubted it. She was too tough to be a push over for anyone let alone the likes of them. The types of guys who had everything handed to them from the time they were born, who came from families that had been entrenched in the community for decades, and had inherited wealth—naw, Gloria wasn't a sucker for any of that. She did seem like she was haunted in some way though.

The same guys that said Gloria put out were the same type of guys Judy would most likely hang out with and marry someday, Sam also knew. And she put out for everybody; he knew that, too. Still, she would land one of those bozos and go through life thinking she was better than everybody else, when in reality she was worse than a prostitute. Sex was nothing but a game for her, but none of the so-called elite would call her what she was. No, instead they'd make up lies about anyone who didn't give a damn about them, namely, anyone like Gloria Wilson. The more he thought about it, the angrier he got, then the faster he drove, and the more he thought.

In light of these things, Sam couldn't understand how someone so naturally sweet as Shannon could have something nasty happen to her. Why wasn't it the nasty ones who got treated like that? Sometimes he wondered how Kathy or Shannon could be Judy's sister. They were nothing like her, and that's the only reason they got to hang around with Holly. Sam didn't want Judy hanging around his kid sister, that was for damn sure.

As pretty as Holly was, he knew those guys, the ones that talked about Gloria like a dog, would do the same thing to her if she didn't put out for them when she got to high school. As pretty as she was, they'd be on her like dogs in heat. He slapped the steering wheel at the thought of it.

"Hey, man," Hank Hall said from the backseat. "We're all pretty upset about your sister's friend. She was a sweet kid. Tearing up the roads, getting busted, none of that is going to bring her back." Hank put his hand on Sam's shoulder.

Sam was glad George and Hank chose to hang out with him. He didn't know what he would have done, many times, if not for their stable influence. Sam turned his head slightly and smiled at Hank, slowing the '55 Chev at the same time. He had to keep his thinking straight.

"Hey guys, why don't we make it over to the fairgrounds. Seems like most everybody is there regardless of what happened last night. We might as well join 'em, see if we can find out anything new?"

The car full of boys all agreed and Sam pulled it out onto Highway 61 heading south. He traveled at the posted speed limits once they reached Rutledge.

Smiley didn't say much more during the ride to the carnival. The kid being killed didn't interest him much anymore. So what, he thought, I didn't know her. But he liked the idea of riding all the rides at the carnival. That would be a gas. But that murder business? Folks were talking way too much about that already. He was sick of the subject. Still, he could understand his friends talking about it. Nobody they knew had ever died, let alone been murdered.

Murder was freaky. Maybe he could do something about it, maybe help solve it. He liked that idea! He'd be a hero for sure! Maybe everybody would quit picking on him cause of his size, then. He salivated at the possibilities for rewards both tangible and otherwise. He considered the suspects. "I heard old Hansen's got a couple guys as suspects he thinks might a done it. Don't know if he's picked them up yet or not," he offered.

"Yea, those carnies, or something, a couple of guys trying to talk to the girls on the Fourth. I was there when my kid sister and her friend told them about them. Maybe it was carnies." A germ of an idea blossomed in Sam's mind.

"Carnies! That's it!" Henry exclaimed. "They're strangers. Don't give a damn about anybody they run across, specially little kids. Maybe one of them did it!"

"What if it's somebody from town?" Sam considered out-loud what Mrs. Conway had said. He also spoke so softly, the others weren't sure they'd heard him right.

"Nah! Man, nobody in town's gonna' hurt a kid! I can't believe that." Dennis, who was in the front seat next to Sam heard him plainly. He was adamant. He brushed aside Sam's idea that it might be someone they knew. That just wasn't possible.

Sam was almost convinced by Dennis' certainty that he almost forgot what Mrs. Conway had said about reasoning intuitions away. He grabbed a beer from the brown paper bag that lay on the floorboards under the radio in the front seat. Nah, it can't be anybody we know, he thought as he pulled the tab and took a long draw off an ice-cold brew, could it?

Smiley sat between George and Hank, both large for their age, in the backseat, and felt like a dwarf. Yeah, he thought, it would be great if I could solve this.

Sam slowed down even further as they approached Rutledge's Main Street. He didn't want to get stopped by any cops; he wanted to get to the carnival. He, too, entertained a fantasy about catching whoever it was that hurt Shannon. If some son-of-a-bitching carnie hurt her, he wanted his chance at the bastard. He heard the description Renee and Holly had given the cops. He'd look for them at the carnival. Dennis' idea that it couldn't be someone they knew just might be right, he thought as he drove through town.

He cruised slowly down Main Street proper, hoping to see what, he didn't know. He felt something though, as he drove past the grocery store, and wondered if the old lady was there. What would she think about the carnie idea?

As they slowly passed the store, Sam could feel something funny, now, something dark, hanging in the air like fetid storm clouds waiting to bring forth torrents of rain, hail and wind, to destroy everything in their path.

No wonder his old man picked this place to move to. It's as evil as he is; he must feel right at home, Sam thought angrily.

While they drove past the grocery store, Mrs. Conway stood in the doorway smiling at the sight of Sam and his friends.

As she did, Sam "knew" there was a counter-force working against the evil, a counter force that was even stronger and ready to fight the evil, all from glimpsing Mrs. Conway in the doorway.

"Man, there's that crazy old woman," Henry said from the window seat across from Sam. Everyone turned to look at her in the doorway except Sam, who kept his eyes on the road. "My old man says she thinks she can hear from God . . . you believe that?" Henry was both astonished and bewildered. How could a woman think she could hear from God, and an old one at that! She must be nuts, he figured.

"Hey, she's all right," Dennis said. "She's always been pretty good to me. I like her."

Sam smiled at that. He was glad to hear it. He still couldn't muster the courage it took to tell his friends that she'd been good to him, too, though.

As they drove past her, Mrs. Conway sighed. She knew where they were headed, what they were looking for. She shook her head in pity at Sam, who, she knew, wasn't brave enough yet to stand against his friends. He would come around though. Sometimes courage had to be developed. She liked the way Dennis was coming along, and although he did not have Sam's potential, he had potential of his own, admirable potential at that. She sighed again as she turned and went back inside her humble grocery store.

Sometimes she wished she didn't have so much potential herself. It was often more of a burden than she cared to bear, but what was she to do? God dealt her a hand. She'd have to play it out. She certainly wasn't going to curse the gifts He'd given her. Still, sometimes, it was a burden. And though she knew the boys were headed to the fairgrounds looking for trouble, she also knew they wouldn't find any. Hansen had already gone by heading in the other direction with two men, whom she assumed were suspects, in the back seat of his cruiser. They weren't the ones though. They didn't do anything. The real culprit was right here in town. Who was it though? That, she still couldn't see. He had to be powerful if she couldn't see him.

After the boys drove by, Mrs. Conway decided to lock up the store for the day. Townsfolk were used to her closing at odd hours. Most didn't come in there for groceries. They bought from her simply out of sympathy. She didn't care. The grocery store was just a way to stay in touch with her neighbors. When people get old, nobody much wants to visit them. As long as the store stayed open, she'd always have some visitors. Wasn't that what life was about, visiting with folks, doing things for your neighbors, friends, family? She thought so.

She locked the front door, turned over her open sign to the back, which said closed, and slowly made her way to the darkened corridor leading to her back door. She stopped short as she reached the screen door leading out onto the back porch. As she touched the door's handle, a bright, blinding light flashed through her mind, illuminating an older male standing over a little girl. But the vision was too foggy; she couldn't make out his features, but she got a general idea of his size.

As quickly as the light flashed inside her head revealing one picture, it burst again revealing another. The same male figure stood over a young girl's bed. He got onto the bed with the child climbing up and mounting her. Mrs. Conway knew what was happening and was powerless to stop it. It made her sick. She still couldn't make out the man's features, tell who either figure was, but she got a strong impression it was father and daughter. She also got the impression it was happening right there in Rutledge.

She shook her head in disgust at both visions and said, "Lord, why do I have to witness such trash? Now I've got to wonder who this little girl is. I've got no way of helping her, and what about little Shannon? Jeez! If I have to see this, let me help!"

When she came out of her revere, she found herself still standing in the back hallway. She rubbed her eyes as if to clear the vision from inside her head, and looked out into the bright afternoon sun that shone in through the screen door. She could see Sugarplum grazing quietly in the field.

It sure was quiet—still like—a bit too quiet. She couldn't hear the birds, or insects, or people. The air was heavy, muggy, sweltering. Tornado, she thought as she slowly made her way to the back landing walking off it onto the lawn and looking up at the sky.

Storm's coming, she almost said out loud when Joseph Wilson's name popped into her head. "Oh my God," she said no longer worried about anyone seeing her talking to herself.

Chapter Fourteen

When Sam and his friends arrived at the fairgrounds, Henry insisted he did not want his cloth car seats smelling of horse manure, so they had to hunt for a parking space that was out of sight of most fairgoers. Sam didn't want to be seen, anyway. He didn't want Henry's folks to find them either for fear they would make Henry take the car home. They found a place behind the midway far enough away from the front gates, so that no one going in would be able to distinguish the car too easily, and upwind of the animal barns so Henry was happy. No smells drifted to them except those of cotton candy, popcorn, and a myriad of perfumes tinged with the smell of human sweat. They could hear the sounds of happy screams as those riding the rides reveled in the excitement. The din stirred up the boys' desire to get inside and enjoy the rides themselves.

All six walked from the car shoulder to shoulder making their way through the throngs of people as they headed through the gates. Most veered off into the midway while others headed to the animal barns, or 4-H buildings, to view exhibits on display by craftspeople, such as quilts, many types of art-work, metal work, wood work and sewing.

The midway was where Sam thought he'd find who he was looking for. Slick dicks, he called them. Hustlers who thought they were somebody. Hustlers who thought they were dealing with a bunch of small town hicks. It was always that way. How many times did these bad boys need to get their asses kicked by locals before they understood that they couldn't just waltz into town and harm those living there? Sam wondered.

Carnies always picked on girls, too, some of which deserved to be picked on, like the local girls who thought they were hot stuff, the ones that knew more than anybody else, who thought they could handle any man who crossed their path; with small town boys, maybe, but with carnies? Not likely, carnies knew more about scamming small town girls, than small town girls could possibly fathom. The small town girls were way too naive.

If a carnie did cross the girl's path, more often than not that small town girl was left with a present to remember him by, a gift that took nine months to arrive, and she'd be lucky if she never saw that carnie again, so would the kid, or so Sam thought.

As the boys walked determinedly down the midway, adult fairgoers gave them a wide birth. They looked tough dressed in the garb of rebels. Even their faces marked them as trouble as their countenances were etched in angry marble, each young man thinking about how he wanted to get his hands on the freaks that had killed Shannon.

All except Smiley. As the smallest of the group the other boys flanked him square in the middle. George and Hank, sixteen years old, and already six feet tall, acted as guards to the group flanking the others at the outer edges. The two young farm boys were intimidating in stature belying the fact that inside they were like two friendly pups, eager to play. Their faces, marked by acne scars and reddened by the sun, along with their well-developed bodies, gave them an ominous demeanor, something they were aware of and cultivated. They used it to keep others at arms' length. Both had been hurt deeply by comments made about the fact they were farmers, about their parent's being farmers, to let many get too close to them.

Sam was aware of all that as they walked through the midway. It didn't hurt that they all looked as tough as they did. Nope, didn't hurt a thing, he thought. It was Sam, however, who led the group with Dennis as his second in command, flanking Smiley and Henry, who took center stage, (Henry, who had been a friend of Smiley's since grade school, always stuck close by him). They didn't have to pretend to be hardened by life, they were, and it showed in their eyes. They weren't as big as Hank or George, but they were much more menacing to passersby. And though sometimes he and Dennis didn't get along, Sam had nothing but respect for Dennis who took care of his mother and siblings while his father drank himself to death. Dennis had earned Sam's respect.

As the group approached the Tilt-A-Whirl, they could see that the ride generated a big crowd. Sam stopped and looked around taking in their surroundings then walked over to the fun house, directly across from the ride to the south, where he pulled out a Camel cigarette from his T-shirt sleeve, lit it, and leaned against the fun house wall. He offered the pack to his friends who followed his lead.

Sam hadn't openly said he would be looking for anyone at the fairgrounds, but the others could see that's what he was doing. They looked, too, although they didn't know for whom. None of them knew that the two men Holly and Renee had described to the police worked at the Tilt-A-Whirl. By coincidence, it sat right in the middle of the mid-way where the boys could see everyone coming and going.

Smiley had an idea who they were looking for. He had heard that the girls described a couple of guys in town yesterday who had been bothering them. He knew the description they gave the cops, too, suspected the men were carnies. Since he was the smallest of the six, Smiley slipped in front of the others, still smoking his cigarette. He wanted to be the lookout spotting the culprits first. It might even make him a big man with the guys, and everybody in town, for that matter.

"Who we looking for, Sam," Hank asked?

Sam looked at him not a little surprised.

"Hey, I wasn't born yesterday. Doesn't take much to figure out why you wanted to come here. We're right behind you, man." George stood beside Hank nodding his head in affirmation. None of the boys liked the fact that little Shannon Thompson had been murdered. They all knew who she was because she was always tagging after Judy, and everyone knew Judy. She couldn't be missed. Hell, most of the boys in Willow River and Rutledge had a thing for Judy so they were always good to her little sisters.

Sam described the men the girls had talked about at the restaurant, and the group kept an eye out for the two looking in every direction scanning the crowd. There were so many people, though.

Sam was amazed. How could so many adults bring their kids out to a carnival after what had happened? He couldn't fathom it. He swore he'd never be like one of them when he grew up. The group watched as the minions strolled through the dust-laden midway, some arm in arm, a lot of them with little kids holding cotton candy, making messes of themselves and the clothes they wore.

Teenagers, mostly, were hanging out around the rides, and some played games. Many couples went into the Fun House. The boys figured the guys were going to try to cop a feel off their lady partners once inside. Some guys walked out red-faced, which caused no end of delight for Henry and Dennis in particular, Dennis remembering his recent adventure with Renee.

They watched as young girls strolled by wearing tons of make-up to look older. They didn't fool the six who stood and watched them pass by, though. Sam shook his head at the sight, knowing that the teeny boppers were setting themselves up for all the predators circulating the fairgrounds. He watched those running the myriad of rides, and saw how the little made-up girls got free rides from the carnies. He could tell because those running the ride never took ticket stubs from them.

Standing there scrutinizing their surroundings, the boys were also being scrutinized. Adults showed a mix of reactions to them. Women often smiled at them in a way they all knew to be seductive. He wouldn't admit it to the others, but Sam thought it amazing that a grown woman would look at him like that. They reminded him of the way Judy looked at him when she wanted sex.

The men walking with these same women could see what the women were up to, too. Those men would challenge the boys, and then thought better of it when they took a good look at Hank and George, then at Sam and Dennis who were the most menacing. They looked at Smiley, too, could tell he was not too bright, and at Henry who seemed to just be there. The men often tried to entice Smiley away from the others hoping to get him alone so they could take their anger out on him. But Smiley was not stupid, contrary to popular belief, just a little slow, and he was well aware of the men's intentions. He wouldn't budge from beside his friends knowing if he did those bozos would work him over, but good.

As the group continued to lean on the Fun House wall in spite of the hawker yelling at them to get away from it, they saw some of Willow River and Rutledge's elite pass by on the midway arm-in-arm with their families. Sam found them intriguing. From the looks on their faces, he could see some were happy to be there, but most looked distracted, as if they couldn't understand what so many people found interesting in such a low life amusement.

But what Sam was really looking for, he couldn't find. The boys gave up after awhile, and having no money themselves, decided they'd be better off hitting the road in Henry's car, maybe having a few beers at the lake.

Chapter Fifteen

Renee didn't like his smell. It wasn't rank on the surface—he actually smelled good. But there was something underneath, something extremely unpleasant about Pastor Joseph Wilson's scent. She looked over at Holly sitting next to him, took her hand and squeezed.

They weren't long into the drive to the fairgrounds when, as Old Man Spur talked to the pastor, Renee first felt something along the inside of her legs, at first so gentle she wasn't sure something was actually there, then digging, hurting, probing her legs apart.

What the heck is that! She thought, quietly trying to wiggle around in an effort to get away from what she guessed had to be Wilson's fingers. Holly sat forward in the seat with her head propped up against the back of the front seat between her parents.

Renee was terrified; the probing got worse, hurtful. Stop it! She thought throwing a glance at her legs to see his fingers when she felt them force her legs open. She sat there, mute, stunned, too frightened and horrified to open her mouth. What is he doing! She screamed inside herself.

His fingers probed more intimately. She dug her fingernails into his skin as she tried to force him away from her by hurting him. She stole a glance at him to see him smirking at her.

Holly never sat back in the seat. Renee was left to suffer the molestation unabated until Old Man Spur turned the big Cadillac into the fairgrounds parking lot. It was with great relief that the twelve-year old felt the unwanted hand leave from between her legs. All during the molestation, Pastor Joseph Wilson kept up a pleasant conversation with Mr. and Mrs. Spur.

Renee just wanted to escape the confines of the filthy car. When the car pulled to a stop, she shakily reached for the doorknob, opened it, and tried to get out, but her legs wobbled so that Holly had to grab her and hold her up. "Hey! What's wrong, Renee! Jeez, you look awful."

Holly's comments only incurred the interest of the adults, something Renee did not want. "Renee, are you okay?" Mrs. Spur asked when she noticed how pale Renee was.

The child was just fine when we left the apartment, Mrs. Spur thought, as she cast a discreet look at the pastor who was feigning concern for Renee as well. He was so concerned, he wanted to make sure she could get on each ride safely. He suggested to the Spurs that he ride the rides with the girls, to keep them safe, he told them.

Old Man Spur bought every thing the pastor said. Mrs. Spur protested, which garnered her nothing but a dirty look from her husband who grasped her arm so tightly it hurt. Her instincts screamed at her that whatever was ailing Renee, the pastor had something to do with it. Still, she couldn't be sure.

When Pastor Joseph Wilson got on the Ferris wheel with the girls, he seated himself in the middle. Renee was petrified. Not only did she have a fear of heights and the Ferris wheel, she was terrified he would place his fingers inside her again. She was in shock. Midway through the ride as tumultuous thoughts raced through her mind, and her terror of heights yanked at her insides, the combination wreaked a benefit she could not have anticipated if she tried. She fought off the sickness. But as she became more terrified of his hands trying to probe her, and her fear of heights grew with each flight the ride took into the sky, her stomach reeled in rebellion. She tried not to vomit, fought it every step of the way, but vomit she did. She had enough presence of mind, however, to lean over the pastor instead of the railing, which she was terrified of falling through, with the majority of her half digested dinner spewing into the pastor's lap.

When she finished, she was both embarrassed and delighted. She couldn't have gotten a better revenge if she had planned it, and though she had not felt his hands on her during this ride, Renee sensed that he had still been up to something. As the ride finally ended, and she stumbled off it weakly getting no help from the pastor, she looked over at her friend, Holly.

This time it was Holly who looked pale and in shock. Since Renee had been sick on the ride, other adults didn't pay too much attention to Holly's pale skin. She was probably suffering the same fear her friend had suffered. Both girls were weak in the legs and wanted desperately to get away from the pastor, and as they looked around, they could see that the Spurs were nowhere in sight.

But the pastor certainly was. He scowled at Renee as he yelled, "You little idiot, look what you've done! You've soiled my good suit!" He wasn't too concerned with the fact that she had been sick enough to vomit on the ride, although the carnies were. They didn't like to clean up messes like that, but it happened all the time. They brought the girls to a nearby concession stand where the people running it cleaned Renee up, and made both Renee and Holly sit for awhile giving them some 7-Up to settle their stomachs.

The pastor walked off, and left them alone where many waiting to board the ride noticed his behavior, hearing how he had talked to Renee when the trio got off the Ferris wheel. He never bothered to tell the girls where he was going or where to meet up with the adults.

The adults milling about the ride were shocked by his behavior, but the girls were joyous. Since the pastor always dressed like a pastor, everyone knew what he did for a living, deciding his behavior toward the children was anything but Christian. Though the girls were elated he was gone, neither knew what to make of what had happened to them. Both were so ignorant in matters sexual, they couldn't broach the subject with each other because of their fears.

Each thought they would be suffering horrific repercussions after what had happened to them. Immediately, both were seized by feelings of guilt and shame, as if somehow his molestation of them was their fault. Were they to blame? Each asked themselves that question never voicing it for fear that someone might tell them they were.

The pastor had treated them like dirt.

Renee felt like dirt. Suddenly she felt as if his filth had crawled under her skin and she'd never be able to wash it away. She longed to go back to Holly's apartment and get under the hot water, to let the soap soak into her pores until her skin shriveled up like a prune. She wanted to take a scrub brush to it. Still in shock, their faces pale, many of the adults eating hot dogs and French fries next to them looked curiously at the girls.

"Are you okay?" One old lady asked. The girls nodded their heads to say they were, but the woman didn't believe them.

"Where are your folks, dear?" She asked hoping to get the youngsters to open up.

"We don't know," the girls said in unison.

The old woman didn't like that answer. She marched off and both Holly and Renee were glad she was gone. They didn't want to talk to anyone. Slowly they started coming back to themselves, although neither girl mentioned what the pastor had done to the other. The woman behind the counter at the concession stand surprised them with hot dogs on the house and they ate greedily, especially Renee whose stomach had been emptied atop the Ferris wheel.

"I loved the way you barfed! It couldn't have happened to a nicer guy," Holly smiled through a ketchup-stained mouth.

"Oh! Please, not while I'm eating," and Renee laughed too. Now that she thought about it, it was perfect. In one swoop she managed to rid them of the pastor for good, they hoped.

"I don't think he'll be bothering us anymore tonight, do you?" Holly seemed to read Renee's mind.

They ate and watched, trying to see if their new enemy was approaching them from any corner. They didn't see him, but they did see the old lady coming back, and she wasn't alone. With her was the same cop they had talked to the day before at the restaurant, the one who told them about Shannon.

Sheriff Hansen, after delivering his prisoners to the jail and interrogating them, left again after putting Freboni in charge of the interrogation. He couldn't seem to sit still. Hansen knew the two twits he'd arrested weren't the ones who killed Shannon Thompson. He could smell it, but he had enough other stuff on them to hold them for quite awhile. If the only good he could garner from arresting those two was so that Freboni got to practice his interrogation techniques, so be it, he thought as he approached the girls.

Hansen had gone back to the fairgrounds sensing something wasn't right there. Something was going on. He didn't want to be bothered by the old woman when she had accosted him on the midway telling him two little kids looked funny, but what the hell was he to do? He followed her in spite of his reluctance, and as they approached the concession stand, and he saw which two kids the old woman was referring to, he was so delighted with the old woman he felt like kissing her. He silently thanked her and knew that this was a chance to get a real break in the Shannon Thompson murder case. He could tell as he approached them, that the girls didn't look right. What the hell had happened to them? He wondered. He could also see that the girls were getting ready to ditch him by scampering into the crowd. Something was wrong here, every instinct inside him screamed.

He darted away from the old woman so quickly, when she turned to see what had flashed past her peripheral vision she saw nothing but color dart past the backside of the concession stand. The sheriff was nowhere to be seen. As he surprised the old woman, so were Renee and Holly surprised when he stepped out in front of them as they tried to dart off into the crowd.

"Your friend over there tells me you two are in trouble," he said to them in his sternest, most authoritative voice. He wanted them to understand that he was in charge.

"No sir," Holly piped up. "We aren't in any trouble. Just got a little sick on that ride, didn't we Renee?" Holly turned to Renee to get back up to her comments.

"Yeah, that's right officer. We're okay."

Hansen wasn't buying it. "Come on back here and sit down; the three of us are going to have a little chat."

As they moved back over to the concession stand, Hansen beckoned the old woman over and had her sit with the girls. "This here lady tells me there was a man with you on the rides. Said he looked like he was a pastor or something, and that neither one of you looked too good when you got off the ride. She said that man was yelling at you. Is that right?"

"Yes," Renee said wondering just how much to tell this big policeman. Would he arrest her for being dirty? She thought he probably would if he knew just how dirty.

"Who was with you," Hansen asked. Something tickled his flesh. He knew he was on to something.

"Pastor Joseph Wilson, Sheriff," Holly said and started to sob. First, her father for the very first time in her life had yelled at her, a man supposedly of God had molested her, and a cop was going to find out and tell everyone, and one of her best friends had been killed not twenty-four hours ago. Jeez!

Renee started crying too. This was too much. Were there no adults they could trust?

Hansen, knowing that this was way too an emotional outburst for what he had been asking, sensed that other things had happened to the pair between the time he had talked to them the day before and now.

"Where has this pastor gone to?" He asked the still crying girls.

Both shrugged their shoulders. They didn't know where he was.

The old lady moved between the two and put an arm around their shoulders. Hansen gave her his card. "If these two tell you anything more tonight, call me. I'm going to see if I can find their parents. I know who they are and can spot them in the crowd."

The old lady nodded as Hansen strolled away. Shortly thereafter the girls gave the old woman the slip and darted off into the crowd as well. The little old lady remained seated on the bench where they had all been sitting, knowing in her heart what had happened to the two girls. It had happened to her once, too, a long, long time ago. She had never been able to tell anyone, either.

What the girls didn't know was that while Renee was throwing up on the pastor, Sam and his friends were leaving the fairgrounds. Both the girls searched the thongs of faces in the crowd hoping to see him, and that he had changed his mind about coming, but it didn't look like he had. They became discouraged.

"Why don't we get out of here," Renee said just loud enough for Holly to hear. "I don't like it here. We could walk home."

"You know, that's the best idea I've heard all day. Dear Old Dad can hang out with the pastor all he wants, but I'm not riding in that car again with him, ever!"

The way Holly said it caused Renee to glance sideways at her and wonder if something had happened to her, too, yet she didn't ask. They made their way through the crowds never seeing again Holly's parents or the pastor, although they passed the Cadillac as they walked out the fairgrounds and onto Highway 61 to walk the mile home. It was a nice night for walking. The moon shined brightly, stars too, and the air was just warm enough with a gentle breeze that tossed their hair behind them as they moved quietly down the road.

Neither girl had given any thought to Shannon when they decided to leave the fairgrounds on their own. Had they, they might have been scared into staying where they were among throngs of people. About half way home, when they walked alone down the deserted highway not sprinkled with overhead lights, and the dark seemed to settle around them like a shroud, Renee said, "Jeez, it's spooky out here. Maybe we should go back."

"Yeah, it is," Holly agreed, but the idea of going back to where her folks and the pastor were, spooked her even more, "Nah, let's just keep going. We're almost to Rutledge, anyway. We'll just stay together and run into the ditch every time a car comes by. We should be okay." Holly's voice wasn't full of the confidence she hoped to convey with her idea, but she dearly wanted to get home where it had always been safe before. "I don't want to be around my folks and their new friend—do you?"

"No, I do not! No offence, Holly, but their friend is a creep!"

"Big time creep, if you ask me. I kind of hope Mrs. Conway is up. It's not that late. She's pretty nice. I wouldn't mind spending some time with her, would you? Maybe we could sit outside by the paddock together."

"That sounds nice. Hey! Here comes a car. Come on!" Renee whispered vehemently as her heart leapt into her chest at the sight of two headlights coming at them from the north. They ran down the embankment into the deeply trenched ditch and flattened themselves against it until the car lights passed. Renee was sweating when they climbed back up onto the highway.

"I've never been so scared in all my life! What were we thinking? Shannon was just murdered by somebody and we're out here walking by ourselves in the dark?" Renee was trembling.

"We have to quit thinking about that and get to town. Come on!" Holly started trotting down the middle of the road where they could make out the white lines that separated the two lanes. Again, car lights came into view this time traveling from the south, and the two slid down the embankment into the ditch to hide until the lights were out of sight.

This time as the car passed on the road overhead the girls could hear voices coming from it, teenage boys, one of which Holly recognized as Sam. The convertible top was down so the boy's conversation carried on the wind. The girls realized this too late. Had they been on the road when Sam drove by he would have given them a ride home, and they would have felt safe with him in the car. They scurried up the embankment as fast as they could and onto the road, but the car was speeding towards town, and it didn't look like anyone in it had seen them.

When Sam first cruised unknowingly past the girls as they hid in the ditch, he reached the fairground limits, and pulled to the side of the road only long enough to look in his rear view mirrors. Something was bugging him tonight. He made a U-turn in the middle of the highway and screeched the tires burning rubber as he reversed directions and headed back toward town. As he stepped on the gas pedal, he thought he saw something in the middle of the road, but then it disappeared out of sight. The car was going too fast for him to tell, but he thought he saw two girls walking down the middle of the road. No, that couldn't be, he thought, not tonight! But as he reached the town limits, he hit the brakes again, and the car worked to come to a halt leaving rubber all over the freshly tarred roadway. The Chevy rocked and shook as it dropped from 70 mph to zero in a matter of seconds while the passengers braced themselves against the dash in the front and the front seat in the back. George and Hank in the back seat had to hold Smiley down so he wouldn't be hurled into the front.

"Hey Man! What the hell are you trying to do? Kill us!" Dennis was shook up by the sudden stop. He hadn't had time to see why Sam stopped.

"Is that the girls back there?" Sam asked ignoring his friend's complaints and turning around in the seat. They all turned then to see two small figures running toward the car and waving their arms. When the girls reached the driver's side door, they were out of breath. Sam said, "What the hell do you two think you're doing? Get in the car." He didn't wait for them to answer any questions.

Dennis hopped in the back with George, Hank and Smiley and the girls jumped in the front seat between Sam and Henry. "Jesus Christ! Shannon was murdered you know, and you two are out here walking by yourselves! What's wrong with you?" Sam was so angry Holly was stunned into silence, so was Renee.

"I thought you two were supposed to be at the carnival with the folks? Where are they?"

Holly started to cry before any words could come out her mouth. So did Renee. Sam looked at them in shock and thought, if any son of a bitch did anything to either one of them, I'll kill 'em.

They didn't stop crying once Sam pulled up outside the apartment building, either. The other boys sensing something bad had happened to the girls jumped out of the car and walked down to the Willow River Bridge without Sam saying anything to him. He remained seated in the front seat of the car with the girls. Sam found some tissue in the glove compartment and gave it to them.

"I want to know what happened," he said quietly. But the girls couldn't open their mouths to say anything. After waiting ten minutes, Sam said, "Okay, I'm going to take you upstairs. I think you need to go to bed, sleep it off. When you're ready to talk, tell me. I'll take care of it for you."

"No! We don't want to be alone," Holly managed to choke out through her sobs. "Take us to Mrs. Conway's, please!" She pleaded. She didn't want to be home when her parents got there. She didn't want to see them. When push came to shove, her father had treated her as badly as he had treated Sam, although she doubted he would have forced them to ride with the pastor if he knew what the man was really like.

"All right, I'll go see if she's up. Don't get out of the car until I come back." Sam got out, and shut the door quietly knowing that Henry was just up the road keeping an eagle eye on it. Sam knew the guys wouldn't come back until the girls were out of the car. He signaled them. They would keep an eye on both girls until he got back, too.

Sam quietly crossed over the old lady's wooden porch and knocked softly on Mrs. Conway's door. It was eleven p.m. She's old. She might be in bed already, he reasoned. Sam was surprised when she answered the door almost before his knuckles could rap lightly on its doorjamb a second time.

Before he could say a word, she said, "You go and get your sister, boy, her and her friend, and you bring them in here to me. They'll sleep over at old Estelle's house tonight. It'll be fun. Now, shut your mouth before it gets filled with mosquitoes and go get the girls, boy."

Sam shook his head as he walked back to the car to tell Holly and Renee they could spend the night at Mrs. Conway's. The girls looked so relieved Sam had to wonder what had happened that would frighten them away from their own house. He could see they were scared, more scared than they had been over Shannon's murder, although that had to play a part in this somehow. Something was wrong, big time. When they were ready to talk, he'd be there but he wished that time were now.

He brought the girls to the downstairs apartment. "Now, son, you run upstairs and get these children some fresh clothes, pajamas, clothes for tomorrow. And don't go forgetting underwears, you know, bras and panties?"

They all looked at Sam's face and saw the blush climbing his neck. Renee was horrified at the thought of Sam going through her underwear.

It was then that Sam noticed the strange smell coming from Renee and the odd stain on her shirt. Mrs. Conway had smelled it no sooner than she walked through the door. She didn't know what happened yet, but suspected by the time the night was over she would.

Sam did as he was told and by the time he came back downstairs, Renee was in the bathtub and Holly was sipping a soda at the kitchen table holding a wet washcloth to her forehead. "You go on with your friends, now, son. These girls will be okay. So will you, but, if I were you, I wouldn't make a point of telling your folks where they are for the night. They'll sleep safely here, and that's best for now."

"I'll see you in the morning." Sam said to Holly as he slipped out the screen door. He wasn't crazy about not telling his folks where they were, but, he reasoned as he walked back to the car, the folks would probably be partying tonight anyway and wouldn't come home themselves. He hoped that would be the case. He walked to the bridge where his friends were still throwing stones into the river. He didn't say anything to them. He started tossing stones, too.

Chapter Sixteen

It was humiliating. Sam saw her underwear; not only that, she rode in the car next to him smelling of vomit and hadn't even realized it! What must he think? The hot water soaked into her skin, relaxing her and the lilac flower bath salts filled the bathroom with their perfume. Renee daydreamed of Sam, glad he could take her mind off the bad things that had happened. Otherwise, she would be dwelling on them instead of something good, him.

What had happened to her in the car? It was wrong, she knew that, but just what was it, and was it her fault? How could a grown-up put his hands between her legs? Was it because he was a grown-up—or because he was a pastor? Was he allowed to do that kind of stuff? She doubted it, had not liked it, and felt dirty. She took the bath brush and scrubbed at her skin hard trying to rid her memory of him. It didn't work. She doubted he had the right to touch her; her body was hers, not his. Greatly relieved that Mrs. Spur had told her about the facts of life, she knew this time she wasn't pregnant, but what was it he did to her—was it sex? Who could she ask? Did Holly know anymore than she did? Maybe Judy, she thought hopefully, if she knows as much as Holly says she does.

Something else troubled Renee as she scrubbed her skin raw in the bathtub. What would others think of her if they knew? Would they think she was dirty, too, that it was her fault? Did she lead the pastor on in some way? How could that be—she didn't even know what that meant? How could she have led him on? Was she now one of those loose girls she heard the boys talk about, the ones they said were easy? How could that be if she wasn't even sure what being easy meant? And worst of all, why hadn't she tried to stop him? Why hadn't she sensed he was up to no good? She had always sensed danger in the past. Of course, she had sensed danger before she got into the car, so had Holly. How could either of them have avoided it? How could she have avoided the adults? How could she defy them? Why had Holly's parents made them go? Couldn't they sense the danger? It seemed as if Holly's father would do anything that slimy old pastor asked him to. Was he blind to the old buzzard?

Renee knew the answer to that question as soon as she thought it. Old Man Spur was always trying to move up in the world, scheming to better his circumstances. He had lost a lot of money over the years trying to get rich quick. She guessed that was why he insisted on moving to Rutledge when the chance to buy the restaurant came up. He could be a big fish in a little pond, finally get some recognition he thought was long overdue, maybe some respect, too.

Renee had spent enough time at the Spur's to know Holly's mother put up with a lot from her husband. She didn't understand that, either. It seemed like the exact opposite at her house. Her dad put up with a lot from her mother, but neither of her parents used violence against one-another or the kids, like she had seen Old Man Spur do in his home, and tonight, for the first time, how he had yelled at Holly. That had never happened before.

Soaking and scrubbing there in the tub, Renee couldn't see how violence solved much of anything. It might feel good, she thought realizing that bopping Old Man Wilson over the head with a cast iron skillet was something she might enjoy.

She considered talking to her mother about what happened, but dismissed that idea. All her mother ever counseled her to do was to shut up and not mention anything in fear that the neighbors would think badly of the family. How could she ever help with this?

Renee considered talking to Mrs. Conway and liked that idea, but would she know what Renee was talking about? Did she know what sex was? Renee wondered.

Was what Wilson had done to her what having sex meant? If it was, she didn't want anything more to do with it. She didn't like it.

She tried to change the thoughts raging through her head by concentrating on Sam when it came to her that Sam might someday want to do the same thing to her. That thought brought fresh grief to her spirit.

For the first time in her young life, despair crept into her mind. She sunk deeper into the claw-footed bathtub using her toes to turn the hot water spigot on re-heating the cooling bath water. It felt good to let the hot water soak into her skin, but she couldn't seem to feel clean.

Her mind wandered to Holly, thinking that maybe she, too, needed to bathe. She hurried out of the tub. As she toweled herself dry, she noticed her skin looked like prunes, all shriveled up from being in the water so long.

While Renee bathed, Holly had busied herself helping Mrs. Conway make up the spare room for her and Renee. Mrs. Conway was so old, Holly worried that she would die at any moment, especially when she tried to move the bed away from the wall to tuck in the sheets.

Holly leapt over the mattress, squeezing between the bed and wall using her thighs to push the bed out away from the wall, so they could make it together. It worked. She took the sheet from Mrs. Conway and tucked it in. Before Mrs. Conway could start on the other side, Holly leapt back over the bed and repeated the procedure.

"You sure do move quick, girl. I thank you for all your help."

"We thank you, Mrs. Conway. We wanted to stay with you tonight. But it might get you in trouble with my dad."

"Don't you worry none about me getting in trouble. I can handle that cantankerous old goat. You just tell me what's got the two of you so worried. Child, I ain't never seen you look so serious."

Holly mumbled something about Shannon, which Mrs. Conway could see wasn't the whole of whatever it was that was on her mind. The child was smart enough to know that that reason would have assured most adults that it was that that was troubling them. It was enough to trouble anybody, but there was more just the same. Most adults wouldn't have bothered to look any deeper, but she wasn't most adults.

"I been thinking about your friend most of the day, myself," Mrs. Conway said quietly as Holly worked tucking in sheets, then the single light blanket that the old woman proffered for their covers. It was hot out, they wouldn't need that probably, but she thought, perhaps the girls felt a need to be covered.

"Do you understand, Holly, what rape means? Do you understand what happened to Shannon, I mean, other than someone taking the poor girl's life?" She handed Holly a pillowcase then a pillow to cover showing her how to do it by doing it herself, and talking as she worked.

"I think I know what rape means—it's sex, isn't it? I mean someone had sex with her, right—or rather, made her have sex—right?" Holly said while watching what Mrs. Conway was doing so she could imitate it exactly as she did. "What I really don't understand is what sex is. I mean, I know some of it, but I'm just not sure . . ." Holly stopped speaking and shook her head trying to put the things she did not understand into words. She thought she sounded stupid.

She had heard from some of her friends that just kissing was having sex, but what about what happened on the Ferris wheel? Wasn't that sex? She wasn't having it, but he was, wasn't he? Why did she feel dirty? Was she guilty of sin? She felt like it. How could that be, though? Why was she feeling so dirty? She didn't LET him do anything, did she? Could she have stopped him? Didn't her parents know? Were they that stupid, or did they just not care? She didn't really believe that, but she had to wonder.

Her father spoke to her now the same way he did Sam. How could he, out of the blue like that, was it the pastor's influence? If it was, how could he turn on her so fast? Why wasn't her mother saying anything? Why didn't the pastor sit up in the front from the start? Was he planning to touch us then? He didn't touch me, but I felt his hand sliding across the seat. Was he touching Renee like he did me on the Ferris wheel? She didn't know for sure but suspected as much. I should have said something in the car, she thought. Why didn't I open my mouth? All these thoughts raced through her mind at lightening speed as she tried to sort it all out in front of Mrs. Conway, who watched her closely sensing some of what might be going on.

She would not put any words in the child's mouth, however, being very familiar in how to report abuse, she would not jeopardize anything that might unfold.

"Rape is someone forcing themselves on someone else, sexually. Rape happens when one of two parties doesn't consent to sexual relations," Mrs. Conway said quietly, acutely aware of Holly across the bed from her. She searched the child's face for a flicker of understanding. She saw what she suspected she would see.

"So rape is anytime a man touches you that you don't want him to?" Holly stopped playing with the pillowcases and stared at Mrs. Conway.

"Sort of. It means anytime someone else touches your private parts without you telling them they can." Mrs. Conway stared at Holly.

Holly sat down on the bed with the pillow clutched tightly in front of her, as if a shield. She gripped it so tightly her knuckles turned white. She put the pillow to her mouth and began to rock her back toward Mrs. Conway.

Mrs. Conway moved slowly to that side of the bed. Tears rolled down Holly's cheeks as she choked back sobs into the pillow.

Just then, Renee came in dressed in pajamas that covered every part of her body aside from her bare feet, neck and head. The lilac scented bubble bath wafted on the air into the room with Renee, a scent Mrs. Conway loved. She sat on the bed cradling Holly in her arms comforting her, and turned to see Renee in the doorway. Renee stood there with the light from the hall backlighting her and Mrs. Conway could see she was also wearing a bra and panties as well as a T-shirt underneath the thin summer pjs. It didn't take much to figure out why a pretty little girl just on the verge of womanhood would want to hide her budding body underneath layers of clothing on a night where temperatures were already soaring in the upper nineties with humidity to match.

"The bathroom's free now, Holly, if you want to take a bath?" Renee said alarmed at her friend's tears. Had she told Mrs. Conway something?

It surprised Renee when Holly burst from the bed, and ran past her down the hall, and into the bathroom where she slammed the door shut. Renee could hear the lock turn. All she could do was stand there staring at Mrs. Conway. "Is she upset about her folks?" Renee asked cautiously. She didn't know if she wanted Mrs. Conway to know anything, either.

"Her friend, Shannon, mostly. I also explained to her what rape meant."

"You did? Can you tell me?" She asked hesitantly.

Mrs. Conway repeated what she told Holly to Renee. Renee reacted differently although it looked like something registered with her at the explanation. "Did that make Shannon dirty?" She asked in a whisper. "I mean does God think she's dirty?"

"Dirty? My heavens no, girl! It wasn't Shannon's fault! No God I know is ever going to blame something like that on a child, for heaven's sake! No, dear, whoever did that to her, or for that matter, who ever does that to anyone, child or adult, they are to blame not the victim. Where did you ever get an idea like that?"

"The guys. I heard them talking about some girl. They said she wasn't raped like she claimed; they said she asked for it dressing the way she did. She had big boobs, too, they said, so it was her own fault some guy wanted to have sex with her, only that's not the word they used. They used the "F" word. I don't know what girl they were talking about."

"Ain't that just like a man? Starts when they're young, too, now don't it. They do all this dirty business, and try to blame it on the girl cause she's blessed with a good figure. I'm telling you child, that they are wrong, and not just a little wrong, but most guys will say that the girl was asking for it."

"I doubt that too many will say those things about your friend, Shannon, though. She was way too young, too innocent, for any of that beeswax, I can tell you! If that don't beat all! I get so mad every time I hear some man say stuff like that I could spit." Which Mrs. Conway almost did before she remembered that she was in her own house, and wasn't about to make a mess she'd have to clean up. She regained control of herself and looked closely at Renee. Nope, this was no time to be thinking about what made her mad, it was time to see what was happening with these girls.

Her temperamental outburst seemed to sooth Renee, which she thought was odd, and now the girl was staring at her so intently it unnerved her.

"Okay, girl, I see you got something serious on your mind. Are you going to tell me about it or do I have to drag it out of you?" She stood up and put her hands on her hips tapping her toe against the hardwood floor of the old apartment.

Renee was sweating, but from fear, not the heat. Inside, her mind played havoc with her emotions. Should I tell her! What is she going to think of me? Should I? No! I can't! She'll be like the others I thought I could trust. I'll tell her my secret and she'll tell some other adult! They'll say I'm lying because he's the pastor! What do I do?

As these thoughts tormented Renee's mind, Mrs. Conway went far away, like she always did when she had a flash of insight. Oh, she was in the room with Renee all right, her body hadn't gone anywhere, but inside her mind was taking her places. She would start to go dark inside, is how she saw it. She couldn't hear any noises coming in from the outside world, couldn't smell anything, or see anything. All at once, it would be as if her senses had completely left her. She was deaf, dumb and blind. She couldn't speak even if she wanted to. It was like her tongue was glued to the roof of her mouth with epoxy glue. Then she would see the bright, white light, and feel the warmth, hot almost, warming her throughout her body, coming from the inside, not the out. And she'd feel an overwhelming sense of joy and peace, even though not everything she witnessed at these times was pretty. More often than not it was anything but. But now, as she stood there facing Renee Good tapping her foot, and looking to Renee as if she was still waiting for Renee's answer, she saw it.

She was at the carnival with the girls, got in the car with them when they left earlier that evening. She saw and felt it all, and knew just what had happened to both Renee and Holly. Her vision wasn't over with yet, however, because she continued to watch the pastor as he plied Holly's parents with drink, knowing that Mr. Spur had a problem with alcohol. He wanted to see what the old man would do when he got too drunk. He thought about seducing Mrs. Spur, she was lovely, but decided against it. Who wanted a used up, depressed old woman when he could ravish all the young girls he could get his hands on. Indeed. He only wished he could have gone farther with the two the Spurs so generously offered up not three hours earlier. If it hadn't been for that visiting snip, he could have. How dare she foul herself on me? He thought. That made him angry. And their enjoyment of it, oh yes, he wasn't stupid, he knew they relished their actions. Well, he would make them regret that, he decided.

As Mrs. Conway listened to the pastor's thoughts, she was at once torn away, and brought back into her own little bedroom to stand in front of the child that was still trying to decide if she could confide in her. She was glad. She'd seen enough of Pastor Joseph Wilson's filthy mind to last her a lifetime. If only that would be the end of it, but she knew it was jut the beginning, and that she hadn't seen it all, not by a long shot.

"I . . . I . . . I . . . don't know what to say," Renee stuttered and Mrs. Conway heard. The old woman moved over to Renee's side of the bed, where the child sat, took her in her arms and embraced her.

"You know, I've just seen it all. The good Lord gives me visions, you know. The pastor, he molested you and Holly tonight, didn't he?"

"He touched me in my private parts! He's not supposed to do that!" Renee was both relieved that Mrs. Conway knew what happened and angry because it had happened. "How can he do that!" She said through hot tears streaming down her cheeks. "But you know what? I threw up on him on the Ferris wheel. He got real mad about that and I'm glad!"

"You're right, he did get mad about that, real mad. But don't you worry none about him. If I have to keep you here with me for the rest of your visit, I'll do just that. Holly don't have to worry none about him either. But I best have a talk with her folks in the morning."

As they talked Holly came out of the bathroom, dressed much the same as Renee and stood at the threshold of the guest bedroom listening. When she started to cry, Mrs. Conway turned, moved over to her and brought her into the room, hugging both girls as they sobbed over what had happened to them earlier that evening. Mrs. Conway assured them that in God's eyes, they were not dirty, but the pastor certainly was. She didn't tell the girls that if the pastor repented for what he'd done, God would forgive him, too. She didn't have the heart to tell them that. Besides, it made her angry every time she thought of some nasty SOB repenting and God forgiving them. She knew full well, though, why Jonah didn't go to Nineveh like God told him to in the first place. It was because he knew the people there would repent and that God would forgive them. He didn't want them forgiven! Why is your countenance so low, God asked him afterward? Well Mrs. Conway knew why it was so low. God's ways are not our ways and His thoughts are not our thoughts. That's probably a darn good thing, she mused.

The girls fell blissfully asleep, comforted by Mrs. Conway, their hot baths, and the feeling of safety they had inside her house and away from the Spurs.

As they drifted off to sleep, Sam stood down by Willow River hunting flat rocks on the gravel road and skimming them across the still waters when he found them. The others had gone. It was a warm, muggy night, nothing unusual for Minnesota in July. The temperature was in the nineties as was the humidity. Sam didn't mind though. It felt good. He worked up a sweat skimming rocks and trying to take his mind off the evening. He wished he knew what had happened to Holly and Renee. He sensed it was something sinister. At the thought, he unrolled his T-shirt sleeve and pulled out his pack of Camels, lighting one as he sat down on the bank of the river to smoke and think.

It's a damn good thing the night is as pretty as it is, he thought as he wiped his sweaty brow on the bottom of his sweat soaked T-shirt and looked up at the sky and the millions of bright stars shinning down on him. He took in his surroundings, listened as the willow trees alongside the river rustled in the gentle breeze, watched as a few bats flew back and forth across the river. No birds flew at night, other than predators, and these were too small to be one of those, Sam knew, meaning they were bats. Instinctively he brushed his hand through his hair, even though nothing had flown remotely near his head.

He could hear the distant din of people enjoying themselves at the carnival as the sounds drifted on winds down to him. He liked that the noise was muffled; he was alone, but not really. That's what he liked the most. Sometimes he just had to get away from the noises people made, from their nasty behaviors. He'd never understand it, human behavior, as long as he lived, he thought. He shook his head thinking of how in his young life he had been treated by his folks and total strangers. It was hard to keep thinking you were anything worth a lick of beans when those closest to you keep telling you you were nothing but a punk . . . telling you that every chance they got.

He took a long draw on his unfiltered cigarette. It eased his tension some. Something about smoking took the pain away, brought comfort. He had a hard time even admitting he was in pain. He certainly couldn't go tell anyone else about it. A guy couldn't go getting soft or people would take even more advantage of him, that's what the old man kept saying. With a caustic snicker, Sam thought that if the old man said it, it had to be garbage, but he didn't know any other way.

The sound of feet shuffling through the dirt on the road caused Sam to lift his head and look in the direction of the sound. Up on the bridge Dennis Hanson stood quietly. He hadn't noticed Sam. Dennis, too, took up rocks skimming them across the water. Sam watched for a short time then cleared his throat.

Dennis jumped at the sound. "Man, what the hell are you doing sitting down there in the dark? Are you trying to scare me to half to death!"

Sam started laughing; he couldn't help it, "Sorry, man! I just couldn't resist. You know you should be taking in your surroundings a little better! You weren't even looking around!"

"So? Why the hell should I look around! I've been coming to this river since I was a little kid, ya' know!"

"Yeah? Well, how many times, since you was a little kid has another little kid been murdered right here in town?"

Dennis shrugged his shoulders. He hadn't thought of that. "Yeah, but she was a girl! Nobody's bothering boys!"

"You mean that nobody's bothering boys . . . yet! If somebody is freaky enough to hurt a little girl like they did Shannon, then they're freaky enough to do anything, I say."

"Jeez, Man, I never thought of that! Ya' think?"

"Not to change the subject," Dennis continued, "but you know Gloria Wilson, right? The preacher's daughter? Well, you know what a big mouth Francine has, she said Gloria is a tramp cause she won't pay any respect to the pastor. Now I don't take much with what Francine says, but Gloria doesn't pay her father much respect. I've seen that myself. And it seems real odd to me. I mean, he's her old man. The way she acts, you'd think the pastor is as bad as our fathers."

"Maybe he is," Sam said out loud, but more to himself than Dennis realizing Dennis may have hit on something that had always bothered him about Gloria. "She seems kinda' sad to me. Does she to you?"

"Yeah, yeah, she does. She could have any guy she wants, but she don't look at us like that, you know?"

"Yeah, I've noticed. Do you think maybe the preacher has something to do with that?"

"I don't know, but I know Francine swears by him! Goes to every Sunday and Wednesday service and is constantly talking about the man! Jeez, she gets on my last nerve! Pastor this, pastor that, and for god's sake, don't let her come around you after she's had a counseling session with him. She comes in all flushed and happy, doesn't give a damn about what's happening at home, says we're all just a bunch of heathens anyway, and going straight to hell!"

"That seem right to you?" Sam prompted Dennis to tell him more. He felt compelled to look at the pastor through other people's eyes, to try and get a handle on the man. He didn't trust him, and if Francine were his sister, she wouldn't be going to any private counseling sessions with him, that was for damn sure!

In a flash, Sam realized what had been bothering him about the man. He had noticed how the preacher was always looking at the young girls whenever there was some function outside the church. He noticed, too, how many young women, like Francine, were fawning all over the guy; even Mrs. Thompson fawned all over him.

He wondered if Shannon ever had. He doubted it. She was too young to care about that kind of stuff. Women reacted to the preacher in the same manner that they reacted to him, sexual. What was up with that? Was he coming on to them?

Sam considered this and decided that it was time to start going to church. What better place to get a good look at the guy? He thought, smiling at the genius of his new plan.

"Hey, Dennis, guess what we're doing tomorrow?"

"What, Man?"

"We're going to church."

"Oh please, you're not going to start sounding like Francine, are you? Cause I don't need it and there ain't none of those folks in church gonna wanna' see Dennis Hanson sitting among them!"

"All the more reason to go," Sam said quietly. His silence ended the conversation, as he knew it would.

Well, I'll be damned, Dennis thought, I'm going to church tomorrow.

Chapter Seventeen

Mr. and Mrs. Wally Spur sat playing Bingo at a booth run by the local Lions Club when the pastor rejoined them. Restaurant patrons had plied both with too much alcohol.

"Where's the girls?" Wally Spur slurred as the pastor sat down next to them.

"Oh, they went off to ride more rides with some of their friends." Wilson said hoping that neither Spur would catch the aroma coming from his pants.

He had walked the fairgrounds until he found the men's restrooms. He went inside and did what he could about removing the soil from his pants. The scheming little whelp that vomited on him must have been aiming deliberately for his crotch, he thought as he tried to clean the mess. He had to stand inside the toilet for a long time trying to dry his pants, at least some. It wasn't of much use. He walked out determined to find the Spurs and garnered some strange looks from those swarming through the hot, dirty midway with him. By the time he finally found the Spurs, he was almost completely dry.

Before the pastor arrived to join them, Mrs. Spur had been worried about the girls. She didn't like the pastor regardless of how he tried to put up a holy front. Wally was determined that the girls stay with the man and she didn't like that, either. This was the first time he had ever forced Holly to do something she didn't want to do. Why? What was going on? She also knew that if she nagged him too much about it, his already foul mood would get even worse. Instead of saying anything to him, she sat quietly, keeping her concerns to herself and feigning gaiety to keep him happy. Well, the good pastor would not be riding in the back seat of the car with the girls on the way home. She'd plan some sweet way to get him in the front while she sat with the children.

When he showed up at the Bingo booth without the girls, she felt both relief and alarm.

Mr. Spur, on the other hand, had been drinking so much he didn't even recognize the pastor when he sat down beside him. Oh, the man looked familiar, but he couldn't quite place him.

The pastor, noting the confused look on Wally Spur's face, smiled and said sweetly, "It's me, Wally, Pastor Wilson. You know the one that let you drive his Cadillac to the fair, the one who paid for your family's admission into the fair?"

Mr. Spur didn't like the tone in the stranger's voice. It sounded holier than thou to him, "Well, ain't you something?" He slurred as he leaned into his wife who sat on the other side of him.

She always sat to one side of him to make sure he was playing his cards correctly. No matter what her husband did in life, she couldn't deny the fact that he was lucky. So lucky that he rarely played a game of chance that he didn't win. Those winnings had helped the couple through many a tough financial time. She was so familiar with his ways of being and doing, she swayed gently to her left to accommodate his leaning into her.

Her husband had a hard time of it growing up, dealing with things, she reasoned. He was weak. She knew that, accepted it. She may not like the way he did the children, but he was her husband and she'd be damned if she wouldn't stand by him, no matter what.

She knew he drank too much. He was doing it today. When those demons got a hold of him, he just couldn't stop. She hated the way that others looked at him when he was drinking—knew it demeaned him in their eyes—that's why she had a soft spot for Dennis' father. She couldn't help it. She knew the men were tormented.

As she watched her husband with the pastor, she could see that the pastor didn't think too highly of him, either. His face belied the fact that he held Mr. Spur in contempt. She wondered what he was up to. Why was he hanging around Wally all of a sudden? She had had one too many beers herself and couldn't grasp it. She'd be lucky if she remembered anything that had past between the three of them the next day. By the look in the pastor's eyes, a predator's eyes, she had the presence of mind to decide she would drink no more that night, and did not.

As for the pastor, he gloated over the Spurs' inebriated condition. This was just how he hoped he'd find them. He asked the booth attendant for a Bingo card, and he too joined in the game. No one else playing Bingo thought much of a pastor playing the game as well. After all, most churches had Bingo nights to earn money for their parishes.

What Wilson didn't anticipate, however, was the fact that Wally Spur couldn't seem to loose, no matter how drunk he became. He found he was rankled with jealousy at the man's luck. He was also displeased with the way Mrs. Spur hovered over the old man and made sure his every need was attended to. How could such a lowly, drunken, ugly old man, he thought, get so lucky?

Sheriff Hansen found the Spurs when he stepped under a tent awning hoping to find a place where he could sit down and rest a minute, maybe have a soda pop. There they sat at a table playing Bingo. Hansen saw them as he noticed the sawdust strewn ground and smelled its sweetness, which always conjured up scenes of his woodshop, and his wife when she used to help him. She had had a knack for carpentry, which always amazed him.

A slight breeze through the open tent carried with it aromas from all over the midway. Cotton candy, roasted peanuts, hot dogs, coffee, even the smell of fear and sex could be delicately scented upon the wind. Adulterers were slinking off for a tryst, and kids were sampling their first seduction in the back seat of someone's car, all just feet away from the midway itself.

The carnival was always like that. Hansen could never make up his mind whether he liked the carnival for all of that, or was offended by it.

As he stood under the tent resting his tired feet, Hansen saw that Wally Spur could do no wrong in the Bingo parlor. He noted with interest the preacher's condescending looks at Spur. The kid's mom was as hot as ever. Man, she is a beauty, he thought, and couldn't figure out how someone that looked like her could have a husband who looked like Wally Spur, and be devoted to him ta' boot!

He watched the pastor get up and make his way to the beer booth bringing back full beer cups to sit in front of the Spurs even though it was obvious Wally Spur was drunk. Mrs. Spur had three full beer cups in front of her, but wasn't touching any them. Hansen already knew how the stain on the preacher's pants got there, enjoying the idea of the kid barfing on him. He didn't like him, considered him a person of interest simply by observing him with the Spurs.

He walked over to their table. "Ahhhmm," he cleared his throat. Everyone looked up at him. "Hello, Mrs. Spur. This must be your husband?" He waited to be introduced. He noted the angry look in Wally Spur's eyes as she introduced him. Was that jealousy? He turned to look at the pastor, and Mrs. Spur introduced him, too. Hansen shook his hand. Mr. Spur hadn't offered his.

Hansen turned his complete attention to the pastor wondering if any of the rumors he'd heard about the man were true. He didn't like the cold, clammy feel of his palm. He didn't like the look in the man's eye, either. It was cold and hard with no warmth. He saw that same look almost every day, every time he arrested a hardened criminal. That same look was never in the eyes of the local drunks who got themselves in trouble by being an annoyance to folks. It was never in the eyes of a petty thieves, either, the ones who stole because of circumstances.

But there it was in the pastor, crystal clear to Hansen, who'd seen just about everything one human being could do to another. Nope, this man of God was anything but.

"Pastor," Hansen said congenially betraying nothing that was going on in his mind, "I heard you might have taken two young girls on the Ferris wheel earlier. Is that correct?"

"Yes, yes I did," Wilson said, smiling. "You know, one of them threw up on me. I'm afraid I lost my temper with her. You understand. I had to wash the mess off the front of my pants in the bathroom. I'm afraid they still smell of vomit."

He stated only what was clearly visible to the sheriff. Smart, Hansen thought, and said, "Whose children were they that rode that ride with you?"

"They're my kids," Wally Spur slurred looking belligerently at the sheriff, "and if I say they can go on the rides, what business is that of yours?"

"Where were you when they were on the ride with the pastor here?" Hansen asked.

"We was right here, where we've been all night!" Hiccup! Mr. Spur belched slipping off his chair as he tried to stand, swaying on legs not yet rigid enough to hold him up.

Hansen watched the drunken restaurateur try to get to his feet and was ready to assist him if need be, but Mrs. Spur gracefully took Wally Spur by the arm while plying the old man with praise, so he wouldn't feel humiliated. Hansen guessed she smoothed over many an argument with her husband that way.

Old Man Spur brushed her arm off and slurred, "Keep your hands to yourself woman! Don't be clinging to me!" He tried to focus his eyes on the sheriff, squinting up at him as he stood there gently weaving back and forth looking as if a slight breeze might blow him over.

"Where are the children, now?" Hansen asked. He didn't like the drunk before him simply because in his weakened condition he was vulnerable. He suspected that Old Man Spur was just as the pastor wished him to be, the pastor being the vulture ready to attack when the old drunk was least expecting it.

"Thas' none of your damn business," Spur slurred.

"I'm afraid it is, Mr. Spur. There's been a complaint. If those children aren't being cared for properly or properly supervised, they could be put into the care of the Department of Human Services."

"Who says they're not being cared for?" Mrs. Spur said angrily. "They're twelve years old, for crying out loud. They don't need us to watch them as if they were two. The preacher said they were off having a good time with their friends! What, I ask you, is wrong with that? And how is that being neglectful?"

"So, they haven't been back here since the pastor returned, is that correct?"

"Yes, that's right," Mrs. Spur said, "and you still haven't answered my question! What's wrong with them having fun with their friends?"

"Nothing Ma'am, if that's where they are." That said, Hansen tipped his hat to the trio and walked away. He'd find the girls and tell them where the Spurs where if it were the last thing he did. If their parents were too stupid to keep a closer eye on them in light of what happened to Shannon Thompson just the day before yesterday, he'd make damn sure he would and that they were okay.

He could feel the pastor's eyes bore into his back as he walked away. By the proud tilt of the pastor's chin, Hansen doubted that the man felt that he, Hansen, was much of a threat. He liked it when people thought that about him.

His only problem now would be locating the girls. He hadn't seen them on the midway since he left them at the concession stand, and guessed that they were already gone from the fairgrounds. He'd start looking for them at the Spur's apartment. He couldn't rest not knowing they were safe.

Sam and Dennis stayed by the river even though they had finished casting stones. They stood leaning into the metal railing spiting down into the water to see how fast their spit would hit, neither one saying a word, but each competing, hoping theirs would splash first. They watched as a sheriff's cruiser pulled up behind the apartment building, and as the sheriff quietly got out of the car. They looked at each other. Both boy's hearts took a nosedive as each feared for their family. They took off running up the road yelling to the sheriff.

Hansen stopped in his tracks. He hadn't gotten as far as the back porch when he heard the boys calling and saw them running toward him. His heart leapt. He thought they might be about to tell him something he didn't want to hear.

"Sheriff, what's wrong," Sam called softly trying not to wake his Mrs. Conway, Holly or Renee.

"Has something happened to my father?" Dennis cried.

For the life of him, Sam couldn't understand why Dennis cared so much about his old man when all the old man did was drink and humiliate his family in new and more vulgar ways every day.

When they were close enough so that Hansen could talk to them without shouting, he spoke quietly, "Relax guys, nothing's wrong that I know of. I'm here looking for your little sister, Sam, her and her friend. Have you seen them lately?"

"Oh, yeah, they're here. We gave them a ride home earlier. They're sleeping over at Mrs. Conway's tonight. Is anything wrong?"

"No, no, just some people at the fairgrounds were concerned with them. Seems your folks didn't know where they were. The pastor said they were off with their friends."

"The pastor? How did he know where they were?" Sam grew uneasy thinking Holly and Renee had been near the pastor.

"He's at the fairgrounds with your folks. Seems he took the girls on a couple of rides. The girls got off the Ferris wheel sick, some strangers said. One woman was so worried about them she came looking for me. The girls took off a little later, and I didn't see them around the midway. In light of what happened to their friend, I thought I'd best find them. Found your folks playing Bingo with the pastor. The pastor told me the girls ran off to ride rides with their friends. Your folks didn't seem too concerned with their whereabouts. Your dad was a bit tipsy. Does he do that often?"

"He does it enough," was all Sam would say. He didn't like his father much, but he wasn't going to try and get him in trouble with the sheriff. "He usually sleeps off a drunk at the café, so he probably won't be home tonight."

"Are you going to be here all night?" Hansen asked

"Why?" Sam asked, suspicious.

"Well, it seems to me that maybe, in light of everything that has gone on around here for the last couple of days, that maybe a man under your roof is not such a bad idea, someone who has all their faculties about him, if you know what I mean."

No adult male had ever called Sam a man before, or implied that he could be more than a punk kid; Sam was astonished. He didn't want Dennis or the sheriff to know that, however, so he acted nonchalant, as if it were a given that he could protect the women in his house.

"Don't worry none, Sheriff. I ain't going nowhere. Hey Dennis, why don't you stay with me?"

"Naw, Man, I'd better get home. Hell, my sister and my mother are there by themselves, too! I don't want nothing to happen to them, neither."

Sheriff Hansen kept his mouth shut, but he was impressed with both boys. They had more responsibility than most adult men, and handled it well. Everybody in Pine County knew Dennis' father was the county drunk, not just a town drunk. They also knew that Dennis tried hard to keep everything afloat for everyone else in his father's house.

They'd had a few run-ins with the kid, but just petty kid stuff, nothing serious. Hansen thought Dennis would do okay if he could ever get out from under the burden his old man put him under. Before Dennis could leave, Hansen said, "You two boys know much about the pastor?"

Neither boy said anything; they shook their heads, no.

Sam didn't want to say anything that Mrs. Conway had told him about the man. Hansen was an adult, an authority figure, and they usually didn't like kids demeaning one of their own. "I don't like him," Sam said confidently. That wasn't giving away too much and didn't make a hypocrite out of him. He wasn't about to voice his other concerns, not yet anyway.

"Well, you two might as well head on in then," was all Hansen would say. He didn't like the pastor much, either. He shook their hands before he left, and as Dennis walked with Sam to the first floor landing, he said, "The sheriff seems okay, for a grown-up, I mean."

"Yeah, he's not too bad," Sam said. Sam stood on the first floor landing, and watched as Dennis disappeared onto the sidewalk on Main Street heading south to his own house.

Sam knew where Holly and Renee where, so he figured he might just as well camp out on the back porch. It was a nice night and Old Lady Conway had left her chaise lounge out. It would be comfortable out there. He lit a cigarette and looked up at the stars. It was a beautiful night. He didn't expect anything bad to happen, except maybe to run into the old man if he decided to stumble up the staircase going home. Sam suspected that the stairs where hard for the old man to climb, one of the reasons he stayed away so much. Too much pride to let his youthful son know he had a weakness, Sam guessed as the smoke from his cigarette curled upwards and disappeared into the night air. Nope, he doubted they'd be a problem for him this night, so he relaxed into the cushioned chaise lounge contemplating with joy how the sheriff called him the man of the house.

Back at the fairgrounds, Wally Spur was well on his way to be falling down drunk. Mrs. Spur did all she could to keep him as sober as possible, but that was nearly impossible with the pastor continually supplying beer. She gave the man dirty looks from the opposite side of her husband where she sat, while the pastor kept his arm around the old man's shoulder from the other side whispering things into the old man's ear. He smirked at her from across her husband's shoulders. Old Man Spur was too far-gone to notice.

"You have another one Wally, and never you mind what your wife says. You're not too drunk, besides, you've worked hard all day and you've got me to drive you home. I'll take you upstairs to your apartment! Don't you worry none!" He smiled to himself as Wally Spur took the bait and another drink. He shook his head in amazement at how, even in oblivion of the mind, the old man could win like he did. He wasn't having much luck with the old man's wife, however.

"Mrs. Spur, dear," he said over the top of Wally Spur's balding head,

"Enjoy yourself! That's what I'm here for. I'll drive you two home. Don't worry about a thing! You must be exhausted the way you work on your feet all day! Please, have a drink on me. It'll do you good."

No amount of flattery or cajoling would move the woman, God, how women disgusted him. None of them knew their place! Was it any wonder he preferred the sweetness of young flesh? And there were two of them in the Spur apartment. All he had to do was get these two so drunk they didn't know if they were coming or going, and he could do as he pleased right under their own roof! It was a daring plan, which is why he liked it. Of course, they did have that troublesome teenage son, something he might have to deal with, but he could handle that too, if need be. He'd find a way.

When Mrs. Spur refused his offer of another drink for the fifth time, he gave up on her. He'd have to alter his plans, go with the flow, so to speak, wait and see what happened next. He saw that he would have to win Mrs. Spur over before she would trust him enough to let loose. He could do that easily; he'd won over almost every woman in town, but he was sick of women. He liked the sweet, innocent flesh of little girls who could be trained up in the way that they should go.

The thought of going to Gloria anymore wasn't as appealing as it used to be, either. She was getting too old and behaving like most adult women, which disgusted him. She should be delighted with all the favor I've shown her over the years, he thought. What is wrong with her anyway?

As Old Man Spur sloshed his tenth beer over his Bingo cards, Mrs. Spur, who had had enough, said, "Okay, Wally, that's it. We're going home. You've won enough money for the night and we have to work in the morning. You know I need you to help me."

Wally Spur turned his head to the side, and looked at his wife through alcohol-glazed eyes, seeing a blur, and smiled weakly up at her. There was no more of his usual disagreeableness. The pastor had been so nice to him over the course of the day that he was in a genial mood even if his wife insisted they call it a night. She was probably right. He tried to stand, but his legs wobbled so much underneath the table that he sat back down emitting a "woof" for his effort.

Even though the pastor didn't really want to call it a night, he decided it was for the best. Besides, it had been only two nights before when he had had his way with a sweet little thing. He had plied the Spur's daughter and her friend with his attentions this night, too, even if it hadn't been enough to really satisfy him; he'd get to them, if not tonight, then another night. For now, since it was a dangerous time, he'd help the Spurs back home and check out their apartment. It would be easier then in the future, he decided.

"Your wife is right, Wally. Here, let me help you to your feet."

Wally Spur turned to face the pastor, a lopsided smile spreading across his face. He'd found a new, true friend. It was about time. He worked hard to be able to stand, show himself worthy in front of the pastor, but it wasn't much use.

Wilson steadied Spur to his feet on one side while Mrs. Spur took his other arm, and the pair guided Wally Spur out from the Bingo tent, slowly across the midway, and out into the parking lot. Mrs. Spur prayed that the effort would sober her husband, even just a little, but to no avail.

When they reached the car, she helped the pastor place her husband in the front seat, and she climbed into the back. Wilson started the car and headed north back into town. When he reached Main Street and their apartment building, Mrs. Spur saw that he intended to pull alongside it in the rear. "No, Pastor," she said. "When he's like this," she pointed to her husband. "We go to the restaurant. We have cots there to sleep on."

"But, Dear," Wilson said in his sweetest voice, "Wouldn't you much prefer the comfort of your own bed! I mean with me to help you, it shouldn't be hard to get Mr. Spur upstairs!"

"Thank you for your offer, Pastor, but no, we prefer the restaurant." She was firm in her refusal. Wally Spur was a lot of things, but he never wanted his daughter to see him when he was drunk. He was firm in that and would be more than angry if he learned his wife had taken him into the apartment as drunk as he was where Holly might see him. Besides, it was a good excuse to keep the pastor out of her house. She didn't want him there.

Wilson pulled a U-turn on Main Street and pulled up in front of the restaurant where he helped the Spurs inside. As he came out, he looked across the street, upstairs, at the blank windows and wondered if he dared go over on his own. No, it wasn't time yet.

Downstairs, in the first floor apartment, Mrs. Conway stood watch, eyeing the pastor as he came out of the restaurant and stood staring upstairs. She was very glad the girls were with her and not alone up there. She took out her notebook and marked the time. She also managed to get a good look at his license plate number and marked that too.

When he got into his car and left, she went outside to get a breath of fresh air and to make sure the pastor didn't decide to drive down the alley for a good look upstairs. It was quiet out back. She stood by the back door, looking out into the pasture at Sugarplum who grazed quietly in the moonlight.

When she turned to go back inside, she noticed Sam asleep on the chaise lounge. She smiled knowing that he was doing sentry duty, but he was asleep. She went into her house and crawled beneath the covers of her own bed. She'd sleep awhile. Nowadays though, she never slept much. Seemed the older she got, the less sleep she needed. Besides, she could take catnaps all day if she needed to.

Chapter Eighteen

Renee slept fitfully next to Holly in Mrs. Conway's modest spare bedroom; her dreams filled with monsters coming to devour her, hurt her, so much so, she screamed out in her sleep.

Sam, outside asleep on the chaise, awoke to those screams running to the window peering in. Renee lay there next to his sister thrashing about under the covers calling out in her sleep. He was relieved it was no more than a nightmare.

Holly, too, seemed to be having bad dreams, he thought watching her restlessly move about in the bed. Maybe she was reacting to Renee, amazed that neither girl awoke. Well, at least nothing is harming them in the flesh, he considered as he moved back to the chaise still disturbed by Renee's screams. What was frightening her? She had spent the night at their house in Makinen when they lived there, many times, and not once had she ever called out in her sleep—so why now?

He pondered that for awhile, thinking maybe Shannon's death couldn't be sitting too well with either girl. No wonder they thrashed about screaming in their sleep, he would too if it were one of his friends, although he'd never admit that to a living soul. A friend is a friend, especially to a kid. You didn't just loose one in a horrific manner like Shannon and not feel the effects of it. Hell, Shannon's death affected him and how much more had he gone through in life than the girls had? Finally, after stumping out another cigarette, he too, fell back to sleep dreaming dreams of monsters chasing him through the streets of Rutledge.

In the Thompson household, sleep eluded Kathy. To her amazement, there was very little for Judy, either, although she occasionally dozed off on Kathy's bed as the two poured over New Testament scriptures looking for what, they weren't quite sure.

"Remember, Mrs. Conway said that God would teach us what we need to know!" Kathy repeated to Judy for the umpteenth time. She was tired of telling her that. Judy wasn't seeing anything that helped her, a lot of the scripture condemned her, she felt, because she had been doing nothing the way it said to do things.

She read where Jesus came to save people, not condemn them, so she read on, but thought, good God! How can He save me? I've been doing everything wrong! She could barely bring herself to continue, but when she did, she saw that all she needed to do was believe in Him, and repent of her sins. That doesn't sound right, she thought, it isn't enough! Though she had yet much to learn, Judy kept an open mind and read on searching for something that would help them find out who killed Shannon, if that was possible. She also hoped to learn if they (she, Kathy, her parents, or any of their friends) were now in danger.

To her credit, she refused to give up on the Bible until something jumped out at her. She read in Luke 8:17 "For nothing is secret that will not be revealed, nor anything hidden that will not be known and come to light (NKJV)."

She jumped at that. So, we will know what happened if Mrs. Conway is right about this stuff, she thought jubilantly! She wasn't sure yet if she believed but she read on and came to Luke 11: 9,10: "So I say to you, ask, and it will be given to you; seek, and you will find; knock, and it will be opened to you. For everyone who asks receives, and he who seeks finds, and to him who knocks it will be opened." (NKJV)

Judy knew then that they would discover who had killed Shannon. She also felt more secure for herself. She showed the passages from Luke to Kathy, and the two girls got on their knees next to the bed and prayed that what had really happened to their sister would be revealed, and that whoever killed her would be brought to justice. They also prayed for protection. By the time they finished, it was three a.m. Both slipped into their own rooms, under their covers and fell fast asleep. They were weary from all they had gone through, but hadn't realized how much until they each slipped between their sheets laying their tired heads upon their pillows.

In the wee hours of the morning, Mrs. Conway, too, was praying. She didn't have to look up scriptures to know which ones to call upon. She prayed prayers of protection for all the children and prayers that whoever had murdered Shannon would be brought to justice. She stood outside looking up at the stars from beside the paddock fence as she prayed. She couldn't get to her knees anymore, but she knew God was the God of mercy and grace and didn't begrudge her because of her feeble body. She'd had a strong prayer life almost from the day she was born, and after 111 years of praying and talking with God, she was quite comfortable and confident in her knowledge of Him.

The calm, still, beautiful night masked the growing turbulence beneath the surface of Rutledge. Mrs. Conway could feel it in her bones. The Lord showed her pillars of smoke, fire, and flames and she knew they were symbols of hell, as she stood braced against the paddock fence. She held on to a fence post for support as visions danced about in her mind. She'd seen worse than these visions before, so she waited for clear direction, for the path she should take out of the flame. A path she would use to lead the others out. She'd have to lead them out; they weren't mature enough spiritually to do it themselves; they needed her. She saw it then, the path. She knew which of them would make it across the river of flames, and which would not. She shivered, but she was prepared.

She had been on the earth for 111 years; it was time for her to rest. She tottered back to her apartment not feeling the chill that the dew filled grass caressed her bare feet with. The only chill she tried to fight was the one on the inside; this time she would need a lot of help. It would be her greatest battle. She was old now, too, too old to do it herself, but she knew with whom to go for help, who would actually be doing the fighting for her. This fight belonged to God. They all did.

She saw Sam asleep on her back porch as she crossed lightly over it to her back door. The light blanket she had covered him with had fallen beneath the chaise; she bent to pick it up and recovered him with it.

Sam woke-up as the light cover touched his skin, hyper vigilant to his surroundings. He rolled over and smiled at Mrs. Conway. " I was dreaming that an angel was covering me," he said unashamed. He didn't think the old woman would ever tell his friends.

"One has," she retorted then slapped her knee laughing. She was the closet thing to an angel on earth that he was ready to see, and she knew it. "Yup, you and me is going to be good friends, young man. Don't you go forgetting it."

He sat up and smiled at her. For the life of him, he couldn't understand his own tolerance of her. She was annoyingly bossy yet somehow he knew she had his best interest at heart. He wasn't crazy about her always telling him about God, either, hell, how could he be quick to believe something that had never been true in his life, like mercy or grace? If God was so merciful, how could He allow children to be so mistreated by adults? How did He allow someone to murder Shannon? No he wasn't ready to believe in God, but he had to admit, he was pretty impressed with Mrs. Conway, and she sure believed!

"Mrs. Conway," he started, deciding it was time to talk about some of the questions that were bothering him about God. If anyone could help him understand, he guessed she was the one. "If God is as great as you say He is, then why did he let Shannon be murdered? I don't understand that, and frankly, don't think too much of a God that would let children be so mistreated by adults." His chin jutted out in defiance. Whenever he thought of God, which he had been since she had started talking about Him, he felt a need to scream out his own pain and ask why He had allowed him to be so mistreated by his father.

"That's a good question Sam. I can only say this, His ways are not our ways, and His thoughts are not our thoughts. What that means, I believe, and this is after a lot of contemplation, is that we aren't always meant to understand the horrible things on earth other than that Satan is alive and well and doing those horrible things. Satan works through everyone you know, not just the monsters that do horrible things. He finds our weaknesses then gets into our minds to create strongholds, which hold us back, keep us oppressed, so we can continue to be his prey.

As for Shannon's murder, well, Satan has a very strong hold on someone right here in this town, and that's why she is gone. God loved her; she was an innocent. She is with Him right now, I'm very sure. Why He allows Satan to do that kind of work, I don't know. I will never know. Maybe she simply didn't know that God would protect her, had she prayed for protection, or maybe her attacker was on her before she knew to pray; I just don't know. But I do know this, now is the time the rest of the town has to pray for protection! God wants us to pray. We need Him now more than ever!

This probably isn't making much sense to you. Believe me, it has confounded me many a time, God's word I mean, when there's been a tragedy, but when we do learn who did this horrible thing, we'll have to pray that we're strong enough to forgive him."

"Forgive him! Are you nuts? How do you expect anyone to forgive a monster like that? Is that what God expects? I'll give you two guesses what you can do with your God!" Sam stood to his full height, indignant that she would say such a thing. Forgive! The animal murdered a kid! How is anyone supposed to forgive that!

"I understand fully how you feel, Sam," Mrs. Conway moved over to him and stood in front of him, her eyes so soft and friendly, Sam's anger washed out of him. "Forgiveness isn't so much for the sinner, the one who would do so terrible a thing; forgiveness is for us. Forgiveness doesn't mean that we have to embrace the person we're forgiving either, especially if it is someone who doesn't know God and who wants to continue to abuse us out of ignorance. No, forgiveness is for us so that God can forgive us our sins. Remember everyone is a sinner. Jesus said that if anyone even looked at a woman not their wife and had lustful thoughts about her they had already committed the sin of adultery. He also said that if we commit one sin, we're guilty of them all. That's why we need Him, because He washed away all our sins, for those that believe, that is, when He was crucified. He is no respecter of persons either, which means no one is better than anyone else here on this earth. That's why we need to forgive, dear, so that we can be forgiven. And if you find it too hard to forgive, He'll even help you with that. Cast your cares on Him, the Bible says. And don't worry too much if you aren't perfect in everything right off the bat. No one is. You'll get stronger though with more of the Word of God that you get into yourself."

She hoped some of what she was teaching would get through, but she knew when someone was abused, it often took a lot longer to trust anyone, especially God; they always blamed Him out of their ignorance and never Satan, and of course, that's how Satan wants it.

"Well, I'm not saying anything more," Sam said, "because I know you believe and for some reason I feel like I can trust you, but I have my doubts about God. That's the truth of it." He sat back down on the chaise, and looked up to see her pulling a cigarette from his pack and lighting it.

"That's okay, dear. When God is ready, you'll no longer have any doubts . . . You know that cigarette looks mighty good. Mind if I have one?" She said after already taking a drag from the one she lit. "I haven't had a cigarette since the 1920s, used to smoke like a chimney."

Sam was flabbergasted. Mrs. Conway looked like she was born to smoke. He didn't know anyone as pious as she was would ever light a cigarette. She took a long draw off the unfiltered Camel, sat down in a wicker rocker next to her spare room window, leaned back and started rocking the chair quietly while she obviously enjoyed the indulgence of smoking. She uttered not a word until the cigarette was down to ash, then said to Sam, "That was probably the best smoke I ever had." He just shook his head in amazement.

"In the morning, we'll have to get to work. We're going to have to stick together now, and I don't know how you're going to manage that with that father of yours, but the Lord will show us, I guess, since that's His will. You may not believe now, but when this is over, you will. Mark my words." She got up from her rocker then and went inside. Before she shut the screen door, she turned and said in parting, "You're a good kid, Sam. Don't let anyone tell you otherwise. The Lord told me to tell you that. And from now on, all you kids will be staying with me at night, the girls and you. No more porch either. I'll give you a key latter on, and you can come and go as you do at home, but we are all in this together, so we'll have to be keeping in touch. Is that clear?"

"Yes Ma'am," Sam said as he stared at the little old lady in wonder.

At the Hanson residence, when Dennis got home that night it was already eleven p.m,. and when he checked, he found his mother and sister already in bed asleep. His father wasn't home. That was just as well. He turned on the television, went into the kitchen and fixed himself a bologna sandwich, then went back into the living room and sat down on the couch to watch TV and eat. Funny, he hadn't felt tired before, but just as he finished eating, he slipped off to sleep. He fell into fitful dreams where an unseen monster approached his house to devour everyone in it.

Frightened, he fought his way awake, and as the cobwebs of sleep brushed aside, he heard the kitchen door every so quietly either shut or open. He sat up, already fully awake. The TV was now off, and he knew he hadn't turned it off. He was glad though, because the blue-light of the screen would not illuminate him as he tiptoed into the kitchen. His heart raced in his chest, there was nothing he could use for a weapon between him and the kitchen door. He racked his brain trying to think of something. Damn, he thought, even the little night light over the kitchen sink, which faced the highway, was out. Who turned that light off! Nobody in the house that's for damn sure, he thought! Everyone knew how irate old man Hanson got if he came home after boozing and there were no lights on!

Dennis worked up his nerve to slip into the threshold between the two rooms ready to do battle with his fists if need be. He faced the back door inside the kitchen and found it shut and locked.

In a flash of insight, he ran to Francine's room. He opened the door and knew immediately that she was at it again. He couldn't understand why she was always so eager to run out with any Tom, Dick, or Harry who asked her, but she did it all the time.

He thought he just might have time to catch her in the act if he got outside soon enough, so he could see her from the backdoor. It was a very dark night. She must have turned the yard light off too, something else the old man will have a fit about.

But she ain't as smart as she thinks, he thought from behind the pine groove he crept into. He could see Francine talking to someone in a car at the end of the driveway. He crept closer, thankful that she had thought herself so clever. It gave him a chance to hide in the dark and watch her, the same chance it gave her. He got a good look at the car and the man Francine was talking to.

He couldn't believe it when he saw her get into it then take off down the road. Damn her! He thought knowing she was after a man again, this time a married one! He'd beat the shit out of her when she got home if he had too! He was fed up. If the old man wouldn't stay home and be a father to her, he would! Sleeping with anyone who asked was one thing when it was kids his own age, but him! If Dennis had had the courage to admit it to himself, he would have realized that his righteous indignation didn't come from the fact that Francine had the gall to sleep with a married man; it came from the fact that she had chosen this particular married man. The guy was a creep, even old lady Conway said so, and he'd trust her a lot quicker than he ever would the pastor.

He was still in the yard when his father came weaving down the road, wearing his good suit askew and carrying one shoe in his hand. He mumbled about not being able to see.

Knowing that his father would never see him, Dennis ran ahead of him into the house, turned on the yard light, the night light over the kitchen sink, and slipped into his bedroom before the old man could try the doorknob to his house. He heard his father stumble in, fall down, crawl over to the couch and lay down. The house fell quiet and Dennis could hear the sounds of his father's labored breathing. He was relieved. The old man had passed out, that meant his mother would be okay this night.

As he lay there on his bed, he heard his father calling out to Shannon Thompson. Dennis sat straight up in bed and listened intently knowing his father was talking in his drunken sleep.

"Best tell them folks I saw the pastor teaching that little girl a lesson! Best tell them that first thing in the morning. Could show them where, too. Best tell them, best tell them in the morning." He said no more.

Over at the Sands Café, Mrs. Spur had finally laid down after getting Mr. Spur quieted down. Sometimes he got so mad at her and she never understood why. She wasn't doing anything wrong; what was his problem?

She knew that this night Pastor Wilson had been the problem. On the way home, he kept saying how lovely she was. Lovely my ass, she thought, he can't stand the sight of me. He just wanted Wally jealous so he would give me a bad time. He was pissed off because we didn't go over to the apartment. I don't know why, but I know for sure those girls are not going near him again! Let Wally get pissed off. If he tries to make them go anywhere with that two bit son-of-a-bitch pastor I'll leave him!

Mrs. Spur was a little surprised at herself when she thought that. Never had she entertained the idea of leaving Wally before. She was afraid to be alone. She had never been alone her whole life. What would she do if she left him? She'd do the same thing she did with him, find a job and go to work. She made most of the money anyway, what difference would it make if he was gone? That was a new thought. She smiled at it and slipped off to sleep, happily.

Chapter Nineteen

Sheriff Ernie Hansen didn't like it one little bit—two bodies in three days in the tiny hamlet of Rutledge! It was unacceptable and almost too hard to believe, but that's what he had.

Francine Hanson, Dennis Hanson's sister, was found in the ditch off Highway 61 by road workers at five a.m. that morning, laid out in the same fashion as little Shannon Thompson.

Only Francine was older, at least sixteen, more than likely seventeen going on thirty, the sheriff guessed. He knew her reputation, as did most of the men in his office, and he guessed, all the men in Rutledge. She acted like a dog in heat ninety percent of the time. Well, this time, she got a whole lot more than she bargained for.

As he squatted next to the body surveying the sight, he could see that where she lay was not where she had been killed. Nope, someone killed her somewhere else then moved the body, and laid it out just as they had Shannon. Hansen knew he was dealing with the same perpetrator no sooner than he saw the body. Her legs were splayed open displaying her genitals. Her breasts were bared so that anyone could see them. Her head was covered with her own sweater, as if the killer were depersonalizing her; her arms were splayed out horizontally from her torso, and she looked like she might have been constructing a snow angel had it been winter.

There was one difference between Shannon and Francine, besides their age, and that was that whoever murdered Francine, took delight in mutilating her ample breasts, something they had not done to Shannon, who had barely begun to develop breasts.

Was Francine raped? Sex might have been consensual, considering Francine's reputation. Sheriff Ernie Hansen would bet on evidence of sexual intercourse, but the coroner would tell him for sure one way or another. He would also give him the estimated time of death and the cause of death. Sometimes the cause of death wasn't as evident as most folks thought. Francine's wounds were substantial, but they might also be superficial. It was hard to tell from where Hansen squatted beside the body to be 100-percent sure.

By the time the Minnesota Bureau of Criminal Apprehension arrived on the scene, Hansen had finished with what he needed. The MBCA would assist with both crimes, including Shannon's, but especially now that there were two. Two deaths had far-reaching implications, Hansen knew.

He feared the worst. He'd read of cases where men went on killing sprees or murdered people throughout their lives, and were not caught until many had died; they were called serial killers. He prayed that wasn't what he had on his hands, but he already guessed it was. There were two unrelated deaths done in like manner and displayed for discovery so, he guessed, in all probability that was what he was facing. The MBCA would confirm or deny his suspicions, which he had already discussed with them.

As he stood up, he watched the MBCA men move in and make quick work of the crime scene photographing everything. Man, he was glad they were there. He didn't have the manpower or resources to put too many men on the case. He needed help and knew it. His sheriff's department covered all of Pine County, and there were only seven officers in total. A murder investigation had to have priority if he was going to keep the rest of the county's population safe. And even if the carnival were still in town, Hansen knew deep down that no one there was responsible. Still, he had to keep men on top of that, too, because the carnival always brought trouble, so he was really in a fix as far as manpower was concerned.

He would focus his efforts in and around Rutledge and Willow River because they were so close. But since the bodies had both been facing Rutledge, he sensed that whoever was responsible lived there. It was as if they were mocking the town somehow. He and the MBCA were in agreement on that, and about how the investigation should proceed.

Hansen may not have had many murders to investigate over his career in Pine County, but he had a reputation throughout law enforcement in the state for being a dogged investigator who didn't give up until he had caught his perpetrator, no matter what the crime. MBCA investigators had confidence in his intuitive deductions regarding the two murders as well, and felt Hansen, being from the area, could get much more information from locals than they could.

Hansen waited for the coroner to arrive, and the body to be removed, before he got into his cruiser heading toward Rutledge. The coroner knew how to reach him if he was still out of the office when the autopsy concluded. For now, he had other business to attend to, the stuff he hated most about his job; he had to notify relatives of the death of a family member. That was bad enough if that loved one was killed in some kind of accident, but when they were murdered, most times loved ones had a very hard time coming to grips with it.

It was early, 6:23 a.m., when he pulled into Hanson's driveway. Francine was found only a few short miles from home. Hansen wondered if anyone in the Hanson household was even up yet. He stepped onto the creaky front porch and knocked at the door.

Of all the damn luck, he thought, as Mrs. Ernestine Hanson stood before him in her faded housedress and apron with a spatula in her hand. "Ma'am," Hansen started, "is your husband or your son Dennis at home?"

"Is something wrong officer?" She was suspicious. Police came to your house for only two reasons, either to arrest someone or to tell you someone was dead.

"Are they in Ma'am?" he repeated.

"Dennis!" She turned her back and yelled at the top of her lungs. "Harry! Either one of you up yet? There's someone here to see you!" She turned back to the sheriff, "You might as well come all the way in here, Sheriff. I'll get you a cup of coffee."

She looked resigned to hearing bad news, Hansen thought as he came in but remained standing near the door.

"Sit down, Sheriff, ain't nobody in this house going to bite you!" She already had a steaming cup of coffee on the table for him. He was glad. He was beat and had left his house too early to enjoy a cup of coffee.

"Thank you Ma'am. I appreciate it." Before he could blink, he found a freshly baked cinnamon roll in front of him, as well.

"I baked these this morning. Go ahead, try it, they're good."

He ate with relish awaiting either Dennis or old man Hanson to come into the kitchen. He was glad they took their time. As it happened, both men appeared in the doorway simultaneously. They sat down at the table without speaking. Neither one figured Hansen was there to arrest them for anything. Harry knew that if he was on a drunk, they busted him while he was still drunk, not after he'd gone home and sobered up, and Dennis knew he hadn't done anything to be arrested for, so he was pensive.

"Hi, Sheriff," Dennis said smiling at the man while worry lines etched his young face.

Mrs. Wilson went around the table serving the men in her life and their guest coffee and seeing to it there was sugar and cream on the table, too. "Why don't you sit with us, Mrs. Hanson," Hansen said.

"Francine, will you get up! You got chores to do!" She yelled ignoring the sheriff. Damn that girl, she thought. She couldn't get her to do housework hardly at all anymore. She just wanted to chase boys. Nothing good could come of that, she mused.

Dennis tensed knowing it was not good news that Hansen was about to deliver.

Mrs. Hanson sat down, wringing her hands in her apron, angry with her daughter and suspicious of the sheriff.

It was then that Hansen realized she'd been busying herself to shore up her emotions in order to hear what he had to say.

"It's Francine folks," Hansen knew of no other way to bring bad news other than to come out with it. "We found her this morning alongside Highway 61 . . . just like we found Shannon Thompson the other day." He hoped he wouldn't have to use the word "murdered". He hoped they understood without him giving voice to it.

There was silence all around the table. Dennis stared at him. Harry did too, trying to understand what Hansen had said. He shook as he picked up his coffee and sipped the hot steaming liquid. He needed to have the cobwebs blown out from his mind. He shook so badly, much of the hot liquid spilled out onto his hands, but he didn't seem to notice.

"Francine, you say?" He spoke quietly.

"Yes, sir, Francine. We found her this morning."

"You saying she's dead, Sheriff?" Harry Hanson was not taking it in. He couldn't be hearing right. The sheriff couldn't be saying Francine was dead. His wife was just calling her to come help with the chores.

"Yes, sir. Francine is dead. She was murdered. Just like Shannon. We found her this morning."

Mrs. Hanson gasped, got up and ran into Francine's bedroom looking for her. She knew she went to bed last night, she saw her go there and later on even checked on her. She was home. She had to get up to help her with the washing. As she opened the door, and saw the empty bed, she started to tremble. Harry Hanson jumped up to embrace her, and to keep her from falling to the floor. He helped her back into the kitchen and sat her in a kitchen chair.

Dennis still hadn't said a word. It didn't seem real. He was listening. He heard what the sheriff said. But it was just last night that he had seen Francine flirting with the pastor in his Cadillac! How could she be dead? He didn't say anything.

The sheriff stood up, towering over them there in the kitchen where he stood atop the weathered linoleum flooring wondering if he should stay or go. Thirty years of this kind of work, and he still felt uncomfortable bearing bad news. The stunned family remained at the table, seeming tiny to him, vulnerable in the extreme, as they tried to understand what he had told them, just like everyone else he had delivered bad news to tried to do. They couldn't get a hold of it, didn't want to get a hold of it. Sometimes women attacked him when he told them something tragic about their family; he wasn't too sure that wouldn't happen with Mrs. Hanson. Finally, he cleared his throat and turned to leave.

Mr. and Mrs. Hanson didn't look at him; instead, they sat together holding each other tightly still at the kitchen table underneath a dimly lit overhanging light while the teakettle hissed on the stove in the background.

Dennis looked up at Hansen. Even though the blow he had just received had floored him, something at the back of his mind was rushing forward, something the sheriff desperately needed to know. "Sheriff, I'll walk you to your car!" Dennis yelled.

Hansen wondered what the boy had on his mind. He could see it was something. He knew he had to question the family about last night, if they'd seen Francine or when they last saw her, but he liked to give people a few moments to deal with the news of a death. He could come back in an hour, but it looked to him as if Dennis had something to tell him that couldn't wait. He hoped beyond hope that this would be the lead he needed, if whoever was doing the killing wasn't stopped soon, no telling who would be next. As he got to the car, he turned to face Dennis who followed on his heels. In turn, Dennis was looking back at the house as if to be certain his parents hadn't followed him.

"Last night, Sheriff, or really . . . early this morning, I followed Francine outside. She snuck out of the house when she thought we were all asleep. Anyway, I saw her kissing a guy driving a Cadillac. It was the pastor. That was three a.m. this morning. She was alive then, very much alive, Sheriff."

"I'm glad you told me, son. That's important information. Now what I'm going to do is leave your folks alone for about an hour, I have some work to do at the office, but I'm coming back then to talk to all of you, so I'm asking you to stay put, and make sure your parents do the same. Make a list for me of all of Francine's friends. What did she do for fun, that kind of thing. It'll be a big help." He opened the car door and was about to climb inside the cruiser, when he stopped, leaned on the roof of the vehicle and said. "Look, Dennis, the sooner we catch this person, the better off everyone is going to be, and the sheriff's office is going to need all the help it can get, so try and think of anything that might help. I'm also advising you not to go into Francine's room. We'll be back with a search warrant to go through it ourselves. You never know, she might have left something there that will give us a clue. Maybe you could comfort your folks first, let them know what's going to happen so they won't be shocked by it. They're already going through enough, but we have to do what we have to do in order to catch this killer."

"Sure, Sheriff, I can do that. I'll prepare them for what's to happen next. Do we need to go to your office and identify her or anything?"

"No. I knew who she was. I I'ded her already, there was no mistaking it was Francine. I'm sorry kid." He climbed into the cruiser and started the engine. Although he was elated with what Dennis had told him, he didn't want Dennis to know it. When he pulled out onto Hwy. 61 and got far enough away from the Hanson house, he turned on the sirens and sped through Rutledge on his way back to Willow River. He needed to hurry. He had an investigation to delegate, a warrant to get, and calls to make.

The siren woke Sam from a sound sleep and pleasant dreams. He wondered what was going on, as did Mrs. Conway who he found on the back porch drinking a cup of coffee. "You go on in the house and get yourself something to eat. I cooked a big breakfast for everyone. Have yourself some coffee, too. When you finish, I want you to run an errand for me. The girls are still asleep, so be quiet. No sense waking them up this early; they didn't seem to be sleeping too well last night.

"Thanks Ma'am," Sam said as he went into the kitchen then came back out on the back porch with just a cup of coffee. "I'm never hungry this early," he said when she gave him a quizzical look.

"Saw the sheriff's car go into the Hanson place earlier. Didn't stay long. That was him with the siren going through town. Heading toward Willow River, he was. That's what I want you to do. Go over to Dennis' house, and find out what happened. Me, I'm staying right here for now till I know for sure. I'm not leaving the girls alone."

"I suspect we got ourselves another death. If that's true, you need to tell me, but you also need to stay close to your friend. If that is the case and you aren't back here within the half-hour, I'll know. Then I'll keep the girls close to me all day. It won't be too hard. But you stay with Dennis, find out anything you can from the sheriff. If it's what I think it is, he'll be back to the Hanson's shortly. Okay?"

"Yes, Ma'am, but are you thinking someone in the Hanson family was hurt like Shannon?"

"Yes, Dear, I am, and if that's the case, the only one that it could be is Francine."

Sam's coffee consumed, he put the cup on the wooden railing surrounding the back porch and said, "I'll go now." He wanted to ask her to pray for him, but he couldn't, wasn't comfortable with it yet, wasn't even sure if he believed, so he jumped the railing and started trotting south, toward Dennis's house. He sure hoped she was wrong about Francine, but what would the sheriff be doing at the Hanson's if something wasn't wrong?

Inside Mrs. Conway's apartment, she heard the girls stirring in the guest bedroom. She wouldn't burden them with her vision of last night. She'd wait for Sam to confirm it then she'd tell the girls. They had to understand the danger they were in.

Sam stopped, looked back at Mrs. Conway. She saw him and yelled, "You go on over and help your friend. He needs you." She didn't bother to tell Sam that she knew exactly what was going on because she saw it in her mind's eye, everything, from Francine's tryst with the pastor, to the sheriff being elated with Dennis' information. This was a dangerous time, possibly the most dangerous because the sheriff didn't have any evidence yet to put the pastor where he belonged, and he certainly couldn't trust in an old woman's visions to convict the pastor of murder. He'd have to gather evidence and it would be hard. She knew that the preacher was clever, very good at covering up. But what she relied upon were the scriptures that said nothing done in private would go unrevealed. Anything done in the dark would be brought to the light. She also knew that the nightmare wasn't over yet. Someone else was going to die.

When she heard the girls in the kitchen, Mrs. Conway picked up Sam's empty coffee cup and stepped inside her first floor apartment as the girls helped themselves to coffee. "Ain't you a little young for that?" Mrs. Conway asked, but had no intention of making them stop.

"My mom lets me drink it all the time," Holly lied.

"She does not," Renee said to her friend a bit disgusted that she would lie to Mrs. Conway. "We thought we'd like to try it, is all," she said to the old woman who still stood in the doorway.

"Well, don't worry about it. You can try it this once, but you won't be drinking anymore of it, is that understood?"

"Yes, Ma'am," the girls said in unison. The smell of pancakes and bacon and eggs permeated the small kitchen and the girls looked ravenously at the food. "You go on and eat. We have a long day ahead of us, and you'll need your strength; how else you going to tend to Sugarplum?"

The girls looked at each other. "You mean it," they said together looking at Mrs. Conway who sat down at the kitchen table with them.

"Yep, sure do. You are going to stay with me today. We may go visit the Thompsons together, later, but we'll see how the day goes. If I'm going to walk that far, I'll need you with me. That sound okay with you two?"

"Yeah, sounds great! I guess my folks never came home last night," Holly said wistfully.

"No, they stayed at the restaurant like they do when they've been out. In fact, I think I'll go talk to them while you two eat, make sure they don't mind you staying with me and all," Mrs. Conway said as she eased herself up from the chair. "You two go on and eat. I can cross the street okay with no help. Besides, I like to visit with your mother, Holly, but sometimes we talk about stuff not fit for little girl's ears," she said smiling as she looked back at the two girls eating in her kitchen. They looked back at her through generous smiles and mouths smeared with maple syrup.

It was 7:45 a.m. as Mrs. Conway crossed the Main Street of Rutledge to get to the Sands Café. Mrs. Spur had been up since 4:30 a.m. preparing the kitchen for breakfast customers, some of whom were already enjoying their meals when Mrs. Conway tottered in the front door. Mr. Spur was still in the back, asleep.

"Go wake him up. We've got to talk." Mrs. Conway said when she learned Mr. Spur was still asleep. She spoke in a tone that left Mrs. Spur no choice but to do as she was told, although she really didn't want to wake her husband. Anytime she had done so in the past, his behavior toward her and the children throughout the day was vicious. She dreaded going near him.

As she opened the door to the tiny back room where Mr. Spur habitually slept off his drunkenness, she found that he was already awake, and apparently in a good mood as he was humming to himself when she entered.

"Mrs. Conway is out front Dear," Mrs. Spur said tentatively expecting her husband to make a rude remark. "She wants to talk to us. I guess the girls spent the night at her place last night." She spoke quietly, but he heard her.

"Oh, did you tell them they could?"

"No, I never said anything about it."

"Well, come on then; let's go find out what she wants. I'll call her into the backroom where we can talk away from the customers. Tell Joe to fix me some breakfast. Have you eaten?"

"Yes, I made something earlier."

He didn't say anything else to his wife as he moved quickly toward the front of the restaurant and invited Mrs. Conway to come into the back with him. He even offered her his arm and helped her into the booth next to the jukebox. Mrs. Spur, who bore a fresh pot of coffee and three cups, soon joined them. Their day waitress had just shown up, so Mrs. Spur no longer had to wait on customers, and could enjoy a few minutes off her feet.

When everyone was settled and Mr. Spur was enjoying his breakfast, Mrs. Conway said, "The girls spent the night with me last night." She waited for Mr. Spur's response.

"I heard," he said sipping his coffee.

"Seems you might not know something I found out yesterday. Something you should know." She waited again for his response.

Old Man Spur was now wary. He could smell something awful coming and didn't want to hear it, but knew he had to, "Go on."

"They were upset last night, the girls. Not too upset mind you, but depressed like. Seemed like they had something on their minds, both of them, something they didn't want to talk about, but were terrified of."

Mrs. Spur was now alarmed as well. She knew something happened the night before, she sensed it. It didn't seem right that the girls would run off to be with their friends at the carnival and leave the pastor, like he said they had. It just didn't seem right.

"We got to talking in a-round-about way, while they were taking their baths, very long baths I might add, and both of them, on their own, and by themselves when speaking with me, almost came out and said they were molested. Renee was terrified she was going to hell and that she was somehow now "dirty." Holly was subdued, I guess you'd say, not her bubbly self. Neither one of them wanted to say anything about it. I guess from the way they were acting that it was an adult that did something to them. I ain't exactly sure what, but considering everything that's gone on around here lately, I'm asking permission to let the two of them stay with me for a few days. I'm home all the time. I won't let them out of my sight. I know you two have to work, so it would be easier for you. I'll keep trying to find out what's going on with them, but I have a feeling it'll take a little time."

Mr. Spur didn't like the sounds of it one bit. Who the hell did she think she was, trying to scare him like this! He held his temper though as he considered the situation. Before he had a chance to say a word, Sam walked through the back door and sat down next to his mother.

"Have any of you heard?" Sam looked so pale and so out of character that even Old Man Spur refrained from any smart remarks, and since all remained silent, Sam added, "Francine Hanson was found dead this morning, murdered just like Shannon Thompson. The cops told Dennis that they found her in almost the exact same spot they found Shannon, and she, too, had been raped."

"No!" Mrs. Spur gasped unable to believe it, "another girl! My God, what's going on?"

"You keep them girls with you for now, Mrs. Conway, but we'll be checking up on them every now and again. I don't want them alone. Sam, you stay with Mrs. Conway, too, make sure the three of them are okay at all times, especially at night." Mr. Spur was unnerved for the first time in his life. He was terrified for Holly. Although he didn't want to admit it, he suspected that what Mrs. Conway had told him about the girls was true, too. He didn't really trust the pastor as much as others suspected he did, especially after the man had been so eager to get him drunk. Oh he remembered that all right and a number of other things. Tending bar for so many years of his life, he had witnessed much of the nasty side to human nature and knew that anyone attempting to drunken his neighbor was up to no good.

"Jeez, Dad, I was going to go back over to Dennis'. The family is in rough shape. Dennis is trying to hold everything together on his own. Some of their family is coming up from the Cities but they won't be there for a long time yet. Can I stay at least until they get there? Besides, the cops are coming back to search Francine's room. They should be there any time now. Dennis is really going to need some support. His parents are beside themselves."

"I never thought of that. All right, go back over there until the rest of the family gets there. But at night, I want you at Mrs. Conway's. Get there at least by 7:30 and stay there. It isn't going to hurt you any. You know we have to work, so we can't get home until late."

"If you get any information from the cops when they're at the Hanson's, come back here and tell me," he said to Sam as he was about to leave, then he looked at Mrs. Conway, "and you need to tell me anything that the girls tell you about yesterday. If someone did molest them, maybe the two incidents are related. The police should know."

"You're going to make them tell the police!" Mrs. Spur almost shrieked, "My God, Wally, how much humiliation do you expect them to suffer?"

"Better a little humiliation now than dead bodies later," he said coldly and matter of factly. "Besides, if they were molested, they didn't do anything wrong. Wrong was done to them."

With that Mrs. Conway got up and left wondering, as she crossed the hot tar of Main Street, about Mr. Spur. Maybe there was something redeemable about the man, yet. Well, she wouldn't bet on it, but she'd pray for him just the same.

Chapter Twenty

It was in Francine Hanson's room that Pine County Sheriff Ernie Hansen found the most telling evidence against Pastor Joseph Wilson. Her journal was full of evidence that could convict the dear pastor of statutory rape, if nothing else.

Francine had loved the pastor, hung on his every word, according to the diary. She was fifteen years old when he first seduced her, inside the church no less; he told her it was God's will that she give herself to him.

Humph, thought the sheriff, God's will my ass! Even though the sheriff himself was devote, he saw too much in his line of work to readily accept anyone claiming to be a prophet of God, like the pastor had told Francine he was, especially if the so called prophet told folks things contrary to scripture. People were gullible, he knew. No woman was put on earth to be used by any man, let alone a man supposedly of God.

Francine had been the perfect victim to someone like the so-called prophet, pastor, Hansen could tell that, too, from her diary. She had low self-esteem, felt unloved, eagerly awaited attention from a man, any man. Kids at school ridiculed her because of the poverty she lived in, her drunken father, and her with her amply endowed breasts. Yep, he thought, she was an accident waiting to happen. He sighed, thinking of the outcome. It was unfair.

The more he saw in his line of work, the more he knew that the book of Revelation was true, especially about Satan waiting to steal the little children. It was like he waited for women in the delivery room, kneeled at the foot of the their bed in the doctor's position, holding a catcher's mitt awaiting the child to come forth from the womb so he could snatch it away from the will of God. It seemed to be getting worse, too, not better. Every time he thought of Shannon Thompson, he knew it was worse. What kind of man could do such a thing?

The sheriff dwelled on these things as he and his men worked gingerly, going through Francine's meager belongings.

They found a note to her friend Sharon Fry filled with hope. Francine thought the pastor would leave his wife for her. Hansen shook his head at the sadness of it. Maybe she threatened to tell his wife they were having an affair. A clear motive for murder, or maybe she threatened to tell the church elders that they were lovers. That too could be a motive for murder, but the sheriff didn't really think the church elders would take her seriously. After all, she did come from the Hanson family and nobody in Rutledge or Willow River thought too highly of them. They were poor, white trash with a drunk for a father. Yep, that threat wouldn't have been too serious, he decided as he continued to probe the residence for more evidence.

Still, he didn't want to get too set on the idea that the pastor was the killer. He wanted to keep an open mind and had to work at it, and as he did so, the crime techs methodically worked the room searching for trace evidence, taking away anything that might remotely lead to her killer.

In the living room, Mr. and Mrs. Hanson huddled together on the couch too grieved by the loss of Francine to think clearly. Dennis and Sam sat there too, waiting for the police to finish. Neighbors had already begun to bring gifts and condolences. Food piled up in the kitchen as people heard the news and worked to do something for the grieving family.

Most of Rutledge, population 350, knew the Hansons, although many of the women couldn't say they had ever invited them into their homes to visit. They didn't see them at church much, either, except for Francine. Many of women of the church thought the girl foolish, slovenly about her appearance, and addle brained, but smart enough to go to church, so they would give her the benefit of the doubt. No one, even those that actively disliked Francine had wished her dead. And they certainly hadn't wished any evil to befall little Shannon Thompson.

Instead of pulling the village apart, the horrors that the townspeople faced drew them together in support of everyone, including the Hansons. Even the Spurs were coming under the caring wings of the townspeople. No one wanted to see anything bad happen to any one of the young girls, and since there were two young girls now in the Spur's home, the townspeople kept them in their prayers daily.

When some of the townswomen showed up at the café after hearing of Francine's death, Mrs. Spur was more than surprised. They told her how they thought her son Sam was doing a fine thing by staying with the Hanson family, offering support while police ransacked the house looking for evidence.

Mr. Spur hid himself in the kitchen when the women came in, and smiled as he listened to them compliment his wife about their son, feeling a sense of pride in the boy, pride he had never felt before. Of course, his opinion of Sam hadn't changed, but if the kid wore his name, he might as well do something worthwhile. Sam owed it to him for taking care of him all these years.

As the day turned to dusk, the streets of Rutledge went quiet, even though the town had many children, none played in the park, or rode their bikes, or went swimming at Willow River Lake. Even Willow River was quiet taking what was happening with their neighbors seriously and praying that young girls in their town wouldn't end up as bodies along the highway. Doors in both towns were kept locked. People pulled their shutters closed tight at night, for fear some unknown stranger would creep through a window, and into their homes while they slept. No one believed that a killer walked among them. It had to be a stranger. No one they knew could do such a thing.

As the day wore on at the Hanson house, Dennis found that if he was to keep his father from totally falling to pieces, he was going to have to go to the liquor store, and get the man a pint of something. When the clerk wouldn't sell Dennis anything because he was underage, the storeowner quietly paid for a pint of whiskey, and slipped it to Dennis outside. He knew Dennis never drank, but that the old man probably needed a drink pretty badly by then. He hadn't seen the old man all day, and he was usually the first one there in the morning, beating the clerk, nine out of ten times. The man was an alcoholic. They couldn't just give up the booze because it was a bad time. It was always a bad time for an alcoholic. Besides, he had heard that an alcoholic could die from with-drawl. He didn't want Hanson to die. Hell, half the time it was Hanson's money that kept him afloat! Nope, he'd give the man the booze. Might do it tomorrow and the next day, too, maybe even send him a case. Hanson's money had seen him through some rough times over the years, so now if it was payback time, so be it.

No sooner, than Dennis came in the door at home, the old man was on him pleading for the bottle. After Dennis gave it to him, he slipped into the bathroom and took a long draw. Immediately his body went into relief and the jitters that had threatened to turn into something worse left him. He went back into the living room, and sat back down next to his wife.

She knew what he was doing, could smell the liquor on his breath, and wished with all her heart that she could stand the taste of booze herself so she could drown herself, and not have to think of Francine or what had happened to her. She loved her daughter, but knew she was wholly inadequate when it came to being a mother. Francine had watched her mother take all her father had dished out over the years, and she knew Francine didn't respect her because of it. When it had been her time to get married and bear children, she was taught that you stuck by your husband regardless, which is what she did, and she'd be damned if anyone was going to make her feel bad about it. Besides, she loved the man, and he loved her. He couldn't help that his body went into such horrors when he tried to give up booze, so much so that he always went back to drinking. She saw him once in the throws of the DT's and it wasn't pretty. Still, Francine was part of her heart, too, a big part, and the sorrow she felt at her loss was incomprehensible to her; it was just too big.

Dennis, too, suffered from the loss of Francine, and was glad that the responsibilities of the moment were on him. He didn't know what he would do if he hadn't had anything to do. He went to the garage and closed it up with a sign that said, closed until further notice. He knew most folks would understand that that meant until after Francine's funeral. As he watched his folks try to deal with everything and take it all in, he knew, too, that he'd be the one to bear the burden of shouldering the responsibility for it all, right down to the funeral arrangements.

He also tried to keep his mind from attacking him. Why hadn't he chased Francine down when he saw her standing outside by that car, to make her come back in the house? At least he would have tried to stop her from leaving! He saw her outside! Why? Why? Why? He anguished over the question all day. He was glad Sam was there and a diversion, for Sam helped him take his mind off of Francine, and what he had seen her doing the night before. But Sam couldn't stay forever and when he left that evening at 7:15 p.m., the thought of facing the night alone almost brought Dennis to the point of taking one of the many bottles of booze that the liquor storeowner had sent to the house, and drinking himself into oblivion. If it worked for the old man, why wouldn't it work for him? He couldn't do it. He had seen how much damage liquor had cost his family, and he just couldn't bring himself to take even a sip of the whiskey that so generously took up space in the kitchen.

When his parents went to bed, and he stood alone on the back porch looking out at the starless night, Dennis' thoughts moved on to revenge. He felt that if he could somehow avenge Francine's death, perhaps his own guilt would subside.

At Mrs. Conway's, as Renee watched Mrs. Conway leave the apartment to go across the street to the restaurant, even though she felt somewhat better, inside a panic arose as the old woman hobbled out the door. She didn't want to be alone! Holly couldn't protect her from anything! What if the pastor somehow knew they were alone and came over there. How would anyone see him if he came in the back door? She froze to the chair with her fork perched ready to take a bite of pancake, while maple syrup dripped off the food onto her hand and down her arm.

"Hey, wake up! You're getting all syrupy!" Holly exclaimed.

"Oh. Sorry. I was watching Mrs. Conway, got lost in thought."

"Hey, Holly, what are we going to do if the pastor shows up here and we're all alone? I'm scared."

"Yeah, I am too, but look," Holly pulled out a steak knife from under the table, which Renee figured she must have had hidden in her lap.

"Hey! Where did you get that?"

"I snuck it last night after Mrs. Conway went to bed. Boy, she sure doesn't sleep much! It wasn't easy. And guess what? Sam spent last night on the porch right outside our bedroom window! He was watching over us! Isn't that great?"

"Sure it's great, but is he going to be able to fight off whoever it was that killed Shannon?"

"I've be wondering about that myself, that's why we've got to make a plan, some kind of protection plan . . . in case something happens." As they studied their dilemma, neither girl had heard yet of Francine's death.

"If he comes in the back door," Renee said, "we'll beat feet for the front door. We should head for a place that has a lot of people, like the restaurant."

"Yeah that's a good idea, but remember my dad? He was kissing up to the pastor last night and look what happened to us. Around him may not be the safest place to be."

"What about Sam and his friends? We could tag along with them, if they'd let us. I mean there are six of them. One attacker couldn't fight off six of them and us too!"

"But you know how Sam is, Renee. He isn't going to want us tagging along with him anywhere. Neither are his friends. We're just going to have to rely on one another. Mrs. Conway will help some, but she's so old, there isn't much she can do."

"Okay, then. If he comes in the back door, we should still run for the front door. If we stick together, we'll have a better chance. Maybe we could make it to the Thompsons. They'll take us in, especially if they know someone is after us. What do ya' think?"

"I think that's a very good idea. Kathy doesn't like the pastor either, and neither does her dad. Yeah, that should work."

"Do you think we should tell Mrs. Conway of our plan?" Renee wanted a back up plan. Whoever killed Shannon had to be smarter than they were, and he was surely a whole lot meaner than they could imagine.

"Yeah, I think we should. Maybe we should tell Sam, too . . . just in case. He'll know to come looking for us there, at least."

"Okay, it's settled." With that, the girls entwined their pinky fingers and made a pledge to rehearse their escape plan, and remember just what to do if faced with either the killer of Shannon, or the pastor. They would not allow themselves to be alone in his presence.

After breakfast, they cleared the table and washed the dishes. Renee washed while Holly wiped, quietly working when Renee cleared her throat and said, "Holly, if I tell you something will you promise never to tell anyone, especially my parents or Sam?"

"Yeah, sure," Holly grew uneasy.

"The pastor, yesterday, he put his fingers on my private parts."

Holly threw down her dishtowel, and turned to face Renee who was facing her. Her mouth hung open. She said, "He did the same thing to me . . . on the Ferris wheel! The bastard." She didn't shout or scream when she called him a bastard, which was twice as chilling to Renee.

"God, I'm glad I threw up on him!"

"Me too! That was a sight!" They laughed at that remembrance while going back to washing and wiping the dishes. Both were relieved to have aired what had happened to them. After they finished sweeping the floors and straightening up their bedroom, they heard the front door open and both, apprehensive, ran into the kitchen to see who was entering the house. They prepared for their flight to the Thompsons, but relief washed over them as Mrs. Conway came into the apartment with Sam at her heels.

"Come on, you two. Come sit down at the table. We've got something to tell you."

Mrs. Conway was so sober, as was Sam, that fear washed over them both.

With everyone seated, Sam blurted out, "Some bastard killed Francine Hanson last night. You know . . . Dennis' sister?"

The girls weren't sure they heard correctly, "What?" they said in unison.

"Francine Hanson was killed last night, just like Shannon Thompson." Sam said again.

This time the horror of Sam's words took root. "No!" again, in unison.

"Afraid so," Sam said wishing he could have spared them the truth. "That means you two are going to have to be real careful from now on. So should Kathy and Judy; you make sure you tell them that when you go over there with Mrs. Conway. I've got to go back over to Dennis' for now, but I'll be here tonight keeping watch. Mom said you two can stay with Mrs. Conway since she and dad have to work so much. She said it would be safer that way. Just don't go off by yourselves anywhere."

The girls, who had not been given any time to deal with their grief over Shannon, and after they had faced an enormous ordeal themselves the night before, didn't take the news of Francine's murder well. It wasn't so much that they knew or cared about Francine too much, but she was a kid, like they were, and she was Dennis' sister, Dennis, Sam's best friend; the grievous amount of stress the two had faced in just two days was almost too much to bear. Each girl burst into tears, and wept there at the round claw footed table in Mrs. Conway's kitchen, so hard that the old woman had to bring them Kleenex, and hug them to get them to stop sobbing. Finally, they ran into the bedroom they shared in her apartment and threw themselves on the bed, weeping uncontrollably. It was early afternoon before either of them emerged once again. Both had cried themselves to sleep. They woke up puffy eyed and groggy. They found Mrs. Conway on the back porch quietly rocking in her rocking chair.

"You two been through a lot in the last couple of days. Come . . . sit down beside me. Sit quietly for a little while. Let the pretty afternoon sooth you."

Holly wondered how the day could be so beautiful when two young women, one, the sister to her very good friend, were dead, murdered by some monster that might now be roaming the streets of the tiny village. How could it be?

Renee wished for the first time in her life that her parents would show up unexpectedly, and take her home, although she wasn't going to say anything to Holly about it. Besides, how could she leave Holly now? They had to stick together. She knew that if her folks had any inkling that something like this was going on in Rutledge, they'd come get her so fast her head would spin. No, she had to keep quiet about this to them, had to stay and help Holly.

As all this was happening in Rutledge, reporters in Willow River had gotten wind of the story and were awaiting a press conference with Pine County Sheriff Ernie Hansen. It was a hot story. After the first blip on Shannon Thompson's murder had hit the AP newswires, the big papers of Minneapolis/St. Paul also made plans to send reporters and photographers to Rutledge.

Once the news of Francine Hanson's murder got out, they'd swarm all over the area seeking out the story. Not much was known about serial killing or killers in the 1960s. As such, the idea that in all probability it was happening in a small rural area was a major news story. Willow River's small newspaper first released the story of Shannon only the day before and already the locusts were swarming to descend on Rutledge, while the girls sat on the back porch with Mrs. Conway watching Sugarplum eat contentedly in the field. It was a calm, balmy afternoon, without a cloud in the sky.

"Storms a comin'" Mrs. Conway said as she rocked and looked out at

Sugarplum. "Yep, and it's gonna' be a big one."

Chapter Twenty-One

As Saturday afternoon wore on, the temperature rose, but the wind did not. It was still, muggy and oppressive, seemingly without air as people slowly made their way to, and fro carrying out their daily lives.

At the Fry household, Sharon, Francine's best friend, learned of Francine's death shortly after four p.m. She passed through the living room where her mother sat watching the early news broadcast out of the Twin Cities, while taking a break from a grueling day of housework. Saturday was laundry day and Sharon's mom liked things just so, so the clothes where hung outside to dry while others were put into the wringer washer to be made clean. The Fry family wasn't wealthy enough to afford an automatic washing machine such as the Thompsons boasted, but Mrs. Fry never let things like what others had disturb her. She had heard about the Thompson's new appliances at various committee meetings from Mrs. Thompson herself, but the woman's bragging never impressed her. She was content in her life with her husband and child and circumstances, so that nothing anyone else did or said disturbed her much. She was without envy or jealousy at others' superficial blessings.

Since Shannon's premature death, however, she was disturbed and had taken to watching the news as much as possible, all of which rattled her quiet, confident manner. Then when her husband came home early Saturday afternoon and told her about Francine's death, well, that was almost too much. Francine had spent so much time at their house she felt almost as if she were her daughter. Oh, she knew of Francine's misguided behavior, and had tried to teach her how to live wholesomely, but Francine was so hungry for love, she couldn't seem to resist any man's attentions. Mrs. Fry loved her in spite of that, understood why she behaved as she did, and always tried to show the girl she was worth more than the girl herself thought she was.

Mrs. Fry was also very concerned how her own daughter Sharon would take the news of Francine's death.

As Sharon passed by the couch, the newscaster said, "this morning, Pine County Sheriff, Ernie Hansen told reporters that a deputy discovered the body of a seventeen-year-old girl, who has yet to be identified, alongside Highway 61, which runs north and south through the small town of Rutledge. Linemen, who had been working on overhead wires near where young Shannon Thompson's body had been found only days before, found the body, just north of that city a half mile, seeing something odd in the ditch. Hansen reported that both bodies had been placed in exactly the same posture, so he surmised that the same perpetrator committed both murders. The sheriff's department does not have a suspect in this case. We'll keep you updated when more on the events unfolding in Rutledge come to light.

Sharon froze mid-step at the news; her mother, who was about to take a sip of ice tea, froze and looked up at her daughter. She hadn't heard the girl come into the room. It was as if time had stopped. Just then, Mr. Fry walked into the house.

"I think you need to know something, Sharon, that your mother and I learned earlier today. Here, sit down on the couch." She did, next to her mother. Her father went on, "The body they found this morning—it was Francine, dear."

Mrs. Fry put her arm around her daughter's shoulders immediately with the news, embracing her as the teenager began to sob. Mr. Fry sat down opposite his wife and held Sharon, too, trying to take away some of the pain.

Sharon wailed; through her sobs she asked "why." Why was Francine dead? Her mother rocked her as if she were once again the tiny baby she brought home from the hospital seventeen years prior.

Mr. Fry was at a loss for words. He said, "What in God's name is going on?"

One-hundred miles away, as the Fry family came to grips with the news of Francine's death, the Good family, visiting their daughter Diane and her husband Ralph in Bloomington, watched the same newscast.

"Oh my God!" Mrs. Good stood up forgetting all else and insisting that the family leave immediately and rescue Renee from Rutledge before anything could happen to her.

As she fussed and fumed about Renee in Rutledge with a killer, the weather portion of the news came on, but she didn't hear what the weatherman said. He was predicting severe weather all up and down the line that Highway 61 traversed. Not one of the Good family members heard him.

Mr. Good, and Mike, too, had been watching the newscast and were as alarmed for Renee as Mrs. Good. While the youngest children did not grasp what was going on, Diane hurriedly packed her family's bags. She, too, was frightened for Renee. The Good family started for the front door to leave just as the Bloomington air raid siren started blasting. Diane, with her husband Ralph, led the group to the door standing outside as the air raid sirens began wailing.

Everyone stood at the front door wondering what was going on. All they saw were the greenish yellow skies with utter like swells protruding from their bellies. The air was unnaturally still, hot and humid. As they stood there, the air started to move, slightly at first then in great gusts as the clouds started swirling around them.

"Oh my God!" Diane said.

Ralph yelled simultaneously, "Everyone inside! Tornado! Hurry up!" He could barely make himself heard as the air roared around them. They grabbed the youngest children in their arms, and hurried back inside the house and downstairs into the basement where Ralph turned on the transistor radio to the weather channel.

The storm, the weather caster said, was more sever than they feared and tornado watches were posted for all around the Twin Cities area. He warned that if an air siren bellowed, anyone within ear shoot needed to get inside and downstairs to their basement to take cover as it meant a tornado had been sighted in the area.

While they listened to the newscaster, the Good's car was being lifted up and carried about fifteen miles away where it landed in a farmer's field killing two dairy cattle.

The severe weather pattern was right in line for Rutledge. As the Goods rushed to the basement in Bloomington, in Rutledge, Sharon got hold of herself insisting she go to the church to pray for Francine. No one in Rutledge was paying attention to the weather forecasters, either.

Sharon would stop by Francine's house and pay her respects to the Hanson household as well. Mrs. Fry wanted her to wait so she could prepare a dish for Sharon to take to the Hanson's, but Sharon wanted to get to the church. "Oh, go ahead dear. I'll get this ready and take it over to Mrs. Hanson myself. I can pick you up over there if you like. I'll be a couple of hours yet so you'll have plenty of time?"

"That sounds good, Mom. I really want to get to the church. I'll catch up with you at the Hansons." With that Sharon ran out the back door fearing that her mother would have second thoughts and call her back in, considering everything that had happened in the past two days. She did not, however. Still resting in her false sense of security, it did not register in Mrs. Fry's mind, that there was a killer loose somewhere among them, someone who killed young girls—like Sharon.

As Sharon got to the small church, which resembled a country chapel, she slipped in through the front door, which rarely, if ever, was locked. The church was empty. She, out of habit, went to the pew on the north side of the church and sat where she sat every Sunday. She got down and started praying for Francine and Shannon. She was so involved in her prayers she didn't hear anyone come in.

"Hello Sharon." A melodious voice said.

Sharon gasped and jumped at the sound of her name. When she looked up, she saw the pastor sitting within a few feet of her.

The hairs on the back of her neck stood up. She felt the tingle of fear rush down her spine. "Hello Pastor," she said meekly as she slowly got up from her kneeling position flexing her muscles as she moved. "I didn't know you were here. I hope I haven't disturbed you." She felt chilled to the bone even though the temperature inside was ninety degrees and climbing with not a lick of wind to ease the burden of the sweltering heat.

"Oh, Dear, you aren't bothering me. I didn't even know you were here. You know the church is always open to the devout," as he spoke, the pastor inched imperceptibly closer.

Every corpuscle in Sharon's body screamed at her to get out of there. She moved to the end of the pew quietly. He saw and countered her movement by standing and moving to the other end of the pew, effectively cutting off any means of escape through the front door. It was if the two were playing Chess with their bodies.

Since Sharon had attended this same little church all her life, she knew every nick and cranny of it, and she also knew there was a side door right behind her, a door that was also rarely locked. She prayed as hard as she could that when she made her rush for freedom, the door would be open and remembered the scripture that said, "No weapon formed against me shall prosper." And, "Yeah, though I pass through the valley of the shadow of death, I will fear no evil." And, "If God be for me, who can be against me?"

It was as if the pastor read her mind, "You know dear. I locked that side door before I came in here," he said smiling sweetly at her.

Sharon fought down her fear. Then, from a place she didn't know she had, a calm overcame her, and all fear washed away. She felt peace and strength. She confidently started for the front door saying, "Well, thank you Pastor for letting me use the church. I have to go now." To her great surprise, the pastor did not try to block her path.

When she got outside, however, that same sense of urgency to get away from the pastor and the church overcame her, and she lit out of the churchyard running as fast as she could to the Hanson house, which was right next door. She sighed with relief when Sam answered the door to her frantic pounding.

"Hey Sharon, what's wrong? You look like you've seen a ghost!" Sam was alarmed after taking a good look at Sharon, Francine's unflappable friend. He didn't know her except to see her with Francine around town, but she always looked like she was very self-possessed. Standing in front of him now, she was as white as a sheet.

Sharon immediately rejected the idea that she could tell Sam Spur about her encounter with the pastor, how her hair had stood on end as he moved in toward her. She didn't know Sam very well other than to see him around town with Dennis. Dennis was another matter, altogether; they had grown up together attending the same schools since kindergarten.

Sharon came into the Hanson house, and paid her respects to Mr. and Mrs. Hanson before taking Dennis aside to tell him everything that had gone on in the church. Dennis felt a chill crawl up his spine at what she said, but didn't tell her that he saw Francine with the pastor the night before. Sharon also told him that her mother was coming over later, but she wanted to go home now rather than wait for her mother to get there. She wanted to get as much distance as she could away from the pastor. She still felt uneasy being in such close proximity to him.

Sam walked Sharon home because Dennis felt he couldn't leave his parents alone.

When she came into the house with Sam Spur, Mr. Fry could tell she was frightened. Her skin was a ghostly white. Sharon couldn't bring herself to tell him what had happened in the church. Sam had to, as Dennis had told him everything. Mr. Fry did not like it. He didn't like the fact that his wife was now next door to the church at the Hansons. He reasoned she would be okay. No grown woman had been hurt. He would make sure she knew of the incident in the church with the pastor and their daughter, however. He'd tell her when they went to bed. They would figure out what, if anything, to do about it.

Before he left Sharon's house, Sam made sure her father understood just how dangerous it was to let any young girl go off by herself until the killer was caught, even to church. What he did not tell Mr. Fry were his suspicions that the church was especially dangerous.

Mr. Fry had never met Sam until that day, but by the time he left, Fry liked him. "How old are you, son," he asked as he walked Sam to the back door.

"Fifteen, sir," Sam said as he headed down the gravel driveway toward Main Street.

Mr. Fry shook his head and thought, seems a lot older than that, as he went back inside praying that his wife would get back and soon. He didn't like the looks of the sky.

As he walked back to Dennis' house, Sam thought about everything that had happened in the past few days. It seemed surreal. How could someone he knew be murdered, two people he knew—his sister's friend—now his friend's sister? None of it made any sense. It was as if he were in a nightmare from which he couldn't awake.

At the Conway residence, Renee and Holly spent the afternoon with Sugarplum. No one ventured over to the Thompson house. Mrs. Conway said the air was too thick for her to be walking anywhere, besides, a storm, a big storm, was coming, she could feel it in her bones and she wanted to be close to the basement.

The one thing in the world that frightened Mrs. Conway was a tornado, and she knew it was tornado weather without ever turning her television set on or listening to the radio for a weather report. Newscasters were warning of an impending storm, and talking about Rutledge and the two murder investigations there, but she never heard them.

Mrs. Conway wouldn't have listened to newscasters even if she had turned on the TV. She didn't really need to hear what they had to say. She already knew about the murders, and as for the storm, she could tell by the wind, the humidity and her aching legs that it was approaching. She also knew that it wouldn't be there that afternoon, but would hit sometime in the wee hours of the morning. She was glad of that because the longer it stayed away, the more chance there was that it might pass over all together, but she simply couldn't afford to take any chances. It wasn't as if she could move very fast. She was well aware of the intense damage a storm like the one that was coming could do to her if she didn't prepare.

A tornado had killed her husband so many years before she couldn't quite remember the date anymore. She remembered the destruction, however, in horrible detail. Her husband had been out in the fields plowing when that storm came out of nowhere, seemed like. It lifted him and the tractor up into it, and deposited them somewhere on the other side of the county. He had to be identified by his dental work, the storm had battered him about so badly, he wasn't recognizable any other way.

It was bad enough that it had stolen her husband, but it also hit their house and left it in ruins. If she hadn't run for the basement when she saw it for the first time as it was hurling through their fields, no telling what would have happened to her. Her husband dead, her house fit for nothing; the tornado left deep and abiding scars, the kind that never really healed.

Now she stayed close to home whenever she felt bad weather on the horizon, thanking God for her aching joints, which alerted her to potentially dangerous storms. At 111 years of age, her running days were over; she had to stay close to home.

It was no different now that so many other horrible things were going on inside the village. So instead of taking the girls over to the Thompsons, Mrs. Conway let them groom and ride Sugarplum on their own while she sat rocking in her rocking chair on the back porch watching them. The girls were like gazelles running and frolicking with the horse in the field. God worked through Sugarplum His healing on the girls as they doted on the big racehorse in the field, she could see as she rocked. The girls were young enough and fast enough that they could make a swift dash for the basement if a storm was coming, and she'd call to them in plenty of time.

Tomorrow, being Sunday, she expected to see the Thompsons in church, even though she rarely attended services, so she'd pay her respects then. Desperate times call for desperate measures, she thought, so she'd step foot into the little church once more because there was a great need for it now. A great need for healing for the whole town.

If the Holy Spirit led her to say a thing or two about the pastor in church, she'd do that too. She would keep her mouth shut until the Holy Spirit guided her, spoke out of her mouth. Just as Second Corinthians 11:12-15 states: But what I do, I will continue to do, that I may cut off the opportunity from those who desire an opportunity to be regarded just as we are in the things of which they boast.

For such are false apostles, deceitful workers, transforming themselves into apostles of Christ.

And no wonder! For Satan himself transforms himself into an angel of light.

Therefore it is no great thing if his ministers also transform themselves into ministers of righteousness, whose end will be according to their works. (NKJV)

Nope, can't hide from God, she thought as she rocked her chair back, stood up, and took another look at the sky. She sat back down, spit off the porch railing, and once again started rocking her chair to the beat of an inner rhythm as she looked out across the yard at the girls in the field riding Sugarplum in the afternoon sun. It was a blissful, calm scene right out of a Norman Rockwell painting, a contradiction in terms considering the events of the past few days. No matter, she thought, this too shall pass. If the girls get an afternoon reprieve, so be it.

Her eyes glazed over and her mind filled with images of the past removing from her sight the things physically in front of her and replacing them with inner visions. She couldn't help but remember her husband every time the weather got bad. She never fully understood how God could take such a lovely person off the face of the earth at such a young age then let her continue on without the man of her heart for another eighty, or so years. Sometimes, all she wanted was to go to her Maker so she could be with her husband once more. She didn't understand why He wouldn't let her go. As she rocked it came to her that this was why she was still here. She was here to protect the children as best she could and teach them some things about Him before she could go to her final rest. She sighed with happiness knowing that soon it would be her time.

She came out of her reverie when she heard, "Hey, Mrs. Conway, are you okay?" It was Sam back from Dennis' at 7:30 p.m. on the dot. When she realized the time, she looked out into the field and panicked seeing that the girls weren't there.

"It's okay, Mrs. Conway," Sam said when he saw the concern on her face, "They're inside cooking dinner."

"Cooking?"

"Yeah, you fell asleep, so they decided to do something nice for you. That okay?"

"Asleep! When did I fall asleep?" She didn't wait for an answer, "and of course it's okay if they cook! But what on earth can they be cooking?"

"Come on in and find out. I think you'll like it." Sam took her arm and helped her inside.

With Mrs. Spur's cooking instructions given over the phone, the girls had made sloppy Joes with a fresh tossed salad and Jell-o for desert. They added hot spices to the sloppy Joes and hoped the dish wouldn't be too hot for Mrs. Conway. They needn't have worried. She loved spicy food, although she didn't eat a lot of it anymore, saving it for a treat every now and again.

When they finished eating and washed, dried and put away the dishes everyone sat back down at the kitchen table. Sam told them everything he had learned at Dennis' earlier in the day. Mrs. Conway told them of the storm that was coming, that would probably reach them by that evening, so they all stayed up and watched the late news, confirming her report.

They learned then that television crews were on their way to Rutledge when a tornado had hit and had taken out part of Highway 61 leaving the crews stranded about forty-five miles from town. The weather had calmed since, and no tornadoes were expected to strike again overnight, but the roads were littered with debris and closed due to downed power lines. The newscaster said that they wouldn't be opened until sometime the following day.

Chapter Twenty-Two

A sweltering, humid day Sunday, July 6, but even so, everyone in the tiny village of Rutledge headed off to its tiny Protestant church, an unprecedented event. The only church in town, it had served the community for over 100 years even as its congregation grew smaller, and smaller, and smaller, thanks, in part, to neighboring farms loosing their battles with nature and the world system of operations. This new trend began forcing families to leave their farms, which, in turn, began the onset of corporate farming practices.

Schools began to shrink forcing consolidation as rural folks left for larger metropolises. This saw grocery stores, clinics, an array of other businesses, even churches, being hit hard financially.

Many churches had to close their doors as their congregations dwindled, and the tithes and offerings that supported them trickled away, which was one of the reasons the Thompson family had been such a boon to the Rutledge church. Not only were the Thompsons generous with their tithes and offerings, but they paid for the pastor to be there as well, a gift to the community.

The pastor did not have to rely on tithes for support. It was a godsend, most of the congregation thought, as they didn't believe in tithing anyway. More to the point, they had very little to tithe on.

That is how Pastor Joseph Wilson stood in front of his parishioners that hot July 6, 1963 morning with the overhead fans blowing softly throughout the small room not alleviating anyone's discomfort. This unprecedented day even had Mrs. Conway sitting along a back pew close to the door with the Spur and Hanson children. The Fry family sat next to them with Sharon sitting between Sam and Dennis. Renee and Holly watched for Judy and Kathy and waved to the girls as they came in, and sat in the front row with their parents. The girls had not had time to talk since the day after Shannon was murdered. They hoped they would be able to after church.

Wilson stood at the front of the congregation smugly looking on as the Thompson family walked in. Mrs. Conway watched him closely. Since most of the town was afraid of her, she wasn't bothered by well-wishers, which allowed her the freedom to study whomever she choose, which of course for her meant the pastor, someone she distrusted immensely.

As the congregation moved about the church welcoming one another,

Mrs. Conway was conspicuously left out, as were the Spur children because they sat with her. Most town folks were beginning to accept the Spur family, however. A number of women decided they would go to the restaurant to warn the mother and father about Mrs. Conway, and to invite them to church. Perhaps they simply didn't know that the old woman was strange.

Much whispering concerning the Thompsons swept through the pews as well. Mrs. Thompson was decidedly not herself, and though most of the women and men felt a great deal of sympathy for the couple at the loss of their child, they did not have much sympathy for her in general. It was Mrs. Thompson who always bragged about her family, showing off all her wonderful possessions, and they paid the pastor's salary, now didn't they? If they were wealthy enough for all that, then they really didn't deserve much sympathy. They could buy away their troubles, take a cruise or something to go away and forget.

And so what if Mrs. Thompson hadn't seen fit to apply make-up or go to the beauty parlor to have her hair done as she always had in the past, since before she always flaunted her affluence throughout town, and acted like she was better than everyone else? Why should they ply her with sympathy? She wouldn't want it from those so beneath her, many decided. Most of the townswomen were in complete agreement on that.

The Hansons were another matter, altogether. They had to stay in the same house, do the same things every day that they did when Francine was alive, and go on as best they could. They couldn't escape their circumstances, and they never acted like they were better than anyone else.

Though these same women had nothing but good to say about Francine after her death, they hadn't said too many nice things about her when she was alive. Everybody knew Francine couldn't keep her pants on. Really, the girl had such a sex drive, she was an embarrassment to everyone at church. But now that she was dead, well that was different. In their hearts, however, most parishioners "knew" Francine had gotten what she deserved.

And being an acute judge of character, Pastor Wilson knew exactly how the town was treating Mrs. Thompson in her hour of need, and he couldn't have asked for a better result. He relished the snide remarks he heard as he passed through the congregation welcoming everyone, and eyeing the children as they sat in the pews with their parents. He knew just which ones were vulnerable and how he could insinuate himself into their lives. People were so easy to manipulate it wasn't even much of a challenge for him anymore.

He wanted a challenge. Shannon, who he thought would be, hadn't been much of one, as it turned out. Her parents had schooled her about being obedient to adults in authority, so it was relatively easy for him to coax her into letting him in the house, even when she didn't like him. And she didn't like him; he knew that, that's why he chose her.

Francine had been another situation all together. He enjoyed her vulnerability for some time before she died. It was too bad she had seen him with Shannon. It was not smart for her to tell him so, either. Tsk, tsk, tsk, he thought as he eyed the other young girls in church. He erred with

Shannon but he'd be much more careful now. He had to be. This was just too good a situation to mess up.

The do-gooder Thompson parents were who he enjoyed watching the most. They thought they were really something special, they did. Paying his salary, him being a big-shot lawyer who thought he was so smart! Well, how smart is he now, Wilson wondered as he watched Ralph Thompson from behind, while he listened to Mrs. Gertrude Heppleworth speak words of fear for the town because of what was going on. He listened to the old woman with one ear knowing that she thoroughly enjoyed the excitement the tragedy was causing.

As for Mrs. Heppleworth, she listened to the news just like everyone else in town and knew that newscasters were on their way there at that very moment. Perhaps she'd see herself on TV! Besides, her daughters and grandchildren didn't live anywhere near Rutledge, thank the Lord, she thought, so what did she have to worry about? She never uttered those thoughts to any of her neighbors knowing many of them were terrified for their children.

Pastor Wilson enjoyed seeing people squirm. He remembered the time he took his daughter Gloria's dog Mutt out and shot him then through him over the fence into the field of a neighbor, a man who was always yelling at her, for this, that, or the next thing. He figured she'd blame the neighbor, but somehow she had known that it was he who had killed her dog. He used that incident to his advantage to get her into bed with him that first time, and it worked slicker than anything he had ever tried before. She was scared of him! It was beautiful, but he had to admit he was tired of her. She wasn't a little girl anymore. She was a rebellious, trifling teenager that nothing seemed to scare.

The best days of his life were when he had pastored the country church up near the Canadian border, and they had lived on that little farm just outside of International Falls. It sure was easy to get away with things out in the country. He missed that. Country girls seemed to be so much more sophisticated when it came to sex than city girls, too. Maybe that came from watching all those animals mating or something, it turned them into smoldering cauldrons of fire just waiting for the right man to come along and ignite their flames. He missed that too, and the girls were all so robust, his loins tingled at the thought of the more than one girl he had seduced inside the rectory there. He remembered that as fondly as he remembered pastoring their parents while seducing their children! It was funny. Most parents worried that their darling daughters were going to go too far with the boys they dated—if they only knew! He loved the fact that they didn't, and that he could walk among them superior in the knowledge that he could do anything he wanted and there was nothing they could do about it. Then the parents would invite him to their house for a meal and he'd sit beside all of them, parents and children, at the dinning room table; he enjoyed it so much, he couldn't express it in words.

But that wasn't enough, anymore. He wanted more power. His needs seemed to be growing exponentially. When he killed Shannon, it was better than any sex he had ever had, and he'd had plenty of that! That was what made it easy to get rid of Francine.

His sex drive had almost gotten out of hand with Sharon Fry the day before, however. He almost couldn't control it. He didn't like that. He did not wish to loose control, ever. That was a sure way to get caught and he liked what he was doing too much to give it up.

That is why, as he walked among the pews Sunday, what he was really looking for was his next victim. He had to satisfy his lusts. He stopped short at the thought—why does it have to be a girl? Though this idea had never occurred to him before, he found himself relishing it. Imagine, controlling and over-powering another male? He decided that would be even more gratifying if it were possible. So it was that he left off his well-wishing and climbed up to the podium to stand in front of the congregation.

He had been so lost in thought, he hadn't noticed Mrs. Conway in the back pew.

As he stood there wrapped up in his thoughts of overpowering a young man, and scouting the congregation for his next victim, his eyes fell on Dennis Hanson. Wilson had never noticed the young man before, but felt now that he would be perfect. Strong, it would take effort to subdue him, young, it would take strength to out last him, and an innocent; extreme arousal at thoughts of raping him and forcing himself on Dennis almost overwhelmed Wilson standing there at the podium.

It was when his eyes traveled the length of the pews to fall on Mrs. Conway that a shiver climbed his spine with the effect of cold water being poured on him. He gazed back into that pair of ancient eyes that bore into his soul and trembled. Witch! He thought as she unnervered him with an unrelenting stare.

No, I am not a witch you liar; it's the Holy Spirit! Though she uttered not a sound, he heard her.

"Suffer not a witch to live!" he shouted bringing the congregation to their seats with a start turning all eyes in rapt attention on him, just the way he wanted it. "We know we have a witch in our midst—someone who hides among us. What else could bring such destruction on our young! She sits with us today!" He said pointedly staring at Mrs. Conway so everyone knew whom he was talking about. The congregation grew uneasy with his accusations, the same accusations they hid in their hearts.

Mrs. Conway knew it, too. She stood up, her frail frame shaking, but not due to advanced age, but to righteous rage. "Who do you think you are accusing, you heathen hypocrite," she barely whispered the words but the church had grown so quiet, everyone heard her, gasping at her audacity. "You stand up their pretending to praise God all the while planning on which child you will molest next. Your own daughter! You should be ashamed!"

At this, Gloria, who for the first time in years attended church, turned in her pew to stare at Mrs. Conway, her face drained of color. How does she know? She thought trembling at the horror of her shame. She wouldn't look at her father.

"The witch speaks! Accusing the one sent by God to shepherd the sheep!" Wilson's voice boomed throughout the small room.

"You're no shepherd. You belong to Satan and you always have. Well, your deeds are being brought to the light, and don't you forget it. Those here grieving for their young need to be stoning you for the horror you have brought among them! Laughing to yourself at how gullible they all are. Well, God is not gullible and He is not mocked. Your day is coming. Mark my words, PASTOR," Mrs. Conway mocked him with her tone.

"Stop! I'll hear no more of this! Have you no shame," in the front pew Mrs. Thompson stood staring back at Mrs. Conway screaming at her. "The pastor has been nothing but gracious to this family and to the church. How dare you say he has done something vile, you old crone! Everyone in town knows you've mocked him since the day he arrived. Yet you have the nerve to come into this church, after years of being absent from it, to mock him who has served this whole community, someone we need now in our worst hour! How dare you?"

At this Mr. Thompson stood up and took his wife by the arm. This was the first sign of life he'd seen in her since Shannon's death, and though he didn't agree with what she was saying, he was glad she was among the living once again. He tugged at her arm and whispered in her ear to calm down. He gently placed his hand on her shoulder and reseated her while he remained standing.

"I think this has gone far enough. Mrs. Conway, my wife extends her apologies. Please forgive her. She grieves too hard for Shannon. She is not herself. As for any Sunday service, perhaps we should all go home and pray on our own." Before he finished speaking, Mr. Thompson turned and addressed the pastor.

"Sir, I don't think it wise to accuse our oldest and dearest citizen of witchcraft, either. This is a house of God and no one is convicted of any sin unless two or more members of the congregation accuse them of the same sin, and no one else in this room brings any such accusation against Mrs. Conway. It's Mrs. Conway who has inspired my two daughters, Judy and Kathy, to read the Bible, it wasn't you." He paused here to let that information fall on the elder's ears, for them to realize what he had just said.

Pastor Wilson's face went white with rage at Mr. Thompson's rebuke.

"No, I think perhaps Mrs. Conway was right when she instructed my daughters to pray to God for help. She's been instructing the other children of the town to do the same. Instead of accusing her, we need to be thanking her for the inspiration she has been to them during a most terrible time. And perhaps the rest of us should follow suit, go home, and sit with our families and pray for the well-being of all of them, young and old."

With that, Mr. Thompson took his wife's arm and stood her up. Her eyes shot daggers at him showing everyone she was not happy with him. Kathy and Judy followed their father's lead smiling at everyone as they walked toward the back exit, and making sure Renee and Holly saw them. They smiled at Mrs. Conway too. They were relieved their father had come to the old woman's aid. No one else had.

Discomforted by the outburst between the pastor and Mrs. Conway, then Mr. Thompson, the congregation almost flew out of the pews and out the front doors in a hurry to get away from the little church, and those involved with the argument. Many were slyly espying Mrs. Conway from the corner of their eyes, as well as the pastor, as they scurried out the door wondering what the old woman had meant. Was there really something going on with the pastor and his daughter? Mrs. Conway had made so many remarks like that over the years most townsfolk believed her. She was eerie that way, knew the stuff they hid in their hearts, which is why most folks stayed away from her.

The pastor was an odd one that was for sure, but so was old Mrs. Conway! Everyone in town knew that! Maybe she was a witch, but why or how could a witch get children to read the Bible. No one doubted that Mr. Thompson spoke the truth. His reputation for integrity was solid throughout Rutledge as he repeatedly showed himself to be wise, honest, humble and brilliant in his dealings. As the town was so small, Thompson had had dealings of some kind with everyone in it, even the children as he coached the Little League baseball team, even helped his wife oversee the Brownie camping trips.

Everyone in town decided that day that they too should pray for their families, and though most didn't really believe that God still worked miracles or protected them in their daily lives, it couldn't hurt to pray for protection. If Ralph Thompson were going to do it, they would do it too, and if old lady Conway prompted him to pray, then she had to be okay too, didn't she?

The pastor seethed as he made his way out the door behind the rectory, his private entrance. Mrs. Conway had ruined his shinning moment. He wanted her out of the way so badly he could taste it, like vile bile in his mouth.

Mrs. Conway stayed in the back pew of the church as everyone else fled. Sam, Dennis, Renee, Holly, Sharon and her parents stayed glued to her side. Sam was so alarmed, he thought someone might try and attack her.

Before Mrs. Conway could make her way out of the church, one from the congregation called the sheriff and told him what had happened there that day. Sheriff Hansen was very interested, noting to himself that he'd be paying the old woman a visit. He admitted to himself that sometimes she unnerved him too, but what could he do.

His pastor once told him he thought the old woman was a prophet. Most times prophets, real prophets, didn't tell people what they wanted to hear. Got stoned to death in biblical times, too, people got so upset with them. Sheriff Hansen had never met a real live prophet, that he knew of anyway, didn't even know if they were real, but, he decided he'd approach that possibility with an open mind. Perhaps his pastor would go with him, pick up the biblical slack, so to speak, that he had in his life, let him know if she was the real deal, cause he didn't know how he would be able to tell.

Besides, if she could give him a lead, it was worth the effort. A lead was a lead, and he didn't have any to be able to afford to disregard one, even if on the surface it might seem flighty.

While the sheriff considered how to approach Mrs. Conway, Sam and Dennis were helping her down the church steps. Mr. Fry, too, was trying to help. He ran ahead of the boys and brought his car around to give the group rides home. Mrs. Fry, however, had other ideas. She invited them all to their house for Sunday dinner. She had already started a big pot roast and there would be more than enough for everyone. She would not take "no" for an answer.

Mrs. Conway couldn't remember the last time anyone in town had ever invited her for a meal. She surely didn't expect anyone to after the day's disruption of church services. She never liked to think about it, but she had been lonely for adult company for a long, long time, and being invited out meant a great deal to her.

None of the children protested. Dennis and Sharon found they had a lot in common. Very bright, Dennis was often overlooked in school because of his family. Teachers assumed he was slow. They pushed him aside no matter how well he did on a test, or when called on to answer a question they posed. Treated as if he would never amount to anything, no extra effort was ever exerted by any teacher to encourage him toward intellectual pursuits.

Teachers never showered much attention on Sharon, either, all though she consistently did well with homework and on tests. She too was passed over more often than not when teachers called upon students to answer questions. A quiet, unassuming child, she wore no makeup, didn't flirt with boys, and wore unbecoming clothes to class so as not to draw attention to herself. No adult, other than her parents, showed any interest in encouraging her either, no matter how brilliantly she performed at any given task.

Both knew how the other was treated having attended the same schools together since kindergarten. Dennis and Sharon also shared a connection to Francine, both having loved her deeply regardless of her behavior.

Francine had brought Sharon home with her a million times, but Dennis had always been too busy trying to take care of the household to pay much attention to her. She was so skinny that her presence had been diminished by Francine's robustness.

Everyone could see as they sat at the Fry's dinning room table to eat dinner, that Sharon and Dennis had finally noticed one-another. The level of conversation passing between the two was noticed by Renee and Holly, too. Listening to Dennis, Mr. Fry was particularly impressed with how he had worked so hard to keep his family together.

As Sam sat there listening, the elder Fry impressed him with his loyalty to his friends and family and how attentive he was to Mrs. Conway.

When dinner was over, and the dishes washed and put away, again everyone got into the Fry car to travel to the Hansons. Dennis' folks were happy that someone from town thought to visit, and offer condolences in person, most had sent their children over with some sort of food, but the adults hadn't come.

At home, Gloria Wilson sat quietly in her room abashed at Mrs. Conway's statements in church. How could she know? The girl wondered when she stumbled home to the modest ranch house behind the church. Had anyone guessed what the old lady had meant?

She prayed that no one had noticed her slipping out of the church. She couldn't look at her father. She was too ashamed of him . . . and herself. It must be my fault, she thought, sneaking downstairs into the basement recreation room, and going behind the bar to take a swallow of scotch whiskey she knew her father kept there. If he could rape her, she could drink his liquor, she reasoned as she looked about the room. She wanted a way out.

That was when she heard the back door open, and the sound of her father's footsteps overhead. She could tell from the sound who it was, she had listened intently to it so many times in the past trying to hide from his advances. She didn't know where her mother was, though she too had been in church. She always went to church.

The back door opened once again, and this time Gloria heard the sounds of her mother crossing over the kitchen floor to the stove. She could tell exactly where both parents stood. Her father was opening and closing doors throughout the house, so Gloria guessed he was looking for her. She knew he never looked for her mother. How long before he found her, she wondered as she heard him cross back into the kitchen.

"What did Mrs. Conway mean, Dear?" Gloria heard her mother's soft voice question quietly when her father's footsteps moved closer to the basement door.

"What?" He never really listened to his wife, but for some reason he stopped and turned to hear her this time.

"What did Mrs. Conway mean? 'Your own daughter,'" she said. "'You should be ashamed.' What did she mean Dear?" Mrs. Wilson clutched the sink so hard her knuckles were white. Never had she been so alert, so intent on hearing what her husband had to say.

"She's an old bat who wants me thrown out of the church! She didn't mean a damn thing!" He screamed at his wife for having the audacity of even mentioning Mrs. Conway in HIS HOUSE! HOW DARE SHE! "And who do you think you are that you should bring that old bat's accusations up to me!" He bellowed so loudly that Gloria, for the first time in her young life, was afraid for her mother.

"I'll tell you who I am," Mrs. Wilson said quietly, but with authority. "I'm your wife. Do you remember what that means? Somehow I doubt that you do. Remember me? I'm the one you promised to love, honor and cherish, just like I did you. Remember, you are to love your spouse as Christ loved the church? Do you remember that?" She really didn't want him to answer; she already knew that he didn't love her and that his opinion of her was one of contempt. What he didn't see was that she had gone into the drawer underneath the stove where she retrieved the massive butcher knife her grandmother had left her. The one her grandmother had used when she lived on that isolated farm in central Minnesota and an escaped mental patient had attempted to break into their tiny house. Her grandmother had taken the knife and chased that man out of her yard and off her property when she was no more than five feet tall and weighed all of 100 pounds soaking wet. The six-foot-four-inch tall man ran for his life. Now Mrs. Wilson held the same knife in her hand and let the remembrance of her tiny grandmother's courage soar through her veins.

"And don't think you're going downstairs to look for Gloria," she said quietly as he turned and placed his hand on the basement door. "You are done harming our daughter, Dear, so I advise you to get your hand off that door handle, or I'll remove it for you." Mrs. Wilson spoke quietly, coldly, deadly, bringing the knife in front of her, fondling it as she spoke.

As Wilson had the presence of mind to look back at his wife, he saw something in her he had never seen before, and it caused him to slowly, finger by finger remove his hand from the basement doorknob. He could now see the knife his wife held in her hand, knowing the story connected to it, and how she felt about it. Never in a million years did he expect his mousy little wife to use it on him, but at that moment he was unsure of what she would do. He backed slowly away from the basement door moving imperceptibly toward the back door. He thought it wise to get out of the house for now. She would answer for this outburst later, when her resolve left and he regained the upper hand. He could find a way to dispose of that knife latter, too.

Gloria heard him back away from the basement door toward the kitchen door, and yelled up to her mother, "He's going to make a break for it Mom! Be careful!"

As she yelled out, Wilson bolted for the door and flew out of the house. He jumped into his Cadillac and sped out the driveway spitting gravel as the vehicle's tires spun out on the road.

At the sound of the Cadillac roaring away, Gloria ran up the stairs and bolted the door. She ran into the living room to bolt that door, too, not really taking a close look at her mother as the elder Wilson woman ran about checking the locks on all the windows still brandishing the knife with the eighteen-inch blade.

When Gloria felt secure that the house was locked up tight against her father, she took a long hard look at her mother. She no longer saw the mousy little woman she had always seen before. In front of her stood a tiny, dignified woman who had the countenance of a fearless warrior.

"Your father has keys to both doors, so we're going to have to block them if we want to be safe tonight. When we're done with that, you and I are going to have a long talk."

Gloria was not happy at the sound of having a long talk, but guessed that perhaps the day she had always dreaded was upon her, and she resigned herself to speak the truth, no matter how much it hurt her, her mother, or her father. It was the only way out.

Chapter Twenty-Three

It was late afternoon by the time Mrs. Conway, the Spur children and Renee Good returned to the apartment building. Foreboding clouds hung low in the overcast sky. A strange, green tinge lit up the sky's underbelly while dark gray clouds hovered above. The air was still and quiet, with not so much of a sigh of a breeze wafting through it or a bird singing in the background. The temperature soared in the mid-nineties with humidity reaching 100-percent.

Mrs. Conway gasped for air as she slowly made her way up the sidewalk to the back porch and climbed the steps to sit down in her rocking chair there. The girls helped her, hoping she would be okay. Mrs. Conway was all they had to protect them from the evil that permeated the town. The old woman seemed to have an in with God, whose protection they were all praying for. They had nothing else. No one was able to protect Shannon. No one protected Francine, either. What good was it to have a man around, they wondered. Shannon had her father and Francine had Dennis. They both were murdered.

As Mrs. Conway sat down in the rocker she let out a "wooff," startling the girls.

"Are you okay, Mrs. Conway?" Holly asked.

"Yes, dear, I'm fine. But you know what, I'd really like a cold glass of lemon-aid. Could you get me one . . . with lots of ice?"

"I'd be glad to Ma'am," Holly yelled already inside the kitchen pouring the cold liquid into a tall glass filled with ice.

Sam sat quietly across from Mrs. Conway and Renee. "You know, Dear," she said looking at him. "It's going to be storming hard anytime now. You know where my basement is?" She raised her eyebrows to the question. He nodded his head. "Good. Now, when I tell you, do not question me, give me any back talk, just do as you're told. Do you understand?"

"Yes, but I've never argued with you before. Why do you think I'd argue with you now?" Sam was a bit offended that she would think he wouldn't listen to her. He was crazy about her, although he didn't let on. It wouldn't do for his friends to think he was smitten with an old woman. They'd never let him hear the end of it.

"Don't get your knickers in a twist, there kiddo, it's just that when this storm hits, things are going to start happening fast and furious around here, but they're not for you to undo. It's in the Lord's hands now. We've done all we can do, so we'll stand when the time comes. But, we have to be safe downstairs in the basement to stand. One of us is going to be swept up in the other storm that's coming, but you are not to worry. The Lord is with her. You have to trust now. Can you do that?"

Sam didn't like the sound of that. "Trust! Trust? What the hell am I supposed to trust? My old man beats me; we've got a lunatic in our midst that is murdering my friends, just what the hell am I supposed to trust!" No one was more surprised by his outburst, than Sam.

"God, Dear, God. He's with you even though it doesn't seem like it. He's with you; He's with all of us. He's heard our prayers. The Thompson girls are on their way over here. Why don't you take Renee inside and help Holly bring out six glasses of lemon-aid. The girls won't be here long, their father will be picking them up, but they might enjoy some lemon-aid while they sit here on the back porch and talk to us. They have a lot to say."

Sam gave Mrs. Conway a wary look but did as she asked. He wanted to be alone with Renee anyway, to see how she felt. Sam shut the screen door softly behind him as he entered the kitchen where Holly stood next to the antique claw footed table pouring lemon-aid into tall glasses that were already filled with ice. "Where's Renee?" Sam asked coming into the room.

"She's in the back changing clothes." Holly seemed subdued to Sam.

"You okay?"

"I'm as okay as I know how to be, considering. I miss Shannon."

Sam moved over close to his little sister and hugged her. "Yeah, I miss her too. She was a card."

"I don't know how Kathy can stand it without her?"

"Mrs. Conway said that Kathy and Judy are on their way over here. Maybe you can find out then. Oh, yeah, she said to pour them some lemon-aid, too."

Holly wondered how she could know that. She hadn't called anyone since they'd been back from church and no one had called her. She poured the lemon-aid anyway while Sam walked to the back of the apartment.

He found Renee coming out of the bedroom into the living room. "Your family has been in church about as much as mine. Do you believe what Mrs. Conway's been saying?" Sam stood in front of Renee with every muscle tense, as if ready to spring into action if she said anything remotely similar to what Mrs. Conway had said.

Renee sensed something deep underlying Sam's question. Something he really wanted to know about her. She answered carefully.

"Even though I've just met her, she seems to me to be telling more truth than I've ever heard any adult tell. She seems to know things, too. I believe she's right about God." Renee could think of nothing more to say, but she saw Sam physically relax as if all the tenseness he had hidden washed away. She knew she had said the right thing. But she said none of it to please him. She believed every word she had spoken. She was also afraid. "If it is real, I mean if God is real, doesn't that have to mean Satan is real too? I mean, it seems to me that there is always an opposite, like good/bad, night/day, light/dark, that kind of thing. It also seems to me that evil has been working overtime in this town since I got here. Doesn't it seem that way to you?"

Sam had never thought of it that way before, but Renee was right, things had been pretty bad since she got to town. He was also very impressed with her. She was so young, he thought, to be so right. "Yeah, looks like you've caused havoc around here. What's up with that?"

He smiled broadly, and Renee fell in love with him all over again. It seemed to her that every time he looked at her, her spirit rose up with joy so wonderful it was hard to put in words other than to say she felt elated. She raised an eyebrow in mock shock then said, "I guess I have more power than I knew," she tossed her hair back from her face and started into the kitchen with her head thrown back in mock supremacy.

It was Sam's turn to fall in love.

As Renee reached the kitchen, Kathy came through the back screen door. Renee stood by the table helping Holly put the lemon-aid on a tray. They all headed back outside onto the porch. There the girls hugged each other, crying. Even Sam hugged Kathy telling her he was sorry about what had happened to Shannon. As they embraced, Judy strode up onto the back porch.

It was a turning point for Sam. Although he walked to her, too, and embraced her over the loss of Shannon, both she and he knew that it was the embrace of friendship, not as lovers, as it had been.

Renee's heart broke as she watched them thinking things were same as always between them.

When Sam stepped back from hugging Judy, she took Kathy's hand, and they all turned to look at Mrs. Conway. No one said a word. Everyone quietly took a glass of cold lemon-aid and sipped.

The Thompson sisters moved to sit on either side of Mrs. Conway, who sat her glass down and picked up one of each of their hands. Holly and Renee sat on either side of Sam facing the old woman and Thompson sisters. All were lost in thought, not speaking.

The air hung hot and heavy around them, as if it were a tangible thing, an old wash rag that needed wringing of excess moisture. Not a leaf stirred in a breeze.

"We've been praying," Kathy said quietly to Mrs. Conway in particular but to everyone else as well. "Judy and I, we've been praying upstairs with the family Bible, looking over scriptures to see what we should say." Judy nodded her head in affirmation.

"We've all been praying, too," Mrs. Conway said without ever asking either the Spur children or Renee if they had. She knew they had.

"After what happened in church today, I'm afraid for you, Mrs. Conway. I mean the pastor called you a 'witch'! Why would he do such a thing?" Judy wanted to know.

"He's afraid of me; that's why. He wants to discredit anything I say or do. But he can't stop God from working through anyone God chooses to work through. It just happens to be me right here, right now. You know,

God uses the weak and foolish things to confound the wise."

"Yes, but are you going to be safe? I mean what if the pastor is the one doing the killing. Somehow I think he is. If not that, he's at least an evil person. He's been doing something to his own daughter! You said that yourself! I heard it." Judy said. She had been aghast in church when Mrs. Conway had said that, started thinking about Gloria, and believed what the old woman had said was true. She was aghast at her own blindness toward a girl she had called friend, at the shallowness of her own feelings toward Gloria. That all shifted there in church when she realized the truth.

"Now I don't want you to hold it against Gloria because she is his daughter. She's just a child too, and he's been hurting her a whole lot longer than he's hurt anyone here. She needs your love, not your scorn. Do you understand me?" Mrs. Conway looked piercingly at Judy. She was well aware of Judy's weaknesses. The girl wore them as if a badge. Of course, with her mother teaching her how to be proud, she couldn't expect too much from her—yet.

"Look, Mrs. Conway, Gloria is my best friend, remember? I'm not going to do anything to hurt her, but if it is her father that's killed Shannon, I don't see how she's ever going to be able to live in Rutledge, and be part of this community! I'm not saying that to be mean, either."

"You might be right about that, Judy, but you be careful with her. She's under enough pressure as it is. Remember, it's her that lives in the same house as that man. Think about it. How would you like to live there?" She let that sink in. Judy said nothing else so Mrs. Conway had to believe that she was at least contemplating the thought.

A gentle breeze caressed the girl's cheeks as they sat listening to the others talk. "Did you feel that Mrs. Conway? Maybe it's going to cool off after all." Holly said quietly.

Initially, what Holly said didn't register. "What was that?" Mrs. Conway asked.

"The breeze? I said maybe it's going to cool off after all."

Mrs. Conway's face went pale. The one thing she feared most in all in the world would be hitting sometime soon. She could sense the electricity in the air. Her senses went on red alert, She started commanding everyone off the porch.

"You two, get in there and call your father, NOW!" She screamed at Judy and Kathy as she pulled herself up out of her rocking chair.

"Renee, you get down to the barn and turn Sugarplum loose. You leave open the paddock gate too, in case he has to run for his life.

Sam, when those girls are done on the phone, you get on it, and call the Hansons, then the Frys and you tell them a tornado's coming, to get in their basements! MOVE! EVERYONE! MOVE!" She ordered with such conviction and fear that everyone scrambled up out of their chairs and headed out to do as she told them.

"Holly!" she yelled as Holly attempted to get to the paddock with Renee. "You let Renee handle the horse. You come back here and get this porch picked up. We don't need any extra glass breaking and blowing about! Renee, you hurry up now and get on down to the barn. I want everyone that's staying with me back on this porch in ten minutes. That's all the time we have, now, MOVE!"

As Renee ran across the lawn down to the barn, she saw the Thompson car pull-up beside the apartment fence, and Judy and Kathy run out and jump into it. She was sure the girls would warn their parents about the coming storm. As she ran, she found it harder and harder to brace herself against the wind that picked up velocity with every step she took. By the time she actually reached the barn, the wind whistled about her like a vacuum sucking the air out of the sky.

She had to fight the wind to throw open the double barn doors and get inside. As she did she found Sugarplum stomping his feet and dancing about his box stall like a maniac. His high-pitched screaming reverberated throughout the small stable bouncing off the walls and coming at Renee like crazy demons screeching in frenzy. She had all she could do to keep from running back outside in a panic, the screaming was so intense. She swallowed her fear and made her way to the box stall door, sliding it open along its runner. She was glad she had left the gate to the field open, because Sugarplum didn't wait for the door to completely open before he pushed it aside and made a mad dash for the barn door. In a flash he was gone and she was alone in the barn with the whistling wind rocking the rafters.

Or was she alone? Her skin crawled and the hairs on the back of her neck stood up. Someone else was in the barn with her. She stood at the center of the aisle looking around expecting to see something out of place, or someone, but there was nothing.

She braced herself, and headed for the barn door intending to run with all her might back up to the house. Just before she reached the barn door threshold, an arm jutted out from behind the door and blocked her path.

Like a stealthy predator, Pastor Wilson popped out in front of her, quiet as a cat with a Cheshire grin spread across his grotesque face. He had hidden himself behind the stable doors when she opened them. He had been waiting, knowing that someone would come down to the barn to release the horse. He knew Mrs. Conway's reputation for being fond of the animal and he had seen the girls grooming it, knew they liked it, too. It didn't take much contemplation to figure out what they'd do in view of the approaching storm. He hadn't heard any weather reports, seen any TV to tell him a tornado was coming, but he knew, saw it in his mind. What perfect timing, he thought. He couldn't have prayed for a more opportune time to take advantage of his scheme.

Besides, his need was too strong to deny anymore. He had waited too long already. Francine had been so long ago and she had been so cooperative that it hadn't been much fun, nothing like Shannon. He needed someone like Shannon to satisfy him now, and he didn't really care which of her friends would be his next victim. Renee would do nicely. She would satisfy him while he waited for his chance at Dennis Hanson, whom he really wanted, believing that a victory over another male would be much more satisfying.

Outside the wind grew stronger by the minute. Holly had managed to help Mrs. Conway into the basement fearing for the old woman, because for the first time since knowing her, she saw fear on the old woman's face.

Holly had already come to rely on her strength and wouldn't know what to do if that failed her. How could she hold up with everything that had happened to her and Renee over the last couple of days, Shannon's murder, their molestation, Francine's murder? How could they get along if Mrs. Conway wasn't there to help them? As they slowly made their way downstairs, she wondered what was taking Renee so long to get back.

Sam ran to the restaurant to check on his parents, as the wind grew stronger. He was worried about his mother. Both Mr. and Mrs. Spur were listening to the weather reports on the radio once a customer had told them a bad storm was on the horizon. They had their radio tuned into the local station, but there were no reports of a tornado. Still, just by looking out the large plate glass windows at the front of the restaurant they could see the wind howling, how oddly the sky looked, and people scampering to get inside.

With that, they began their emergency procedures. Mrs. Spur was just about to lock the front doors when Sam came rushing in. Mr. Spur removed the cash from all cash drawers, sent employees to the basement, and was about to head down there, too, when Sam arrived. Sam told them where Holly and Renee, were and where he was headed, then ran back out. Mrs. Spur tried to stop him, but he never even heard her above the roaring winds. He needed to get back to Mrs. Conway. The urge was so strong, he battled against the winds that pushed him backwards two steps for every step he managed forward.

Regardless, he made it to Mrs. Conway's back door, and looked down toward the barn to see Sugarplum run out of the field and down the road over Willow River Bridge, then out of sight. He figured someone had to be down there to let the horse loose. He watched waiting to see if anyone came out of the barn, but when no one did, he fought the wind to open the screen door, and push himself into the apartment running downstairs to safety knowing he would find Mrs. Conway, Holly and Renee there.

Pastor Wilson had a plan. He knew just the place to wait out the weather. He dragged Renee out the back stable door, which faced the river. He knew no one would be out there now anyway, with the storm raging, but he didn't wish to take any chances. He was right, the coast was clear. He had his hand over Renee's mouth and his arm around her neck dragging her along with him as he sped down Willow River road. He had to hurry, the wind was horrific. Trees were toppling, branches were being strewn about in every direction. He had to duck more than one tree limb flying through the air like torpedoes all the while managing to keep his arm around Renee's throat and his hand over her mouth so she could neither scream nor get away. It didn't matter much, he knew if she did scream. No one would be able to hear her above the winds. This was such a perfect time for his perfect place.

He fought against the forces of nature pushing him backward, and finally managed to reach his destination, an old root cellar that he had found once while strolling through the woods, the same root cellar he had taken Shannon to.

Renee was terrified. As the wind howled around them she saw branches flying about as well as glass, tin off roofs, debris of all sizes and shapes;

she desperately wanted to run for the safety of Mrs. Conway's apartment, her basement, her arms. But the pastor's grip on her was too tight. She dragged her feet as he dragged her along doing whatever she could to slow him, but she couldn't scream out. She decided she'd rather die in the storm than at his hands, and fought back tears as he brought her along effortlessly. Her heart sank when he pulled her down into a dark, dank, damp underground room.

She smelled rotten potatoes, stale vegetables, air that seldom was renewed to the fresh breezes that blew above, and grew even more terrified. She knew that because of the tornado no one would be out looking for her. She screamed out on the inside of herself pleading with God to help when all of a sudden, a great peace filled her. Calm settled over her entire being. She knew then she would be okay, and all she could think of was the scripture that said that under the name of Jesus Christ, every knee would bow, and that she, too, could cast out demons as a believer. She had doubts on that score, her being a child and all, but along with the peace was the assurance that it was true. She would not let go of God, of relying upon Him. She had nothing else. Since the pastor still had his hand over her mouth, she could say nothing, so she waited as calmly as she could to declare the word of God against him.

The winds howled ever fiercer above them. Wilson wondered if the door would hold against them. It was locked with just one two by four laying horizontally across it, in the doorframe where it was secured in the door jam. Standing in the middle of the dug out, he listened as the wind whipped at the door.

It's almost as if it's trying to get in here, he thought, as the door shook in the doorjamb. He was so focused on the storm, he took no thought of Renee still locked in his embrace as he drug her about the room looking for the safest place to wait it out.

Tornadoes rarely lasted long, so he deduced that he had seen the worst of it already, had stumbled through it to get to his hiding place. All he'd have to do now was wait for it to die down. He looked about the dank, smelly room that he loved so much, searching for the farthest corner when he saw something he had never noticed before. On the northern most wall, about midway down was what looked like a doorway. He looked at it, then at Renee, the door, then Renee once again. He looked over to the cot he had stashed down there and removed a handkerchief from atop it. The same cloth he had used to bind Shannon from crying out, he'd use to bind Renee as well. He managed to get the cloth into her mouth before ever removing his hand completely from it. She had no time to scream out. He then tied her hands behind her back with a piece of cotton clothesline he had stashed there. He tied her feet, too, then placed her under the steps of the dugout. If the door burst because of the wind, it would drag her out into it, and maybe that'd be for the best. No one could ever tie him to the bonds he used to tie her.

When he finished, he hurried over to what looked like a door. He held a lit candle in his hand using an old tin can as its holder as he examined the space. He pried at it with his fingers but couldn't get it to budge, all the while the wind seemed only to get louder thrashing against the door violently. He had to hurry. He found a stick and managed to get it behind a loose edge enough so that he could reach behind the opening and pull the door all the way out, which he did. He held the candle in front of him as he examined what lie beyond the open maw.

To his amazement, he saw a room that was about six and a half feet in height and six feet across. It was dry, smelled sweet and had clean floorboards that looked as if they'd been cleaned only that morning. To the north end of it was a small cot with a chair in the northeast corner. On it was a small book; he couldn't make out the title from the doorway. On the west wall was a small bookcase with a number of volumes in it. On the bed lay a clean coverlet and he could see that sheets were atop the mattress.

He studied the back of the door, and saw a piece of rope attached to it horizontally, so the door could be pulled closed behind anyone going into the room. But where was the fresh air coming from? That question was answered quickly when he saw a piece of pipe coming out of the roof of the room and felt a blast of air shoot down through it. Perfect! It was perfect! He was so excited he almost forgot to retrieve Renee from under the steps.

She tried with all her might to wiggle the handkerchief out of her mouth. She rotated her jaws back and forth, back and forth, working it loose by pulling it tightly then letting it go with each side to side movement of her jaw. All the while she worked the gag, she watched to see what Wilson was doing. From her place under the step, Renee could see there was a neat little room behind a door he just opened. She could see part of the bed, a coverlet and snatches of the wooden floor. It looked a whole lot nicer than the room he had her in now. But it was odd that such a room should be hidden off an old root cellar that she knew she was in.

She hadn't been in town long enough to know that the root cellar belonged to Mrs. Conway. Back when Mrs. Conway kept a big garden she had it built, but used it for more than just storing vegetables. Renee didn't know that Mrs. Conway once used the other small room to hide women and children running from abusive husbands. She didn't know the room once shielded children beaten and abused by their families. No one in town knew that Mrs. Conway ran an underground-railroad of sorts starting in Minneapolis. No one in Rutledge knew this, but Mrs. Conway was well known in the Twin Cities for her ability to hide families away until they could start a new life somewhere. The root cellar was used to help the helpless escape dismal circumstances that had no chance of improving. She not only gave abused families a way to escape their circumstance by providing a safe hiding place, she also gave them money to start over again; how much was always dependant on the individual.

Wilson would have been horrified if he had known. Women were not to leave their husbands regardless of circumstance. Once married, they belonged to their husband. He didn't hold with the scripture that said a man should treat his wife as Christ treated the church. That his body belonged to her, as hers did to him; nope, that couldn't be true as far as he was concerned. Women were less than men; everyone, even they, knew it, and if they didn't stay in their place, their disobedience was to be beaten out of them.

One of the reasons he held Mrs. Conway in such contempt was that she had no man to teach her her place. He would love to beat the old crow himself, and if given the chance that was exactly what he intended to do. In fact, he thought he might enjoy beating her more than he did having fun with the girls!

Renee squirmed as Wilson turned to look at her again. His eyes were dead in the eerie candlelight. He looked vile, coming at her as he stood up and crossed the room to where she was under the stairs. As he did, the wind outside whistled even louder above them, the noise growing to such intensity that it sounded as if the whole forest they were in was crashing down around them.

Wilson stopped to listen watching the door violently shake above him. To hell with it, he decided; I'm saving myself! He turned back around and ran for the little room, tucking himself inside and shutting the door before Renee could understand what she was seeing.

She realized he was saving himself, and was going to let the storm kill her! He ran and hid and left her right underneath the door that rattled so loudly, she greatly feared it would come off its hinges. Just as the realization struck her, the gag came out of her mouth enough for her to yell, "Be still!" She shouted at the wind. "Lord Jesus Christ have mercy on me! Lord Jesus Christ have mercy on me! Lord Jesus Christ have mercy on me!" All she could think of to say was the Jesus prayer over and over and over again without ceasing. As she prayed, she yelled it out loudly praying Jesus could hear it above the storm then realized the winds didn't sound as loud. She prayed even more fervently, because she needed all the help she could get.

Even if the storm stopped, she would still have to deal with Wilson. She believed in Jesus. She believed that Mrs. Conway was good, the one who knew the true path because she was the one who said to pray to Jesus. Renee prayed louder and the wind died even more. The door quit rattling and before she knew it, the bonds that held her hands and feet somehow came loose. She sat terrified for one long moment looking at the inner doorway, expecting Wilson to come out after her any second. Then from somewhere deep within herself she mustered the courage to run for the steps. She took them two at a time preferring to be up and out of the root cellar, and into the storm than to be held captive anymore by someone she sensed meant her mortal harm. She was at the top of the stair sliding the two by four back when she heard the door to the little room opening. She flew the door back and was up and out of the root cellar so quickly, Wilson hadn't even made it out of his hideaway before she was gone. The storm still raged, but Renee ran for her life into it, happy to be away from Wilson. She dodged fallen branches, jumped over fallen trees, and made it back to Mrs. Conway's' as if on wings. She threw open the backdoor even though it had been locked and was down in the basement with the others before Wilson made it up the stairs of the root cellar.

Chapter Twenty-Four

When he stepped up out of his office basement, where he had retreated at the onset of the tornado, Pine County Sheriff Ernie Hansen couldn't believe his eyes. Everywhere he looked—total devastation. Houses were now matchsticks, agitated as if they had gone through a washing machine cycle, much of their debris lying in the street in front of his office. He saw tin roofs twisted and turned like rubber bands lying all about, cars and trucks dangling from tree limbs, and the occasional oddity, a house still intact.

The air was eerily calm, no breeze ruffled his hair, the sky was a brilliant cerulean blue, birds chirped from crippled tree branches as if nothing had happened. Hansen felt like he was stepping into an episode of the Twilight Zone. But he couldn't dwell on it. He had too much to do. He turned and with Freboni, who had climbed out of the basement behind him, helped his office staff up and out, and got their two prisoners locked back up in their cells. His office had escaped relatively unscathed, and already their backup generators were running. His office was prepared for any contingency. Hansen didn't know yet how far reaching the tornado had been, but he had his dispatchers checking into it.

The sheriff's office phones, however, remained ominously quiet. Hansen didn't like that one bit. It couldn't be good. He prayed that the loss of life would be low. Loss of property, he knew, would be another matter.

The two dispatchers still working rushed to tell him they managed to contact two off-duty deputies, one right there in Willow River, and the other in an outlying area. They and their families were okay, but both had lost their homes. Where were they going to house tornado victims?

Again, dispatchers gave him the news that the school in Willow River, too, had escaped serious damage. Hansen radioed back his deputies and told them to get their families over to the school. The officer in the country, even though only a few miles away, would have a difficult time doing that so Hansen advised him to see if there was anywhere out there where survivors could be housed until they could get roads cleared from Willow River. Hansen was relieved to find his men and their families had escaped the tornado unharmed, even if they were facing devastating losses.

Other deputies living in outlying areas began to radio in. No one could use the telephones as lines were down. Hansen ordered the men to begin search and rescue efforts near their own homes and to work their way back to the office in Willow River, getting as many people to a shelter of any kind as much as possible.

Dispatchers learned from the National Weather Service that the tornado had been rated an F4, and had cut a swath of destruction through the area such as had never been seen there before.

Hansen prayed that everyone had gotten to shelter in time before the tornado struck. There hadn't been much warning.

In light of the natural disaster, everything else he had been working on had to be put on the back burner—including the two murders.

For the first time since his wife had divorced him, Hansen was glad of it. His daughter was safe, off on a vacation to Yellowstone National Park with her mother and her mother's new husband. He never thought there would be a day he would be thankful his ex-wife had re-married, but he was this day. Nothing could have made him happier than knowing his daughter was safe, so he concentrated his efforts on his neighbors and friends. He radioed the state patrol in Wyoming to get a message to his ex-wife and their daughter that he was okay. Even their home had been left relatively unharmed, so she could come back in two weeks as planned.

When he had everything as organized as well as he could, Hansen found his truck intent on getting to Rutledge. A foreboding had settled over him, a force driving him, and he felt it urgent that he get there. Something was wrong there, aside from the tornado, and it compelled him forward.

Driving the four miles to Rutledge proved a much bigger challenge than he anticipated. Downed trees, downed power lines, and overturned vehicles all slowed him. At each vehicle, he had to stop to check and see if anyone were somewhere close by. He found no one. It felt eerie that so many cars were abandoned, yet no one was near by, washing him once again with a feeling of foreboding, and renewing that sense that he had stepped into the Twilight Zone. How could they have escaped? Where did they go?

Downed power lines lay sparking in ditches alongside Highway 61. Hansen couldn't search inside the ditches for people that might be lying there in need of help because of exposed wires, but he got as close as possible to see if anyone lie out in the open. He radioed the rural co-op, ICO Power Company to send trucks and men, and asked that they immediately cut the power. Management was already at the ICO Power Company organizing their efforts for restoration. They would be working to cut power to downed lines as quickly as possible. In the meantime, Hansen called out to anyone who might hear him as he walked alongside the ditches as closely as possible, hoping someone might answer him. As he approached a large culvert running to either side of the road, he got the response he had been praying for. People started emerging from the culvert, which they had used for cover from the tornado, when they heard him calling. Slowly, one at a time, people stepped up on the far side of the road, safely away from the downed power lines. To Hansen, they looked shell-shocked, dazed, dumbfounded by what they had just experienced, and some were still very afraid, he thought, judging by their appearance. He could see it in their eyes, in the way they held themselves, tense, as if ready to bolt back into the culvert at the slightest provocation.

Almost every vehicle owner who had abandoned a vehicle along

Highway 61, he accounted for, and apparently they were suffering from only minor scratches and cuts. One he suspected had a broken arm, but that seemed to be the worst of the injuries. As power company trucks arrived at the scene Hansen enlisted them to transport all those he found in the culvert to local hospitals. Because of the danger posed by the downed lines, the power company sent out two more trucks to work on that problem, after assuring the first two truck drivers that it was all right to help the sheriff and get the injured to safety.

All the while he dealt with the immediate emergencies, Hansen still felt compelled to get to Rutledge, growing edgy with impatience as he was forced to proceed at a snail's pace. The overwhelming foreboding grew with each inch he progressed.

In Rutledge, at the Sands café, Mr. and Mrs. Spur worked their way out of the basement. Their help followed. Joey, the cook, an avid weight lifter, helped Mr. Spur push the basement door open. As it finally gave way, they gazed out on the sky, a clear, cerulean blue and tranquil, with no restaurant ceiling or walls to obstruct the view. The restaurant was nothing more than a pile of debris. As they slowly turned 180 degrees, they saw the whole town was obliterated until they looked to the other side of the street and saw Mrs. Conway's apartment building still sanding. Mrs. Spur sighed with relief.

Their waitress, June, a seventeen-year-old from Willow River, sobbed, as she stepped up and out into the daylight, the devastation was so complete. Mrs. Spur put her arms around the girl, all the while thanking God that she and Wally had been smart enough to insure against acts of God. Joey helped June through the ruble while Mr. and Mrs. Spur slowly climbed over fallen timbers, restaurant equipment, broken glass, a mangled array of pots, cooking utensils, the cash register, candy bars and gum wrappers, all that was left from underneath the counter where the cash register had stood. Menus lay about helter skelter throughout the tangled mess, as well. At the sight, Mrs. Spur, too, broke down and sobbed. All that she and Wally had worked so hard for, was gone.

When the Spurs looked out at the village, they saw that almost the whole town had been decimated. Three buildings were left standing. One belonged to Mrs. Conway, which meant they still had a home to go to, the church steeple they could see over the treetops so they assumed the church, too, still stood, and the Hanson's garage, just two blocks down on the other side of Main Street from where they stood, was still there, too.

As June bawled that she wanted to go home, Wally Spur looked out to the west of where the restaurant once stood, and saw the Thompson family climbing out of the wreckage that was once their home. Similar scenes popped up from the other homes within his line of sight. Families scrambled up and out of the ruble as if the ruble were giving birth.

The Frys, too, climbed up and out of what was once their home, Mr. Fry looking about to see if anyone else emerged from the devastation. He helped his wife and Sharon up out of the basement, and they silently made their way through the ruble toward the restaurant. Everyone they saw was headed in the same direction. They all met at the Spur's, and together they all quietly looked about at the ruble they had once called home.

"We need to start searching, make sure everyone is okay and help those that aren't," Mr. Thompson said with authority after taking it all in. No one questioned that decision. "Henry (Fry), you take Joey and start on the south side of town. Wally, you and I can start on the north. Judy, you, and Kathy go check on your friends, but that building is still standing, so I'm guessing they're okay. But we need as many able-bodied people that we can find to search out and help those that are in trouble."

The girls took off running for Mrs. Conway's store. Mrs. Spur sighed with relief, for she was anxious to know if Holly, Sam and Renee were okay, even though she believed they were.

"Mrs. Spur, you and June take the west-side of Main Street and work your way back, everyone calling out to those that might still be inside the ruble. Check vehicles too. Some may have tried to ride out the storm in their cars." Mr. Thompson then headed off with Wally Spur to see if there was anyone in need of assistance.

Mrs. Roberta Spur took a moment to watch as they walked away. She thought them an unlikely pair, but said nothing. She continued to try and sooth June's fears. The girl would not be able to go home for some time, even if someone could drive her. The roads had to be a mess if the storm was so strong it left this much devastation in its path, Mrs. Spur reasoned while they approached the first house.

"What are we going to do if we find someone hurt?" June whined as Mrs. Spur called out at the ruble, "Is anyone there?"

"We're going to help them, that's what we'll do. If we find someone beyond help, then we'll mark the place and go on, now get a grip! This is no time to be thinking of yourself. Others need our help!"

June tried to concentrate on others, but she dearly wished that she could get home to help her own family, see if they were okay. She knew that would be impossible for some time, so she would do what she could right here until she could get home. That's all anyone could do.

At the first house, Mrs. Spur and June found a young couple. They couldn't get their basement door open for all the debris resting against it. The two women pulled and prodded until enough debris fell away that the young man inside could push the door open. As he stepped out, behind him stepped his wife and two small children, one eighteen-months old, and the other about three-and-a-half.

June picked up the three-and-a-half-year old, and the trope went on to the next house, the young couple deciding to help the women look for other townspeople, too.

When they finished their side of the street, the group, along with all the others they had found, headed back up Main Street to in front of what was once the Sands restaurant. From the south came a group of what looked like war refugees, and another group of shell-shocked looking people approached from the north.

Mr. Thompson, who Mrs. Spur could see was the authority figure for the later group, started issuing commands. "We'll go down to Hanson's garage. I think that'll be big enough to hold us all. Has anyone gone to the Hanson house yet?" He yelled out to the crowd. From the back of the group, Dennis, with his father, emerged from the south. The elder Hanson looked like he had aged fifty years from the last time Mrs. Spur served him in the restaurant.

"Dennis!" Mr. Thompson called out, clearly glad to see the youth alive, "I'm afraid that your garage looks like the only place left standing that can house everyone. Do you have the key, and can we gather there?"

"Of course," Dennis said softly and turned to help his father back the way they had come. Mrs. Hanson had remained at the back of the group, but as Dennis and her husband approached, she fell into step beside them. Mr. Thompson hurried his wife along stepping alongside the Hanson family, now united in more than one tragedy. Mrs. Thompson reached out and took Mrs. Hanson's hand, astonishing those close enough to see the gesture. Mrs. Spur saw and was thankful that they each had someone to lean on. No one else she knew had suffered the types of losses these two women had suffered over the course of the last few days. It was awful.

As that thought rushed through Mrs. Spur's head, from behind her she heard familiar voices calling her name as well as the sound of running feet. She could not, however, see anyone threw the throngs of people surrounding her.

The dazed and shocked group surrounding Mrs. Spur gently moved aside to let the children pass.

"Mamma!" Holly called, "Mamma!"

Mrs. Spur froze where she stood waiting for her child to emerge from the wounded lot surrounding her.

As she saw her mother, Holly broke into tears running straight into her mother's waiting arms. She couldn't stop crying. Behind her came Renee, also sobbing, with Sam bringing up the rear. Mrs. Spur had a momentary thought for Mrs. Conway, but it flew from her mind at the joy of seeing her children alive. With two sobbing girls hugging her, Mrs. Spur embraced her son as hard as she could while not letting go of the girls.

Mr. Spur turned back at the sound of his children's voices and was relieved to see that they were okay, although he kept on walking at Mr. Thompson's side heading for the garage. Sam saw and figured the old man was just doing what the old man always did, ignoring him. He thought it was just one more way of telling him that he didn't matter.

When the group finally stopped hugging one-another, Mrs. Spur pushed Holly back and asked, "Where is Mrs. Conway?"

"She's okay, Mom. She decided that she would stay in her basement and pray. That's what she's doing, she's praying for everybody. She said an even bigger storm was coming, one that we needed God's help with. She said this storm was God warning us that a worse storm was on the way."

When people surrounding the Spurs heard what Holly said, they panicked, all afraid at the news that another storm was coming, taking what she said to mean another tornado. No one doubted anything the old woman declared now, but they prayed that this news wasn't true. They started to mumble and talk amongst themselves, their grumbling reaching the front of the crowd and Mr. Thompson.

He stopped in his tracks. Everyone was almost to the garage now. Most walked slowly as many were hurt, but not seriously. He moved to the back of the group to where Holly stood talking to her mother.

"Look, everyone," he said loudly turning to the crowd, "continue on to the garage. Dennis Hanson will let us in. Sit down and rest. We'll get to the bottom of Mrs. Conway's message and find out if we have to go under ground again. We'll be okay, just keep moving!" Mr. Thompson, who had a melodious voice, reassured everyone calming their fears. They trudged slowly on. Mr. Thompson gave his attention to Holly. His own daughters, Judy and Kathy, stood alongside the Spur family now walking with them to the garage.

"Holly, what exactly did Mrs. Conway say?" Mr. Thompson asked her quietly.

"She said we should all gather together and pray. She said a bigger storm is coming. We are going to need God's help with it, but all we have to do is gather together and pray. He would fight the battle for us."

"You're sure of this?"

"That's it exactly, Dad," Kathy offered. "Mrs. Conway said that to us as we were leaving her basement. She's okay Dad, but she doesn't want anyone with her now because she's going to be praying. She said she's been interceding for the town. She wants us all to gather at the garage. She said that by no means should we go to the church. But we need to pray."

"I don't like leaving an old woman alone. It's not right. I'm going back to get her and bring her here." Mr. Thompson started off back up Main Street to Mrs. Conway's.

"No Dad! She doesn't want you there! Can't you just listen for once?" Judy was angry with her father believing with all her heart that the old woman knew what she was doing.

"Mind your mouth young lady, and take yourself and your friends down to the garage! Do it! Now!" No one had ever seen Mr. Thompson angry, including Judy and Kathy. They didn't say another word; they headed off to the garage.

No one said a word yet about Renee's episode with the pastor, either, but the Thompson sisters kept her close, feeling a kinship with her because of what she had been through. Both girls believed that Renee had probably escaped death by a miracle. Holly, too, stuck close to Renee's side as did Sam, who was appalled at the thought of almost loosing her.

When Renee had come running into the basement screaming, Mrs. Conway had to slap her across the face to get her to calm down. Renee was so terrified she could barely tell them what had happened. When she finally managed to get the story out of how the pastor had abducted her from the barn, and had taken her into an old root cellar, Sam went into a fit of rage; the women were thankful that the storm had forced him to stay inside.

Renee described the place Wilson had taken her, and Mrs. Conway recognized it immediately. She had had visions of the pastor with little girls, but had never been able to see exactly where they were. She knew now. What would she do about it? No police officer would listen to her story of having visions. They would dismiss her as senile. If she had evidence, that would be a completely different matter.

Besides, no one in town knew about that root cellar except the pastor, she thought from listening to Renee. She wondered how he had come upon it, and didn't like the idea of him being in it, contaminating it with the demons that possessed him.

What he didn't know, she was sure, was that she had a way to the root cellar through her own basement. Her husband had built tunnels to it some seventy years before with such fine craftsmanship that they were as strong and steady as the day he built them.

Also, from what Renee had said, it didn't seem to Mrs. Conway that the pastor had ever discovered that secret room until today. If he was as terrified of the storm as she suspected he was, from Renee's description, he hadn't discovered the doorway leading to the passageway to her apartment either. If he had, they probably would have seen him sometime during the storm. The door to the tunnel in Mrs. Conway's house was simply a door that she never locked. It looked like any other door and anyone going into her basement, or coming from the root cellar, had merely to turn the knob to open it. She had never considered locking it, as sure as she was that her root cellar was unknown to everyone in town but her.

And if he did what she guessed he would after Renee had escaped, he was out and gone now so she'd be safe heading down the quarter-mile tunnel with little to disturb her. The weather sure wouldn't be able to stop her there, underground. This was what she had hoped to do as she sent the children up and out of the basement to be with the townsfolk. It was best for everyone to pitch together in this horrible hour of need and she knew it. This crisis would bond families tighter than they'd ever been bonded before. It was the one good thing storms did do.

She also intended to do what she told the children she was going to do, pray. That's how she got through every day. That's why she was protected from so many disasters. She prayed continually, with every breath and every step she took, whether it be sitting still or busily working, she prayed continually.

So, as the children rushed upstairs and out of the house, Mrs. Conway decided it was time for a snack to give her energy for the work ahead. She found a box of crackers and sat back down in her old rocker she kept downstairs. She rocked awhile praying as she munched on the meager fare, so she would be strong enough to make the trip down the tunnel.

That's where Ralph Thompson found her when he came uninvited into her house and downstairs into her basement.

"You've got your nerve, boy, busting in on an old lady like that! You trying to scare the daylights out of me!"

"I'm sorry, Mrs. Conway, it's just that the girls said you were going to stay here alone, and I was worried about you."

"What you got to worry about me for? Can't you see the storm did nothing to my house! You blind?"

"They also said you said another storm was coming, one that will be much worse than the first. Now I'm asking you to explain that to me, so everyone can take greater precautions. This is no time to be speaking in parables!"

"Just do like I told the girls to tell you. Pray. That's all you got to do. It wouldn't hurt none if you all got down on your knees and prayed, either, but I know some of them folks aren't going to want to do that, but if a few of you do, that'll be okay. Pray hard. If you don't know what to pray, just say, 'Lord Jesus Christ have mercy on me,' and keep saying it. That'll do you all for now. I'll be praying with you, too. I just won't be there in the garage. I'll be here."

"I have to insist that you come with me, Mrs. Conway. This is no time for you to be by yourself."

"You can insist all you want to, boy, but I'll do as I damn well please. Now, you need to leave."

"I'm not going anywhere without you."

"Don't put on any high and mighty act with me, Mr. Big Shot Lawyer! You don't run me! I pay my taxes, obey the laws of this land! You ain't ordering me anywhere!"

"Settle down, Mrs. Conway. With the killings and the storm, don't you think you'll be safer with the rest of the town, together?"

"Oh, that—don't you fret about me any. I got the good Lord on my side. He won't let anything bad happen to me until he decides its time to take me home. And as old as I am that could be any time now anyway. If it is, that's between me and Him, not you folks. I got things to do here yet, and I need to do them alone."

"What, like using that underground-railroad of yours for something?"

Mrs. Conway stood up when she heard Thompson entering her house, and remained standing all through their conversation, and for the first time in her 111 years, she was shocked speechless. She sat down.

"You needn't look so surprised, Mrs. Conway. I've guessed what you've been up to a long time ago. Did some research on it, too! Found out when your husband passed away, what he used to do for a living. No, I'm not as dumb as you seem to think. And I'm pretty sure how you've managed to get them people in and out of here for so many years without most folks even guessing what you've been up to."

"Well, I guess your parents didn't waste no money sending you to school. So what you think you gonna' do to me? I'm a little too old to go to jail." She came back to herself rocking gently back and forth in her rocker.

"I don't plan on doing anything to you. But I do have a question. Is it possible that the killer found out about your hideaway? Maybe used it when he killed Shannon? I have to know."

"I'll be honest with you, Mr. Thompson. I know the killer found that root cellar. I also learned that he hadn't discovered any of the secret hidden rooms except for one, and he didn't do that until today during the storm. He damn near killed little Renee, Holly's friend that's visiting? But the little whip beat him at his own game, and came running back here to us after he'd kidnapped her from my own barn, and drug her down into my root cellar. I'm betting that's where he killed Shannon, if you want to know the truth, cause it's the one spot around here no one seems to know about. I'm fixing to head to it right now, hoping I'll find some evidence. That's why I don't want nobody here with me."

"And the second storm I was talking about, that one's up to God to fight; it has to do with the evil that lives here in Rutledge right now. That's worse than any tornado, causes more havoc. But you people keep praying. It won't hurt none of you and will keep everyone safe. Gotta' pray for others, too, not just yerselves."

"Don't you think it would be better if I went with you? I do know a thing or two about evidence."

"That may be true, but how are you going to hold up if we do find something of Shannon's. I'm going to need you to stay strong if you're with me."

"I'll do my best."

"Well, all right then, but first you go and tell the rest of the folks what I said about praying. Just tell them that you want to stay with the old lady, so she won't be alone, and make out that I'm too feeble to make it to the garage. They'll believe it. And have them two girls of yours lead folks in a prayer. They'll do a good job. Sam, him and Dennis will, too. Encourage them kids. God's listening to them."

With that Mr. Thompson headed back upstairs running all the way to the garage. He hoped against hope that there would be some kind of evidence that could be used against the killer of his little girl, and of Francine. He wanted to catch their killer so badly he ached for the chance. He knew, too, that he had to use caution, so that he didn't mess up any evidence police could use to build a case against the perpetrator. He prayed as he ran that he'd have enough wisdom and strength to restrain himself if they did find something.

He also needed to assure himself that Renee was okay, that Judy and Kathy were safe. He knew he couldn't rely on his wife to protect them, but he'd take Dennis and Sam aside instilling in them the need for the children to stick together. He'd talk to Mr. Fry too; he seemed a stable, loving parent, someone who would look out for others, not just himself.

He had no doubts that he would leave the garage and return to help Mrs. Conway.

Chapter Twenty-Five

All about the garage people milled, shell-shocked from the wrath of the tornado, most having lost homes they'd lived in all their lives. The Fourth of July weekend had been too much for some: first Shannon's, then Francine's murders, and then the tornado. What more were they expected to go through? How could God desert them so, and why had He allowed Shannon and Francine to meet such premature deaths? They couldn't understand any of it, and their pastor wasn't there to comfort them.

Bits and snippets of conversation floated over to Sam and Dennis who paced in front of the garage doors. The air was quiet, warm, the sun shinning brightly against the wasteland of homes blighting the horizon; all seemed surreal to the boys as they gazed about themselves still unable to comprehend fully all that had gone on in the last few days.

Dennis, however shell-shocked, felt proud that the community had come to his family for shelter in their time of trial. It was the first time anyone had come to the Hanson family for anything in all the years they had lived in Rutledge. Oh sure, most had their cars fixed by him in the garage, but never had they been as decent to his parents as they were being now. He watched his mother being cared for by ladies of the church who had never even been to the house to visit her in the past.

He didn't know if he should be happy for her or scream at them for leaving her alone all those years. He knew how she suffered from loneliness, never having anyone to talk to because her husband was the town drunk. And her husband, his father, was rarely home, all she ever had were himself and Francine, and now Francine was gone, too. What was she going to do? At least the tornado hadn't destroyed the family business or home. He thought that was some kind of miracle, too.

When Sam first came to him about praying, Dennis had wanted to deck him as he had done him the day before for stealing a kiss from Renee. Pray! Pray to who? Pray for what? Against his initial rejection, Dennis did pray, had even gone into his mother's bedroom and retrieved the family Bible, read a few scriptures.

Funny, he seemed to find just what he was looking for by merely opening the book. He read scriptures about being adopted by God into His family even if his own family rejected him. How could that happen? He wondered to himself, and then paged through the book some more. Each time he stopped, he found scriptures that touched him where he hurt the most. It was odd. Was it coincidence? Was the Bible really the living word? He didn't know, not for sure, but he kept reading; he prayed, too, even though he had never prayed before, didn't really know how.

He had prayed like the dickens once the storm started without realizing that was what he was doing. It came almost unbidden. He didn't want his family to loose anymore than they already had. Maybe that's why the house hadn't blown down as so many others had. But, he guessed, probably a lot of other townspeople had been praying too, yet their houses were destroyed. Why?

"Hey, man, you okay?" Sam asked bringing Dennis out of his reverie.

"Yeah, man, I'm fine. I was just watching my mom over there with those ladies from the church, you know? Nobody in town has even given her the time of day, not that I've ever seen, now look at them hovering over her like she was their long lost relative, or something."

Sam watched, too. He knew what it was like to be an outcast, but he couldn't fathom going through that for thirty, forty years without leaving town! How the hell did she do it, he wondered?

He looked around the room seeking out his mother when his eyes caught sight of her at the back of the garage. She was tending to someone's wounds. The garage sink, where she was, still had running water, although Sam didn't know how that could be since the tornado knocked all the power out for everyone else.

"Oh, that's just cause we have a private well. We're not connected to city utilities. Pops wouldn't have it. We have a gasoline-operated generator, too. I got that going right after the storm. I guess Pop's done something right with his life!" Dennis smiled at Sam knowing he would understand the irony of that statement.

"Looks like the good old townsfolk need to be beholding to your folks." Sam grinned at Dennis.

"Yours ain't so bad, either," Dennis pointed out Sam's mother still by the sink cleansing wounds and Sam's father, who sat next to Dennis' father with his arm around the man's shoulder, comforting him. Dennis' dad looked like he'd been through the worst beating of his life.

"You think your old man is in need of some booze?" Sam asked cautiously.

"No, man, we've got a house full of it. Didn't one bottle break in that tornado! Can you believe it? Not one single bottle? It didn't so much as jostle them. Maybe that's for the best though, cause this is no time for the old man to be going into the DT's. It'd make these here upstanding folks mighty uncomfortable right now. Besides, it looks like they've been through enough, too."

While the two boys talked, Renee, Holly, Kathy and Judy huddled together in the garage office. Renee told Judy and Kathy in detail what happened to her in the old root cellar with the pastor. The rest of the town hadn't found out about her kidnapping yet. The girls were trying to decide if they should tell them.

"I'm keeping my mouth shut for the time being," Renee said. "People have been through enough for the moment, unless of course, someone wants to go to the church. We should all start yelling then. We can't let anyone else get hurt." Her assurance, that someone else most certainly could be hurt at the pastor's hands, unnerved the other three. Silently, each one determined to stop anyone foolish enough to seek the pastor's help.

Holly put her arm around Renee's shoulder. Kathy moved over to hug them both.

"I bet he's the one who killed Shannon," Judy whispered out loud, more to herself than to the other girls.

"Yeah, that's what I think, too." Renee said quietly. "I bet he took her right where he took me. I know this much, when the sheriff gets here, I've got a few things to tell him! I don't care what happens to me, someone has got to listen, or he's going to keep on killing!"

"You're right. But for now, maybe we should just get back out there and see if we can help anyone in anyway. There's got to be something we can do. Maybe baby-sit some of the little kids so their parents can decide what they're going to do." Judy surprised Kathy with her offer of service. It was a first.

What a mess, Hansen thought as he slowly cruised through what remained of Rutledge. He couldn't get far, however, as Main Street was nothing but rubble. He parked his truck at the north end of the city limits and started walking.

Everywhere trees were torn up by their roots, branches scattered across the streets; what were once houses were now only rubble, looking as if they had gone through a barrage of war incited missile attacks, as they lay strewn this way and that. A toaster rested on top a mattress. A child's teddy bear lay inside an oven whose door had been torn from its hinges. He saw a typewriter lying inside a busted open tool chest. Everywhere glass and shattered timber lie along the roadway.

As he moved slowly along, Hansen shook his head in disbelief. Rutledge must have been directly in the path of the tornado to receive such damage, he thought. As he approached the main shopping district, he was amazed to see Mrs. Conway's apartment building and store still standing. It didn't look too bad, either, except for a missing shingle or two. A single solitary glass had been broken out of a second story apartment. He checked the front door to the store and found it locked. He then walked around to the back and checked the downstairs doors. They too were locked tight. He went back to Main Street and continued on.

Across the street there wasn't much left of his favorite restaurant, but its sign still hung from an exposed wire that threw off sparks as flashes of power shot through it when it brushed against the fallen tin roof.

When he looked south, Hansen could clearly see that the Hanson garage still stood. He wondered, as he walked around, and over, strewn rubble, how he could organize a search party and start looking for survivors. He wondered if he would find any, and doubted it. To his astonishment as he approached the garage, and could look up from his debris-strewn path, he saw that it was full of townspeople as the doors to the garage stood wide open. He was relieved, thinking that the death toll would be great, but from the throngs of folks standing idly by, perhaps it wouldn't be too bad. He felt great relief at the sight.

Dennis noticed the sheriff first, as he stood just outside the garage bay doors smoking a cigarette. He threw his cigarette down instinctively, thinking the sheriff would try to ticket him or something, but he was glad to see him, regardless. "Hey Sheriff!" He called when the sheriff was still a half a block away. His shouts garnered the attention of everyone inside. Most immediately flew out the doors to converge on Hansen as he approached the garage, everyone speaking at once.

They were traumatized, Hansen could tell, because everyone tried to tell him, at the same time, their trials during the storm. He waited until they expelled that rush of emotion having told their harrowing exploits for the first time to someone outside their community. When it grew quiet, he said, "It looks like everyone is here. Is that correct? Do we need to start looking for others?"

The townspeople were dumbstruck, as they turned to look at one another blank eyed, as if for the first time realizing they hadn't asked themselves that same question. "I think everybody's here, sheriff," Dennis said as he searched the crowd one more time. A few heads nodded in agreement.

"Where's Mrs. Conway, Mr. Thompson?" Hansen asked when he couldn't locate either of them in the crowd.

"Mrs. Conway wanted to stay inside her house and Mr. Thompson went over to stay with her," Renee told him holding her breath as she waited to speak to him alone.

"What about the pastor? I don't see him here." Hansen stated. He also didn't see the pastor's wife or daughter.

"We haven't seen him," someone shouted from the back. "Shouldn't we be out looking for him, make sure his family is okay?"

As the townspeople contemplated going out to search for Wilson and his family, he was out trying to reach the little bitch that got away, he thought, but that's okay. There will be other chances to get at her; I'll make sure of that. Who is she anyway? Nothing but some loser farmer's kid! Nobody's going to give a damn if she turns up missing, nobody, especially the police." He was speaking out-loud although he didn't realize it.

Wilson knew how the police operated. The only people they ever attempted to deliver up to the law were poor people or lower middle class folks. They were too afraid of wealth and power to do anything to them if they committed a crime, but poor people were easy targets.

That's why Francine was so easy to get to. Even if she had changed her mind about their sexual exploits, and had tried to expose him, nobody would have believed her over him. Besides, she had loved basking in his power. Power was something he had a lot of. He told everyone in town what to do, why wouldn't she bask in it? She was thrilled with him as a lover too, he was sure of that.

He thought he might miss her tender mercies as he made his way through tornado-strewn debris to his house.

God—a super power? What a laugh, he thought. God's wrath! He snickered. He had defied God successfully, hadn't he? He had made it through the tornado safely, too! He'd continue right on with his work and nobody could stop him.

Women couldn't be allowed the power they sought, he thought as he trudged forward. They were useless, meaningless nothings, fit only to serve men as slaves, to cook, clean and lie underneath a man, oh, and of course, to do whatever man wanted them to do sexually. It wasn't all that hard to get them to cooperate either, he learned; he had had a lot of help over the years.

Women had been well trained over the centuries to be good-little obedient girls. How lovely for him and how easy it was to conquer them just by telling them it was God's will that they please him in every way, even when they were young. That worked almost every time.

It hadn't worked on Shannon Thompson though, so he had to deal with her rebellion swiftly and with due diligence. She was a child. She needed to do as she was told. It gave him great pleasure to discipline her.

He saw, too, that all of her friends were in just as much need of that same discipline. Contrite, contrary minded little whelps, that's what they were.

Wilson made it to the edge of town. He saw that houses had been blown apart with such force, they were nothing more than twigs strewn about. Only instead of carrying debris in just one direction, debris had flown about in a circular fashion at the belly of the downspout, he guessed.

Wilson made it into a culvert on a road he didn't recognize scurrying to the safety it offered him, crouching down and crawling to the south end where he could watch, look for anyone who might also be out and about. He did not wish to be seen. He had a perfect view of the destruction from that end of the culvert.

For the first time since the storm had begun, he wondered where his wife and daughter were. He hoped they were dead. That would garner him a lot of sympathy from the whole town, and all those lovely little girls would knock themselves out trying to comfort him. How easy to get rid of an unwanted wife, he thought. She was a help in the most menial of ways, but he could hire someone to replace her, even get someone to do the work for free if he wished. He would be a martyr. He liked that idea.

Back when the tornado bore down on the village, inside Wilson's house there was an even greater storm brewing as Gloria told her mother what her father had been doing to her for years. To Gloria's amazement, her mother did not believe her. Her face turned deep red with rage as Gloria spoke, and she slapped her daughter as hard as she could across her face.

The blow enraged Gloria. Gloria slapped her mother in return. "You know what he's been doing. You've known it all along! Why haven't you stopped him Mother! Listen to me! He's been molesting the girls at the church, too!" Gloria held onto her mother's shoulders as she screamed in her face trying to make herself heard above the storm that raged outdoors.

"How dare you," the elder Wilson woman shrilled at the top of her lungs. "How dare you speak of your father like that! A godly man, doing the Lord's work—how dare you defame him to me, your mother—his wife! What is wrong with you? You whore of Babylon! You speak filth!" Mrs. Wilson attempted to slap her daughter once again, only Gloria caught her hand in mid-strike and held it back.

"Man of God? Man of God! How dare you call that evil son-of-a-bitch a man of God! He's been raping and hurting girls everywhere we've gone, and you've done nothing but hide your head in the sand so he could keep on doing it! Man of God! You will go to hell just for saying that!"

This time Mrs. Wilson was so angered that she freed her hand from Gloria's grip, and landed a solid open handed blow once-again across her daughter's face. She seethed with anger at what Gloria said, "You little tramp. You better pack your bags and get the hell out of here! I won't put up with a heathen like you in this house, do you hear me! Get out! Get out! Get out!" As she screamed, she inched closer and closer to Gloria's face backing her up until Gloria stood motionless with her back against the wall. She stood stunned by the hatred she saw in her mother's eyes, the hatred she heard in her mother's voice, her own mother.

Gloria deflated with the emotional blows her mother struck her with. She had always thought that if her mother really knew what was happening to her because of her father, she'd stand up for her, save her, somehow. She had hoped for that moment for more years than she cared to remember, but now, now it seemed that all her hope was in vain. She started to shake, standing there against the wall, trembling so badly she thought she were in the throws of a seizure. But the Bible verse, "even though your mother and father forsake you, I will never forsake you," popped into her head from out of nowhere, it seemed, and the quaking stopped.

The verse seemed to lurch itself into her through her navel causing her to know that Christ had just adopted her into His protection. Peace flooded throughout her being, and brought tears to her eyes. With that sudden knowledge, she let out her breath in a quick expulsion. As she did, the tornado hit full force into their house sucking her mother up into its 210 mph winds that circled overhead screaming out like angry banshees.

The storm beat down on everything with wind and debris as her mother was swept away. Gloria fell to the floor while the wall she had been standing against collapsed on top of her, covering her where it remained until the storm's furry passed.

Pastor Wilson knew nothing of this as he crouched inside the culvert. When he saw that his house was destroyed, he gleefully hoped his wife and daughter had been too. Nothing but ruble remained where his house once stood. He knew, too, that he would be needed more than ever after this tornado just by looking at the devastation that lay all around him. His mouth watered at the thought.

God's wrath, he snickered. Yeah, well, maybe it was, maybe God wasn't unhappy with him after all; maybe he was God's weapon against all the evil women of the world! Humph, he thought, it was a brilliant idea, one he hadn't thought of before.

But deep down, he didn't believe in God anymore than he had before. It was a storm. Weather conditions had been perfect for a tornado, that was all. They had all been warned of the possibility of a tornado by weathermen. If there were such a thing as God, then warnings wouldn't be possible.

Wilson climbed out of the culvert. Slowly and covertly, he began to make his way to his house, but wasn't exactly sure where it was any longer. If not for the part of the church that still stood, the church steeple, he wouldn't know positively that his house, or its ruble, lay strewn nearby. He didn't see anyone else about, and that was good. He wanted to search the rubble, to find what he was looking for in private. Everything else could wait.

As he approached what he thought were the remains of his house, he listened, tried to hear if anyone cried out for help. When he heard nothing, he figured his wife and daughter had been killed in the storm, and if that were true, they'd turn up later. He wasn't going to go searching for them.

He'd play the victim later if he had to, too, but for now he had to get to the church and see if anything incriminating had been uncovered by the tornado. Slowly he made his way over and through rubble. He saw things that didn't belong to his family lying in amidst things that did. A souvenir from a state park someone visited; a shattered photo with its frame all eschew resting on top of the bed that belonged to his wife's mother, personal items everywhere. Theirs, and other people's things, mixed in with shattered timber, torn insulation, wires, and shattered glass. He had to be careful where he placed his feet.

Even though he didn't much care if anyone was dead or not, the damage that the storm wrought unnerved him. It had lasted less than five minutes, and in that time, everything that the whole town had worked for, and maintained for more than 100 years, was shattered and lying at his feet. He stood a long minute looking around at his home, and at what once was the town. Even most of the trees were gone. Those that remained where scared, too, and some contained the remnants of what was once a family car, a tractor, and even a plow rested in one.

He saw that the store downtown still stood and immediately grew angry at the sight. He hated Mrs. Conway with a passion, and wished to God that she had been killed, but he doubted that she had from the looks of things. Oh well, he thought, you can't always get everything you want.

He saw, too, that the Hanson's still had their garage. As he stood staring at it, he noticed a few people walking up Main Street, and heading toward the garage that was just north of his house on the south end of town. He watched for a brief second then ducted down behind rubble as more and more people emerged from the wreckage and headed for the garage. He would wait until they were all inside then he would make his way to the church, which once sat behind the garage, but for the most part, was now just so much rubble. The only thing still standing strong was the steeple, which towered over the town. There were things stored in that steeple that he didn't want anyone else find—incriminating things. He had to get to it before anyone else did.

Chapter Twenty-Six

The National Guard was on its way to help the people of Rutledge, thanks to the sheriff. The Salvation Army had already arrived setting up shop in the garage, serving meals, tending wounds, and getting those who needed it, warm clothing. Even though it was still hot and humid, many people were cold because of shock. Medical help was on the way, too.

Hansen thought it amazing how fast he and his deputies had been able to start the whole recovery effort moving. The tornado hadn't caused much damage anywhere else, except for a few outlying areas, so he concentrated his efforts where they were needed the most. His officers managed to move stalled or abandoned vehicles off Highway 61 leading in and out of town so medical emergency vehicles could get through. Surprisingly, not many were hurt badly, so his efforts could go immediately into searching the debris for anyone who was still missing. Even that didn't seem like it would be a major rescue effort for most of the townspeople were right there in the garage. Mrs. Conway, the Wilsons, Mr. Thompson, they were all unaccounted for yet, however. One teenager who had slipped out of his house before the storm was also missing. He didn't know of any others.

Hansen began his efforts by placing deputies at the outskirts of town on the north end. He paired them in groups of twos with each pair given an area of two blocks wide and two blocks deep to walk and search thoroughly. When finished with that area, they would continue through town walking two block by two block squares until they reached the south side of town. Each group stationed next to the other was to remain in that position. No two-paired team would move ahead to the next area without the other two-paired team, assuring that nothing went unsearched.

As the sheriff worked to organize the search and rescue parties, Renee waited impatiently to talk to him, alone. She had approached him to speak with him earlier, but he was curt and dismissed her telling her she would have to wait.

As she walked away from him dejected, he wavered, but simply couldn't take the time for the kid at that moment. He made a note to seek her out once he was assured everything was proceeding smoothly with the search. That had to remain his priority.

As that got underway, he took a deep breath and looked around him. It was the first moment he'd had since arriving in Rutledge two hours earlier to take a deep breath and assess the situation. Renee sat by the front doors of the garage watching him. He motioned for her to come over to where he stood next to a cruiser that one of the deputies had the foresight to drive into to town once the roads had been cleared.

"Okay, kid. What is that you want to tell me?" Hansen towered over Renee like a giant. His six-foot-seven inch frame rose up into the sky blocking the sun from view as Renee stood there looking up at him.

She looked nervously about her first, still not saying anything.

"Look, we can get in the car and talk, would you like that?"

She nodded and after getting comfortable inside, she told the sheriff everything that had happened before the storm. He took notes and although his face revealed nothing, looking as if it were carved in flint, he was, on the one hand elated. The kid sitting next to him had been smart enough to get away, and had not been hurt too badly. He also knew that now he had a witness that could really make a case against the pastor. It would not be easy otherwise.

His growing suspicions about the pastor being the killer of Shannon Thompson and Francine Hanson where now being confirmed by the waif sitting next to him, a little thing probably weighing less than a 100 pounds, he figured. She had outwitted one smart cookie, too, and had managed to stay alive, to his great relief. He didn't think he could bear finding another murdered child in his midst.

But he didn't want to assume, yet, that the pastor was for sure the killer. Oh, the man was off all right, and he'd be able to book him on charges of kidnapping and attempted rape, for sure, just for the molestation of the girls the night before, which Renee also revealed to him, but he'd need more solid proof that the pastor was his murderer.

He knew it was never a good idea to feel that there was only one suspect. A good cop had to keep an open mind, cover all the bases, try, and look at every possibility. It wasn't always easy, especially when he sensed he was on the right track, like now. But his other suspects, the carnies, had checked out. They couldn't have killed the girls, at least not both of them, and he could tell both girls had been killed by the same person.

"Do your friends know what happened to you and Holly at the fair yesterday?" Hansen asked this because he could see that three young girls were now hovering about the garage door entrance staring at the patrol car. Renee couldn't see them as she sat facing Hansen.

"Yes. They're the ones who insisted I tell you as soon as possible. They are worried someone else is going to get hurt."

"They're right. You let them know that. You did the right thing by telling me, and don't you worry. What that pastor did was kidnapping, and it's more than illegal. He may well have been attempting to hurt you, too, I think you're right about that, and if we get more evidence, we'll be able to charge him with that, too. If that root cellar checks out the way you think it will, we'll find it there. You've been a great help. Don't you forget that . . . oh . . . by the way, you are going to have to give a statement to one of the patrol officers when they get back. We have to get this on record. Okay?"

"Yes, I guess so . . . Can I go now?"

"You sure can." Renee opened the door and was swinging it wide when the sheriff said, "You girls stick close together, and to the garage with a few trusted adults until we catch this guy. He's still out there somewhere, okay?" Renee nodded her head.

"Why don't you tell Sam to come here. I need to talk to him, too."

Renee looked over to the garage at Sam who was talking with Judy. Together, they looked much different than at any other time she had seen the two together before. For the first time she didn't feel a pang of jealousy as she watched them. Both teenagers smiled at her as she approached.

"Sam, the sheriff said he'd like to talk to you."

"Okay, kid," he said as he rubbed her head and headed off to speak with the sheriff.

Renee fumed that he should dismiss her so in front of Judy, her arch nemesis in her love for him. Would he ever see her as anything but a kid!

"You know, he's really pretty decent," Judy said absentmindedly as she watched Sam walk away from her. "I can't believe I have been so mean to him."

Renee just looked at her. Her heart sank. "You mean you like him more than you did before?" She asked timidly.

"Yeah, I do, but in a different way. I see him differently now. I was just using him before, for sex, you know, but now, well, I don't think I can do that anymore."

No, Renee did not know. She still didn't know for sure just what sex was, but she did know instinctively that she had escaped from finding out through violence. When this was all over, if her mother didn't pack her up and take her away forever, she was going to find out exactly what Judy was talking about!

Back at Mrs. Conway's, as he ducked his tall six-foot-three-inch frame down so he could get through the underground tunnel leading to the root cellar, Ralph Thompson wondered how any man had made it through this passageway before. Then he chuckled to himself, for not many had. It was an escape route for abused women, mostly. He wondered if he was the first man to lay eyes on it and thought he might be, aside from Mrs. Conway's husband, who had built the tunnel in the first place. Man, he must have been something, Thompson thought as he followed Mrs. Conway slowly along the dimly lit walkway.

How many years had they been using the tunnel? How long had women needed to escape abuse? Well, he knew that answer from his own work— for as long as there has been such a thing as marriage. Why did men seem to think it was okay to beat up their wives? He would never understand it. From the women he saw in his office, he knew that many had escaped death at their husband's hands, by a very narrow margin. He also knew just as many didn't. He prosecuted their husbands for first-degree murder often enough. Those men rarely understood that beating their wives to death was a bad thing, and the brutality of it never ceased to confound him.

He wished he had known about Mrs. Conway's activities before, though. He could have directed a few of his clients her way, but he guessed that was why she and her husband, now just her, had been so successful over the years. Few knew about them.

He needed to see the root cellar proper, too, needed to know if it was where Shannon had been murdered. He suspected the pastor was the culprit, hadn't liked him from the first time he laid eyes on him, but he didn't want to assume he was the killer, not without more proof. He wanted the right man to pay for his daughter's rape and murder, wanted to kill the man himself.

For Francine he wanted justice. Not many within the system would give her death much consideration because of who she had been, the family she was from, but he would make sure he did. Francine, he felt, was the key. She would lead him to the one who killed Shannon and he'd be ever grateful to her for that. He would make sure she got as much attention in death as Shannon did in life. It was the least he could do.

Before anyone had begun searching the town, Wilson skulked around the churchyard looking for anything that might incriminate him. He knew the sheriff had arrived and was over at the garage, not fifty yards away, so he had to be very careful not to make noise. He didn't want to be found just yet. He could overhear everything being said and knew when the sheriff organized the search party. He was glad they started at the other end of town, but that still didn't leave him much time. He'd make sure a search party found him by the time they reached the south end of town. He hoped that wouldn't be for a few hours yet as he poked his way through ruble, bent over at the waist, working to remain hidden from the labyrinth of eyes just north of where he searched.

Though debris lay everywhere, Wilson recognized the churchyard easily. He did the church proper as well, could tell where everything had once been. Slowly, methodically, as quietly as possible, he lifted off wood and tin and drywall looking carefully underneath it all, searching for anything incriminating, plotting his next move, where he'd let the search party find him.

When he found a few of his hidden items, he sighed with relief, glad he was the first to search the area. He found one of Francine's bras that she had left him as a souvenir. Maybe folks would have thought it got over into the churchyard because of the storm, but he couldn't take that chance. He enjoyed it now as much as he had the day she left it for him.

God, no one had breasts as large as hers! He could almost touch them, even now. He almost wished he hadn't killed her, but she had left him no choice.

He also found the scarf Shannon had been wearing around her neck the night he picked her up in his Cadillac. He liked the smell of it too, remembering how he had enjoyed taking her innocence away from her, her screaming at him as he did. It was very different with Francine. She gave herself willingly, and he had loved it. She taught him things he didn't know were possible. Still, she was no replacement for innocence.

No one seemed to know Shannon had changed clothes when she left the parade that day, that's why he had the scarf to remember her by. When she answered his knock on the door, she was ready to come back out and find her friends. She had put up a fight, resisted. He even had to wipe up a little blood from the nose bled he gave her; and she may have lost one of her shoes in the struggle, but how tantalizing it had all been! The more she fought, the more aroused he had become. At memories of Shannon's abduction, his mouth watered in anticipation of his next deflowering. He couldn't wait.

In the meantime, he tried to find his way to the church basement entrance. He would hide the things he'd found in the rubble down there with his other souvenirs. He liked to keep little mementos of each girl he'd seduced. Until Shannon, he hadn't murdered anyone, but he had raped plenty. How easy it was, too, to threaten those girls into silence. The allure of the power he had over them as their pastor, confessor, made him tingle, but never as much as with the taking of human life, what a power surge that had been!

He was often awed, and somehow disappointed, that his wife and Gloria didn't seem to have a clue, know he possessed items from other lovers, and had hidden those items under their noses for years. It was so easy in fact, he was bored with it. People were always enamored of him; he could do almost anything and get away with it. And, he had to admit, the danger of possible discovery excited him almost as much as the murders themselves.

From where he worked, he could hear conversations going on at the garage. He knew Renee was there, as were the other girls. She'd tell the sheriff of his abduction of her, he was sure, but maybe, just maybe, in all the confusion, he could get to her and finish her off before she had that chance. She was just a poor farmer's kid after all. Her folks weren't even from town! It would be her word against his if she got to the sheriff before he could get to her, and even if she did, who would be believed over whom? He was confident the sheriff would honor him as much as everyone else always had.

In the past, he'd always managed to convince adults of his innocence if one of his flock went to them with a complaint. He felt confident he could do it again. Still, he wanted to get to Renee simply because she had the temerity to get away from him. It would be a joy to throttle her and feel her life ebb from her body as he enjoyed her flesh. He'd drag out the pleasure for a long time, too, make her die slowly just so she'd know who was really in charge.

Renee's escape had unnerved him more than he realized, he discovered as he worked through the debris-laden ground. No one had ever even attempted that before. He found he liked the challenge of it, thought it was stimulating. She wouldn't be as easy a prey as the others, making her all the more enticing. The more he thought about it, the more he anticipated getting her alone once again, and doing what he wanted with her. It aroused him more than he thought possible.

He fought to keep his mind on the task at hand. He didn't need to get careless in the midst of so much turmoil. As for the tornado, he couldn't have contrived a better circumstance if he had planned it himself. In all the confusion, it would be even easier to recapture Renee, and secret her off amid the storm debris somewhere. It would be a long time before all the debris was cleared away. He'd be able to hide away better than he ever had before, and he could do anything he wanted to her in any one of a 100 homes. He could have his way with as many as he wanted, too, as he noticed none were being careful about protecting themselves any longer, forgetting the danger they had been in, being so traumatized by the tornado. All he had to do was listen to people talking to tell him that.

One by one, perhaps, he would grab all of Shannon's friends and make quick work of them, too. Thoughts of recapturing Renee aroused him to fever pitch. It would take more than just one little girl to quench that thirst, now. At that moment, he wished Gloria were there with him. She was always good at relieving those pressing, intimate needs, that needed quenching immediately.

That was the only thought of remorse he gave toward his daughter whom he assumed perished in the storm.

Across town, while Wilson was relishing the idea of recapturing Renee, the first thing searchers found was the teenage boy who had disappeared in the storm. They stumbled upon him as they searched the northern most block of town. They came upon a German shepherd and a Golden Retriever lying close to something on someone's front lawn. As searchers approached, the dogs snarled, emitting low growls. From a distance, the dogs looked okay, although blood could be seen in the grass where they lay. Searchers pushed in closer, seeing that something lay between the two dogs that they were protecting. As they drew closer, they saw the body of a young man, and as they drew closer still, the dogs whimpered, got up and moved away from the boy.

By this time those searchers had called out to fellow searchers, and as more arrived, some with experience handling animals captured the dogs easily, and checked them over for injuries.

When the searchers examined the unconscious young man, they found his left leg was severely broken, as was his right arm. They supposed he had been pelted with debris, possibly some of the two by fours they found lying about the area. An ambulance arrived, and whisked the young man off to the nearest hospital. He hadn't regained consciousness, but the EMT's told searchers his vital signs were good, so he'd be okay.

A vet, too, had arrived and told them the same thing about the dogs. They'd be okay, too. In fact, they were in such good shape, the vet suggested that the search party use them to sniff out injured people, and rescuers jumped at the opportunity. The vet joined the search handling the German shepherd himself.

Though the search party took its time going through debris as they made their way to the garage, no one else was found on the northern end of town. Searchers stopped for a break once they reached the garage, then a team of five, including the vet with the dog, decided they'd finish the search behind the garage. No other houses were across the street. All that remained to be searched were the church and the pastor's house, they thought.

Searchers started in the Wilson's yard as Mr. and Mrs. Wilson were still missing. They spread out and walked the fields with the vet in the lead. The big German shepherd lowered his head frantically making his way across the cornfield lying south of the house.

The tornado had cleared a large path through that, too. The field was heavy laden with odds-and-ends of houses, doors here, a toy there, someone's photo album stuck in a corn stock, even a set of dishes were strewn about in the corn. That was all but ignored by the dog that kept his nose to the ground making a beeline for one particular row of corn. There, he made a mad dash in a straight line, pulling with such force on the leash, the vet had to fight to keep up with him. Once he reached a large pile of debris, the dog stopped dead in his tracks and started to whine.

The vet guessed that something or someone was under the old mattress, some broken boards, scattered bits of a barbed wire fence, and other odds-and-ends, but he didn't want to be the first to look under it. By this time, other members of the search party had come up behind him, panting as they tried to catch their breath, the dog leading them faster than many had traveled in some time. Searchers began removing debris, piece by piece, and as the vet feared, underneath it all they found a body, that of Mrs. Wilson, broken and bloody and obviously dead. As her body was uncovered, the dog sat down on his haunches and started to howl, letting out the eeriest sound that the searchers had ever heard. It was as if he mourned for the dead.

The people back at the garage all grew silent at the sound, knowing something bad had happened to someone they knew. The howling was too ominous to mean much else.

The dog continued to bay. The more intense he became, the more agitated the people in the garage became, and one by one, and two by two, they trickled out into the field to find out what the dog was howling about.

The only ones left inside the garage were the girls. Finally, Renee could stand it no longer and went running out before her friends could stop her.

"I'm not going out there!" Holly was adamant. "There's probably somebody dead out there!"

"Hey, you don't have to convince me, kid!" Judy said. She certainly didn't want to see a dead body, either! Neither did Kathy, although she didn't say anything. She was too worried about Renee, and was tempted to run after her.

"Maybe we should go with her. You know the sheriff said we should all stick together? Whoever killed Shannon might be out there," Kathy said quietly.

"Well, the whole town is out there. If she isn't safe with the whole town, whom is she going to be safe with, for crying out loud!" Judy had her hands on her hips again yelling at her sister.

"I guess you're right," Kathy conceded.

Holly moved outside and stood at the back of the garage, watching. She could see everyone in the field. There were so many people. She couldn't see Renee specifically, but then she could be in the front of the rest of the townspeople hidden from view, she reasoned.

Chapter Twenty-Seven

Renee ran out of the garage heading for the field where everyone else had gathered. She didn't want to be with the other kids. She had an overwhelming desire to be with the adults.

She slowed down as she walked past what was left of the church, fearing the pastor might somehow be inside and lunge out at her from some dark recess. She stepped cautiously past the church steeple, which stood naked and alone against the stark blue sky and amid vast mounds of tornado-strewn debris.

Renee thought it ironic, the steeple standing alone such as it was. Maybe God was trying to tell everyone in town something. Her skin broke out in goose bumps as she approached the largest pile of debris figuring it had to be the bulk of the church as she saw a pew here, a hymnal there. She also saw pieces of stained glass window scattered about the dirt; she stepped cautiously over boards with long nails sticking up out of them. She made her way over bits and pieces of a tin roof that had dislodged from some village home to land in the churchyard. As she went, she continued her vigil, making sure she had an escape route planned in case the pastor did jump out at her. What really gripped her attention as she trekked through what was left of the church, however, was the howling dog.

As she listened, she forgot herself and her surroundings, and ceased to pay close attention to either. She became so engrossed in the dog's wailing that her insecurity left her for she could see that the town's adults were only a few hundred feet in front of her. She ignored the hackles on the back of her neck as they stood up attributing them to the howling dog, the noise so eerie in the bright sunshine. If she had been paying more attention to her immediate surroundings, she would have recognized the feeling for what it was—a danger signal.

As Renee focused on the adults in the field and the howling dog, Pastor Joseph Wilson could not believe his luck. Here was the little twerp right in front of him, and all she was doing was staring off into the field where everyone else in town was. Not only that, she was about to walk right to him—he was so blessed! That was all there was to it! No one could have this kind of luck and not have it come from a divine source. Luck, combined with his cunning, would serve him well this day, he thought.

He glowed, knowing that he would get his desires and the little twerp who had escaped him earlier would still be his. All he had to do was wait these last few seconds until she positioned herself just right before he grabbed her. None of the townspeople knew she was there, he could tell, as they all seemed fixated on something in the field. He rested on his haunches, ready to spring, much like a lioness waits in the tall grass as she stalks her prey anticipating the exact right time to move in for the kill. He would have to be quieter than a cat if he wanted to secure this prey away from all those prying eyes just ahead. Not much can take a kill from a big cat in the wild, and he intended the same to be true in his world. If he didn't wait for the exact right moment, everyone from town would want to deprive him of his hard-earned meal.

As he watched Renee draw ever closer, Wilson's mouth salivated at the thought of enjoying her young flesh. This one had escaped his grasp once, but she wouldn't be doing that a second time.

Across town, and underground, they were coming up out of the root cellar when Mr. Thompson offered Mrs. Conway assistance with the steps. She refused, slapping his hand away in disgust, saying, "Just how many times do you think I've been up and down these steps, Sonny? I never asked for help before and I ain't about to start now." The two decided to go back to the garage outside rather than through the tunnel. Both felt an urgent need to assess the tornado damage.

Mr. Thompson ran his hand over his face in frustration. She was a hard woman to get along with, but he was glad she had at least let him tag along with her to the root cellar. There they had found evidence that Shannon had been there, and he could not wait to find the sheriff to tell him about it.

As Mrs. Conway climbed up the last stair of the root cellar into the open, Thompson took the time to take a good look about him. The tornado damage was extensive. He had a hard time absorbing it, making it real in his mind. Though he had already seen much of it, he hadn't comprehended it, he had been so intent on searching for Shannon's killer. Now, with some evidence to help in the investigation of Shannon's death allowing him to put his focus elsewhere, he began to grasp the magnitude of the whole town's situation.

As Mrs. Conway stepped out into the bright afternoon sun, she too, had a hard time digesting what she was seeing. At 111-years of age, she was the oldest living person in Rutledge, and she remembered well its humble beginnings. She was the village's oldest living citizen, and had lived through the entire history of it. She was saddened to see it brought to such ruin in one fell swoop.

From where they stood, however, they could not see everything.

"Never thought I'd see the day," Mrs. Conway said out-loud although she was speaking to herself and had not directed her comments to Thompson.

"Nor did I," he offered anyway, knowing what she meant.

"How much of the town is gone?" She asked for the first time since the tornado had hit.

"Everything, but your place and the garage, everyone went there after the storm, but I think I told you that?"

"Yeah, you did. Anybody get hurt?"

"No one that I know of; of course when I went to your place, no one had even looked yet, but it seemed like most folks were at the garage."

"Well, that's good I guess. Now come on young man. Me and you got to get to that gas station. Maybe the sheriff is there by now. Let's get the lead out."

With that, she took off walking so slowly Thompson had to force himself repeatedly to take smaller steps to keep in step with her. She may not want my help, but she might need it, so I'm sticking by her, he thought. But it frustrated him. He wanted to run to the garage and find the sheriff. His sticking close to Mrs. Conway proved to be the right thing, he saw, as they reached the bridge over Willow River. The tunnel bypassed the river, but to go back to the garage outside, they would have to cross the bridge. It was in bad shape. Part of it was twisted so that it no longer rested on its foundation. It looked as if a giant hand had come down and twisted it half way open, and it rested on a severe angle to one side. Luckily for them, the edge of the metal beams on the north side still remained flat enough to walk across though they twisted out over the river, but were stable regardless of the list.

Below the bridge, Willow River rolled on, its calm façade masking the fact that beneath its waters strong currents sucked everything underneath in its tow hurtling them downstream. The current could suck a person under quickly taking the life out of them so fast, they wouldn't be able to save themselves were they to slip and fall into it, and both Thompson and Mrs. Conway knew it.

Slowly, cautiously the two made their way across. The river unnerved Thompson for the first time in his life. He couldn't help but look down as they crossed the bridge on its twisted beams, because of the shape of the steel, they had to walk across to get over it. Water splashed up onto the steel girders, making them slippery and treacherous. Thompson forced himself to stay calm; he had to help Mrs. Conway. Mrs. Conway seemed perfectly secure as she crossed the bridge holding onto twisted steel as she slowly inched her way across. Since she moved so slowly anyway, Thompson wasn't sure if she was just slow or if she were being cautious. He was not going to ask.

Finally they reached the other side, and Thompson hopped off the girder with delight relishing the firm ground under his feet. Mrs. Conway just got off the bridge, stood next to him for a brief moment, then slowly started heading toward the garage saying, "Now you just take yerself a break there, Sonny. I know that river scared you some."

Mr. Thompson looked at her, exasperated. How does she know? Disgusted, he forced himself to move ahead. This time he worked to stay behind her. He didn't need any more of her observations at the moment.

His peevishness left him quickly as he forced himself to think of the mission they were on. He couldn't wait to find the sheriff; he had so much to tell him. Lost in thought, he found himself passing Mrs. Conway once again. Once again he forced himself to slow down. She deserved much of the credit for finding who killed his daughter and he would not forget that. The least he could do was force himself to walk at her pace.

Over at the churchyard, while Mrs. Conway and Mr. Thompson were making their way to the garage, Wilson grabbed Renee. It was easy. She was focused on getting to the group of folks in the field, and was not paying close attention to what surrounded her. After covering her mouth and choking her just enough to knock her out, he drug her downstairs to the basement of the church, which earlier he had discovered was still okay and easy enough to get into. He hoped that whatever had drawn the town's attention in the field would occupy them long enough for him to remove Renee to a more secure location, but he was safe for the moment.

Rescue workers wouldn't be getting to the church to cleanup for a long time, he reasoned, but they had not searched the area, yet, so they might show up for that. In which case, where could he take the girl to finish what he started earlier? The root cellar was out of the question. It would be too hard to get her through the labyrinth of tornado-strewn debris to get there, for one thing. Besides, he didn't know who owned the place and couldn't take the chance of being discovered in case the whelp had told anyone about it, and they decided to see how it had fared during the storm—so—where then? It came to him just where he needed to go. It would be perfect. Again, the storm had blessed him more than he could say.

Renee, coming out of unconsciousness, began to stir. Lucky for him he kept supplies in the church basement. They would serve him well. He moved over to the supply cabinet on the far wall where he found just what he was wanted. He couldn't remember why he kept the ether, but was glad he had as he poured the liquid on a rag and went back over to Renee to cover her nose. That would knock her out for a while. He didn't want to mark her too much by continuing his chokehold on her, but he needed her to stay quiet just the same. This was the next best thing to knocking her out. It wouldn't take much, either. The sight of her lying limp in his arms aroused him, but he forced his mind onto other things. He had to be careful if he wanted to toy with her awhile, and he did.

What the townspeople gawked at, and the dog howled for, was Mrs. Wilson who lay mutilated in the cornfield not fifty yards from her own back door. The tornado had twisted and torn her almost beyond recognition. Townspeople grieved at the sight. She had been popular with many women of the church. She was the first to care for someone in need, to cook, and to help anyone who needed it. Townspeople were ashamed to admit it, but she had been the only one who had really been nice to the Hanson family.

After the shock of the tornado wore off and they realized that it was in the Hanson's garage that they were being cared for, many of the townspeople felt a deep sense of shame. They had systematically shunned the Hansons since before anyone could remember, now here the Hanson family was nursing them back to health. The sight of Mrs. Wilson lying so battered and bruised in the cornfield brought that truth home to them.

A few didn't like it, either.

"Why don't we find a better place to hold up in until we can get things settled," one man noted as they all stared at her body.

"Yeah," one woman said, "there has to be someplace where decent folks can take shelter instead of at the town drunk's garage. I mean, really, is that any place for a good Christian woman, inside the dwelling of a heathen prone to strong drink?"

A few others murmured the same sentiments.

"Seems to me it's been them 'heathens prone to drink' that have behaved in the most Christian like manner," one man, standing to the back of the crowd said. He garnered dirty looks from many of those standing around him.

"You folks with your noses in the air, I suggest you go home and find yourselves your own shelter if you think you can. Maybe it'd be best if you stayed here helping others, including the Hansons, like they've been doing for you. I didn't come here to listen to any petty quarrels over whose better than whom, either, but to help get everyone here back on their feet, and to make sure everyone's okay. And I do mean everyone! Besides, we still have Mr. Wilson to find," the man said.

Sheriff Hansen felt the same way, and wasn't too keen on those standing around him voicing negative sentiments against the Hansons; he had all he could do to fight down telling them all where they could get off. But people were still missing. They had to find them, and they would all damn well cooperate or he'd throw them in jail. Not such a bad idea, he thought as he found a blanket and covered Mrs. Wilson with it. Immediately those mumbling against the Hansons started pitching in once again. The dead woman had inspired nasty things from the crowd. Hansen wondered why.

Finally, across town and ever so slowly, Mrs. Conway huffed and puffed as they reached the garage, the effort of the long arduous walk showing on her frail body. But instead of stopping, she kept right on walking confounding Mr. Thompson. "Estelle! Where are you going," he cried.

"Gloria Wilson needs help. She's trapped and unconscious. If we don't get her help soon, the child is going to die!"

"How do you know that and how do you know where she is?"

"The Lord told me. Now you gonna help me or what? Get the lead out if you are. There's a wall fallen in on top of her; I'll need help lifting it off."

He trotted up next to Mrs. Conway wistfully looking at the garage as they passed by. He thought it odd that no one seemed to be inside, at least he didn't see anyone. As they turned off Main Street and walked into the church parking lot, he could see why. Everyone seemed to be in the cornfield just past what was left of the pastor's house.

Mrs. Conway went nowhere near the church proper, instead veering off to her right and heading southeast across the churchyard. She made a beeline for a debris pile that lay strewn about a small area where a neat green grass lawn, which didn't appear to have been disturbed in the storm, looked absurd alongside the destruction lying about it.

Still huffing and puffing, Mrs. Conway said, "She's in here, Thompson. Go in there and see if you can find her. I don't have a flashlight or nothing, so do the best you can. Call her name; maybe she'll answer."

He did as he was told, but was angry with Mrs. Conway for speaking to him as if he were a child, him a well-respected man of means. He choked down the gall rising in his throat and did as she instructed. He doubted that he would find anyone, but decided to call out anyway.

"Gloria," he whispered loudly then wondered to himself why he was speaking as if he were in a library. "Gloria!" Louder. This time he thought he heard a response. He stood near a fallen wall, but much of the roof covered it making it near impossible to reach, as did the other walls, which seemed to have fallen against it. A myriad assortment of other debris filled in every other conceivable space around the one t-pee like wall that still almost stood upright. If anyone were underneath that wall, they stood half a chance of surviving as it blocked off the rest of the debris that overwhelmed the space.

Mrs. Conway stood outside the debris pile, and was about to say something, when Thompson held up his palm indicating she should keep quiet. He heard the noise again. This time it sounded as if someone were moaning. He listened harder and as the moans became more frequent, he was able to zero in on their location. He grew so intent on his purpose, he didn't notice that Mrs. Conway had taken off again.

She headed out into the field. Thompson would need help and she could see the others out there. She hoped beyond hope that the sheriff was there by now, too. They needed outside help. Her prayers where answered when she saw the big man lumbering toward her. With him were some strangers she didn't recognize, and between them they were carrying a gurney of sorts with something that looked like a body on top of it. Behind them, she saw the whole town walking toward her. She stopped. They'd have to come to her now. She was too tired to go any further.

As they met, she told Hansen about someone being caught in the pastor's house while one of the younger EMT's with the group picked her up, and proceeded to carry her back to what remained of the Wilson house as she directed. She, however, got so angry with the EMT she punched him in the back trying to force him to put her back down on the ground. She'd use her own two feet to get where she had to go, thank you very much. But since the young man carrying her was a devout body builder, there wasn't a thing she could do about it. He wouldn't listen to her spitting and sputtering about being able to take care of herself, either. She, weighing about ninety-five pounds, wasn't too big a burden for him to bare, he being only nineteen-years old, and weighing over 200-pounds and standing well over six feet. Hell, he'd carried heavier survival gear with him on National Guard outings! He laughed at her fussing about letting her down, which infuriated her all the more.

When everyone reached the pastor's house, however, Mrs. Conway became as quiet as the others except as she directed the sheriff to where Thompson had gone into the debris pile. She was glad now that the sheriff had such strong help as the young man who had insisted on carrying her sat her down, and began helping the sheriff move debris.

As Hansen called out to Thompson, he heard muffled voices coming from inside the debris pile near a wall that was almost standing upright, but precariously at an angle. It appeared to be supported by more debris lying underneath it. Not the strongest nor the safest load bearing support, Hansen thought as he listened intently for more sounds to direct himself to Thompson, and whoever else might be lying beneath the pile of trash he found himself standing in. It was hard to tell exactly where he was, but he figured it was somewhere inside the Pastor Wilson's house, or rather, where the house had once been. He listened intently then heard clearly Thompson calling out to him. He walked into the debris pile where he discovered an almost door like opening leading into the chaos. It was amazing. Here, not one piece of debris could be found. He could see the floorboards of the house, walking down what looked like a hallway. To his right sat what was left of the wall, angling off the roof, but leaving a V-like opening on both sides. He hadn't ventured into the other side yet, but thought he heard Thompson calling to him from the other side of the wall.

Thompson had found his way to Gloria easily enough. It was almost as if the storm had left him a path to get to her. He wondered if God had made it. When he reached the girl, he found her unconscious, periodically awaking enough to let out a moan. Soon he was joined by the sheriff and the EMT's who quickly assessed Gloria's condition, and had her loaded onto a gurney and out of there quicker than the others could respond. Soon ambulance sirens were blazing and Gloria was rushed to the hospital in Willow River.

By that time, everyone in town had gathered outside the pastor's house. Most were relieved to find that Gloria was okay. They wondered where her father was, knowing that Gloria's mother was dead. What kind of condition would they find him in?

Chapter Twenty-Eight

The pastor, realizing, to his delight, the perfect place to hide and do as he wished with Renee, lugged the drugged twelve-year-old up the 111 steps of the steeple belfry. She was easy to carry, being drugged she didn't put up a fight, and upstairs, he knew, he would have the best seat in the house to keep abreast of his situation. Out of the tower, he could see everything happening around him clearly, but no one could see up into it. It was perfect.

He hadn't reached the top yet when he heard the townspeople outside somewhere near where his house had been. He supposed they were trying to rescue either his wife or Gloria, but he didn't care, not really, what the results of their efforts would be. Their voices were muffled inside the tower so he didn't learn through eavesdropping if his family were still alive.

The 111 steps began to tell on him, however, once he reached the seventieth step. He had been out and exerting himself for a long time already that day. He was no longer a young man, although he kept fit and trim, lifting weights every other day and jogging five days a week. At forty-five-years of age, he could no longer keep up continuous efforts for twelve hours without feeling the effects of that effort on his body. Knowing he had a cot upstairs he decided that once he reached the belfry, he'd tie Renee up, put tape over her mouth, and set her aside up there, then lay down for awhile. He was sure that would be okay, since the town couldn't possibly consider it a need to climb into the tower, one of the only still standing structures in town, to look for him. They'd be searching debris piles for his lifeless body. He liked that idea.

Over at the garage, townspeople gathered together around the desk inside Dennis' office. No one thought of the garage as belonging to the father because he was always too drunk to work, but Dennis was always a presence there except when in school.

Mrs. Conway was given the most comfortable seat in the room, Dennis' office chair. Dennis loved that chair and was glad he had a chance to do something nice for the old lady who had always been so nice to him even when the rest of the town treated him like dirt. He hoped she enjoyed its comfort as much as he did after a long day. After being in school all day, he often had to work until ten or eleven p.m. to keep his family going.

Sam stood with Dennis to the side of the file cabinets behind the desk. The office was large and accommodated many of the men from the town. Except for Mrs. Conway, the women decided to busy themselves fixing meals for the men who had labored hard doing back-breaking work moving debris to rescue the few found trapped beneath debris piles. Everyone had been so busy that at first they didn't notice that Renee was not with them.

"Why don't you and Renee see what you can find for paper plates and utensils so we can serve the men something to eat before they continue searching," Mrs. Spur said to Holly, who after her mother had returned from the field, hadn't left her side. Kathy and Judy hovered about the adult women as well, hoping to help their mother and the others.

Holly looked about her then, realizing that she hadn't seen Renee in quite some time. She had not been with the group of adults when they returned from the field. She looked for Judy and Kathy in the crowd, saw them, but could not see Renee anywhere. "Where is Renee? Mom, have you seen her?"

Mrs. Spur stopped working, held her breath, stood straight up, and searched the large, cavernous mechanic work stalls for Renee, holding her throat in terror. Inside she wanted to scream with fright, but quietly and quickly she left the women's side, and went into the office where the men worked planning their next foray out into the storm tossed town.

Mr. Spur sat on an oil can to the left of the younger men, listening, waiting to hear what he could do to help in the search efforts. He noticed his wife immediately, angry that she came into the office flaunting her beauty in front of all the young men. He had all he could do to refrain from jumping up, knocking her down, and throwing her out the big double garage doors.

What really angered him the most was that when she walked in, the room went silent, so much so that he could hear the breathing of those standing around. Even Hansen went quiet at her approach.

At the sight of Mrs. Spur, the hair on the back of Mrs. Conway's neck stood up and she knew one of her little ones was in trouble.

"Has anyone seen Renee, Holly's friend? Is she in here?" Mrs. Spur hoped beyond hope that Renee had wanted to join in the search efforts, and was comfortably protected within the safety of the office and her friends and family.

"She's not in here, Mom," Sam replied with a sickening feeling plunging his stomach into knots he thought would make him vomit. "Isn't she out there with you?"

"If she were, son, I wouldn't be in here asking if she were here, now would I?"

Sam knew that, he was just praying that his mother was wrong and that Renee was safely with the women of the town. She wasn't.

What the townspeople didn't know was that Renee was only yards from them in the belfry. Renee tasted something bitter in her mouth as she came to, metallic like; she wanted to vomit, felt something gagging her and realized her mouth was taped shut with duct tape. A cool breeze sent chills throughout her small frame.

She couldn't remember why, but something had her on the alert, cautioned her not to reveal that she was awake. She warily opened one eye a slit to take in her surroundings. She looked without turning her head to try and figure out where she was, and while she did, she tried to move her fingers but found them bound together behind her back. Her muscles ached. Cautiously she tried to move her feet, but found them bound as well. She couldn't move. She was tied up!

She could see the steeple bell above her, the open casements to her left, and knew that somehow she'd managed to climb the steeple steps, but how? Slowly, through the cobwebs of her mind, what happened came back to her. Wilson had grabbed her and held his hand over her mouth so tightly and quickly she hadn't had time to call for help! He must be up there with her!

With that thought she shut her eye and listened intently. She heard nothing at all except the gentle breezes blowing through the tower. She cautiously opened her right eye a slit to see if Wilson were on that side of her. She didn't see him then, either. Her back was to a wall, so he couldn't be behind her, she reasoned, then more confidently she opened both eyes.

"Well, well, well, look what we have here. The little birdie has finally come back to life."

A chill, like she'd never experienced before, ran down Renee's spine. How the pastor could see she was awake eluded her, but he saw, all right. He was hiding behind a pillar and stepped out as she opened both eyes, smiling at her like a Cheshire cat. She was terrified.

At the garage, Mrs. Conway excused herself to use the bathroom, or so she told the men in the office. What she was really intent on was getting to the church steeple where she knew Renee was being held captive. The minute Mrs. Spur had come looking for Renee, the Lord revealed to her exactly where the child was, and what Mrs. Conway had to do in this her final hour.

The old outhouse was still behind the garage, which, on this day the townspeople were thankful to have although they'd been complaining about it for years to the city council, saying it was an eyesore and should be removed. The city council never took their complaints seriously as the toilet was out of sight of Main Street, and as they knew, but never bothered to tell the townspeople, was actually out of the city limits on the edge of Hanson's property. Knowing Hanson as they did, they did not wish to incur his wrath or he'd berate them continually every time they had a city council meeting; he'd done it before when they had tried to stop him from operating his business. City drunk though he might be, he still was a force to be reckoned with if they over stepped their bounds, and crossed over into his territory.

And so it was that the old out house remained and Mrs. Conway slowly made her way there. She also decided it was the best place to get some privacy. She needed a little time alone with God so He could reveal His plan. He'd never cared much where she was before when revealing something to her; she doubted He'd care now, especially under the circumstances. And she sure couldn't go home to meditate on it; she was too darn old for all the exercise she was getting. He knew that too, and that her body had seen better days.

She wasn't inside the outhouse long before she knew everything she must do. No one was outside as she opened the door, so she began her trek to the steeple.

Upstairs, Wilson was too intent on Renee to bother looking over the casements at the ground below. He smiled down at her, then squatted alongside, slowly rubbing his fingers over her cheeks. She flinched backward at his touch.

"What's the matter Dear, are you afraid? You needn't be afraid of me, of what I'm offering you. It'll make a woman out of you. You've been waiting for the chance; I know. You look at Sam Spur with such fondness. Imagine how pleased he will be when he finds you know how to really please him," with that Wilson bent over and kissed her on the cheek.

Renee tried to scream, and started to gag with the tape still over her mouth.

Wilson chuckled, enjoying her discomfort tremendously. He ran his fingers down her long, gangly legs, smiling at her as he moved, then tugging at the ropes so that the pressure was relieved some. "See, Dear, how when you're nice to me, I do something nice for you in return? That's how it works in the real world, you know. You scratch my back; I'll scratch yours? Surely you've heard that, even if you are so young?"

As Wilson began his attack on Renee, at the hospital in Willow River, Gloria Wilson fought to regain consciousness. Through her fragmented thoughts, she knew there was something she wanted desperately to tell the police, and as she fought to come up out of the darkness, she began to recall what it was that she so desperately wanted to say.

She arose from the abyss, but before she could come all the way up she saw a light. It burned brightly and called to her with an overwhelming sense of love. There was something wonderful for her there, and she desperately wanted to get to it. Instead, she saw herself twenty years in future talking to young girls, all of whom had gone through similar things she did at the hands of their biological fathers and stepfathers. She saw herself surrounded by them, encouraging them to rise above the circumstances they'd been born into, with God's help, teaching them that God loved them, and that they could be everything He'd purposed for them to be. Then, in another burst of brilliant white light, which she thought might burn her up, Gloria came to, and found herself lying in a hospital bed with a sheriff's deputy sitting beside her.

Hansen had stationed the deputy there to inform Gloria that her mother had died and that her father was still missing. When the deputy saw that she was awake, he did just that thinking that he could leave his boring post after reporting the news, and get back out into the action to help all those people in Rutledge that really needed it. He was dying for some action.

He grew impatient with Gloria as she started to tell him all her father had done to her. She was sad her mother was gone, but at the same time felt that her mother had left her long ago. She grieved for what could have been, but never was between them and was sorry for her mother's failings. She felt she had to press on in telling about her father, however, as others might loose their lives if she didn't. She was sure he was the one responsible for the deaths of Shannon and Francine.

Not too far into the tale, the deputy's attitude turned around 180-degrees as he realized he had information to crack the biggest murder case the county had ever seen. His boss would be pleased, and he now had plenty of reason to get over to Rutledge. When he was assured by the doctors that Gloria was stable and in no danger, he took off running for his squad car.

It was then that Deputy Andy Freboni pulled into the hospital parking lot, and seeing the other deputy's cruiser, pulled up alongside it. Freboni was in charge of the office when Hansen was out in the field and knew to check with the hospital on Gloria Wilson's condition. Both he and Hansen suspected the girl might have plenty to say.

Deputy Harris, excited by what he'd learned, told Freboni everything when he ran into him in the parking lot thinking it would grant him leave to get to Rutledge. Instead, it put Freboni on red alert. He ordered Harris back inside to guard Wilson in case her father showed up. Freboni was in radio contact with the sheriff and knew Pastor Wilson was still missing.

Though Harris was disappointed, he realized this new mission was much more important than he originally thought. He'd be guarding a material witness to the biggest crime to hit the county in over seventy-five years. He'd guard her all right, with his life if he had to. He wouldn't miss it for the world.

Freboni turned on his sirens and headed to Rutledge. He had things to tell the sheriff that wouldn't do to repeat over the radio. Besides, the four miles between towns wouldn't take too long to traverse.

Before everyone in the garage realized Renee was missing, Sam and Dennis's Willow River friends, Henry Sampson, Hank Hall, George King and Smiley Rains gathered at Hank's folk's farm to saddle up the elder Hall's quarter horses, with their parent's blessings, and make their way to Rutledge. The young men figured the roads would be too impassable with debris to make it to Rutledge in Sampson's '55 Chevy. The only one of the group not an experienced rider, Smiley Rains, rode double with the most accomplished equestrian, Hank. The big quarter horse he rode handled two riders easily especially since Smiley was of such a small stature.

Their parents made lunches, filled canteens and packed their saddle-bags full of first aid supplies they figured might be needed in Rutledge. Willow River hadn't sustained too much damage, but some of the outlying areas had, and the young men's parents decided it was there that they were needed most, but knew their sons worried most about those in Rutledge.

Riding in tandem, the young men managed to keep their horses paced at a steady lope as they jumped over fallen trees, veered around strewn machinery, dodged fallen power lines. They saw the power company trucks out along the highway, with men working to get the power poles back up in place, and the power lines reconnected to town. They saw people walking toward town, apparently missed when sheriff's deputies came through. The boys offered the stragglers water, a welcome relief for most as the sun scorched down upon their shell-shocked bodies. None of the young men had ever seen anything like the tornado destruction, and the more they rode, the more frantic they became to find their friends, fearing the worst. Their horses maintained a steady pace with apparently no ill effects as they willingly trod along the debris-strewn path with no shying away from unexpected birds taking flight or unexpected animals running across their paths.

As the boys were making their way to Rutledge on horseback, Mrs. Conway climbed the first ten steps, rested, then continued climbing. This war, she knew, would be her last. That was okay, though, she thought, for it would be a welcome relief to go to her final rest. She'd be with her God, with her husband, whom she hadn't seen or heard from in seventy years or more. For years after he died, she saw him in her dreams waving at her. But the last time he visited her, all he did was smile down at her. She knew in her heart, then, that it would be the last time he visited. It dawned on her the morning after the dream, that he had been visiting her for her sake, not his, and that his smile told her that he knew the worst of the grieving was over for her, and that he could go to his final rest. No words were spoken, but she still "knew" in her heart, that is what the dream foretold. And God had been proven right by it, too, for she was no longer seeped in grief for the man she loved most on the earth, but could continue on without him.

Still, his visits had been nice. She still waited, too, longed for the day when she could spend eternity with him and her God. Her body was worn out. She felt it with each flight of stairs she ascended.

As she climbed, she prayed, continually. The battle belongs to the Lord, she kept saying. She was merely His instrument. She had no idea how she, in and of herself, would battle the man who awaited her in the steeple. He knew she was coming, too, of that she was sure—step by step, she inched her way upward.

Wilson did know she was coming, and awaited her with relish. He saw her creeping toward the steeple, knew she was coming for him. He smiled. As he waited, he fondled Renee as he had in his Cadillac when they went to the carnival. How sweet she was, trying to fight him, her legs and arms bound. Wasn't that the cutest thing? She couldn't escape, neither could the old woman in pursuit of him. He thought it odd she didn't bring the rest of the town with her, or her champion, the sheriff. Well, he wouldn't worry about it; he'd come up with some unusual ways of tormenting her tired old body, too. He'd been waiting for a chance to get at the old hag for a long, long time. He'd relish this golden opportunity.

It was as if the town had blinders on. No one in the garage thought of searching the church tower for Renee. Instead, the sheriff started a search party of two by two beginning at the north end of town once again as he began new rescue efforts. No one questioned his authority.

In the garage, Dennis stewed over what was happening, but said nothing. He didn't think they should start searching for Renee at the north end of town. He wanted them to start at the south end. He didn't know why, but he was frustrated with the sheriff. When Hansen made no effort to include him or Sam with the rest of the searchers, Dennis took Sam aside.

"We ought to be out looking for Renee, too," he said.

To Sam, it was as if Dennis were reading his mind. "Yeah, man, that's what I think, too, but I think the sheriff is going in the wrong direction. We should start at this end."

As he spoke, Wally Spur came into the bathroom where the boys were talking and heard everything they said. "So, you think you're smarter than the sheriff, do you, boy? Why don't you take your useless, good for nothing, ass out there, shut your mouth, and do what your betters tell you to do? Think you can do that, punk?"

Sam held his tongue.

"Why don't you take your slimy ass out of my bathroom and get out there and help the sheriff, or are you too old and useless to be of any help?" Dennis did not.

Wally Spur drew back his arm to punch Dennis in the mouth, and as he did, he took a good look at both the boys, dropped his arm, and went back out into the garage to work with the sheriff in searching for Renee. He didn't care much about the kid being gone, but Holly did, and he wanted to ease her mind from worrying. He didn't have much use for the Good family, anyway, they being nothing but a bunch of hick farmers. He couldn't understand how his wife could befriend them like she had, but thought she was probably chasing after old man Good—and them kids of theirs? Nothing but a bunch of no good trash, just like the bunch he was forced to raise. God, but he'd be glad when the last of the little illegitimate bastards were out of his house! It would be a relief.

Sam said nothing to Dennis about telling off his father. Dennis didn't mention it either; both boys had to struggle against their own parents and they both knew it. Neither felt superior in any way to the other, just bonded. Sam thought about thanking Dennis, but didn't feel right about doing that, either.

As the adult men spanned out across the north end of Rutledge, Hank, George, Smiley and Henry rode into town. The horses, as if smelling danger, danced about the debris, seemingly frightened by something. As the four made their way single file down Main Street, they saw the sheriff, two deputies, and a number of townsmen walking their way. The horses snorted, and danced about the streets at their approach.

"Hey, Sheriff," Hank said. "You seen Sam Spur or Dennis Hanson?"

"Yeah, they're down at the Hanson garage. You boys go see if you can help anyone there. We might need horse power later, if you don't mind."

"Sure Sheriff, we'll be glad to help any way we can, horse power included." With that the boys headed in the other direction to meet up with their friends at the garage. They were delighted to know Sam and Dennis were okay, but kept their elation in check not wishing to seem insensitive to the others who were going through a lot by the looks of the town.

In the belfry, Renee, so frightened she wanted to vomit, and so disgusted by the pastor putting his hands all over her body, fought back the urge to throw-up, knowing, instinctively that she would choke to death if she did because of the tape over her mouth. Her arms ached behind her as her bonds held tighter with each attempt she made to ward off the pastor's touch. Her legs, too, were bound too tightly for her to move them. Oh, how she wanted to kick him where he'd feel it most! She squirmed in an attempt to get away from him, but couldn't escape. She saw, too, that the more she fought the more excited he became. He seemed to enjoy it. She mustered every bit of strength she had to not move, to lay there like a lump; perhaps he'd get bored and leave her alone.

At the garage, Holly, Kathy and Judy held a conference in the bathroom trying to decide what to do. Neither Holly's nor the Thompsons' mothers wished the girls to join the search, fearing that they'd become the next victims to the murderer in their mist, none of them realizing who that might be.

"What are we going to do? We have to do something!" Holly was terrified for Renee. She thought of running out to find Sugarplum, saddling him and searching for her best friend on horseback. If she found her, then Renee could jump up behind her and they could make a swift escape; the pastor could never catch them because there was so much debris scattered about. He'd never be able to use a vehicle of any kind.

"I think we should stay here like our folks want us to," Judy said, to which Kathy was not surprised. Judy might like to cause trouble with her mouth, but when it came to facing it, she was a coward.

"I'm with you, Holly; whatever you want to do! We have to find Renee!" Kathy said.

"Somehow I don't think that Renee is on the north side of town. I get a feeling she's real close. Have either of you seen Mrs. Conway lately?"

Kathy and Judy looked at each other, silently shook their heads "no" then looked back at Holly.

"I bet she knows where Renee is, went off to find her on her own. Jeez! She's so old! What does she think she can do?"

As she spoke, the girls heard a commotion out front, so they cautiously left the bathroom to see what was happening. Holly's eyes fixed on the horses standing outside in front of the garage's double doors.

When she could pull her eyes away, she noticed Sam and Dennis with their friends from Willow River hitting one another in the arms, doing all the silly things boys did when they greeted each other, especially if they hadn't seen each other for awhile. She was glad that Sam's friends thought enough of him to come looking for him, and knew in her heart that's what they were doing, all though none of them mentioned it.

She turned, looking directly into Kathy's eyes, and they seemed to know instinctively what the other was thinking. Together they looked at Judy who shook her head "no," but who pantomimed locking her lips tightly. Holly and Kathy knew she would tell no one what they were up to.

The girls quietly slipped over to the big doors, none of the boys noticing them as Judy sauntered in the boy's direction capturing their attentions. Holly quietly slipped her foot into a stirrup, lifting herself quietly up onto the back of a big bay gelding. Kathy did the same thing on a big palomino mare. They rode the horses off so quietly, even the horses' stable mate didn't notice their absence.

As they rode away, Mrs. Conway climbed up the ninety-ninth step into the church tower. The Lord spoke to her now telling her what she must say when she reached the tower. She was confident. Yes, this may be her time to die, but it no longer mattered. She had served the Lord for almost 111-years and He was well pleased with her. She was confident that the pastor would fall under the name of Jesus to which every knee must bow. She was also sure that Jesus would help Renee recover from the abuse she was going through. There wasn't a lot she could do about that. Her old body wouldn't let her move any faster than it was going. She couldn't have told the others, either, even though she wished to save Renee from the terror she was facing. God had plans for Renee that she would see later on included this pain.

Mrs. Conway no longer questioned God and why He let things happen the way He did. It wasn't as if He couldn't stop it. One move of His hand would have ended the pastor's reign of terror easily, but folks were folks and they turned to evil ways too easily. They seemed to have to learn the hard way that His way was the best way; sometimes that included children. How she wished it were different. If she had her way, no child would ever see any pain of any kind. She also knew that some of the most devout worshipers of the Lord were those that had gone through horror after horror, coming out of it, and realizing that it was the hand of God who brought them out. They were the ones that worshiped Him with their whole hearts, honored Him and reverentially feared Him. The ones personally invited by Him to be His servants. It was a mighty and glorious thing, she knew, something that unless it was personally experienced, wasn't revered as much as it should be. Most folks thought that God was dead, or a myth, a superstition. But those people simply weren't called by Him and would never know His glory. That was another hard lesson she had had to learn over the years.

Now, with every bit of strength that was hers, she'd make it all the way upstairs and teach those same lessons to the so-called pastor of the church. Those that are supposed to lead the sheep of His fold, but consistently lead them astray, especially angered the Lord. They would meet His wrath, something she never wanted to know.

As she made her way upward, outside the girls raced their horses to the field where Mrs. Wilson was discovered. Holly thought perhaps they'd find a clue there, something that might help them locate Renee. Instead, they found nothing, and rode slowly back up the path the others had made earlier on their route back to the garage. Maybe there was something there.

In the garage, Judy held the boy's attention for quite sometime, which gave Holly and Kathy plenty of time to get away, but she couldn't hold the boy's attention forever, especially Hank's, because he wanted to care for the horses that brought them to Rutledge before they went out to help the sheriff in his search.

"Where the hell are Roscoe and Lady!" He exclaimed as he carried water buckets to the horses for them to drink. Everyone turned to look seeing only one horse now at the garage doors.

"Where is Holly?" Mrs. Spur said almost at the same time, her voice betraying the terror she felt as she realized her youngest child was not among the women.

"And where's Kathy?" Mrs. Thompson echoed. She turned to Judy. "Do you know where those two are?" She grabbed Judy by the shoulders, her fingernails digging in to the tender skin beneath her shirt.

"Ouch, Mom! Let go of me!"

"You better start talking young lady or you're going to get it a whole lot worse!" Mrs. Thompson growled out her comment scaring Judy so badly, she blurted out, "They took the horses and are out looking for Renee."

Sam and Dennis were on the other horse so quickly, Hank had no time to try and stop them. He and George ,acting swiftly, took off too quickly for anyone to protest. Smiley and Henry stood inside the garage looking at all the stern looking women staring back at them as they shifted their feet in unease. They didn't know what to do.

On the north side of town, the search party had thought that all the townspeople had escaped the tornado. They were wrong. Their new search at the north end of town offered up an elderly couple who hadn't had time to make it to a shelter, the sheriff deduced from the looks of things. Their mobile home had been tossed and turned in such a way it looked as if it had gone through a paper shredder.

The German shepherd, handled by the vet, found the elderly man's hand sticking out of a debris pile that looked to have once been the couple's kitchen. When the men lifted off the sheets of tin covering the man, they found his wife beside him. The couple were still holding hands.

Hansen radioed for the county coroner, and waited for his arrival while fellow searchers continued their search. A number of Rutledge residents, coming out of their own shock from loosing their homes, remembered that a number of Rutledge's elderly lived in the region where they found the dead couple, so they went about meticulously searching, hoping to find survivors. Rutledge's population being small, 350, they didn't expect to find many, either way, alive or dead, but they wouldn't rest until they felt that every square inch was searched.

In total, six other elderly couples were located with no more fatalities among them. The elderly population of Rutledge lived in a trailer park for the most part, where they kept their living expenses to a minimum and enjoyed one-another's company socially. It was easier for them to travel between homes on foot in their secured off little portion of Rutledge, too. Most had grown up and lived their entire lives in the village, except for two couples who had moved there from Willow River, friends of those already living there. The men enjoyed fishing in Willow River, which, for the most part, lazily crept along at the edge of the retirement village. The ladies played bridge, had a sewing circle where they made quilts and knitted hats and gloves for the less fortunate, giving the garments and blankets away at Christmas. They cooked, enjoyed their grandchildren and families when they came to visit, and generally lived peacefully and happily together. Since none had ever experienced a tornado, this one had come as a complete and utter shock to them. Though most didn't have basements, there was a community shelter, which housed the Laundromat, which was where searchers found the couples. They had all been monitoring the storm on their televisions and radios. The couple that perished did not believe Rutledge would see the storm deciding to ride it out at home. The others had all gathered in the shelter an hour before the storm hit, and took refuge in the one room without windows, which housed the heating system for the shelter. When searchers finally reached them, they were all greatly relieved, but as a path was cleared for them to come out, and they saw the damage done to their beloved homes, most were devastated. It only got worse when they learned their beloved friends had perished as well.

All seemed to be in good physical condition, but the medical examiner, by this time on the scene at their friend's house, insisted that the sheriff have the couples taken to local hospitals for overnight observation. The sheriff complied. They'd need shelter and a warm place to sleep that night anyway.

It would take awhile for them to decide what to do about their homes. Insurance companies would have to be informed. It shouldn't be too difficult, Hansen realized, as they had more than enough documentation to prove they'd been devastated by a natural disaster. As he talked to the couples, he learned that all were heavily insured and none would take too big a hit as far as losses were concerned. He was glad. He didn't know how much clean up would cost, but figured it would be substantial. The elderly couples would have to pay for that, too.

Hansen shook his head as the last of the couples was loaded up and taken to area hospitals. They requested they all be housed together, so Hansen radioed ahead to make sure they were. Area hospitals were happy to comply, wanting to help in any way they could.

He still had nine-tenths of the town to think about. They would all need a place to sleep for the night. Where was he going to house them? He was pondering that question when Mrs. Ralph Thompson and Mrs. Wally Spur came striding up to him with such a look of determination on their faces, he didn't think anything good would come from their appearance.

"Sheriff," Mrs. Spur said, "my daughter has run off on a horse with her daughter," she pointed to Mrs. Thompson, "to find Renee. She is missing. Did you know that? There is still a murderer on the loose! Have you forgotten?"

"No, Ma'am, I haven't forgotten. Do you see what's happened here? I have a lot of things to contend with right now, but I have certainly not forgotten there is a murderer loose somewhere around here. I do know Renee is missing. We were searching for her when we found all these other people."

"That's good, but I'm terrified for Renee right now, not these other people, for my daughter, for her daughter," again Mrs. Spur pointed to Mrs. Thompson who hadn't opened her mouth.

To Hansen, Mrs. Thompson looked strange. On the surface, she was calm, composed, but when he looked into her eyes, he saw such terror, it was hard to look at her. She seemed to be searching the crowd, maybe looking for her husband, he thought.

"I know Shannon is around here someplace, Sheriff, can't you help me and my family find her? She's been hiding for days. I don't know what's got into that girl. Now Kathy has run off, too, on a horse no less. Never should have paid for those riding lessons! Acted like Annie Oakley, she did, jumping up on that horse from behind and taking off like she was Roy Rodgers. Never seen the beat in all my life! Is my husband around here somewhere?" She looked about the debris, the milling search and rescue workers, looking through everyone at something no one else could see.

From out of nowhere came the lone woman, the one who had sat at the Sand's Café the first day Renee arrived in town. Quietly, without a word, she approached Mrs. Thompson, took her arm, and gently steered her back away from the group. The two lone women walked slowly back toward the garage. No one said a word. Many of the men in the search and rescue party where the same ones who bought the lone woman liquor anytime she happened to be at the Sand's when they were. They had all been friends with her son, knew the father, and had visited the family in their home. They knew what the women shared, fought off a sense of grief for the pair, and wished they could do something to comfort them.

One of the men approached the sheriff. "We can't do much more around here. You think maybe it's time to get busy and go after that ass hole that's been hurting them kids? Me and the boys over there, if nothing else, would like to kick his ass." The man nodded to his friends who continued to watch the two women walk slowly back to the garage.

"Yeah, let's go; don't think he's around here." Hansen said taking Mrs. Spur's arm and leading her, too, back to where the rest of the town waited. He ordered the men to spread the word that the search and rescue efforts were over. It was time to go man hunting. And he knew just where to look.

Chapter Twenty-Nine

When she reached the 110th stair, Wilson stopped what he was doing to Renee, smiled and waited for the old woman to turn the corner up into the steeple loft where he could get a good look at her. Stealing a glance at Renee, he regretted not having time enough to satisfy his lusts on her, he would though, soon enough.

Mrs. Conway sweated profusely, something she rarely ever did anymore, but the effort of climbing 110 stairs took a lot out of her. She was surprised at how much. How was she going to fight this devil if she had barely enough strength to climb into the loft proper?

No matter, she thought, be still and know that I am God! How she prayed He'd be there when she needed Him, that His words would be in her mouth when she needed them the most, the right words! She'd seen Him work before, knew that even if Jesus had come to save the world, He had not come to change one word of the Old Testament, only to remind everyone that they were to have only one God, the true God, and to love their neighbors as themselves. She'd heard preachers say over the years that if someone had Jesus, they didn't need God, didn't need to know the Old Testament. How dumb was that, she wondered? How could any man, who had ever had a son, think that a third party might accept the son but not the father? How would the son feel? Would he honor someone who didn't honor his father, especially when it was Thee Father, the Holy of Holies, with no evil in Him? Jesus did come as a savior, but He never denied His Father, how could anyone living think they could? Those were questions that had prayed on her mind for years, were her reason for leaving the church. She'd be damned if she would let some twit who preached falsely be her shepherd.

The Lord is my shepherd, I shall not want, she thought to herself as she climbed the 111th step, and stood a moment resting before going into the steeple tower proper. The landing hid her from view just enough so she could have a moment to steal herself for the battle she knew was about to begin.

What she didn't know was that Holly and Kathy were about half way up the stairs behind her, quietly climbing up to the tower. They left the two horses downstairs by the steeple tower door.

Sam and Dennis were not disappointed. Their horse went straight for its stable mates in front of the steeple doors. The two young men jumped off, and raced into the tower and up the stairs, "knowing" that this is where they'd find Renee. George and Hank were right behind them having run after them when they took the last of the three horses ridden to Rutledge.

Sam guessed that Mrs. Conway was in the tower, too, as was the pastor.

As the search party reached the garage and learned what had happened with all the children, they immediately set out to the south end of town where townspeople had seen the children go.

Most of the folks still inside the garage were suffering the aftershock of the tornado, too numbed by the devastation surrounding them to even remember the horrors of the days preceding the storm. None of their children had been harmed, so it was easier for them to forget that, even with the Hansons sitting in front of them. They had enough presence of mind, however, to note the things going on around them, to be able to tell those concerned with the investigation what was happening.

Hansen was thankful for that. He didn't know what he'd do otherwise. Just as the search and rescue teams were heading out to start their search, Freboni came speeding into the parking lot in front of the garage, sirens blazing. He took a moment to tell the sheriff everything Gloria Wilson had told Harris, confirming all Hansen had suspected.

As Freboni was doing that, Mrs. Conway stepped into the steeple proper.

"Well, well, well, look who we have here," Wilson taunted. "It's so nice to see you, Dear. It must have been a struggle, all those steps and all. What are you now, into your hundreds?" His voice dripped honey as he smiled at the shriveled up old woman standing in front of him. How could he have feared her? She probably weighed ninety pounds, didn't have an ounce of muscle on her skinny bones. He shook his head at his own stupidity.

Renee watched in horror as Mrs. Conway, breathing hard and holding onto the wall for support, made her way into the steeple. She couldn't cry out, her mouth was still bound, yet she tried to scream at her to go back with her eyes making noises behind the gag that stifled her.

Mrs. Conway noted her, saw the terror in her eyes, knew it was more for her than for herself. She looked away. Most people made wrong assumptions about a person based on their outer appearance. This battle belonged to inner strength, not outer, however, as most battles did.

What would Wilson think then? She wondered, smiling because she knew he, too, misjudged her. She never got angry about being misunderstood anymore. It often worked to God's advantage.

Staring the pastor in the eyes with a look of fierceness so bold he looked away, Mrs. Conway got on her knees. She raised her hands to heaven and began to pray. Speaking in tongues, the old woman uttered noises that neither Renee nor Wilson understood. It didn't matter. She was speaking with Angels, not them, and they didn't need to understand. As her prayers grew louder, fiercer in tone, Renee noticed a change in the atmosphere. Something was happening. A breeze began to blow, gently at first, then faster. After Mrs. Conway prayed for only a short time, Holly and Kathy came bounding into the steeple proper almost knocking the old woman to the floor; Mrs. Conway ignored them, praying louder and louder in a language none could understand.

Though he wanted to run at her and knock her in the head, Wilson found himself glued to the wall at the farthest edge of the steeple away from Mrs. Conway and Renee, who was secured to the eastside. Mrs. Conway continued to pray in the middle of the floor as he huddled at the northwest side of the tower.

Holly and Kathy ran to Renee undoing her wrists, mouth, and legs. Renee tried to scream at Mrs. Conway to stop, but found her mouth as bound without the gag as it had been with it. Holly and Kathy, too, found they could not speak. The three huddled in the corner and began to pray, too, asking God to help the old woman, and them, escape from Wilson.

Once the girls began praying, Mrs. Conway stopped. Although they uttered not a word out loud, she knew what they were doing. She stood up. "Ezekiel 25:17—And I will execute great vengeance upon them with great anger and they shall know that I am the Lord, when I lay my vengeance upon them!" (NKJV)

As she spoke, Mrs. Conway made her way to Renee laying both hands on her head. The others could feel a tremor beneath them as if the tower itself shook with the might of the Lord's words. It was slight at first, but growing in strength. With the tremors could be heard thundering footsteps as up the stairs the four young men came bounding with all the might and vigor of their youth into the tower. First to the doorway, Sam looked in with wonder witnessing a grown man cower in a corner as tiny Mrs. Conway, next to three young girls, recited verses from the Bible, now in plain English.

He didn't cower long. At the tremor, Wilson moved with the speed and agility of a cat, at Mrs. Conway, ready to rip her tongue out for her audacity, challenging him, the town's preacher, quoting God's word against him!

Sam perceived the move, but couldn't respond fast enough. Wilson grabbed Mrs. Conway so quickly, Sam took but one-step into the room before Wilson was at her throat. Dennis rushed in behind Sam as did Hank and George, their big muscles, toned from years of hard labor on the farm rippling with desire to tear the pastor in half. The four lined up like offensive linebackers of a football team eyeing the pastor and ready to strike at a moment's notice.

Wilson, holding tightly Mrs. Conway's throat, dropped his hold one second while watching Sam as he slowly approached the two.

She cried out, "The battle belongs to the Lord! Get on your knees and pray!" She did not want the young men involved in this. God would have His way, but they were not to be His instruments, not this time. She knew, too, that the men climbing the steps behind them couldn't save her either.

The three girls, too terrified for Mrs. Conway to look, bowed their heads in prayer.

Sam led his friends to their knees and they, too, bowed down in prayer although it went against the grain of each and every young man. They were young, strong, and full of energy; they wanted to grab the pastor and punish him for what they knew he had done.

Wilson was astounded! He couldn't believe his luck. He went to his escape hatch, opened the door, and throwing Mrs. Conway across his shoulders, slipped out of the tower, out of sight of everyone up there. As the door closed behind him, the sheriff and his deputies reached the tower proper to find seven young people on their knees praying.

"Where'd they go!" He screamed at the teenage boys.

In unison, the four, still bowed in prayer, pointed to the doorway.

Before Hansen could utter a sound, four of the search and rescue party, the friends of the lone woman's family, bounded down the stairs heading for the bottom door. Freboni and the other men with the sheriff brought up the rear, and were right behind them. There was no time to see to Renee, although Hansen saw she was okay on the surface. She'd have to stay with her friends for the time being, and he figured with them all praying they were in no immediate danger. He desperately wanted to capture the pastor before he could do anymore harm to anyone else.

Meanwhile, Wilson had to think on his feet. He hadn't contemplated getting away or having to tote an old woman with him, but he'd be damned if he'd let her go. He had known that the secret stairwell in the tower would one day be his saving grace. Whoever had built it, he now thanked in silence. He got downstairs and outside before the searchers reached the tower proper. As for Mrs. Conway, she had galled him for the last time. Outside, he ducked behind a pile of debris here, another there, scurrying toward the root shelter dragging the old woman with him. Why not finish the old bag off there, he thought? It was the perfect place, and he effortlessly carried her away from the church steeple.

Mrs. Conway continued to pray. She did not want the children involved in this; she was frightened they would be scared by what they might see. They'd been through enough already. Most of her prayers centered on protection for the children. For herself, she asked only that the evil person intent on doing her harm would be stopped before he could. She knew that wasn't always the case, witness Jesus himself at the hands of the Pharisees.

What Wilson and the others never would have guessed was that she prayed for Wilson, too, for him to come to his senses before God punished him for good. God, she knew, would forgive him if he repented. Witness Jonah and the wale. Jonah hadn't wanted to go to Nineveh where God had ordered him to go because he knew the sinners there would repent if they had any sense, thereby receiving mercy from God, which is what they did and received. That's why he disobeyed God and went to Tarshish ending up in the whale's belly. Why so low your countenance Jonah? The Lord had asked. Jonah had wanted to see them punished, not saved. Oh, how she understood that.

She knew too well. Jonah wanted to see the Lord's anger on the wicked of Nineveh and when it didn't happen, he was greatly disappointed. She understood that, too, knowing that God's ways are not our ways; His thoughts are not our thoughts, which was a good thing. His mercy and graciousness are for everyone, even the worst of sinners. Sinners like the one who had her in his grasp at that precise moment.

The air hung around them like a wet blanket, sweltering on one of the hottest days of the year. Sweat ran in rivulets down Wilson's shirt, soaking into Mrs. Conway's already sweat-drenched housedress. The same oppressive heat bore down on the men heading out of the tower, a giant book set out to press them like flowers between its pages, slowing them, and making animals, already crazed by the tornado, edgy and angry, even the horses.

Sugarplum, who Renee had set free from the barn before the tornado hit, ran nonstop for miles in the opposite direction of the storm once freed. Dazed and frenzied, he made his way back to Rutledge neighing in a mad effort to find his stable and the one person he trusted implicitly, Mrs. Conway.

But the stable was gone. All he managed to find were three horses, like the horses of the Apocalypse, standing quietly next to the church steeple. Standing briefly with them, he scented the air sensing Mrs. Conway somewhere nearby. Lathered up and foaming, he trotted frantically up and down the pathway, which had been cleared by searchers earlier, neighing unceasingly for his mistress. He was so lathered up he looked like walking shaving cream hot from the can.

As the search party bounded out of the steeple rushing to go chasing after Wilson and Mrs. Conway, Sugarplum turned, saw them, and ran full speed at them, neighing at the top of his lungs, screaming out in rage, angry that they were not his beloved mistress, his ears flattened to his neck and his neck snaking along the ground. Terrified at the sight, the men jumped back inside the steeple doorway as the horse came to a screeching halt just outside it. When one of the men tried to peer out Sugarplum angrily laid his ears back flat against his head, opened his mouth wide and lunged at the man snapping his jaws shut in an effort to grab him. The man was quick enough to pull the door shut before Sugarplum could bite him.

The horse turned on the other horses milling about then, attacking, biting, going after the legs, anything he could reach. He lowered his head, snaking it along the ground, snapping at the other horses, drawing blood so viciously one animal feel to the ground. Just as quickly as the attack began, it ceased, as Sugarplum sped off down the path screaming once again, apparently still searching for Mrs. Conway. The men heard his thundering hoofs gradually fade into the distance enough so that they felt it safe to step outside, and then they scurried out of the steeple.

Sugarplum, running through and jumping over debris, picked up Mrs. Conway's scent once again. He screamed all the louder, hoping the old woman would show herself. He heard something then, stopped as quickly as he had started, and listened, sniffing the air. Sensing something was wrong with his mistress, Sugarplum ceased his screaming, put his nose to the wind and started trotting toward the odor he knew so well, still with his head and neck snaking along the path like a giant anaconda searching out its prey. Mrs. Conway's scent was mixed with someone else's. Danger lurked. He laid his ears flat back along his neck, and slithered his head about through the grass, running as fast as his racehorse sleek legs would carry him.

Wilson heard the horse, too, and didn't think much of it. Mrs. Conway also heard. She knew from the sounds of it that Sugarplum had gone off the deep end. She'd seen him do that once in his prime when he was about seven. She never understood why it had happened, but realized with terror that it was happening again. She'd seen the stallion bring down horses in the crazed state he was in, and dreaded the thought of what he could do to a man. She started to shake.

Wilson noticed. She must be in shock, he thought, stepping faster so he could make it to the shelter with her. He didn't want her dying before he could have some fun!

She heard the pounding of hoofs growing louder. She wanted down! Wanted to get behind a tree or hide in some debris where the horse couldn't reach her. She'd seen what a stallion could do to a human by biting them, hell, they could remove a lot of flesh that way and if they wanted to kick and bite, well that would be the end of it, and not a pretty way to go. Sugarplum may be her horse, but from the sound of it, he was beyond being able to discern her from anyone else.

"Hey, Wilson, why don't you make me walk! Can't help me much, you oughta' enjoy that."

He was getting tired. He sat her down on the ground, stood erect, and stretched his back. No one seemed to be following and he'd already made good time getting to the root cellar. He could afford a second's reprieve, he thought.

Just then, as he looked down the path he had just traveled at the sound of hoofs thundering over it, he saw Sugarplum racing right for him. He reeled in terror at the sight of the horse, his neck snaking about the ground, his ears plastered to the back of his head, the lather soaking his body.

Wilson turned, horrified, knowing the horse belonged to the old woman, to grab her and put her in front of him, but she had already made it to a pile of debris, and was sheltering herself in among some fallen branches and brambles like a rabbit hiding from a lynx. He had no time to move before the horse was upon him.

Sugarplum, full of the scent of Mrs. Conway, but without seeing her, went all the way over into madness. He charged Wilson with his teeth bared, grabbing him by the shoulder, drawing him up into the air as he reared, throwing Wilson so that he feel belly down in the dirt underneath Sugarplum's hoofs. Sugarplum reared up again coming down with both hoofs on Wilson's head, stomping Wilson to death.

Frenzied and hot, the heat bore down on Sugarplum as his heart pounded wildly in his chest. Already nineteen years old, he was getting up in age for a horse, and though he was in fine shape, the heat, exertion and extreme stress were too much. He rose high into the air screaming his victory over Wilson's inert body, then without ceremony fell, all 1,200 pounds, atop Wilson, as dead as the man lying beneath him.

Mrs. Conway watched in horror as her beloved pet had turned to mince meat the person of the parish pastor. She gasped as Sugarplum fell atop the man, scrambling as fast as she could from underneath the brambles that had been her hiding place. Her old body, tired and distraught at the sight of her good friend, Sugarplum, lying dead atop the man who tried to kill her, wanted to keel over. The animal she had cared for almost nineteen years had stopped the man who had killed two children, and molested who knew how many others. Slowly she ambled over to the horse, his still hot body lathered up like shaving cream. She could make out Wilson's feet from beneath Sugarplum's frame, but that was all. She sat down and took the animal's head in her lap, softly crying in grief at his demise.

The heat bore down on her, too, relentless. She, too, had been through much that day. Too much, she thought. Silently, she prayed to God, asking Him to take her home. She'd seen too much, needed to rest, tears ran down her cheeks as she lifted her head to heaven asking for God's help once again. Through the tears, she smiled, and lay down in the grass next to Sugarplum still cradling his head in her arms.

The search party found them there in the grass, Sugarplum's head in her lap, a smile on her lips, her tiny body breathing no longer.

Back in the steeple, after praying for a longtime, all the children left the tower. The girls thought of searching for Mrs. Conway, but Holly decided it would be better for Renee to go to the garage where the women could look after her. With Sam's encouragement, the girls did just that, quietly walking around tornado-strewn debris to the garage where they were welcomed with relief. Mrs. Spur was delighted to see Renee alive.

The boys followed the path all the others had taken and came upon the search and rescue party, which included the sheriff. They, too, saw Mrs. Conway lying in the grass, holding Sugarplum's head in her lap, looking as peaceful and happy as they had ever seen her.

Though Sam felt a horrific bolt of grief surge through him at the sight of Mrs. Conway lying there dead, he couldn't help but marvel at how happy she looked. He wondered if she was with God. Had God reached down to get her? Had Jesus?

It was awhile before the boys realized that Sugarplum had killed the pastor and that the man who had terrorized Rutledge over the past few days lay dead beneath the horse.

As the rescuers trekked back into the village, it was with great relief that Holly watched Sam in the lead walking toward her as he made his way back to the garage to inform everyone there about what had happened.

"Hey! Look you guys, here comes Sam!"

As he drew closer and she could see the look on his face, dread welled up inside both Holly and Renee. Behind Sam came Dennis, Hank and George, all looking beaten, tired and grieved.

"Sam, you've got to help us find Mrs. Conway! Wilson is going to do terrible things to her if we don't find her!" Holly cried.

"We already found both of them," Sam said, defeated. "You all better sit down."

As the boys entered Hanson's garage to talk to the girls, the rest of the townsfolk still there gathered around them to hear what they had to say. Mrs. Spur, Mrs. Thompson and Mrs. Hanson were all worried about Mrs. Conway, as was the strange woman Mrs. Conway had befriended.

Though Mrs. Thompson hadn't had much good to say about the old woman over the years, she felt deep gratitude to her now after her husband had explained to her that the old woman had gotten their daughters to read the Bible. She had been trying for years to get them interested in scripture but seemed to loose ground on the issue yearly.

Still searching for Shannon, she continued to fret over why her youngest daughter wasn't with the rest of the crowd, was worried that she'd been hurt in the storm, so much so that as she approached the group standing by the garage doors, she continually rung her hands in her skirt.

Kathy and Judy watched their mother through veiled eyelids, worried that she would never be okay again.

Holly and Renee paid too much attention to Sam to notice their friend's mothers' peculiar behavior.

Sam removed his cigarettes from his T-shirt sleeve, took one out, lit it, took a long draw off it then said, "The pastor's dead. Sugarplum killed him." A gasp went through the crowd. Most of the townsfolk had no idea of their pastor's behavior since coming to town.

Sam cleared his throat, "That's not all." He took a long look at Holly and Renee sitting there watching him, hanging on to his every word. Looking them both in the eyes, and forgetting that so many others were in the garage, too, he said, "Mrs. Conway is dead, too."

Holly and Renee, in unison, gasped, shocked.

"The doctor said she simply passed away. It was her time. She had been doing so much lately, then with all that went on during and after the storm and with the heat—it was too much. Her heart gave out. She lay there in the grass, when we saw her, smiling, holding Sugarplum's head in her lap."

"The vet said the same thing about the horse. Said the animal was twenty years old or better, and with the tornado and going crazy like he had, it was too much for his heart, too. It was as if they died together."

"He saved her life, you know. The pastor was going to kill her, just like he did Shannon and Francine." Another gasp ran through the crowd. All had been so involved with their own losses due to the tornado, they hadn't given much thought to the horrors that had surrounded them only the day before, and were wholly unaware that the pastor was implicated in those horrors.

Sam hadn't been paying attention to Mrs. Thompson, so he didn't notice that she stood behind him as he spoke of Shannon. Sam's words lifted the veil of fog that had hovered over her mind since first learning of Shannon's death. The truth he uttered finally sunk in, so, as if for the first time, she grasped what had happened to her youngest daughter. It was as if Sam had taken all the power his young body had to offer, swung his right fist into her stomach, and pummeled her, his words had such an effect. She doubled over, lamenting so grievously she humbled everyone surrounding her, her grief over her daughter so deep, her wailing tortured them.

Kathy and Judy ran to her, thankful that finally she grasped Shannon's death. Perhaps all was not lost for their family, the girls hoped. They couldn't know the guilt that weighed on their mother's shoulders, however. She wailed for her daughter, true, but she also bemoaned the fact that she was instrumental in bringing Wilson into their community, the man who murdered her daughter, and Mrs. Hanson's daughter. She wondered how she would ever live with the horror of it all as her two living daughters hugged and tried to comfort her.

As this was going on, the search party, the sheriff, Mr. Thompson,

Freboni and the other deputies walked up to the garage. The coroner's van slowly drove by pulling out onto the highway bearing Mrs. Conway and Pastor Wilson to the coroner's office where he would perform autopsies officially determining their cause of death, although he already knew what it had been for both of them. The sheriff had already called in a big shovel to dig a hole to bury the horse.

At the same time, from the south end of town came the Good family car, Mrs. Good, having been terrified for Renee's safety because of the tornado, had forced her husband and family out on the road early so they could get to Rutledge and check on her.

All the phone lines were down so she couldn't call, and felt they had no other choice but to get there. Luckily, road crews had worked to open up Highway 61 before them.

When he saw all the people milling about the garage, Mr. Good turned in there where he found his daughter, much to his great relief.

Mike was there, too, happy to see Sam and Holly and the rest of the Spur family was okay, too. The first thing Mr. Good did was to offer his help to anyone who needed it with tornado cleanup.

The Good family unloaded their station wagon making it available to anyone who wished to go anywhere. People were just beginning to realize they had to find a place to stay for the evening.

Old Man Spur, still contemptuous of the farmer and his family, accepted the Good family's offer to put them up in a motel for the night, feeling it was his just due. Mrs. Spur was grateful that her friend, Mrs. Good, was there to help them through the night. Things had been so traumatic she hadn't had time to think of tomorrow or what would happen in the future. She needed the friendly nurturing Mrs. Good brought with her and was thankful for it. As usual, she was ashamed of her husband's brisk behavior toward Mr. Good. She wondered if he was jealous of him, too.

Mr. Good found a motel in Willow River where he rented separate rooms for the boys and the girls as well as the Spurs. After such a long, traumatic weekend, and hot day, Renee and Holly were exhausted. They hugged each other goodnight, each stealing away to read the Bible, for a little while before going to sleep, looking for a comforting word concerning Mrs. Conway and Sugarplum, the horse they loved.

Renee also wondered how she would tell her parents about what had happened to her. Would she tell them? She didn't get along with her mother all that well, and wasn't comfortable talking to her about anything. All her mother ever said in times of crisis was to not mention anything to the neighbors.

Sam told Mike everything about Wilson, and what had happened to Renee. She hadn't said a word to her parents about it. Mike decided he wouldn't either, not until she did.

Too, the sheriff took the Thompson family with him to Willow River where they also went to a motel to spend the night. Mrs. Thompson, though still sobbing, seemed to be herself once again, and for that Mr. Thompson was eternally grateful. He loved her unconditionally and wanted her whole, and in his life no matter what. Their daughters needed her whole again, too.

Sheriff Ernie Hansen went to his office. He spent the night there, not wanting to go home to an empty house. Even with a job well done, he felt empty. Witnessing much in the way of human behavior over the years, he still couldn't come to grips with the evil he knew lurked in everyone, including himself. Mrs. Conway was right, it was God everyone needed so they could rise above their own evil natures. They sure weren't doing it on their own.

Epilogue

In the ensuing years following the tornado, the village of Rutledge rebuilt itself. Though still not a big city, it stayed afloat like it had in the past. Then when the freeway was built, about a mile east of the city proper, Rutledge ceased to grow. The restaurant became a bar that locals patronized faithfully. Mrs. Conway donated her building to the town in her will, which they sold at market value. The store is gone, being used now as an apartment, but the apartments upstairs where everyone lived remain fully rented to this day. Even the rickety back stairs leading to the upper floors remain as they were in 1963, as strong as they ever were.

The Spurs left Rutledge later that year for California, deciding it would cost too much to rebuild.

Renee and Holly drifted apart ceasing to write to one another as each made new friends, and began their separate adventures into adulthood. Holly married a prosperous man, opting to stay home to be a wife and mother. Renee, a college graduate, became a psychotherapist specializing in helping young girls through rape and molestation. Also a devout Christian, she applies techniques from scripture in helping young girls through those hurdles that they don't know how to overcome on their own.

Sam joined the Marines as soon as he was eighteen, and was sent to Viet Nam where he was killed in battle. He, too, was a devout Christian, and held in high regard amongst his platoon.

Smiley Rains joined the Marines, as well, and although he hadn't seen Sam for seven years, not since the Spurs left Rutledge, the two ended up in the same platoon. He was there when Sam was killed. After he got out of the service, he came home, but was never the same again. He moved out into the woods to live as a hermit.

Hank Hall and George King didn't have to join the service as both young men were needed at home to help their families. They took over their family farms and thrived, both marrying and staying friends throughout their lives. They remained friends with Dennis Hanson, too, and the three often left packages in the woods for Smiley. Smiley had told them what happened to Sam, some of the other things he had seen during the war. Hanson, King and Hall make sure Smiley wanted for nothing until his death in 1988. Some speculated that Smiley committed suicide. His three friends knew it was Viet Nam that killed him. He simply quit eating.

Dennis Hanson still runs the garage in Rutledge. He didn't leave even after both his parents passed away by the time he turned eighteen. His father died of kidney and liver failure, and his mother died shortly thereafter. Dennis believes she died of a broken heart. Dennis never took to drink like the townspeople predicted he would. Instead, he, too, is a devout Christian attending church regularly where he serves as an elder. He married Sharon Fry, who teaches school in Willow River, kindergarten, and they have five children. The elder Frys took Dennis as their son long before he married Sharon, treating him accordingly, the first real fathering he had ever received. He loves them dearly, as he did his own parents.

The Thompson family rebuilt their home in Rutledge, and is flourishing as before, except that now Mrs. Thompson is a much humbler person gracious to all that pass her way. She went out of her way to befriend the Hansons and the woman who lost her family in separate car accidents. The women are now inseparable.

Shortly after the tornado, Judy Thompson was spotted in Minneapolis, while on a shopping spree there with her mother, by a modeling talent scout, and went to New York City where she became a celebrated fashion model. Kathy went to law school, graduated with honors and came back to practice law with her father. She specializes in cases of rape, murder and molestation of young girls.

And though all lost touch with Gloria Wilson, she followed the same path as Renee, helping young girls, as a psychologist, with molestation and rape issues. She moved to Wyoming, changed her name, and worked hard to overcome her own issues brought on by her parents.

A new pastor was brought to Rutledge after the church was rebuilt, a man sensitive to all the heartache caused by Wilson. A devout man, sensitive to the needs of others, he was, and is, a welcome respite to the congregation in need of his sensitivity. He's been there forty years, now.

On a plaque he had made and hung in the foyer of the new church as a reminder to the past and how Satan works, he had inscribed a quote from 2 Corinthians 11:14,15, which says: And no wonder! For Satan himself transforms himself into an angel of light. Therefore, it is no great thing if his ministers also transform themselves into ministers of righteousness, whose end will be according to their works. (NKJV)

A.J. Questenberg grew up in and now lives in Northern Minnesota with her Chihuahua Milo. As a graduate of the University of Wisconsin with an art and English degree, she likes to design her own covers as well. As a newspaper managing editor, and before that a cops and court reporter, she gave up that demanding position to write novels trading on her vast experiences for inspiration. Her first novel, <u>Snowbound</u>, can also be found at Amazon.com or through your local bookseller. Ask for it if you can't find it in stock. Also, you can visit her website at, <u>www.AJQuestenberg.weebly.com</u> for updates.

26263326R00141

Made in the USA
San Bernardino, CA
23 November 2015